The Matchbreaker

CHRIS MANBY

The Matchbreaker

HODDER &
STOUGHTON

Copyright © 2006 by Chris Manby

First published in Great Britain in 2006 by Hodder and Stoughton
A division of Hodder Headline

The right of Chris Manby to be identified as the Author
of the Work has been asserted by her in accordance with
the Copyright, Designs and Patents Act 1988.

A Hodder & Stoughton Book

2

A CIP catalogue record for this title is available from the British Library

Hardback ISBN 0 340 83880 9
Trade Paperback ISBN 0 340 83881 7

Typeset in Plantin Light by Hewer Text UK Ltd, Edinburgh
Printed and bound by Mackays of Chatham Ltd, Chatham, Kent

Hodder Headline's policy is to use papers that are natural, renewable
and recyclable products and made from wood grown in sustainable
forests. The logging and manufacturing processes are expected to
conform to the environmental regulations of the country of origin.

Hodder and Stoughton Ltd
A division of Hodder Headline
338 Euston Road
London NW1 3BH

To Lukas Arnold with love from Auntie Chris

ACKNOWLEDGEMENTS

The Matchbreaker is my tenth novel for Hodder and Stoughton. It marks the passage of a decade since I called my fabulous agent, Antony Harwood, from a soggy campsite near St Ives and he told me that Kate Lyall Grant had made an offer for my first novel, *Flatmates*. I can't tell you how lucky I feel to be able to make my living as a writer and how grateful I am to the people who helped set me on this path. So once again I'd like to thank David Garnett, Dylan and Geraldine Gray, Peter F. Hamilton, Guy Hazel, Ryan Law, Helen Pisano and my family for their vital early support.

And for their help during the writing of this book in particular, my thanks go to everyone at Hodder, Joanne Smith at Sunseeker, Reuben Stephenson, James Macdonald Lockhart, James Pusey, Dea Brovig, Sally Riley, Sheryl Peterson and Debbie Deuble (the Three Martini Girls), Tony Gardner, Peter Dailey, Jennifer Niederhauser and my fellow Boarders (without whom, I would have written eleven books by now).

I

I could think of far better ways to spend a Saturday afternoon in June than trying on bridesmaids' dresses. However, that is exactly what I found myself doing one day last summer; sweating like a French cheese in a changing room without air-conditioning in one of London's biggest department stores; trying not to swear out loud as I stepped into a dress specifically designed to bring out the red in my spots. It was a gold dress. Who on earth does a gold dress suit? Not an ash-blonde like me, that's for sure.

Still, the bridesmaid doesn't really get much choice what she's going to wear, does she? And if the bride's special colour scheme for her big day decrees that her attendants look like they're suffering from a bad case of jaundice, there's not much the average bridesmaid can do about it but slap on some extra blusher. Not that there was enough blusher in the world to save me from looking like a convalescent right then. Karen's colour scheme decreed that her bridesmaids look as though they had just been disinterred . . .

'Oh, Lindsey, you look beautiful,' Karen gushed as I emerged from the changing room. I prayed as I did so that no one I knew would walk past. I would have dropped dead for real if anyone I respected caught me looking so grim.

'That empire line is super-feminine,' the shop assistant chipped in. 'And it really does suit you.'

'Try this headdress with it,' Karen suggested.

She plonked a garland of gold polyester roses on my head and the village idiot effect was complete.

Karen had already changed into her wedding dress. The best one could possibly say was that the dress she had chosen was *complicated*. It had more swags and flounces than a set of theatre drapes. And it was pure-as-the-driven-snow *virgin* white. I mean, let's be realistic . . .

Karen resembled nothing so much as Marie Antoinette pretending to be a milkmaid – a train crash of low class meets too much cash, right down to the little white silk and bugle-beaded pouch that dangled from her wrist for those all-important wedding-day accessories. Like her mobile phone. Meanwhile, the shop assistant tugged at the back of my balloon of a skirt and held the waist in tightly so I could see how I might look once alterations to the gold sack had been made.

Hideous. Still hideous.

'Doesn't Lindsey look beautiful?' Karen asked her mother.

Marilyn, Karen's mother, paused long enough in searching through her handbag for nicotine patches to agree.

'She's looks lovely,' she said without looking up.

'See, I knew you'd look fantastic,' Karen persisted. 'Gold really is your colour, Linz.'

'You'll look better in the church. The lighting in here isn't terribly flattering,' said the assistant, noticing my frown.

Didn't I know it?

I'd been in that changing room before, you see. Three times in fact. And each time trying on a dress more spectacularly loathsome than the last. Melanie, the personal assistant, had wanted to see me in peach. Heather, the 'model', thought yellow would go with my hair. Trisha, the yoga teacher, had my 'colours done' and stuck me in mauve.

They were all wrong.

Fortunately, I wasn't to be seen in public in any of those disaster outfits. For years afterwards, the dresses hung unworn in my wardrobe like taffeta scalps. And the gold dress Karen wanted me to wear was going to join them there, I promised my unhappy reflection.

'You'll look like a princess on the day,' said the shop assistant cheerfully.

If the day ever came, I would look like one of the Hanson boys in drag.

'Your dad is going to be so proud of you, Linz,' Karen – the woman who wanted to be my stepmother – assured me.

2

That's right. Karen had wangled herself a pretty spectacular catch. She was my father's fourth fiancée. Fifth if you count my mother, his first and only wife.

Sounds bad, doesn't it? Like Dad was addicted to engagement ring shopping or was the kind of man who didn't follow through on his promises. That's not the case. He just made some unfortunate choices.

Really, I can think of no better man than my father. I know pretty much every daughter says that – whether the dad in question is a prince or a train robber – but I also know I am telling the truth. Give me any fatherhood scale you care to mention and my dad would be right at the top of it.

You see, I grew up without a mother and, with Mum gone, Dad worked harder than you can possibly imagine being two parents' worth of father to me. In fact, he was as steadfast and supportive, protective and loving as two parents, four grandparents and an entire extended family of aunts, uncles and irritating younger cousins.

He certainly didn't have it easy, raising me all on his own. When he found himself in the role of single parent, Dad soon came to sympathize with those articles you read in women's magazines about the difficulty of juggling work and family life. Dad was a high-flyer at university and had a serious career in advertising with all the attendant serious career stresses before he was twenty-five. He was the youngest ever account manager in his firm. He was a partner by the age of twenty-eight. But although he quickly reached the top of his career tree, it definitely wasn't at the expense of our relationship.

Dad was there at every important moment in my life. He saw me take my first steps. He heard my very first word (which, somewhat strangely, was 'Mama'). He sewed name-tags into my first school uniform and cried like a girl with the real mums at the gate as he watched me walk into the playground for the very first time.

He taught me to ride a bike. He taught me to swim. He was never too busy to help with my homework. He made it to every school concert, even if it meant having to slip away early from a meeting (in fact, he once brought an entire commercial film crew to see me play an Oompaloompa in a musical version of *Charlie and the Chocolate Factory*). He took a weekend cookery class so he could bake a cake for me to take into school at harvest festival time (the other 'mums' were gently patronizing until Dad's Chocolate Yule Log won first prize at the Christmas Fayre).

Dad was always there for me. When the time came, he even took me aside and told me about periods and puberty. I don't know which of us was more embarrassed.

But my favourite memory of Dad comes from when I was four years old. As I think about it, I can still smell the fallen leaves mouldering on the ground, the delicate hint of a bonfire for Guy Fawkes' on the air. It's an autumnal smell that makes me smile even now.

We were walking across Hampstead Heath on our way home from the playground. Dad always took me to the swings on a Sunday afternoon. He was holding my hand in his big, fatherly paw. It was almost dark, though it can only have been five o'clock.

And then I heard my first firework. It exploded with a bang that seemed impossibly big and dangerous to a four-year-old girl. Immediately, I burst into tears. I wrapped myself around Dad's leg, almost bringing him to the ground. He scooped me up into his arms. He pressed his bristly cheek against mine and kissed the end of my nose. I buried my face in his neck.

But Dad gently took my face and turned it towards the sky, directing my eyes to where the fireworks still glittered on the horizon above London like shattering stars. He wouldn't let me hide.

'Look,' he said. 'There's nothing to be frightened of. There will never be anything to be frightened of. Not while I'm here.'

Gradually, I loosened my grip around his neck and relaxed. We stood on the Heath for a long time after that, me on Dad's shoulders, watching the graceful arc of dozens of Roman candles as they lit up the November sky. From terrified to mesmerized in a matter of minutes. I knew then that he was right. I didn't need to be afraid. Dad would open my eyes to the good things in life and I would never be afraid or unhappy as long as he was there.

As I was growing up, whenever people found out what had happened with Mum, they would pull a sympathetic face or reach out to touch me gently on the arm as though I needed comforting. But I honestly didn't feel I lacked a thing. I had a complete and perfect family in Dad and me. I couldn't have been happier. And that's how it was for a very long time. Just the two of us. Me and Dad against the world.

3

Nineteen years later in that bridal department, I took off the stupid gold bridesmaid's dress and threw it over the back of the chair in the changing room like a fish-packer discarding stinking overalls at the end of a shift. I didn't even bother to pick the dress up when it slithered from the chair on to the frankly filthy floor. Outside, Karen twittered on to her mother and the assistant as they unlaced the ice-white monstrosity she had chosen for her wedding day.

Not that Karen looked much less tacky in her day clothes. She had come out in her usual shopping attire. A pair of velour tracksuit bottoms with something retarded written in big letters across her buttocks (today it was 'Hard Tail': it should have been 'Soft in the Head'). A matching hoodie. Her Ugg boots: at least two years too late. Looking at Karen's mother, Marilyn, it was easy to see where her dress sense came from. Marilyn kept her nicotine patches in a gold-trimmed Fendi baguette. Fake, of course.

Karen's style had been making me wince since the day I first met her. In fact, I think I started wincing in anticipation the moment I heard Karen's name . . .

She was a personal trainer. *A personal trainer!* What kind of job is that? You can imagine how I felt when Dad told me he had been seeing someone new and that she worked in his gym.

Karen had been recommended by my father's GP. Dad

had been suffering from chronic backache for a while. All those hours at the office and long-haul flights to shoot commercials all over the world were starting to take their toll. After his doctor patched him up and prescribed anti-inflammatories for the umpteenth time, he insisted that Dad sort out a new exercise routine to strengthen his muscles and prevent him from ending up permanently incapacitated. Something Pilates-based might be a good idea. He knew exactly the woman to help.

Karen had, according to Dad, a wall full of certificates in her office. She had studied sports medicine in the United States, trained in some of the best fitness centres in the world, and knew more about anatomy than the average surgeon. She wasn't just a trainer. She was, to use the American term as she did, a sports physician. That didn't make the revelation that Dad's new 'sports physician' was getting to know his anatomy rather more intimately than the average client's any easier to take.

I found out during the Christmas holidays. I came home from a very difficult term at university – feeling quite guilty that I hadn't managed to make it back to London at all until then – and found an unfamiliar hairbrush in *my* en-suite bathroom. Dad didn't look at all embarrassed when I confronted him about the pink plastic bristles covered in long dark hair. Instead, he grinned widely at the memory of something I really didn't want to guess at and said, 'Ah, yes. I've been meaning to tell you. We're going to be three for Christmas this year.'

'Three?'

'That's right,' he confirmed. 'I've met someone fabulous.'

'Someone serious?' I asked, heart in mouth.

He merely grinned.

Oh dear, I thought. 'Where did you find her?'

'I met her at the gym. She's my trainer. She's called Karen.'

Everything – the cheap hairbrush by my bathroom basin, the job description, that horrible name – told me this was a terrible idea.

But it was too late to get out of the rendezvous and so I met Karen for the first time on 22 December. Dad wanted me to meet her before Christmas Day *and* before he shopped for her Christmas present so I could advise him as to what she might like.

What would a woman like Karen like? To be able to answer that, you first have to know what a woman like Karen *is* like. I've already told you what she considered to be suitable attire for a shopping trip to some of the better parts of London. When Karen first walked in to Sardi's, our favourite Italian restaurant, I assumed she must be one of the waiting staff.

'You are joking,' I murmured when the very common-looking girl scanning the tables caught sight of Dad and her face split into a beam of recognition. '*That* is Karen?'

Dad didn't seem to hear me or react to the tone of my voice. He was too busy grinning right back at her. He jumped to his feet and planted a kiss smack on her lips. When they broke apart after an extremely unseemly amount of groping from two grown-ups in a public place, I extended my hand.

Karen shook my hand with such enthusiasm I thought she might be trying to dislocate my shoulder. I gave her the cold, wet fish in response.

'You must be Lindsey. Wow! I've heard so much about you,' she said.

'Wish I could say the same,' I replied. 'But Dad kept you rather quiet.'

The goofy grin wavered at once.

'She's joking,' said Dad. 'I can't stop gushing about you. Can I, Lindsey love?'

I didn't reply. Sometimes it's best to let your silence do the talking. I dropped Karen's hand and went straight back to perusing my menu. I was already satisfied that even if Christmas was going to be ruined, Karen wouldn't make it much beyond the New Year.

'What do you like to eat here, Lindsey?' Karen tried to start a conversation.

'I'll go straight for a main course,' I said, snapping the menu shut. 'No point hanging around.'

Karen never quite recovered her poise that day. She sent her water glass flying and dropped spaghetti down the front of her shirt. She drank too much wine. I think she was hoping it might give her confidence but it merely made her even clumsier. As we left the restaurant she somehow managed to trip herself up on the umbrella stand by the door.

For someone who made her living teaching other people how to have good posture, Karen didn't even seem to be in control of her own body. Her eyebrows were horribly over-plucked and her low-lights were several months overdue a retouch. She dressed as though she'd been raised in a trailer park and had the conversational skills and natural grace of an adolescent chimpanzee. What on earth did Dad see in her? I was extremely relieved when Karen left us to go back to work.

As Dad and I walked through the centre of London together that afternoon and he told me what he was planning to cook for Christmas lunch, I tried to work out why he was so infatuated with a girl who made Britney Spears look like Grace Kelly. It wasn't the first time either. Why was he constantly picking such embarrassing girlfriends?

I decided the issue was that he was subconsciously trying

to find a woman who was the polar opposite of my mother in an attempt to keep from sinking into depression at the thought of what he had lost. Karen was certainly the polar opposite of Mum. There was something so rough about her, with her chain-store clothes and her badly-coloured hair; something so different from the woman who smiled down at me each night from the photograph on my bedroom wall. Beautiful, elegant and understated at all times, my mother definitely wasn't the kind of woman who wore tight purple training pants to lunch.

I resolved to tell Dad that it was OK. I knew what was going on in his head and I understood the rationale behind it. But it was time for him to realize he could love someone who was my mother's equal without fear of getting hurt again. Far better to take a risk on true excellence than continue to date bimbos like this latest one who would give him a quick fix and leave him feeling lower than ever before when he realized how her lack of class, sophistication and general intelligence reflected detrimentally upon him. I felt sure he would know at once that I had hit the nail on the head with my insight.

But I couldn't find the appropriate moment to tell him, and later that afternoon, Dad insisted we go to *Tiffany* to buy Karen's Christmas gift.

'*Tiffany?*' I can't describe my horror.

'Go crazy,' he told me as we stepped into the bright, airy diamond room, busy with slightly frightened-looking guys hunting for last-minute gifts and accidentally buying engagement rings.

Dad nudged me. 'Find Karen's perfect present.'

'What? In here?' I said. 'I don't think so.'

I dragged Dad upstairs and made him buy Karen a charm bracelet in the silver department.

'Silver?' he said, as the assistant laid it before him on a

velvet tray. 'I was planning to spend a bit more than that. Are you sure this will do?'

'Better with her skin tone,' I assured him. I didn't add that as far as I was concerned even that little silver bracelet represented an awful lot of money to spend on someone who wouldn't be around for all that long. There would certainly be no need to buy a silver heart charm for Valentine's Day.

Unfortunately, Karen proved to be remarkably tenacious. That year – my final year at university – I risked my studies and made a point of coming home much more often, since Dad must have been pretty lonely to hook up with his personal trainer . . . Not that he had a chance to be lonely any more. Karen was always there when I got back to the house in Hampstead. Always hanging around in our kitchen, cooking Dad cholesterol-lowering food or whipping up a smoothie. And always wearing that bloody horrible bracelet I had chosen and polishing it on the hem of her sweater as though it was worth more than three pounds in scrap.

By September, she had officially moved in.

And the following Christmas, the very worst happened. A year to the day from my very first encounter with Karen, Dad dragged me to Tiffany again and showed me a bright platinum band set with a single square diamond. Three sodding carats.

'You were absolutely right about silver being better than gold with her skin tone,' he told me. 'So platinum will look even better.'

Dad proposed to Karen on a New Year's trip to Barcelona; on the first day of a long weekend that was cut tragically short when I was rushed into hospital with suspected appendicitis moments after they called to tell me the good news. But now my appendicitis scare (aka The Wind Incident when my father was being particularly cruel) was long forgotten and the wedding I had never quite believed would happen was just six weeks away.

Back in the bridal store, I could hear Karen chatting on the other side of the curtain. The shop assistant asked about her fiancé. Karen giggled and said she'd found one 'second-hand'.

'One careless lady owner?' the assistant asked witlessly, sending Karen and her hideous mother into hysterics.

I raced to get out of the changing room before Karen or her stupid mother said something that might force me to use physical violence in a department store. I felt like David Banner on the brink of becoming the Hulk.

'And this is my future daughter,' Karen said, catching me as I emerged and wrapping her arm around my shoulder.

'Stepdaughter,' I corrected brusquely. 'I don't think many people will make the mistake of thinking I'm your real daughter.'

Karen's face fell.

'Well, I suppose there are just ten years between us,' she said.

'Not that Karen's marrying an old man,' Karen's mother quickly clarified. 'Alex and his first wife had Lindsey when they were very, very young. Isn't much of a bargain marrying a rich old man these days anyway,' she prattled on. 'Not now there's Viagra! It's ruining my life . . .'

Marilyn laughed so hard at her own joke it set off her smoker's cough.

'Er, gross,' I muttered, not knowing which was worse: the thought of some priapic old man chasing tail or the fact that Karen's vile mother was still managing to get laid.

'I'll send this dress off to the seamstress this evening,' the shop assistant said as she shook out the bundle I had left on the changing-room floor. 'It should be back in three weeks' time and then you'll need to come in for a final fitting. Make sure you haven't lost too much weight in all the excitement,' she added.

'No danger of that,' I assured her.

'Especially not if we keep having lunch at Sardi's,' Karen laughed.

Dad was meeting us at his favourite Italian restaurant, having lunch with 'all his girls' before he and Karen went off to sort out some issue with the wedding list and, God-willing, Marilyn went back to her granny flat in Bournemouth and left me alone to console myself in Selfridges.

'Let me just check I've got the date right one more time,' said the shop assistant. 'And the big day is . . .'

'July,' said Karen. 'July the seventeenth.'

Over my dead body.

4

Outside the store, Karen linked her arm through mine as we went in search of a cab. I unlinked my arm from hers to hail one. Karen patted the black leather seat beside her as we clambered inside the taxi. I sat on the jump seat opposite and stared out of the window for the entire trip, merely grunting in response to the questions she'd asked a thousand times since I moved back home after finishing university. 'How are the job applications going? I expect you're itching to get started with your career, aren't you? I know I'd be getting really bored just hanging around at home with a couple of old fogeys like me and your Dad . . .'

'Hmmm,' I replied. I simply wouldn't allow her to engage me. But as we arrived at the restaurant and stepped out of the cab I wove myself between Karen and her mother for the walk to the door and flicked on my smile. I was like Judy Garland stepping out into the spotlight, fresh from downing a bottle of scotch. I could do Oscar-winning happy when I had to.

Dad beamed when he saw us looking so pally.

'My girls!' he called.

We had a group hug, which lasted until Marilyn had another of her coughing fits. Not long then, thank goodness.

Inside Sardi's, the restaurant where Karen first walked into my life and proceeded to ruin it, the waiter showed us to our usual table. Karen sat in the seat that had always been mine:

middle of the banquette, facing out into the room, flanked by
my dad and her mother. It was the best seat in the restaurant –
mine for the fifteen years Dad and I had been eating at that
place before Karen came along and muscled her way in like a
cuckoo in the nest. Now I sat with my back to the room and
complained about the draught from the door, though I flatly
refused to move when Dad offered to swap with me.

I nibbled on a breadstick while Karen talked about our
morning. 'My dress is nearly ready. And Lindsey looked like
an angel in her gown. Wasn't she beautiful, Mum? Didn't you
think she looked lovely?'

Marilyn coughed her assent.

'I looked like a retard,' I said. Everyone ignored me.

'Everything is coming together perfectly,' Karen concluded. 'The dresses are going to be perfect. I checked on
the flower order yesterday. Apart from the wedding list, the
only thing left to arrange is my hen night.'

'Well,' laughed Dad, 'I don't know how I feel about you
having a hen night! What if you meet some handsome stripper
and leave me standing at the altar?'

'Oh, Alex.' Karen shoved him playfully in the arm. 'You
don't really think I'd be swayed by a pretty face and a pair of
impressive biceps?'

And that's when it came to me.

'Why don't I arrange your hen night?' I asked.

It was an unexpectedly effective conversation stopper.

Dad rocked back in his chair and looked at me as though I
had just announced I was going to run the New York
marathon in a fireman's outfit. Karen's mouth dropped open
too but her 'gawping in surprise' look wasn't that different
from her usual expression anyway. Marilyn's eyebrows shot
up to meet her face-lift scars.

'You want to organize my hen night?' Karen managed at last.

'Well, yes.'

'But . . .' Karen began.

I took a deep breath. 'I want to do something nice for my future stepmother.'

Someone spluttered. It might even have been Dad.

'That's, er, really kind,' said Karen. 'But you absolutely don't have to. I was just going to have a couple of drinks with the girls from work. Maybe have dinner somewhere. You could join us if you like.'

'You've got to do something more special than that,' I said.

'Really, there's no need for you to put yourself out . . .'

I knew there was no need. But I was determined. I looked her straight in the eye. 'Karen,' I began. 'I know that things haven't always been entirely . . .' I paused to find the exact right word. '*Comfortable* between you and me.'

Dad put down his silverware very quietly. Karen nodded minutely at the indisputable.

'That's an understatement!' her mother spat. She'd had too much Chianti with her pasta. As usual.

'Marilyn,' Dad said his future monster-in-law's name like a warning, 'Lindsey is trying to talk.'

I ignored Marilyn's pursed cat's bottom of a mouth and continued to address Karen directly. 'I think it's even fair to say that I've been a little bit harsh.'

'Oh no,' Karen protested politely.

'Hmmmmph,' Marilyn growled.

'I have been *very* harsh,' I insisted self-deprecatingly. 'But I'm sure you understand that it's only because I love my father so very, very much.'

Dad gave me a proud little smile.

'I just wanted to protect him from all possible heartache.

Which is why when he said he'd fallen in love with *another* personal trainer, my very first instinct was to scream. After all, you know what happened last time . . .'

Karen snorted with nervous amusement. Tales of her predecessor Trisha, who taught 'yogalates in self-defence', still formed the basis of some of Dad's favourite after-dinner anecdotes.

'And so,' I carried on, 'when you and I were first introduced in this very restaurant two Christmases ago, I was automatically on the defensive. I didn't want to like you and as a result I didn't really give you a chance to make me like you. I was primed to expect the worst and I looked for it. I was instantly dismissive of all your good qualities and magnified the negatives instead.'

'What negatives . . . ?' Marilyn began.

This time it was Karen who silenced her mother with a gentle hand on her arm.

'I magnified the *negatives*,' I said again for effect. 'Of which I have to say I could see many.' I counted them off on my fingers for her benefit. 'First there was the superficiality of your career. Personal training? What kind of job is that for a grown-up? Then I couldn't see beyond your lack of culture. You'd never heard of *Tosca* or *La Bohème*. I even took a dislike to your name. I mean, *Karen* . . . It's hardly dripping class.'

A blood vessel began to bulge above Marilyn's eye. I saw Karen's biceps flex as she held her mother firmly to her seat.

'But I see now how very unfair it was for me to focus on those things,' I pushed on. 'After all, you didn't choose your name and what does it matter if you would rather veg out in front of a soap opera than pick up an edifying book?'

Dad's eyes flashed 'danger' at me.

'It's your choice to fritter your spare time exactly as you want to. I realize now that what I thought of as simply prancing around the gym is actually a very stressful job and you deserve to relax in the way you like best when you get home after a long hard day at half past four. Let's face it, Dad is just a little bit obsessed with his intellectual reading. Perhaps he needs to lighten up. And I'm sure Dad never really enjoyed the opera as much as he always claimed to. He's probably glad he hasn't had to go to Covent Garden since he met you.'

I felt the gentle pressure of Dad's shoe on mine beneath the table.

'I don't suppose he particularly misses being able to discuss current events over breakfast with another equally well-informed adult when I'm not in town either. Ow!'

The pressure wasn't quite so gentle this time.

'All I'm trying to say is,' I gasped, 'I think I've judged you harshly in the past.'

'Hear, hear,' said Marilyn, knocking back the best part of another glass of vino and helping herself to a top-up which set her coughing again.

'But when I saw how you were with Dad, those big red flags quickly started to recede,' I shouted over the hacking.

'Thank goodness,' Karen breathed.

'You're getting married to him this summer and after that you're going to be in our lives for the rest of our lives . . .'

'She certainly is,' murmured Dad.

'Karen, you make my father happy.' I took another deep breath. 'And ultimately, I suppose that is the only thing that really matters.'

'Well said, Lindsey.' Dad squeezed Karen's free hand and made his goo-goo eyes at her.

'So you and I had better bury the hatchet,' I finally choked out. 'And I think we should bury it on your hen night.'

'Thank you,' said Karen. 'That's very . . . very kind.'

'Let's raise a toast to that,' said Dad. 'Lindsey, it's a lovely thought. Well done.'

'You better make this hen night a good one,' hissed Marilyn as we left the restaurant.

Despite Karen's gracious acceptance over lunch, Dad had to persuade her she should really take my offer up. I heard them arguing about it later that night, in the living room of the rambling Hampstead house I had moved back into after finishing my degree.

When I graduated, Dad suggested I might want to carry on living in the Exeter flat I shared with my best friend Gemma for a while but I told him I wanted to be back in London. Dad even offered to continue to pay my rent if Gemma and I found a new flat together somewhere. Perhaps we could look in Notting Hill? But I told him it was a waste of money. Why should he have to pay rent for me to live somewhere else when there was so much space in the house where I had grown up?

Anyway, back to their argument. Listening through my bedroom floor – face down on the rug with a water-glass to my ear – I heard Dad say that by suggesting I organize the hen night, I was offering a genuine olive branch. Burying the hatchet, as I'd put it. Karen said it was still clear to her that the only place I really wanted to bury my hatchet was in her head. I must be planning something. I never did anything nice without an ulterior motive. Remember the time I made a 'chocolate cake' for her birthday? It was an accident, Dad reminded her, that I used chunks of chocolate-flavoured laxative instead of cooking chocolate in the icing.

'Accident, my arse,' said Karen, which was quite a good pun I thought. For her.

Dad begged Karen to judge me more kindly. The way I had always judged her so kindly, Karen scoffed. Sure, sometimes I behaved in a pretty immature way for a twenty-something, Dad conceded (Karen interrupted that comment with another nasty spluttering laugh), but he was sure I was genuinely asking in my own clumsy way for a chance to make amends. And for Karen and I to become proper friends would be the best wedding present we could possibly give him. Wouldn't she give me the benefit of the doubt just this once?

'It would mean so much to me,' Dad wheedled.

'OK,' I heard Karen say at last. 'OK. Just for you, Alex. I'll do it. But only for you.'

She sounded as though she had just agreed to donate a kidney.

5

I made a few calls that night. Sent a few emails. And the following morning I presented my fait accompli over brunch at Lemonia, another of Dad's favourite restaurants, in Primrose Hill. Karen's hen night would in fact be a 'hen weekend', comprising four days with my best friend Gemma in Ibiza. Just me, Karen and Gemma herself.

'Four whole days? With no other guests except you, me and one of your friends?' I saw the panic in Karen's eyes.

'You and Gemma will get along very well,' I promised.

But as you've probably guessed, neither Karen nor I were exactly looking forward to her hen weekend in Ibiza. As soon as I booked the flights I started to wonder whether I had been mad to even suggest it. Four nights with the Queen of Common? Was I a glutton for punishment? Only Dad seemed entirely thrilled with the idea.

Every day I gritted my teeth as Karen asked my opinion on some new piece of wedding trivia. I honestly thought my head would explode if I heard the words 'place setting' one more time.

'Should we designate someone to collect all the disposable cameras from the tables at the end of the night?'

'Probably,' I would mutter and go straight back to reading my book.

'I think I should throw the bouquet right after cutting the

cake, don't you? Otherwise, some of the girls who have to leave early might miss out.'

'Throw it whenever you like.'

'I'm glad you're showing an interest in arrangements,' said my father from behind his newspaper.

I sensed that he was really as irritated by all the stupid little wedding details as I was, but I managed, for his sake, not to say, 'Whichever are most likely to choke you', when Karen asked for the third time which type of sugared almond I preferred.

Just a couple of days before we were due to fly off to Ibiza, I decided to go shopping for some new beach gear. Though I had no intention of taking Karen anywhere we might be seen by anyone I particularly cared about, there was never a good reason *not* to shop. I headed straight for the second floor of Harvey Nichols. Designer collections. No diffusion lines for me. I picked up a couple of sundresses from Mark Jacobs, then I popped upstairs and bought three bikinis from La Perla. I never wear any other brand. After that, I tripped along Knightsbridge, avoiding all chain stores, en route to Harrods. And it was while I was taking that little trip that I got a real blast from the past.

It had been at least five years since I last saw her, but there was absolutely no danger that I would fail to recognize Poupeh Gharani. When I first caught sight of her, she was buying an *Evening Standard* from the man who had the pitch outside Harrods. Paper bought, she leaned against a wall and opened the paper out dramatically so that it covered her entire face, except for her eyes, as though she was trying to hide. But if the gesture was meant to make her blend into the masses that seethed towards the tube station, it really hadn't succeeded.

Let me explain about Poupeh Gharani. She absolutely wasn't the kind of girl who could slip unnoticed through a crowd. She may have been only five feet two inches tall but she always seemed a great deal bigger. It was partly because she was at least as wide as she was high and partly because she always dressed like a Chinese circus tent. On that particular warm afternoon in June she was all in hot pink with gold trimmings. She had what appeared to be a piece of tinsel twisted through her thick brown hair.

I first met Poupeh when she started to attend my senior school. She arrived late, at the beginning of the second year, by which time all the important cliques were already fully formed and pretty much impenetrable. The day before she arrived, our form teacher informed us that we were all to be extra nice to Poupeh Gharani. This was not only her first week at a new school but her first week in the United Kingdom. Prior to that she had been at an American school in Dubai. She was Iranian. Some bright spark immediately asked if she was related to Saddam Hussein.

'Iranian,' repeated Mrs Castle patiently. As a class, we had a Republican's grasp of world politics.

'How do you spell her name?' someone asked.

Mrs Castle wrote it up on the board.

'But you pronounce it "Poop-ee", right?' someone tittered.

'Poo-*pay*,' Mrs Castle enunciated.

'Poop-*ee*,' we enunciated right back at her.

Poupeh really didn't stand a chance. She was the class laughing-stock long before she got as far as the classroom, providing welcome relief for Melinda Haverstock, who had held that far-from-coveted position throughout the first year thanks to a disastrous attack of diarrhoea during double French. (We had one of those horribly strict language teachers who wouldn't let you go to the bathroom unless you asked in French and absolutely correctly. Bit difficult when your vocab stops short at 'Bonjour'.)

'Poupeh will have to sit next to Melinda,' someone suggested wittily. 'If she smells like her name sounds.'

The class erupted with hilarity. So you can imagine my horror when Mrs Castle appointed me and my best friend Gemma as 'ambassadors for the class' and charged us with making sure Poupeh settled in.

We did the job. In the loosest possible sense. We told her where the science labs and the geography room were. We only once directed Poupeh to the strictly off-limits sixth-form toilets instead of the year-two cloakrooms. But after that first week, we never hung out with her again. She was just too embarrassing, always so enthusiastic about everything when it really wasn't done to be excited about anything except the boys at our brother school. The teachers loved her – she was always ready to volunteer. Some of the less cool girls in our class loved her too. But Poupeh Gharani definitely wasn't a girl I had ever intended to keep in touch with.

Now there she was, hiding behind a newspaper on Knightsbridge, like an enormous pink elephant standing behind a skinny palm tree. I froze as though by standing very still, I might make myself invisible, like the children in *Jurassic Park* who stand still to outwit the T. Rex. I could tell that Poupeh was scanning the street from behind that newspaper. It was very unlikely she was looking for me in particular, but thoroughly likely that she would see me anyway. Perhaps she wouldn't recognize me. My hair was longer and blonder than it had been at school and I'd had a small amount of work done to my nose as a present for passing my A-levels. Strictly for medical reasons, of course.

Slowly, moving sideways and backwards, I slipped into the

entrance of Zara with the intention of regrouping and making an escape plan. Did Zara have a back entrance? I'd never been in there before. I bought my Prada-style dresses from Prada. But I was distracted by a very passable Mark Jacobs rip-off just inside the store. I took my eye off Poupeh for just a second and next thing I knew she had grabbed me by the arm.

'Lind-zay!' she shrieked.

'Poupeh,' I squeaked.

'Lind-zay Parker. I thought it was you. What are you doing here? In Zara?'

'Good question. I just stepped into the doorway to get out of the crush on Knightsbridge,' I said quickly.

'I know what you mean,' said Poupeh, fanning herself with the paper. 'It is so hot today and so hectic. How are you keeping? It must be . . .' I could see her making the calculation in her head. 'Five years since I saw you last. In the classroom! Our last day at school! And to think we said we'd keep in touch . . .'

'You did, Poupeh,' I muttered to myself.

'I'm sorry I've been such a bad correspondent. Are you married now?' she asked.

'No.'

'Children?'

'No.'

I said that last with some irritation. Did I look as though I might have had children in the past half decade? I automatically glanced down at my stomach. It was, of course, perfectly flat. I worked out with a personal trainer (at a different gym from Karen's) three times a week.

'Me neither,' Poupeh sighed. 'But that is good, no? We are career women now, yes?'

I nodded.

'So . . .'

'So?'

'So, Lind-zay, what are you actually doing in your career?' She had to ask the one question I couldn't answer.

'Oh, you know. I only graduated a few months ago.' In fact, it was coming up for twelve. 'I'm just taking a few weeks off before plunging into the rat race,' I adlibbed. 'What about you?'

Poupeh tapped the side of her nose and handed me a card.

'I would like to tell you but I'd have to kill you!' she laughed. 'Here, have this.'

'Ha ha,' I said. I guessed that I was supposed to press for more details but I really couldn't be bothered. I glanced at the card. It merely contained her name, the initials PGI and her number.

'Well, I have to get on,' said Poupeh.

I couldn't help sighing with relief. That saved me from having to find an excuse to go.

'But we must get together one evening soon. There is so much to catch up on. Do you have a card too?'

'Oh. No, I don't. Sorry.' I made a 'how unfortunate' face.

'Then give me your number.'

'I can never remember it,' I lied. 'You know how it is with mobiles. Probably easiest if I call you,' I said, without ever intending to do so. The last thing I wanted was for Poupeh Gharani to put me on her friends and family list.

'Do that the minute you can,' she said. 'I want to arrange an evening out as soon as possible! You and Gemma. You still see Gemma, don't you? I'll always remember how kind you both were when I first started at Lady Margaret Heron School for Girls. That joke with the sixth-form bathrooms! How funny. I was so scared but you and Gemma knew that the big girls would be kind to me when they found out I was new. But I must go now.' She threw her arms around me and hugged me until I couldn't breathe, before adding mysteriously. 'I would love to talk some more but I am on an assignment. Goodbye, dear friend! Goodbye!'

An assignment? What was she on about? I couldn't help but watch and wonder as Poupeh bustled about a hundred metres down the street, then leaned against a wall outside Harrods and took out her newspaper again. Strange girl. Why didn't she find somewhere to sit down? Still, at least she hadn't suggested coffee right that moment, or lunch, or anything that might involve horrific amounts of time together. I went back to my own assignment – holiday shopping – in peace. I started at Zara. Really, that Marc Jacobs rip-off was worth investigating.

That evening, sitting at my computer, I instant-messaged Gemma in Ibiza and told her that I had bumped into Poupeh Gharani outside Harrods. 'Well, not exactly bumped into her,' I admitted. 'I tried to hide inside the doorway of Zara and she hunted me down. She gave me her card and said we should meet up. You too. She especially wants to see you again. Oh-mi-god.'

'I guess that means she's forgiven you for writing that love letter to Miss Hobson and signing it with her name, then?'

I had forgotten all about that. Now I had just the littlest twinge of guilt. When the letter was found in the pigeonhole belonging to Miss Hobson, our history teacher, Poupeh's parents were called. The letter was absolutely filthy, full of the wildest sexual imaginings possible (as wild as two girls who couldn't say the word 'breast' without having hysterics could get). An educational psychologist was threatened. Eventually, Poupeh managed to convince her parents and the staff that the letter was a fake but the real culprits were never discovered.

'That prank only worked so well because Poupeh really did fancy Miss Hobson,' I wrote back. 'All the best lies contain at least a grain of truth.'

'You are *evil*,' Gemma replied.

I took that as a compliment. I knew that was what she liked about me.

'What's Poupeh doing with herself these days anyway?' Gemma continued.

'She was being all mysterious. She said she was on an assignment.'

'Perhaps she's joined MI5?'

'Well, that makes perfect sense. The world's least anonymous-looking woman joining MI5. She was probably waiting to meet someone from an Iranian marriage bureau. She's not married,' I added unnecessarily.

'Neither are we,' Gemma reminded me. 'But perhaps there will be some eligible men at your father's wedding.'

'If it happens!' I tapped back. 'There is no way on earth I am going to wear that horrible dress.'

'Ha ha ha,' typed Gemma. 'You're going to look like Little Bo Peep. I'm going to take lots of pictures.'

'I'd break your fingers. Not that you'll get a chance. Looking forward to seeing you in a couple of days,' I said, getting ready to sign off.

'Me too,' mailed Gemma. 'I've lined up loads of hen-night treats. Can't wait to meet your future stepmother. I want to help you make this weekend really *special* for her.'

'Oh yeah. This weekend is going to be really *special*.'

I smiled to myself. I knew exactly what I meant by 'special'.

6

The hen weekend soon came around.

'Pumpkin,' said Dad on the morning we were to fly. 'You have no idea how happy it makes me that you are making such a big effort to be friends with Karen. I'm so proud of you,' he told me.

'Thanks, Dad.'

I held him close. Mostly because I couldn't look him in the eye.

'You will look after her for me, won't you? You'll make sure she doesn't run off with some second-rate Spanish Chippendale?'

'She's in perfectly safe hands with me,' I promised.

'You're an angel.' Dad squeezed me tight against him. 'This means so much to me,' he rubbed it in one last time. 'My two favourite women in the entire world going on holiday together.'

I flinched. *Two favourite women?* I wanted to ask him about that. But Dad was already pulling away from me anyway. When I gave up on his embrace, I noticed that Karen was standing at the top of the stairs with her wheelie case. I wondered how long she had been there, watching me talk to my father. It was creepy the way she wandered around the house as though she owned it.

'All set?' Dad asked her.

'All set,' she nodded.

Dad bounded up the stairs to help carry her case down. Karen clapped her hands together like a medieval princess at his chivalry. I wondered why she didn't carry the bag herself. After all, Dad was the one with the persistently dodgy back and she was the one who could bench-press 180 lb with one arm.

'Travelling light?' Dad joked as he strained to pick her bag up. I could see that the fake Louis Vuitton was dangerously stretched about the seams.

'Watch your back!' I shouted.

'Bend your knees,' said Karen. 'You can do it, Alex. Come on. Remember what I've told you. Engage your core muscles. Breathe out as you stand up. Breathe. Breathe.'

'Jeez,' Dad hissed like a punctured lung. 'Did you remember the kitchen sink?'

'I wasn't sure what to bring,' Karen added to me as Dad puffed his way down to the hallway. 'I wanted to make sure I packed the right kind of gear.'

Looking at her choice of travelling attire, I very much doubted she had. I was wearing my favourite air travel outfit: soft blue denims and a black cashmere hoodie. Anonymous lux, as I liked to think of it. Karen was dressed in the kind of outfit a footballer's wife on her way back from a World Cup match might choose to run the gauntlet of paparazzi at Heathrow: tight white jeans, a pair of high-heeled gold wedges you could smuggle a lot of cocaine in, an enormous pair of sunglasses tangled in her brutally straightened hair. The entire look was the kind of thing I might have worn when I was fifteen and thought tacky pop songstress Anastacia was a suitable role model for daywear. Karen's T-shirt proclaimed that she was 'ready for anything' in glittery pink writing.

I wished I had time to commission a T-shirt that said, 'I am categorically *not* with her.'

'You look fabulous,' said Dad, confirming my suspicions that men really don't notice what a woman wears as long as it's showing a bit of flesh. Or a lot of flesh, in Karen's case. He had no idea how tacky it was to flash so much middle-aged stomach. Especially beneath a slogan. No matter how toned it was.

I knew Gemma would agree with me when we arrived in Ibiza and she met Karen for the first time. If Karen ever got that far . . .

Dad offered to drive us to the airport in his new Aston Martin (any excuse to take it out on a motorway), but Karen told him it would make her too sad. Even though she knew we were only going to be away for four days, she hated to say goodbye to her 'best boy'. So, we called a cab, and Karen did her sniffling and sobbing in the hallway of the Hampstead house instead, while the taxi meter ticked on outside. It was quite ridiculous. After a while, even Dad had to remind her she would be home long before the next episode of *Desperate Housewives*.

Nevertheless, Karen dabbed at her eyes all the way out of London. Which gave me the perfect opportunity to slip a little something special for her hen night into her handbag. Something that might cause her more than a bit of embarrassment when we went through the x-ray machine.

7

By the time we arrived at the airport, Karen had at last stopped snivelling and was instead cheerfully making plans for our first (and only, I hoped) little holiday together.

'You are such a darling,' she said, squeezing my hand. 'I'm so touched that you sorted this whole trip out without me having to do a thing. It's so lovely.'

When the taxi driver stopped, I jumped out as quickly as possible in case Karen was about to move from hand squeeze to full body hug. I waited on the pavement while the driver unloaded our bags and Karen handed over the fifty-pound note my father had given her for our fare. The driver smiled goofily as he gave her our change (he'd rounded the fare down) and wrote out a receipt. Lots of men got goofy around Karen. Pity she had chosen to go goofy back over my Dad.

I let Karen push the luggage trolley while I navigated a passage through the crowds to our check-in desk. The queue was ridiculously long. I had chosen one of those budget airlines and clearly the first place they had budgeted was on the number of check-in staff. Or should that be the number of check-in staff able to do their job? Three of them crowded around one terminal as they tried to restart a computer one of them must have crashed through incompetence.

I didn't need this extra waiting time. I wanted to get through security and on to that flight. I didn't want to be standing in a queue full of pikey scumbags intent on bringing shame on the House of Burberry while Karen pulled 'funny' faces at a toddler standing with her parents in front of us.

Soon they were playing 'peekaboo'.

'Oh, I just love children,' Karen told me when the toddler and her parents had checked in and wandered off in the direction of departures – toddler waving all the way. 'I can't wait to have lots and lots of them with your dad.'

And dilute my inheritance, I shuddered. No way was that going to happen on my watch.

'Good morning, ladies,' said the girl behind the desk. 'Where are you flying to this morning?'

They were checking in several flights at once. I handed over the email printout with our flight details.

'The 1105 to Ibiza?'

'That's right.'

'And if I could just have your passports, please.'

I gave her mine. Karen reached into the breast pocket of her pink denim jacket and pulled out her own passport in its brand-new fake Smythson cover. Also pink. 'Got to have a nice-looking passport when your dad takes me first class to Mauritius for our honeymoon!' Karen had explained to me.

'Don't bother getting your jabs,' I thought in reply.

'Oooh, this is a lovely passport cover,' said the girl on the desk as she tapped in our names one-handed. 'Where did you get it?'

I closed my eyes in shame as Karen confided, 'Camden Market. Seven pounds.'

'I'll have to get over there. And how many bags will you be checking in this morning?'

'Two,' said Karen promptly. She heaved her enormous case on to the belt and tossed my far lighter suitcase after it.

'Has your baggage been out of your attendance at all?' the check-in girl continued. 'Does it contain any sharp objects? And are you carrying anything that someone else has asked you to carry . . .'

'No, no, no . . .' Karen and I recited our part in the security role-play dutifully. The check-in girl duly printed off two sticky baggage labels and attached the tags to our boarding cards. She then handed both the boarding cards and our passports to Karen, who went to put them in her fake Fendi. Except the fake Fendi wasn't there.

She shouted, 'My handbag!' like a woman who thought she'd lost her child.

The white-noise chatter of the terminal was silenced by Karen's shriek. Everyone looked in our direction.

'My handbag! I can't find my handbag, Linz.'

'Where did you last see it?' the check-in girl asked.

'I don't know.' Karen raked her hand through her hair. 'I'm sure I had it a minute ago. It must be here somewhere. It *must* be here.'

But it wasn't.

I just stared at the place where the bag *should* have been – dangling from the hook on the back of the baggage trolley alongside mine. How on earth had anyone been able to get to it and steal it since we'd walked into the terminal? They'd have had to do so right under my nose and I hadn't stepped away from the trolley for a second.

'I'll call the airport police,' said the check-in girl. 'It must have been stolen.'

Karen's face was creased with worry. 'Oh, I hope not. I can't stand that thought. It had all my credit cards in it. And my house-keys. And my little leather photo-holder with that picture of your dad . . .' she said to me.

Not to mention my special hen-night treat.

'If it was nicked in here,' the check-in girl said with a look of appropriate determination, 'whoever did it will have been caught on CCTV. We'll get them. There are hidden cameras everywhere. They won't get away with it. Don't you worry.'

A policeman was already heading our way. I felt my jaw clench in irritation. If the bag was found in the clutches of some scumbag now, it would have to be opened so that Karen could check the contents were still there, and my present would be found much too early and, worse still, could be explained away as having been put there after the bag went missing.

'When did you last see the bag?' the policeman asked Karen. 'Can you describe it?'

'It's pink. A Fendi baguette, if you know what that is.'

'Fake,' I added helpfully.

'And you're absolutely sure you had it with you when you came into the airport?'

Karen frowned hard as she tried to remember.

'I think so. I mean . . . where else would it be? I definitely had it as I left the house. I had it in the taxi. I had it . . .'

The policeman started to give out a description over his walkie-talkie. 'Pink Fendi handbag . . .'

'Fake,' I reminded him.

'You know,' Karen said eventually, 'now you mention it, I'm not entirely sure that I did remember to pick it up when I got out of the cab . . .'

Even as she expressed the possibility, Dad telephoned to confirm it. Luckily for Karen, she had tucked her mobile phone into the back pocket of her jeans.

'What's going on? The taxi driver just came back here with your bag,' Dad told her. 'He was halfway into London when he noticed you hadn't taken it with you. You just left it there on the back seat.'

'Oh, thank goodness,' Karen breathed. 'I knew it wouldn't have been stolen. You can tell that cabbie he's restored my faith in human nature. Honestly, I feel such an idiot. It's because I was so excited about our holiday. I'd forget my head if it wasn't screwed on,' she smirked at the policeman.

The policeman smirked back. 'That's quite all right, ma'am. Happens to the best of us. I'm just glad to have a happy ending for once.'

'You won't arrest me for wasting police time?' Karen flirted.

'Not unless you want me to,' the policeman flirted back.

Dad asked whether he should drive the bag to the airport himself but Karen told him there was really no need. She had her passport and her phone. If I would just agree to lend her some cash for the few days we were going to be away . . . Dad told her to let me know that he would transfer a grand into my current account at once so that I could sort out the spending money. What could I do but say it would be fine by me? I would be more than happy to help. Inside I was absolutely fuming. Karen's gift had cost me a fortune and it really wouldn't be the same if she didn't take it with her to the island.

'Actually,' Karen told me later as we waited at the gate. 'It's quite nice to be travelling light.'

I glared at the three carrier bags full of make-up, booze and suntan lotion she bought with *my* Switch card on our way through the terminal.

8

The flight to Ibiza was a nightmare.

Our discount airline didn't allocate seats at check-in. Ordinarily, I wouldn't have considered flying like that but I had been clinging to the silver lining that if we boarded late enough, Karen and I would be unable to sit together and I would at least have two hours of airborne peace before we arrived in the Balearics.

But when we got on to the plane a suspiciously chivalrous man offered to swap places so that Karen and I could be side by side. I knew he was just looking for an excuse to impress Karen and I said he really needn't bother – I didn't mind sitting in the aisle seat next to the loos (and three rows away from the prospective stepmonster) – but Karen happily took him up on his generous offer and proceeded to talk bloody sugared almonds all the way to the Med. I didn't even manage to finish reading my horoscope in *Heat*.

'You know,' she said as the plane taxied to the terminal at Ibiza airport, 'I really wasn't sure about a hen weekend in Ibiza when you first suggested it, but now we're here, I'm very excited. I think we're going to have a fantastic time.'

I could only pray that Gemma wouldn't let me down.

Gemma, my best friend, was already on the island. Since leaving university, like me, she hadn't had much luck on the job-hunt front (mostly because, like me, she hadn't actually applied for any jobs). She had decided instead that she needed to take some time to chill out and really find herself. It was the only way to work out properly what she wanted to do with the rest of her life. I agreed with her wholeheartedly. Fortunately, Gemma's mother Tanya was all about finding oneself too – she had been doing exactly that for the past forty-seven years – so Gemma wasn't subject to any of the thinly-veiled comments about dossing that I was starting to get from my father as we approached the first anniversary of the day Gemma and I left university with our matching thirds.

Gemma certainly looked as though she had found herself when she picked us up at the airport. She was wearing a voluminous white dress that might have been compulsory garb for someone entering a religious order, accessorized with a pair of brown leather sandals and a big wooden necklace.

'Hey! Lindsey! Karen!'

'Is that Gemma?' Karen asked.

'I'm afraid it is.'

'Oh. She looks much nicer than I imagined,' Karen whispered. 'From the way your dad described her I was expecting the kind of horrible woman you see looking snooty around Joseph at Brompton Cross.'

Which was exactly what Gemma usually looked like.

'I think she might have been taken by a sartorial body-snatcher,' I replied.

I was shocked. Perhaps she'd suffered a blow to her style cortex since I had last seen her in London a couple of months before. In fact, I soon decided it wasn't just Gemma's dress sense that had gone awry. She told Karen that she liked her T-shirt for a start. If it hadn't been for the hideous dress and the 'naïve' jewellery that Gemma herself was sporting, I would have assumed she was being sarcastic. Now I just couldn't be sure.

'I'm really glad you decided to come here for your hen night,' Gemma gushed, as she held both Karen's hands in a gesture that could only be described as 'warmly welcoming'. 'I can't believe we haven't met until now. Just five weeks before you're getting married to Alex!'

'Well, I've invited you to dinner hundreds of times over the past two years but Lindsey is always telling me what a busy girl you are.'

Gemma looked momentarily puzzled as she tried to re-member a moment in her life when she might justifiably have been described as 'busy', except in the sense of 'busy trying on shoes'. Or a time when I had passed on a dinner invitation from my Dad's fiancée? OK. So perhaps I had never actually passed on any of those invitations.

'Never mind. We've got plenty of opportunity to get to know each other now,' Gemma smiled. 'Oh, wow. Look at your shoes, Karen. They're absolutely fantastic!'

'Thank you. I like your beads,' Karen reciprocated.

Gemma's beads were like something a three-year-old brings home from pre-school. What was with all this mutual compliment stuff?

Gemma led us through the airport car park to her tiny Fiat Seicento. I insisted on sitting in the front, pleading a tendency to car sickness, leaving Karen to climb into the back seat with our bags. She looked a bit squashed but I decided it would be a very valuable lesson on the virtues of really travelling light. It didn't seem to quash her enthusiasm, however. She cooed about the landscape for the entire drive.

'It's just so lovely here. I never would have guessed. I expected it to be full of eighteen-year-olds getting drunk and puking.'

'Oh, there's plenty of that goes on. But it isn't the whole

island by any means. I'm really glad you like it so far,' said Gemma. 'My job is to make you feel at home.'

'Where is your villa?' Karen asked.

'Oh, there's no villa,' said Gemma. 'Didn't Lindsey tell you? You're staying on a boat.'

To say that Karen looked surprised is an understatment. Shocked is closer to it. She went green, as though in anticipation of sea sickness.

'A boat?' she said feebly.

'Don't tell me you don't have sea legs?' Gemma grinned. Karen couldn't even speak.

'We had a villa here until last summer,' Gemma explained. 'But Mum got a fantastic offer for it so she decided to sell up. Too many memories since Dad died, for one thing. But my half-brother and I didn't want to leave the island altogether so we persuaded her to buy a boat instead. That way we can be here or in St Tropez, depending on who's partying where.'

Gemma smiled brightly. Karen was still looking queasy.

'Don't you like boats?' Gemma asked her.

We were close to the harbour now. Karen gazed out of the window at the sailboats bobbing in the breeze. 'I'm just not a very strong swimmer.'

'Don't worry,' Gemma laughed. 'I won't make you walk the plank.'

9

I should tell you some more about Gemma.

Gemma's mum and dad were what you might have called a 'power couple' in the late 1980s. Gemma's father, 'Disco Dave' Smith, was a working-class-boy-made-good from Salford. He was a record producer. He had discovered some of the biggest one-hit wonders of the 1970s and made a fortune in royalties.

Gemma's mother, Tanya, was Disco Dave's second wife. She was a Scandinavian fashion model, famous for starring in a series of iconic underwear ads with a Swedish tennis star and later for going on a date with Prince Andrew (though didn't everybody go on a date with Prince Andrew in the 1980s?). Tanya was once described in *Vogue* as 'devastatingly beautiful'. Gemma had inherited her father's looks.

Fortunately, Disco Dave's money enabled Gemma to make up for being short-changed in the beauty department. Gemma's father left an awful lot of money when he died, as well as the enormous houses in Hampstead and Barbados (where Tanya lived almost full-time these days). Most recently, the coffers of his estate had been swollen again by a craze for nostalgic ring-tones based on his greatest hits.

Gemma and I had been best friends for years, though it wasn't an instant thing. When we first came across each other at our North London Prep school, I announced that Gemma's pencil case was really beyond the pale and she found herself ostracized by my altogether cooler gang with their trendy pencil *tins*. She would tell me later that it was a harsh but thankfully early lesson in the importance of looking just right. The following Monday she turned up with a pencil tin that was only available in America (one of her dad's colleagues brought it back on Concorde) and I was the one looking 'last week' in the stationery stakes. I sensed we were almost equals after that.

Eventually we became good friends and by the time we were eleven and moved from our Hampstead prep to the same senior school, we were to each other the siblings we never had. (In fact, Gemma did have a half-brother but he didn't really count. His mother was Dave's first wife, Elaine, the childhood sweetheart he left behind in Salford the minute he got his first big production deal.)

When Gemma's father died of a heart attack in a New York hotel just as we turned fourteen (the woman who called the ambulance swore she was just on turndown duty), we started to build up this little fantasy that we could now become sisters for real. My single father would fall in love with her single mother, they'd get married and we'd all live happily ever after. Unfortunately for the plan, Gemma's mother took up with some fat oil tycoon from Houston shortly after the funeral. (In fact, it later transpired that the fat tycoon had been in the background for quite some time before Gemma's father popped his clogs.)

And then, when the tycoon sodded off with a younger model (quite literally) on his private jet, my dad had already taken up with Melanie – the first of his fiancées post-Mum. And by the time Melanie was history, Gemma's mother was stepping out with a racing driver she had known when she was one of the girls who decorated Formula One car bonnets in the pit lane before the start of the race. When the retired racing driver sped away, Dad was seeing fiancée number two.

When that moment of madness ended, Gemma's mother had already hooked up with some aging playboy lord. And now that the old codger had finally gotten round to dying, Dad was weeks away from marrying Karen.

They were simply never single simultaneously. But I was certain that if they ever were, my dad and Gemma's mum would be a match made in heaven. After all, who doesn't want a Scandinavian supermodel as a stepmother? Although she modelled maybe only twice a year these days, Tanya still got a lot of free clothes.

Just under an hour after we landed, Gemma's little car crunched into the car park by the harbour in Ibiza Town.

We got out. As Gemma unloaded the bags from the back of the car, Karen nervously scanned the boats, wondering which holey old death-trap was going to be her home for the next four days. I thought I'd mentioned that we were going to be sailing, but perhaps I forgot. It was clear now that Karen had been imagining a beautiful villa and a calm, shallow turquoise pool. Life on the ocean wave was another thing entirely. But I wondered whether Karen had imagined a villa half as beautiful as Cala d'Or, the villa Gemma's parents built, had been. Or what a lot of boat you could get in a swap.

'There's the launch.' Gemma nodded over her shoulder.

'Is there going to be enough room for all three of us on there?' asked Karen, looking at the small motor-launch that Gemma had pointed out.

'Of course. There are three full-time staff,' said Gemma in amusement.

'On that?'

'Darling,' Gemma laughed when she realized Karen's mistake, 'that's just to get us to where she's moored.'

*   *   *

It takes a great deal to impress me. After all, I've lived in one of the richest parts of London my entire life. I attended a school where most girls had at least one parent who was a top-flight hospital consultant or a major player in the film industry. One particularly lucky girl had an Oscar-winning father *and* stepfather. My dad took turns driving in a school-run team that comprised a Roller, two Mercedes and a Jag.

At the beginning of every school term the girls in my class recounted holidays spent at second homes in St Tropez and the Caribbean for 'show and tell'. If anyone holidayed in the UK, it was because they had inherited an ancient pile that was open to tourists on bank holidays. So, no, money doesn't impress me at all. But even I let my jaw drop when I first caught sight of the place that was to be our home for the next three days.

'Welcome to the *Afsaneh*,' said Gemma.

Boat? It was the size of a small detached house. Gemma had navigated us through the long lines of cruisers towards the gleaming white hull of a Sunseeker 105 that rose out of the azure blue like an enormous upside-down steam iron.

I didn't know much about sailing but I knew that we were looking at the best part of five million pounds' worth of floating luxury. It was the kind of boat you would see P. Diddy launching himself from the back of. Scantily-clad beauties came as standard with this kind of big boy's toy.

Karen's eyes widened accordingly.

'What do you think?' Gemma asked proudly.

'It's got no sails,' said Karen in awe.

'Doesn't need them,' said Gemma. 'You can get halfway across the Atlantic on one tank of gas.'

'And this is what your mother bought from the proceeds of the villa?' I asked.

'And ring-tone sales of "The Turkey Twist",' said Gemma, referring to one of her father's very worst compositions: a novelty dance-song that had sparked a terrible craze for going 'Gobble, gobble'.

' "The Turkey Twist"? I've got that on my phone,' said Karen.

Now, why didn't that surprise me?

'But what does *Afsaneh* mean?' Karen asked as we pulled up alongside the steep white side of her hull.

'*Afsaneh* means "fairy tale",' Gemma obliged.

That's just what the boat was.

A Grimm fairy tale. I'm afraid to say that the inside of the boat absolutely fitted my expectations. It looked as though Donatella Versace had done the interior decoration. With a hangover. The smooth, sleek exterior lines of the boat were 'complemented' inside by more swags and flounces than Karen was hoping to wear at her wedding. It must make the boat's designers howl, I thought, that the only people who could afford to run them were the kind of people who thought that satin upholstery could be chic.

'Did Tanya choose this?' I asked incredulously. It was hardly her trademark Scandi-style.

'How are you doing?' Gemma asked Karen. 'Found your sea legs yet?'

You hardly needed to have sea legs to be on a boat like a Sunseeker 105. It was so big and so perfectly well balanced, that if you didn't look out of the windows, you could quite easily pretend you were on dry land.

'Do you think you might be able to eat some lunch?' Gemma asked.

'Of course,' said Karen. 'I'll help you make it.'

'Absolutely no need!' Gemma laughed.

It turned out that a cook was one of three full-time staff who kept Gemma's mother's floating insult to chic afloat and at her disposal all year round. There was a captain, an engineer and the cook / stewardess. All of them liveried. It must have cost hundreds of thousands of pounds a year merely to keep them in clean, pressed uniforms.

'You just get yourself freshened up,' Gemma suggested.

Karen was only too happy to agree.

The stewardess led Karen to one of the bedrooms, leaving me and Gemma alone for the first time since she'd met us at the airport.

'Well, this is a surprise,' she laughed. 'The very last thing I thought you would do is arrange your future stepmother's hen night.'

'You're telling me,' I said.

'She's not at all what I expected. From the way you described her, I was expecting her to be a real Chav.'

'Have you gone blind since I last saw you?' I asked. 'She looks like a footballer's wife. That outfit.'

'She's really very nice.'

'Hmmm.'

'But bringing her away on holiday. That's quite a change of stance from you.'

'I promised Dad I would make the effort to get to know her properly before the wedding.'

'Good for you,' said Gemma.

I assumed she was being sarcastic. 'Well, this is absolutely the last resort I'm prepared to go to with her,' I quipped.

'Ah, Karen. What do you think of your room?' Gemma interrupted. Karen had rematerialized behind me.

'Fabulous. Just like a hotel room. I can't believe we're actually on a boat.'

'Let me give you the proper tour. Don't worry, I won't make you stand too close to the edge.'

Karen followed Gemma out on to the fly-bridge. I left them to it. There would be plenty of time for Gemma and me to talk later on.

10

By the time Gemma had finished giving Karen the guided tour, lunch was served.

The stewardess / cook had set out a table beneath the canopy on the enormous fly-bridge, complete with a white tablecloth and sparkling crystal glasses. It was a far cry from rowing around the Serpentine, and even Karen seemed to have calmed down, safe in the knowledge that we weren't about to capsize.

'This is heavenly,' she said. 'You're really pulling out the stops.'

'Anything for the woman who's marrying one of my favourite men,' said Gemma. 'I've had a crush on Lindsey's dad for years.'

I rolled my eyes, popped the cork on the champagne and poured myself the first glass. Gemma narrowed her eyes at me, reminding me that I had breached etiquette by serving myself before the guest of honour. She quickly snatched the bottle back from me and poured a glass for Karen.

'We should have a toast,' said Gemma. 'Karen, I'm very glad you're here. Here's to a fabulous hen weekend and many, many happy years ahead for you and Alex.'

Really, Gemma was laying it on a bit thick.

'Thank you,' Karen smiled. 'You're so sweet.'

Yeah, I thought. What happened?

★   ★   ★

As we picked at our food, Gemma delivered her life story, as though she was determined to make up for all the years I had kept her and Karen apart. She talked about her childhood, her parents, our time at university. Pretty soon, she was telling Karen all about her love life, or lack of it, confiding as though she had known Karen for years.

'I can't believe you're both single,' said Karen then. 'Those boys you knock around with in London must be mad.'

'Perhaps I'm too picky,' sighed Gemma.

'No. It's good to be picky,' said Karen. 'I'm glad I waited for Alex to come along.'

'You're lucky that he did,' said Gemma.

Wasn't she just, I thought.

'You know what,' Karen said then. 'I think you girls would really like my stepbrother.'

I didn't know she had a stepbrother. Or perhaps I did, but the news had gone in one ear and out the other like so many Karen facts, most of them along the lines of: favourite colour – gaudy; favourite music – crap. I tuned in a little while Karen explained.

'My parents split up when I was twelve and my father remarried when I was fourteen. Dad's new wife had a nine-year-old from her previous marriage. I hated him. In the way that teenage girls always hate little boys. It wasn't simply that he was someone else's child and had taken some of my father's attention. He was just so frustrating. He was always booby-trapping the room we had to share at Dad's house. Can you imagine being a teenager and having to share with a nine-year-old? I remember the first time I got my hair permed. I wasn't meant to wash it for three days or the curls wouldn't take. I got home to discover that he had put a bucket full of water on top of my door. It got me right on the head and my perm was ruined. Probably a good job,' Karen laughed, showing a rare awareness of how awful her taste in hairdos was. 'It saved me six months of looking like a poodle. But I still pinched him until his arms were yellow.'

'What's he like now?' Gemma asked.

'Oh, not quite as annoying as he was back then,' she smiled. 'And much better-looking! I'll always think of him as the irritating little twit with the bowl cut but he's very handsome, actually. A bit like John Cusack, I think. And successful too. He's been working abroad for the last few years. He runs his own company. I'm very proud of him.'

'Is he coming to the wedding?'

'He'd better be. He'll be straight off my Christmas card list if he doesn't make it because of some business deal. Especially since I've been nagging him for ages that he needs to put more effort into his private life if he doesn't want to end up on his own. He needs someone to look after him. Wouldn't it be funny if I set him up with one of you?'

'If he looks like John Cusack, then I'm definitely up for it!' said Gemma.

I just snorted. John Cusack lookalike or not, I didn't think Karen's stepbrother was very likely to be my type. I'd never met Karen's father, but having met his first wife, Marilyn the desiccated trollop who smoked like a labdog, I didn't have much faith in Karen's father's taste in women. It was very unlikely that he'd managed much of an upgrade with wife number two and so, by definition, his stepson was almost certain to be as low-class and unsophisticated as his daughter. I could hardly imagine that Karen really had a successful businessman who looked like a film star in her family.

'Make sure you sit me next to him at the reception,' said Gemma. 'I'd let you have first dibs, Linz,' she told me, 'but you'll be on the top table anyway. Since you're a bridesmaid.'

Gemma had to rub that in.

'Oh, I can't wait for everybody to see Lindsey in her bridesmaid's dress,' Karen trilled. 'She's so lucky having such a fantastic figure and her blonde hair looks really wonderful against the gold.'

'What's your dress like?' Gemma asked her.

'It's the dress I always dreamed I'd have. How would you describe it, Linz?'

'Like Marie Antoinette meets Tinkerbell?' I suggested.

Gemma looked horrified at my directness but Karen actually clapped her hands together and laughed. 'You know, Lindsey's probably about right. Maybe it is a bit over the top. But I always wanted a white wedding. When Alex first proposed, I thought I was probably too old to go for the whole big dress thing but then I thought, what the heck, a big romantic dress is sort of timeless and you only get married once.'

'That's what I thought,' I said.

'That I should go for the big dress?'

'No, that people should only get married *once*.'

Gemma looked down into her salad.

'Well, ideally you're right,' Karen qualified.

'Time for another toast. To Alex and Karen,' Gemma interrupted.

Karen raised her glass, but her smile had gone quite tight and for a while after that, we continued to eat without speaking at all.

'Gemma, you've got a visitor.'

It was Karen who broke the silence. She pointed in the direction of the stern, where a very good-looking young man was climbing on board like the Milk Tray man.

Gemma rolled her eyes. 'Oh no.'

'Who is he?' Karen asked. 'Not some old flame you've been avoiding?'

'Worse than that.'

It was Gemma's half-brother Damien.

It's quite difficult at first glance to see how Gemma and Damien are related. Of course, they're only half-sister and brother, but while Gemma had been getting a little tubby of late, her brother was always whip-thin. Gemma had inherited her father's faintly gingery colouring. Damien had his mother's olive skin.

He was wearing a white silk shirt open to the waist and tight bleached jeans. He should have looked like a complete twit, but he was so handsome in that Eurotrash way you see all over Kensington that he was probably the one guy on Ibiza who could carry it off. Even the Bono-style dark wraparound glasses that don't really suit anyone (least of all the U2 front-man) made him look more like a spy than a fly. Damien was extremely exotic considering his mother was a check-out girl from the north of England.

'Hey, Jim-jam,' said Damien, as he pinched Gemma's champagne glass and helped himself to a huge swig as though he was drinking from one of those sports water bottles. 'Hey, Whinge,' he said to me. I just raised my eyebrows at him. I hated the nickname Damien had been calling me by for the past fifteen years. It wasn't as though it really properly rhymed with Linz anyway. 'What's up?'

'Nothing was until you arrived,' said Gemma.

He ignored her and finished off her champers. 'Who is this lovely lady?'

'Karen, this is my brother Damien.'

'Hey, there,' he said.

Damien made the words sound like a wolf-whistle. Then he pushed his glasses up into his thick brown hair and gave Karen the benefit of his big, dark eyes, so dark and chocolatey they were almost black. 'Lovely to meet you,' he said. Karen actually blushed under his model gaze.

'You've missed lunch. Are you going to be on board overnight?' Gemma asked with a hint of irritation in her voice.

'Unless I get lucky,' said Damien. 'Or perhaps even if I do.' He didn't take his eyes off Karen as he said that. She went even redder and stared into her champagne as though looking at the chilled fizz might cool her down. 'What are you three lovelies doing this evening?'

Karen said, 'Nothing.'

'In that case, perhaps you'd like to come along to this?'

Damien handed out three flyers to a club called 'Hot Stuff'. A girl wearing nothing but bikini bottoms stood with her arms wrapped across her chest to preserve her dignity against a background of photo-shopped flames.

'Good name,' I said. Sarcastically. 'Original.'

'Named especially for you,' he told Karen.

This time Karen went a shade redder than I had previously thought humanly possible.

'I don't think we want to go to your sort of club,' Gemma told him, gathering the flyers back from us as quickly as Damien had handed them out.

'Everybody who comes to Ibiza really wants to go to my sort of club,' said Damien smoothly. 'Until later.'

He left us and climbed down on to the deck below.

'Good riddance,' said Gemma. 'Honestly, Karen, my brother is a nightmare. He thinks he's Peter Stringfellow since he started promoting these stupid clubs full of women dancing in cages.' She pursed her lips at the thought.

Karen nodded sympathetically.

'It's all flash cars and drink and girls. Especially girls. No woman can turn him down.'

Karen shook her head and took quite a thoughtful sip of her champagne.

And it was then that I had the first tickle of an idea. Was Karen's love for my father strong enough to prove Gemma wrong?

'But the worst thing is,' said Gemma, 'he's developed a ridiculous gambling habit. He can't resist a bet. He'd bet on anything. Horses, football matches, two flies crawling up a window. He once bet two hundred pounds on whether he could get a persistent floating poo down the toilet in two flushes.'

Karen snorted champagne across the table at that.

'Did he win?' I asked.

'He did not. It took three. He's totally lost it.'

'Perhaps he just needs a little understanding.' I took a look at the flyer. 'A bit of non-judgmental support from his family. You know what,' I said. 'I think we should go to his club tonight.'

Sometimes inspiration comes very quickly indeed.

'But you hate clubs,' Gemma pointed out as we lazed on the fly-bridge later that afternoon.

'I know. But this weekend isn't about what I like or loathe. It's all about showing Karen a good time.'

Karen looked at me over her sunglasses.

'I'm really not that bothered about going to this club if it's not your sort of thing, Linz. I mean, I could just stay here all night quite happily. But we could have a lovely evening at a restaurant instead. A bottle of wine, some girlie gossip.'

'Sounds good to me,' said Gemma.

'But that's so boring!' I countered. 'You can't just go to a restaurant on your hen weekend. You've got to get completely wasted in front of people and do something that will make you blush every time you hear the word "Ibiza" for the rest of your life.'

'That doesn't sound so good,' said Karen.

'Oh, come on. We'll make sure you get home in one piece. What kind of a woman are you?'

Gemma laughed. 'I guess she's right, Karen. Lindsey and I really won't have given you a proper hen night if we don't get you into at least one totally mortifying situation, and my brother's stupid nightclub sounds like a good place to start.'

'Just keep me out of jail,' Karen pleaded.

11

I had no intention that Karen should spend the night in a jail cell, but I was determined that she would find herself in another, potentially more serious, kind of trouble.

After a brief dip in the ridiculously big hot tub on the fly-bridge, we retired to the main deck and started to get ready, applying our make-up side by side at the enormous dressing table in Gemma's room.

Gemma put on a turquoise variation of the white dress she had worn to the airport. I dragged out a fluttery green chiffon number that I had picked up in Barbados the previous winter. Gemma and I were both doing luxury hippy that night, but I suggested that Karen wear the short, hot pink dress that she had worn, rather embarrassingly, to my last birthday dinner.

Karen's dress was anything but hippy. It was instead the kind of ridiculously revealing dress that a glamour model might wear to the launch of a men's magazine. It was definitely not the type of outfit a thoughtful thirty-something woman would have worn to her future stepdaughter's twenty-third birthday.

That night back in London – at my birthday dinner at Sardi's – every man who laid eyes on Karen seemed to lose the power of speech. Including my date for the evening, who barely looked at me all night and talked about Karen even as he drove me home. 'Isn't she nice? Isn't she interesting?' He even said, 'Isn't she clever?' All those qualities men see in a woman when they've really just been hypnotized by a pair of big boobs. I never bothered to answer his calls again.

'Do you really think I should wear this?' asked Karen. 'Aren't Ibizan clubs more casual? I look so much more dolled up than you do. Your outfits are so much more cool.'

'You look amazing. Go all out,' I assured her.

That piece of pink lycra was a knock-out dress and I was determined that it would play some part in the sucker punch I was planning for Karen.

Gemma warned us that the VIP queue at her brother's club looked like a casting call for a modelling assignment and was actually often much longer than the ordinary queue.

'He gives those flyers out to everything in a skirt and tells every single one of them they're on the guest list,' she said ruefully. 'He's probably forgotten that he invited us at all.'

Indeed, when we arrived at the club, we found a queue that snaked all the way back to the airport. Gemma and Karen were ready to give up and go back to the boat. But I insisted that we stay and it wasn't long before a bouncer walked the length of the line and pulled us out.

'You're to go straight to the VIP entrance,' he said.

'What? My brother doesn't usually bother to do me any favours,' Gemma harrumphed, assuming the bouncer had been sent to look for a red-haired weeble dressed in sea-green.

Of course, Damien wasn't particularly feeling full of brotherly love that night either. When we found him in the VIP room, he told us that he had been watching the queue on CCTV and caught sight of Karen's fabulous dress – how could he miss that incredible hot pink – and there was no way he could have us stand outside when Karen clearly wasn't dressed for the cold.

'We are in Ibiza in June,' his sister reminded him. 'It is still sixty-five degrees out there.'

Damien ignored his sister as he popped open a bottle of champagne and charged our glasses. He filled Karen's glass first.

'The guest of honour. To you and your fabulous dress,' he smarmed.

You might have thought I would be irritated that Damien was giving Karen the special treatment, but I couldn't have been more delighted. He was clearly smitten by my father's fiancée and as far as I was concerned that was a very good thing indeed. Perhaps I wouldn't have to prey on his other weakness after all.

Damien led us from the VIP bar to his special table and attempted to rig the seating arrangements so that Karen sat beside him. But she hung back, and Damien ended up sandwiched between his sister and me. Soon Karen was deep in conversation with Gemma again and he had no choice but to turn to the lady on his left. Which was me.

'She's a beautiful woman,' he sighed.

'Who?' I feigned ignorance.

'Karen, of course.'

'She's getting married,' I pointed out. 'We're here on her hen weekend.'

Damien's mouth registered resignation.

'But what difference does that make to you?' I asked.

'What do you mean?'

'The fact she's getting married isn't an impediment to a piece of devil's spawn like you, surely, Damien? Her fiancé's not here right now. And I heard that no heterosexual woman can resist you since you became the King of Clubs. You're a regular Casanova.'

'That's a rumour I'm not going to try to quash,' said Damien, his slightly lovelorn expression replaced by his usual full cockiness once again. He even seemed to have subconsciously puffed out his chest.

'No,' I shook my head, 'on second thoughts, I don't think you could turn Karen's head. Her fiancé is a very special man.'

'Is he really?'

It was clear that Gemma hadn't told Damien exactly who Karen's fiancé was.

'Oh yes. Incredibly good-looking, rich, successful. He's thinking of buying a club like this to run as a hobby. Though I wouldn't have thought he'd have time for another hobby what with looking after his successful advertising business *and* running his racing cars.'

'What car has he got?'

'A new 911.' I chose a car that was just a little bit better than Damien's (his 911 was almost two years old) and saw a minute twitch in his jaw in response.

'Sounds like a man who has everything,' he half snarled.

'Including the most beautiful fiancée in the whole of London,' I reminded him.

At which point Karen obligingly, if unknowingly, gave a dazzling smile in our direction.

'Now Karen's fiancé really is a man that no heterosexual woman could resist. They'd be mad to.'

'How much do you bet me?' Damien suddenly asked.

'Bet you what?' I asked innocently.

'That even Mr Wonderful's fiancée can't resist me? How much?' Damien asked again. 'Come on, bet me. I'm not going to sit here in my own club and listen to your bullshit about this superman. I can have any girl.'

He had walked right into my plan.

12

'Make me a bet,' Damien insisted.

I shrugged, trying to make it look as though I wasn't taking him seriously. 'I don't know. A hundred euros,' I said eventually.

'What kind of bet is that? A hundred's nothing. Five hundred. Make it worth my while.'

'Whatever you want,' I said casually. 'I'm not expecting to have to pay up.'

I could see that the idea that he was less attractive than the mystery man I had described was driving Damien crazy. He had a peculiar shine in his eyes and I had a feeling that the more I scoffed, the harder he would try to prove me wrong. That prospect was very interesting to me.

'But I guess I'll agree to pay you five hundred euros if you get to kiss Karen – a proper kiss, with tongues – before the end of the night.'

'A kiss? I'll get further than that,' said Damien, rising to the challenge.

'I'm going to need proof.'

'Isn't my word good enough?'

'Frankly? No. I want to see it happen. Because how else will I know if it really happened? You've got a vested interest in lying and Karen isn't likely to tell me, is she? We're pretty close, but I know her future husband very well too and I think she would want to keep it quiet if she did get some action this weekend. After all, she is marrying in just over a month and if it were to get out that she hadn't been exactly chaste on her hen weekend . . .'

'So what do you want to do?'

'My suggestion is that you text me just before it's going to happen, then you lead Karen out on to the beach and I will watch from the VIP balcony.'

Damien's club was right on the sand.

'Done. Though it's a bit weird, you know, Whinge. Betting on your friend's honour.'

'I'm betting on her honour because I know she will *keep* it,' I lied. It seemed like the perfect thing to say to make sure that Damien considered he had a proper challenge.

'OK. You're on. Five hundred euros says I get the girl.'

We shook hands under the cover of the table.

'Lindsey,' Karen shouted above the mind-numbing beat of yet another identikit dance-song that wouldn't sound half so good when the punters listened to it again back in a Wolverhampton winter, 'Do you want another drink? I'm just going to the bar.'

Damien fixed her with his very best Peter Stringfellow smile. 'You are going nowhere, my lovely Karen. You girls are my guests at the club tonight and you do not need your money at all.'

With that he clicked his fingers and a mini-skirted waitress duly appeared with another bottle of champagne. Expensive champagne at that. Gemma rolled her eyes, but Karen looked pathetically impressed.

'Cristal! I don't think I've ever *seen* a bottle of this before. Damien, how on earth can we thank you for your generosity?' she asked, unwittingly offering him his first opportunity as she did so.

'Anything for you,' said Damien. 'All I ask is that you let me have the first dance.'

Damien wasted no time in trying to win our bet. He kept Karen's glass constantly topped up, so that by the time Gemma and I had finished our first glass of champagne from that second bottle, Karen had probably had three. When Gemma got up to go to the ladies' room, Damien immediately slid along the banquette into her place right next to Karen and engaged his hapless target in a conversation about her hair (one of her favourite topics). Damien refused to budge when Gemma came back again. She sat down next to me instead.

'Look at him,' she snarled. 'He won't leave Karen alone. He knows that she's getting married and he has a perfectly good girlfriend of his own who is probably staying at home washing his socks tonight. I'm going to tell him exactly what I think of him.'

'Don't do that,' I said. 'He doesn't mean any harm. He's just trying to make sure that Karen has a great hen night. It's very generous of him to give us all this free champagne.'

'Ha! He won't be paying for it,' Gemma grunted. 'When this business goes bust through his stupid showing off, just like all the others before, my father's estate will have to pick up the tab. Damien's got no sense of responsibility at all.'

What sense of responsibility did he need, I wondered. He and Gemma were going to inherit more than they could spend in fifty years of lost nights at clubs like this.

'Let's dance!' Damien shouted.

He stood up and lifted Karen on to her feet. 'Whoops,' she giggled as she almost fell straight back down again. Unlike her booze-hound of a mother, Karen didn't ordinarily drink very much. Her commitment to fitness went above and beyond her working life and she never let herself go overdrawn on her weekly alcohol units. But that night, she was well on her way to being hammered and it wasn't even nine o'clock. Damien practically had to carry her to the dance floor. At least her drunkenness was a good excuse for him to hold her very, very tight. He had to keep her upright.

'He'll try and grab her bottom,' said Gemma. 'Mark my words. My bloody half-brother should carry a government health warning.'

I nodded gravely. But inside I was delighted. Damien's hands were indeed already moving down from Karen's waist towards her bum and she didn't seem to be resisting. Instead, she was leaning into him and laughing at one of his cheesy lines. A win for Damien was definitely in sight. But little did he know it was a win-win situation for me too. I was one digital photograph away from being able to bin that gold dress.

'Let's have some more champagne to toast Karen,' I suggested.

Damien kept Karen on the dance floor for quite some time. But eventually, she broke away from him and headed unsteadily towards the ladies' room. I watched as Damien leaned against a wall and took out a packet of cigarettes and his mobile phone. He lit a cigarette, then started to text someone with the one-handed skill of a person who sends more texts than he should.

Seconds later, the screen on my mobile phone burst into light.

'She's meeting me outside when she comes out of the ladies',' was Damien's message. 'Hey, Whinge. Have your five hundred euros ready, loser!'

Loser? I smiled. I didn't feel like one.

I looked up to see Damien slide out through the club's side

door, a very confident grin on his face. I hoped that Karen hadn't told him she'd meet him outside just to get out of his clutches on the dance floor.

Excusing myself from a conversation about Gemma's meditation class (she'd got the hippy thing real bad), I stood up and headed for the ladies' room too. I arrived there just as Karen was staggering out again.

'You OK?' I asked her brightly. 'Enjoying yourself?'

'I've got to stop drinking,' she said. 'That champagne has gone straight to my head.'

'But if you can't behave badly on your hen night . . .' I began the hen weekend mantra.

Karen grinned. 'I guess you're right. But this very minute, I need to go outside and get some air before I throw up or pass out.'

'Do you want me to come with you?' I asked, all concern.

'No. No need,' she said. 'I'll be fine.'

'OK. Just text me if you need me.'

'I won't need you.'

Bingo.

I didn't go to the loo. As soon as I had watched Karen exit the club using the same door Damien had slipped out of five minutes earlier, I headed for the staircase at the back of the VIP room to find my spot on the balcony overlooking the sea and the scene of Karen's downfall.

I watched Karen trot like a lamb to the slaughter, across the sand to the pile of folded sun-beds where Damien was waiting for her, ready to close the deal.

13

I was elated. Who would have guessed that getting Karen to sign her own death warrant would be so easy? When we arrived on the island, I hadn't imagined for a moment that things would turn out like this: Karen getting jiggy on the beach with Gemma's hopeless half-brother. When Karen was with my father, I don't think Brad Pitt in a loin-cloth could have turned her head. But out of sight was obviously out of mind. As I watched, Damien offered her his hand as she stumbled in the sand.

Now was my chance. I took the lens cap off my camera and fired it up. On the little digital screen at the back, I could just about make out the figures of Damien and Karen on the beach down below. I set the camera to its 'night' setting, wishing I had fixed myself up with an infra-red setting before I came to Ibiza. Little did I know how useful it would have been. However, there was just enough light from the buildings along the beach to illuminate the couple on the sand. With a bit of jigging about on my computer when I got home, I was sure that I would at least get a recognizable image.

I took a practice snap. The flash went off. Karen turned towards it. I sank back into the shadows so that if she looked up at the balcony, she wouldn't be able to see me. After a couple of seconds, she turned back towards the ocean. I crept forward again, like a sniper. Karen had wrapped her arm around Damien's shoulder – possibly to steady herself. They started to walk a little further away.

'Bum,' I thought. If they walked much further along the beach, I wouldn't be able to get a picture of them from the balcony. Fortunately, they didn't go far. And then, to my delight, Damien suddenly sank to his knees on the sand and pulled Karen down with him. A moment later they were both lying on their backs. Damien was pointing up at the sky with one hand – probably telling Karen about the stars, that classic seduction technique. Any minute now, I thought to myself, he will roll over and kiss her. I would get the picture and that would be that. Sayonara, stepmonster. Christmas was coming early. I'd be burning that bridesmaid's dress before she could say 'Cheese'.

I primed my camera for another shot, making sure that they were in the middle of the frame. Then, as though the gods were with me, the cloud that had been covering the full moon moved away so that the beach was bathed in magical silvery light. I decided to climb up on the balcony railings to get the best possible view in these best possible light conditions. Damien was still pointing at the stars.

'Come on,' I muttered. 'Come on. Give her a bloody kiss.'

He was taking too long. While Damien faffed about telling Karen how to recognize the Big and Little Dippers, those pesky clouds were moving back over the moon. What was he doing? She was on her back in the sand. Surely he didn't need a more unequivocal signal that Karen was his for the taking? And when he took her, he would be taking her right out of my life! Please, please, please.

Finally, Damien put his arm down. He shifted so that he was on his side, facing towards her, propped up on one elbow. This was the moment I had been waiting for. Surely. Damien and Karen were definitely about to kiss. I couldn't wait to get back to the yacht and mail the evidence home using the *Afsaneh*'s satellite link.

But in my eagerness to get the best possible shot, I managed to fall off the balcony.

When I opened my eyes, Karen and Damien were standing right above me.

'Don't move!' Karen barked, when I tried to get up. She'd sobered up pretty quickly when faced with an emergency. 'You might have broken something.'

I had definitely broken my camera.

Fortunately, amazingly, my body had come through the twenty-foot drop unscathed. Before she would let me move from my place on the cold damp sand, however, Karen insisted she checked all my bones.

'You probably only got away with it because you were drunk,' she said. 'That would have made you all relaxed. What on earth were you doing up there?' she asked me. 'Pretending you were Leonardo Di Caprio doing his king of the world?'

'I was looking at the view,' I said, as I shifted painfully into a seated position.

I glared at Damien. He looked away.

'Come on.' Karen helped me to my feet. 'I'm sorry, Damien. I think the party's over for us tonight. I'll get Gemma, then we should go back to the boat and put this girl in the hot tub. Oh, wasn't that your Christmas present?' she said when she noticed the broken camera that had been crunched beneath my bottom. 'Maybe it can be fixed. Hopefully you won't have lost all your photos . . .' She pressed the camera's power button. It gave a pathetic little whine.

So near and yet so sodding far.

★　　★　　★

A few minutes after we got back to the boat, Karen's mobile phone chirruped. It was Dad. He had been out late with some colleagues and was calling on the off-chance that we too were still burning the candle at both ends.

'Of course we're not in bed yet!' Karen laughed. 'It's my hen weekend.'

He must have asked how the weekend was going.

'Absolutely great. We spent the day on the yacht and then we went to a club,' she said, before adding as an afterthought, 'And Lindsey fell off the balcony.'

There was a small pause while, I assume, Dad registered the appropriate horror.

'No. She's OK,' said Karen. 'Nothing broken at all. Amazing really. She fell on to sand and I think it helped that she was drunk. You know, when you're relaxed you can survive quite a big drop.'

Another, much smaller pause this time before Karen burst out with, 'Oh, Alex! You didn't! That will totally mess up my table plans.'

And then they were back to talking about the wedding.

I couldn't believe it. Dad hadn't even asked Karen to hand the telephone across to me so that I could confirm, in person, that I had come to no real harm. Karen may have checked my bones but she wasn't a qualified medic. She was only a personal trainer. For all she knew I might have concussion. I might wake up dead the next morning! Or rather, I suppose, not wake up at all.

The last time I had bumped my head – falling off the pony Dad bought me for my twelfth birthday – he had raced me to the accident unit and insisted on a *brain scan*. Now, it seemed, his concerns about my welfare could be assuaged by a few words from a woman who knew nothing, nothing at all, about brains. I half hoped that I would wake up dead, just to teach

Dad a lesson for having stopped giving a toss about me. His only daughter! The number one girl in his life!

Eventually, Karen and Dad finished their smoochy phone call. Thank God she went out on to the deck for the phone sex, I thought angrily. Now she came back into the boat's swanky sitting room looking goofier and more loved-up than ever before.

'Your dad sends his love,' she said.

'Didn't he want to tell me that himself?'

'He sent you a get-better kiss too. Here you are.' She blew a kiss at me.

'Oh, purleese,' I snorted. I got up, painfully, and went to bed.

I could hear Gemma and Karen sitting up on the fly-bridge for hours afterwards. Their laughter drifted down the stairs towards my cabin like noxious smoke.

I heard Karen say, 'Your brother is harmless, Gem. Really, he's just looking for a nice girl to settle down with. That's what we were talking about. I was just telling him that his current girlfriend sounds like a keeper when Lindsey fell off the balcony.'

'What on earth was she doing up there?'

'That's exactly what I was wondering,' said Karen. 'Do you think she's having a good time?'

'Oh, yeah,' said Gemma. 'She's loving it.'

14

I avoided Gemma and Karen for much of the following morning.

They were like a mutual appreciation society. They were dressed almost identically for a start – Karen had persuaded Gemma to swap her kaftan for a bright pink sarong.

'You've got a fabulous figure, don't hide it!' I heard her say.

I set up camp on the opposite side of the boat but when I sneaked a peek at them on my way to the loo, I saw Karen actually plaiting Gemma's hair as though they were twelve-year-olds at a sleepover!

I could overhear their conversation through the bathroom porthole.

'You're a bad influence, Gemma,' said Karen. 'When we get back to London, I'm going to get you to come out with the girls I work with at the gym. Then we'll see how hard-core a party animal you really are.'

'I'm always up for a challenge.'

Karen had never invited me to join her and the girls from the gym except under duress that afternoon at Sardi's.

Over lunch, Gemma announced that it was time for us to see a little more of the Balearics and find out exactly what the *Afsaneh* could do when the captain pulled the throttle out or whatever it is you do on a yacht.

We were going to sail to Formentera. The tiny island off the tip of Ibiza was rumoured to have some of the best beaches in the world. It was a short trip but Gemma was excited about showing us the *Afsaneh* in action.

While the crew prepared the boat to move, we moved back up to the fly-bridge deck, where the ship's engineer had arranged three sun-loungers in a row. Karen and Gemma sat side by side and rubbed in each other's suntan lotion.

'Can I help you do your back, Lindsey?' Karen asked.

I told her I would rather wear a T-shirt, even though I was itching to make the most of the sun. If Gemma had offered I would have accepted. But Gemma didn't.

Soon we felt the throb of the engines as the *Afsaneh* purred into life.

'Here we go! Every time I'm on this boat I feel like I'm in a Duran Duran video!' said Gemma, assuming a glamour girl pose as the boat began to gather speed and Ibiza Town slipped away.

Karen jumped up beside her and started to sing 'Rio'. Gemma joined in, singing into the very same pink plastic hairbrush that had been the harbinger of Karen's appearance in my life two years before.

'Come on, Lindsey. You know the words.'

I stayed seated on the pretence of being in charge of taking photographs. I'd never hated Duran Duran so much in my life.

Thankfully, it wasn't long before we could see Formentera. The white beaches were like a mirage in the bright sunshine. The ship's engineer took us ashore in the little launch that Karen had thought was the *Afsaneh* the day before. Once on shore he set up our base for the day. The cook had prepared food for a barbecue: beautifully marinated chicken and fish. Ordinarily, my mouth would have watered at the thought but that afternoon it stayed quite dry. Gemma and Karen opened yet more champagne and continued to whisper and giggle like schoolgirls. Half a bottle of champagne later, they started getting existential in a 'Chicken soup for the simple-minded' sort of way.

'It's all about allowing yourself to be happy in the moment,' said Gemma at one point.

'I absolutely agree with that,' said Karen enthusiastically. 'And you know what, I can't imagine ever being in a happier moment than I am right now. Except when I'm marrying Alex. I just know I'm going to be so happy that day I'll start to cry the minute I see him at the altar.'

'What about you, Lindsey? Do you agree?'

I could definitely agree that I would cry my heart out if Karen married my father. But 'I'm going for a walk,' is what I said in response to Gemma's question.

'But we're going to start the barbecue in a minute,' said Gemma.

'Just save me something,' I said.

'She keeps walking off when I've just asked her a question these days,' said Gemma.

'She always does that,' said Karen. 'I'm not sure she always hears what you've said. I've told Alex he should try to persuade her to get a hearing test.'

'We used to listen to a lot of loud music when we were kids,' Gemma chipped in. 'Perhaps that's what's done it.'

I stormed on until I really was out of earshot.

Formentera was indeed a beautiful island but the way I felt that afternoon I might as well have been walking through a landfill site within the M25. I was distraught.

While Karen and Gemma continued to bond on their beach towels, I walked pretty much the whole way around the tiny island. In the shade of each and every scrubby little tree, a happy family gathered. People were laughing. Children were playing happily. I wondered how many of them would be so happy in a year. How many of them would be adjusting to the misery of life in a stepfamily instead?

I knew it could happen that quickly. After all, in the twelve short months of my thirteenth year, my life had totally fallen apart.

15

I don't know if Dad ever saw any women *romantically* before
that dreadful year. I suppose he might have been on a date
when he told me he was working late at the office or going
somewhere on business overnight, but he was very discreet
about it if that was the case. It wasn't until I was thirteen that
he actually brought one of those dates home and the somewhat difficult subject of my father's love life first impinged
upon my life.

I didn't think anything of it when Dad came home one
evening and told me we were going to be entertaining over
Sunday lunch. I just made a note to ask the housekeeper to
buy a bigger chicken. Even at thirteen, I was used to entertaining Dad's colleagues and enjoyed the sophisticated
advertising world gossip around the dining table. But it
was clear as soon as I saw our guest upon the doorstep that
this meal was going to be far more significant and nerve-
racking than a simple Sunday lunch with the boss.

I wasn't even expecting a girl. When Dad told me that 'Mel'
was his colleague's name, I assumed it must be short for
Melvyn. For a moment, I was confused. And this Mel –
Melanie – looked as though she wasn't sure she was at the
right event either.

It was only just midday, but she was dressed as though on
her way to a black-tie dinner, wearing a dark plum-coloured
velvet dress that was clinging in all the wrong places and a pair

of killer heels that made me fear for the newly polished parquet. Dad and I were both dressed in jeans. I think I had a baseball cap over my dirty hair. Melanie's bleached banana-blonde hair was so big it had its own weather system. She was wearing more slap than a drag queen. In one hand she carried a bottle of cheap white wine I knew Dad would put at the back of the cupboard while he opened something far better from his cellar. In the other she was clutching a gift-wrapped box. For me.

She shoved it into my hands.

'Surprise,' she said.

Extrapolating from the way Mel had dressed for a casual Sunday lunch that the gift was just as likely to be inappropriate, I tried to get away without opening it in front of her. But she insisted.

'I love seeing people open their presents.'

So I did as I was told. And inside was a Barbie doll. Barbie Equestrian, to be precise.

'I didn't know what to get you.'

'Clearly,' I replied.

There may have been one or two thirteen-year-old girls out there who still liked to play with Barbie, but I'd put away my dolls long before I started senior school. Not having a mother around makes you grow up pretty quickly. Why play house in miniature when you get to play house for real every day? I looked at the doll somewhat pityingly, already making plans to pass it on to the cleaner's little girl, who was just seven and a half. Sensing my lack of interest in her gift, Melanie looked as though she might be about to cry.

But Dad was to come to her rescue. As I struggled to find the words to express my somewhat-less-than-heartfelt thanks, Dad appeared in the doorway behind me. He was still wearing his oven gloves. He put a gloved paw on my shoulder – the one shaped like a frog's head that he had used as a glove puppet when I was small – and said, 'It's very kind of Melanie to think of you, isn't it, Lindsey? Don't forget to say thank you.'

And there was the real surprise.

Don't forget to say thank you???

It was the first time I had ever heard my father speak to me as though I was a child. At least, the first time since I actually stopped considering myself to be a child (at about eight years old, if you're wondering). And in public! I couldn't believe my ears. Our relationship until that point had been characterized by the fact that with Mum gone he treated me as an equal.

Now he held out the hand wearing the sensible oven glove to Melanie and led her into the house, never taking his eyes off her as he did so. She relaxed instantly under his gaze. And though I had never seen it in his face before, I recognized straight away that my father was besotted.

I should have guessed when I saw the effort he put into making that Sunday lunch special. I should have guessed when he came into my room that morning and asked me to help him choose which of three broadly identical chambray shirts he should wear with his favourite jeans. I should have guessed from the way he bopped to Frank Sinatra while stuffing a chicken with lemons.

I thought I was going to throw up. I had the same strange sick-to-my-stomach sensation of humiliation and betrayal I got when I saw the object of my first crush, Andrew, kissing another girl in the dark corner of an under-sixteens' disco at the Hippodrome.

My father was in love with Melanie. He was in love with her superficial prettiness, the humble gentleness that I knew at once was absolutely fake. That lunchtime, every chance he got, he reached out to touch her hand across the dining table. She made doe eyes back at him.

I didn't eat a thing.

Three months after that terrible Sunday lunch Melanie moved in and started ordering new curtains to replace the perfectly decent ones Dad and I had chosen together when we bought the house just two years before. Three months after that, Dad told me they were getting engaged and I was fitted for the first horrific bridesmaid's dress, stomach cramping all the time. And three months after that, I overheard Melanie having a phone conversation with one of her friends during which she said, 'He may be minging, Steff, but at least he's rich. Think of the divorce settlement.'

When my father confronted her, Melanie insisted I was making it up; that I'd been determined to ruin things between them from the start. She loved him. She would have loved him if he didn't have a penny, she protested. She would have lived in a mud hut as happily as that great big Victorian house in Hampstead decked out in her choice of soft furnishings from the Conran Shop. Just so long as she was with him.

'Come on, Dad,' I said, when he tackled me. 'I heard what I heard. I mean, why would I lie to you? And would I ever use a word like "minging"?'

He had to agree that my expensive education had furnished me with a more elegantly detrimental vocabulary than that. Unlike Melanie, who called me a 'vicious little slag' when she next found me alone in the kitchen.

After much hand-wringing and insufficiently hushed late-night arguments that I heard quite clearly through the walls, Dad told Melanie that he believed me. The wedding was called off, she moved out and we were on our own again. Soon after that, Melanie found a much better position at a different advertising agency assisting one of my father's old friends: a very wealthy man with a wife and two small children. We heard six months later that Melanie and her new boss had embarked upon an affair, confirming everything I had suspected about Melanie's gold-digging tendencies.

16

Unfortunately, the peace in our house was to be short-lived.

Just a year after Melanie's departure, Dad flew to California to oversee the filming of a car commercial for one of his agency's biggest clients. He came back from Los Angeles loaded down with the Abercrombie and Fitch clothes I had asked for, and something else I had definitely not requested. Another Sunday lunch was arranged . . .

Heather described herself as an actress. More accurately, she was an M.A.W. A 'model / actress / waste of space'. That car commercial in California was her first acting job. If you can call 'gawping in awe' as a car zooms past the window of a diner 'acting'. Heather was playing the diner waitress. She didn't even have to say 'coffee' and yet her scene took twenty-five takes. A real waitress could have done better. But as far as Heather was concerned, it was just a matter of time before Spielberg requested her show-reel and became her benefactor.

In the meantime, it seemed my father would do.

I suppose I could see what Dad saw in her at first glance. Heather was pretty in a girl-band sort of way. She was certainly better groomed than Melanie. In the event of a fire, Heather would have rescued her straightening irons before anything else. But she was definitely not challenging. She was as dizzy as a kitten stuck on a spin cycle. And I took great comfort from that. I knew Dad liked a challenge. I thought she would last for two weeks.

But within two weeks, Heather had unofficially moved in!

Now that her acting career was taking off, she told Dad, it wouldn't do for her to be living up in Manchester with her parents. She should come down to London and look for a flat there so that she was never more than twenty minutes from a 'go-see' or a casting call. It was a clever move. Dad automatically offered her our spare room for a while and was only too understanding when every flat she looked at turned out to be 'not quite right'.

A month later, Heather was still on our sofa every time I came home from school, reading her 'scripts' (or, more usually, *Hello!* magazine), moving only to attend her gym classes and sessions with a voice coach.

I tried not to freak out too much. After all, she was only in the spare room. And she remained in the spare room after almost four months. There was obviously less to her relationship with Dad than I thought. Eventually he would suggest she moved on.

How wrong I was.

I soon began to long for Melanie's erudite conversation. Heather made small talk. Very small talk. She was obsessed with 'New Age' philosophies, attributing everything in her life, good or bad, to the interference of a benevolent universe.

'You just have to ask for what you want, Linz,' she'd tell me.

'What if everyone asked to be a model?' I said. 'Who would empty the bins?'

'There will always be people whose karma means they have to empty bins in this life,' she said simply. Then she went back to drawing 'psychic pictures' asking the universe for a regular part in *Casualty*.

Where Melanie had spent a fortune on handbags, Heather spent a fortune on handbags and premium rate phone-lines to phoney psychics. I came to learn that once a month she also made a trip to Covent Garden to see a tarot card reader at one of those New Age shops that smell of patchouli oil and open graves. Heather taped those readings and kept the tapes in the bedside cabinet. I found them when I was looking for an old school textbook I thought I might have left there. Of course, I have to admit I listened to a couple of the tapes. And that's how I found out they were getting married.

'I see a wedding on the horizon,' said the reader.

'Yes!' Heather squealed. 'It's just a matter of finding a way to tell his daughter that we're together . . .'

No need.

I tackled Dad that night. I didn't mention that I had listened to the psychic tapes but I did mention that Heather seemed to have stopped looking for a flat.

'Ah, yes,' said Dad. 'You see . . .'

He smiled the same soppy smile he couldn't keep off his face when he got engaged to Melanie. My heart broke.

'I've been thinking about asking Heather to move in with us properly. To move in for ever, in fact.'

I knew at once how she had done it. All that sleeping in the spare room wasn't because she *didn't* have designs on Dad, it was an important part of her master plan. She had played him by The Rules – no sex before marriage – and he was stupid enough to pay the ultimate price for a bunk-up.

'She's a great girl, Linz,' said my father.

She was a nasty, scheming cow.

The engagement was announced and I was fitted for the yellow dress. I was more miserable than ever. Just over a year before, I had been distraught at the thought that my father was going to marry a gold-digger. Now he was planning to marry a dingbat.

But even as the wedding arrangements were made, Heather started to seem a little uncomfortable in our Hampstead house.

'I just don't feel right here all of a sudden,' Heather told me one morning. 'Do you ever feel as though there are malevolent spirits about?'

'Sometimes,' I grumbled, looking straight at her.

But it was to get much more bizarre than that conversation over breakfast,

Dad had always taken a fairly indulgent view of Heather's predilection for astrology and other mumbo-jumbo. Of course, he had no idea that her morning ritual of reading Mystic Meg in the *Sun* was the tip of an enormous premium rate iceberg. It was harmless, he thought. Just a girl thing.

But then Heather started telling Dad about the malevolent spirits too. And not only was she sensing a 'presence', she was actually hearing voices. Voices that told her she wasn't welcome in our house.

Dad laughed. 'Next time tell them to talk to me.'

I decided to take her more seriously. This was something that needed to be probed.

'What are they like?' I asked. 'The voices?'

Heather looked about herself nervously before she answered, 'I think it's a woman and a little girl. Sometimes it's just a whisper. And always in the bedroom,' she said.

Later, she worked out that the voices only came to her when I was in the house as well. She consulted a psychic who decided that I must be the conduit the evil spirits had chosen to make their way to the earth. Apparently teenage girls have a hormonal energy that evil spirits love. Heather showed the psychic a photograph of me and the psychic confirmed that I definitely looked 'troubled'. Heather subsequently told Dad that the psychic knew a healer who would cleanse the house and me of all our troubles for five hundred pounds plus VAT.

'You are being utterly ridiculous,' said Dad.

Naturally, I was horrified by Heather's suggestions. Terrified, even. The whole business was quickly getting beyond a joke. I told Dad that Heather was freaking me out. Dad told Heather that she was the one who needed to be cleansed. By a psychiatrist. Heather protested that she wasn't going mad.

'Evil,' she insisted, 'really exists.'

A couple of nights later, Heather heard the voices say that if she tried to marry my father, she would die on her way to the church. The bridal limousine would spin off the road into a flying buttress and the roof of the church would cave in on the congregation. Her family would be first to be squashed. The devastation would be total.

'There are no flying buttresses,' said Dad. 'You only get those on Norman cathedrals.'

The church they were to marry in was Victorian.

The following night, the spirits revised their threat so that the bridal car would simply spin into the lintel by the front door of St Mary's. The rest of the calamity would be exactly the same.

'Then we'd better not risk it,' said Dad, when Heather relayed this information to him. 'I can't argue with the forces of evil.'

I could tell that Dad was trying to make a joke but after another week of spiritual interference his patience was exhausted. When Heather suggested that they move house and marry in a registry office, he was less than enthusiastic. The spirits were in agreement. Next time Dad went on a business trip and Heather was alone in the spare bedroom, they told her that wherever she moved, they would follow. If she persisted in trying to marry my father, Heather would die on her wedding day even if she ran all the way to a drive-thru chapel in Las Vegas. She'd choke on a hot dog. Be electrocuted by a slot machine. They could make a giant neon Elvis fall on her head if they felt like it. 'Wooooh! Woooo-hoo-ooooh!' they added for good measure.

When Dad got back from his business trip he found Heather gibbering on the sofa in the sitting room. She hadn't slept for the entire week he'd been away. This time Dad insisted that she move out to save her own sanity. The removal van was booked while I was at school. And Heather never came back. Dad sent her money for quite a while. To cover her therapy bills.

It was two years before he brought anyone home again.

17

This time it was worse.

I suppose Trisha was partly my own fault. Now in his late thirties, Dad was getting a little bit tubby. I had been nagging at him to find and stick to a fitness regime. He joined the gym near work. Suddenly he was doing three yoga classes a week without complaining. And then he brought home the yoga teacher.

I should have guessed no man was really that interested in stretching.

'I don't teach yoga. I teach yoga-*lates*. It's fitness fusion,' Trisha said.

Whatever she taught, Dad was clearly impressed by her ability to put her legs behind her ears. There really wasn't much else about Trish to find impressive. She'd dropped out of school at sixteen to run away to Ibiza. Then she met and followed some guru to India and spent eight years on a vegan commune before coming back to London to spread the word in her *leather* New Balance trainers. There wasn't a single moment in the day Trisha couldn't turn into a demonstration of her own physical and psychological flexibility. It was particularly annoying when she used the rail on the front of the Aga as a stretch support while I was trying to have my breakfast.

Trisha wouldn't leave me alone for a moment. She was always creeping up behind me, grabbing my shoulders and yanking me into some difficult posture that would enable the 'chi' to flow around my body more effectively than my usual slumped position. Trisha could find 'chi' where most people only found belly-button fluff. She interfered with what we put into our bodies as well, clearing the fridge of just about every foodstuff that makes life worth living and replacing it with tofu. That I could just about cope with. I could always stop off at Starbucks on the way to school for the essential shot of evil caffeine that would enable me to make it through double maths. But Trisha really overstepped the mark the day she told Dad I needed to go into rehab.

I swear to you. Trisha told my father I ought to go to The Priory. And all because she caught me and Gemma smoking on the balcony outside my bedroom.

OK, so I admit we weren't exactly smoking Marlboro Lights. But it was just one teensy-weensy joint. There was hardly any weed in there at all (we'd smoked most of the ounce Gemma bought from her brother the previous week-end). It was probably *healthier* for us than a normal cigarette. And, believe, me, as far as drug-taking went, Gemma and I were very late starters. There were girls in our class at our terribly exclusive school who had been smoking joints since the first year.

Still, Trisha freaked out. She shouted the odds long and loud enough for the police at Scotland Yard to hear without opening their windows. She didn't even stop when Gemma had a panic attack and started choking on the lungful of smoke she had been holding in her mouth since we first heard the handle to my bedroom door turn and still hoped we might get away with it.

'You could die from this!' Trisha yelled at me, snatching the joint from my hand.

'I think Gemma *is* dying,' I replied as Gemma hurled her

guts up over the balcony and on to the newly-painted patio furniture beneath. The lovely *white* patio furniture. If only we hadn't been on a beetroot juice diet that week . . .

'You deserve to be sick,' Trisha told her. 'Imagine how much sicker you'll feel if you wind up wasting your life smoking crack!'

I could tell it probably wasn't a good time to try to impress Trish with the anecdotal evidence that marijuana smoking isn't addictive and doesn't necessarily lead to the abuse of harder drugs. Her inner *Independent* reader clearly wasn't at home.

Gemma scarpered as soon as she could stand up straight, leaving me to bear Trisha's lecture alone *and* clear up the vomit. I nodded contritely as Trisha reeled off the list of nasties I was asking to be visited upon me by partaking of the evil weed. I swore I'd never touch the stuff again and begged her not to tell Dad. I even went so far as to suggest that all I needed to get my life back on track was a steadying feminine influence such as she might be able to give me. Her discretion over this silly little joint would be the perfect gesture of trust. If she could keep quiet about this minor misdemeanour, it would make it much easier for me to confide in her in the future. Really, there was no need to involve Dad at all.

She said she'd think about it.

But that night Trisha presented the confiscated joint to Dad over the dinner table. Right in the middle of dessert.

'I found your daughter smoking this,' she announced.

'A roll-up?' Dad asked hopefully.

'A *joint*.'

It looked slightly shorter than when I'd handed it over, I protested. Like someone else had taken a sneaky drag. My protests fell on furiously deaf ears. Trisha gave a reprise of the lecture I'd received that afternoon. It was just a matter of time before I was a pregnant crack whore. Dad agreed I was on the road to hell.

His solution? I was grounded for the *entire* summer. Sixteen years old and I couldn't leave the house without a chaperone. Not even to buy a pint of milk. My mobile phone was confiscated. The holiday in Ibiza that Gemma and I had been planning for months was cancelled. Trisha even went so far as to call Gemma's mother to let her know what had happened. Fortunately, Tanya was out that day – in fact, she was away for the whole of July – so Gemma, doing a marvellously close approximation of Tanya's mid-Atlantic drawl, picked up the phone herself and assured Trish that yes, my best friend would be grounded too.

I thought Dad would calm down after a while – he hadn't exactly been a model of teenage propriety himself – but my grounding endured from the first day of the summer holidays until the very last. Instead of going to Ibiza with Gemma, I had to accompany Dad and Trish on a boring tour of the Italian Lakes. I missed the three major house parties (all of them at Gemma's place) that were to form the topic of just about every conversation in the sixth-form common room for the next two years. My boyfriend Marcus dumped me because I couldn't go out in the evenings and he got tired of coming round for lunch and a quick fumble in the kitchen while Trisha was on the phone in the hall.

Every so often Trisha would tell me that it was 'for my own good'. Which was why it was somewhat galling when, later that very same year, on her way back from a yoga retreat in Thailand, Trisha was arrested at Bangkok airport with quite a substantial amount of cocaine stitched into the lining of her carry-on bag.

Luckily for her, Dad knew some fantastic lawyers and she

didn't end up in the Bangkok Hilton. But the incident did lead to their break-up . . .

So there you have them. My father's former fiancées. The three witches. A gold-digger, a flake and a drug addict.

You've got to understand it didn't make me happy that my Dad's love life was such a soap opera. But what kind of daughter would I have been if I had been happy for him to marry a bitch like Melanie, who would have bankrupted him at Prada within a single fashion year? Or crazy Heather, with her voices? Or Trish, the hippy hypocrite (with a surprisingly materialistic penchant for Hermes)? Between them those girls had the spending lust of a Selfridges' fashion buyer and the brainpower of a hamster. With concussion. I swear to you, Heather used to follow the words with her finger as she read her gossip mags. Trisha quoted liberally from the words of Cuban revolutionary *Shane Riviera.*

They just weren't suitable. I wanted my father to be happy and I couldn't see how on earth he would be happy in the long term with the idiots he hooked up with during those dark dating years. He was college-educated, well-read and cultured. He was well travelled; a man who could hold his own with anyone from the postman to the President of the United States. He needed a woman who could match him in intellect and sophistication as well as look good on his arm (when it came to arm adornment, Trish, Heather and Melanie were about as classy and attractive as a faux gold identity bracelet). Dad needed a classically beautiful and professionally successful woman, not some old gold-digger who would see the house in Hampstead and the fabulous cars, hear 'ker-ching' and hand in her notice at Burger King.

I know he would have felt exactly the same way had I brought home the guy who checked the tyres on my Mini or the charmer who sold me my cigarettes at the tube station. Both very cute but clearly without prospects. If I'd turned up with anything like the male equivalent of Dad's consorts, he would have done everything he could to prevent me from making a terrible mistake that could ruin the rest of my life. Everything and anything.

Of course, Karen had been right. I had no real intention of burying the hatchet on our trip to Ibiza. Rather, I was still intending to *drive* a hatchet between her and my father. Ibiza had seemed like the perfect place to do that. After all, it has a reputation as an Island of Sin.

My plan had been relatively simple and old-fashioned. I'd get Karen to misbehave and catch said misbehaviour on camera. There were so many different ways she could cock up: drunkenness, drugs, deception. I could make a slide-show. My ideal scenario would be to catch Karen drunk as a skunk and snorting cocaine off the abdominal muscles of a nightclub dancer. I had ways of making her do it, I was sure.

But it was becoming increasingly clear to me that Karen was on an *unwavering* trajectory towards marriage and step-motherhood. She wasn't about to be obligingly unfaithful. She could hold her drink better than I could. And I now knew for certain that she wasn't about to be found with drugs in her fake Fendi as she tried to slip through airport security. In less than a month she would be Mrs Alex Parker and that would be that.

Back on the beach at Formentera, I decided that there was only one way to deal with the way I felt: I needed a drink. Nothing alters your perception and dulls the pain quite so quickly as alcohol on an empty stomach (except perhaps, Ecstasy on an empty stomach). When I got back from my walk, I announced that I would have a glass of champagne after all. In fact, I would catch up with the other girls by having three in quick succession.

By the time the *Afsaneh*'s engineer announced that it was time to go back to the yacht, my nose had started to go numb – first sign that I was rat-arsed. I tried to get to my feet, only to stumble and land back on my bottom in the sand.

Gemma and Karen both reached out to catch me.

'I don't need any help,' I said. 'I just tripped over the picnic rug.'

I caught the concerned glance they shared.

The engineer wasn't put off so easily. He held tight to my forearm as I stepped into the launch. He insisted that we all wear life-jackets for the two-minute ride to the *Afsaneh*, and when we reached the boat, he practically carried me on board.

18

On board the *Afsaneh*, the cook had set out an array of snacks and a cooler full of bottles on the fly-bridge so that we could really enjoy the sunset. I took a beer and knocked it back in two big swigs. I reached for another one before Karen had the top off her first.

'Steady on, Linz,' said Gemma. 'You'll be over the side of the boat if you keep on drinking like that. You know what a lightweight you are.'

'You're not my mother,' I snapped back.

'She's right though,' Karen chipped in. 'Don't go leaning over the edge if you start to feel like vomiting.'

'You're definitely not my mother,' I added needlessly.

Soon the sunset part of our 'sunset cruise' was almost over. The sun dipped into the ocean, still looking so hot that you half expected to hear a sizzle as it disappeared. Now the wind picked up as it always did when the sun went below the horizon. It was still light enough to see without artificial help, but the pinky-purple sky would soon be inky-blue. The sea already looked colder and darker, much less inviting than it had done when we arrived at Formentera. I pulled my hoodie around my shoulders and tried not to fall asleep. In my doziness, I could hear Gemma proposing a cocktail at one of the bars on the harbour when we docked.

'I'm going inside to change the music,' she said then. 'And

to see if we've got any life-jackets for when Lindsey tries to stand up again.'

'I don't need a life-jacket,' I snarled.

'Whatever you say, Linz.' Gemma and Karen shared a sympathetic glance.

'Lindsey,' said Karen after a little while during which we had both sipped another beer in silence. 'I think you and I need to have a little talk.'

'A little talk?' I bristled instantly as she adopted the 'grown-up' tone with me. 'What about?'

'About you and me.'

'What is there to talk about?'

'I know what you've been trying to do,' she said. 'I know that you made a bet with Damien that he wouldn't be able to seduce me to make him try and encourage me to be unfaithful.'

'I don't know what you're talking about.'

'Lindsey, please stop treating me like I'm an idiot. Damien came straight out with it when I refused his advances. He said if I kissed him he would be willing to split the money. I suppose you were hoping for a reason to break up me and your father. Anyway, I'm willing to forget all about it if you are. I don't want to interfere in your life just because I'm getting married to your dad, and I hope the feeling is vice versa. Truce?'

I said nothing. I was going to give Damien so much hell.

'Come on, Lindsey. I'm over it. This is all going to seem hilarious one day soon. Let's just shake hands and try to make the best of the rest of the weekend *and* of having each other in our lives. Really, this will all seem very silly after the wedding. Let's call a truce.'

That's when I turned on her. 'How dare you patronize me? I don't want a truce with you. I just want you out of my life. If you'd given up on Dad it would be doing you a favour too. Don't you see that?'

'No, I don't,' she said plainly. 'Enlighten me.'

'Do you honestly think that you have a chance of making this marriage work? Do you? Karen, you're so mismatched you might as well be from a different species. My dad is an educated, sophisticated, successful man. You've got where you are on your big plastic boobs.'

'My boobs aren't fake,' she pointed out patiently.

'*Whatever!* Do you think it would be easy to be married to a man like my father? Do you honestly think you've been accepted into Dad's circle? Do you think that his friends are any happier about him marrying you than I am? Don't you think they laugh at you behind your back the way they laughed at all the dimwits who went before you?'

'I get on just fine with your father's friends. They're all perfectly nice to me.'

'*To your face.* Of course they are. They're polite enough people. And sure, they were all thrilled for him that he was getting laid again. But he was never meant to *marry* you. Behind your back they call you "the bimbo". And they'll keep calling you the bimbo after you're married. And one morning Dad will wake up and it won't seem like harmless teasing any more. He'll realize that marrying a joke like you has made him a great big joke to the people who really matter. And he'll hate you for that. If you marry my father, you will ruin his life.'

Karen looked as though I had slapped her in the face with my words.

'So, you see. It would be doing you both a favour if you would just give up on him now. I'm saying that as a friend.'

'As a friend? You're saying that as a spoiled brat who really needs to grow up, get her own life and keep her nose out of her father's business,' Karen snorted.

'I'm sticking my nose in because I care about him.'

'If you cared about him you'd see that what really concerns him is not whether I've got any A-levels but why you are still mooning about the house like a teenager now you're nearly twenty-four. Your inability to get a job and start acting like an adult is much more worrying to him than the fact that his friends might laugh at some of my outfits.'

'He's never said anything about me having to get a job.'

'Because he doesn't know what to say! He's been beside himself with worry about you since you came back from Exeter. He's worried that you're depressed.'

Karen attempted to bring the argument down a notch by placing a caring hand on my arm. I shook her off.

'The only thing depressing me is my father's ridiculous taste in women,' I spat back.

'If you loved him you would want him to be happy and I make him happy. I love your father, Lindsey. And he loves me.'

'He doesn't love you. He's in *lust* with you. And you don't really love him. You love the big house in Hampstead and the car and the credit cards. You just love all the trappings.'

'I've got my own career and my own credit cards, thank you very much.'

'Are you telling me you wouldn't rather have his platinum ones?'

'I'm not even going to dignify that with a response.'

'Because you can't honestly tell me that you wouldn't, can you? You will never be my stepmother,' I told her then. 'You're a gold-digging bitch and I mean to make my father realize that before he makes the biggest mistake of his life.'

All the time we were arguing, Gemma was looking out to sea from the other side of the boat. I was shouting so hard that my vocal chords were starting to hurt but every exclamation I made was whipped away by the wind before Gemma could hear it. She had no idea whatsoever that anything was wrong.

And neither did she turn round in time to see me stand up to walk away from Karen and Karen try to keep me from walking away from her by grabbing me by the arm and me push Karen away from me once, twice and then a third time with so much force and anger that this time she flew backwards over the safety wire like an Olympic high jumper. Straight over the safety rail and into the sea. It happened so suddenly she didn't even have time to shout 'Help'.

It's very difficult to have an idea of how fast a boat is moving unless you have a relatively stationary point upon which to focus. Now Karen was my stationary point. It took a few seconds for her to fight her way up to the surface after she fell in. When she finally made it, she popped up like a seal, looking around her in bewilderment. And at first she was facing away from the boat. I imagined her eyes wide with fear as they locked upon the empty horizon to the east.

She whirled around quickly and waved her arms to make sure that I'd seen her. I didn't wave back. I think she might have shouted too. I thought I could see her mouth moving but it was hard to hear over the sound of the ocean and the powerful engine of the *Afsaneh* eating the sea-miles between Formentera and Ibiza Town. Fast as a seabird. Faster than anyone could swim, particularly if they weren't a terribly confident swimmer. Soon Karen's head was indistinguishable from a buoy. By the time Gemma strolled around the prow to join us, I could no longer see Karen at all.

19

'Woman overboard!' Gemma shouted.

She had me stand ready with a lifebelt while she raced to the captain and demanded that he bring the boat around. It wasn't easy. The *Afsaneh* didn't have the turning circle of Gemma's little Seicento and Karen was drifting all the time.

And though the captain soon had every one of the *Afsaneh*'s searchlights trained on the water, it was getting very dark. At one point the little launch was dispatched in the direction of what turned out to be an old football.

When the captain finally admitted that he was at a loss as to what to do next, the police were radioed. They promised to mobilize the lifeguard at once and a helicopter was soon wheeling out to sea above our heads.

I couldn't speak. I didn't say another word until we were safely back in Ibiza Town and the captain and engineer had taken me and Gemma ashore. Then the only word I managed to squeak was 'tea' when someone asked me what I needed.

'Shock,' said the policewoman who wrapped me in a blanket.

Hangover would have been closer to the truth.

Gemma actually threw up.

We were suddenly surrounded by policemen who wanted to know exactly what had happened. Where we were heading. Where we had been when Karen fell overboard. The exact second the accident had happened. The captain and one of the lifeguards pored over a map of the sea marked with wiggly blue lines that meant nothing to a landlubber like me but everything to someone who knew the tides. They quickly worked out where Karen might be drifting and made plans to dispatch help accordingly.

'Are there sharks out there?' I managed to ask weakly.

There were no truly dangerous sharks in the Mediterranean but there were some strong currents, and though it wasn't as cold as the Atlantic, it wouldn't take long for someone to start getting tired and begin to suffer the effects of hypothermia. Particularly if they weren't wearing a lifejacket.

'There are lots of boats out at this time of year,' the lifeguard said optimistically. 'Perhaps someone has already picked her up.'

I remembered hearing Gemma comment on how strange it was that we were the only boat for miles when we were just five minutes off Formentera.

Gemma and I spent much of that night on a bench in the police station. Side by side. Holding hands tightly. Actually, Gemma was holding my hand tightly. When she finally released it so that I could go to the bathroom, my fingers were white as a cadaver's from having had all the blood squeezed out of them.

We didn't talk much. My mind wandered. I ran over what had happened and yet couldn't quite remember. It was as though I hadn't been there. As though it had happened in a dream. Only fragments of our argument drifted back.

After a while, I found myself having a guilty fantasy instead about the kind of outfit I would wear to a memorial service. I imagined my beautifully stricken expression as people consoled me on the loss of the woman who would have been my stepmother. I imagined the kind things I would say about her. She was a beautiful, generous woman. Her loss would hurt me as much as my dad . . .

Who would do the catering for the wake, I wondered. I flicked through a mental rolodex of caterers. Perhaps the wedding caterers would do us a deal. Who would we invite? I suppose there was no way of getting round inviting her mother. Or perhaps there was. Marilyn could have her own memorial service for Karen. Dad and I would have something more intimate and classy. Marilyn didn't have to come to that. I settled on Prada for the outfit . . . I already had a great funeral dress from there. Though perhaps I could buy something new. I thought about all these things – I found I couldn't stop myself – but I don't think for one moment that I really truly thought Karen would be dead.

Soon it was pitch dark. We heard the helicopter heading back towards land. Gemma rushed outside to the landing-pad still wrapped in the blankets the kind policewoman had given us when we disembarked. I followed a little less excitedly. The helicopter crew jumped down and I could tell from the set of their shoulders before they took off their helmets and revealed their faces that the rescue mission had not been a success.

'Go back out there!' Gemma shouted in imperfect Spanish. 'It isn't too late.'

The pilot shook his head. 'It's too dark for us now,' he told her. 'We'll look again tomorrow morning.'

'But by then you'll be looking for a body!' Gemma wailed.

The pilot shrugged his shoulders. I wrapped my arms tightly around Gemma in an attempt to stop her shaking. 'It's all my fault!' Gemma cried. 'I never should have insisted we took the boat out. I shouldn't have allowed everybody to get so drunk. I should have insisted everybody wore life-jackets all the time.'

'We need to phone her next of kin,' said a policeman gravely. 'Do you know who her relatives are? Does she have a husband?'

'Almost,' I said in a very quiet voice. 'She was going to marry my father.'

'Then I think you had better phone him,' said the police-man.

'She's dead!' Gemma wailed as the policeman bundled us into his car and drove us back to the harbour. 'If they want you to call the next of kin that means they think that she's dead!'

Is that what they meant? I wondered how I was supposed to react.

Gemma had completely lost it. She cried and wailed like a one-woman Greek chorus. At one point I thought I might have to slap her. For my part, I didn't know what to do. My eyes might have got a bit watery but I think that was more to do with tiredness and an early-onset hangover.

I eventually called Dad from the galley of the *Afsaneh*, well away from the wailing in the sitting room, where Gemma was being comforted by her brother and the cook.

'Dad,' I was surprised to hear my voice quaver for real as I told him, 'we went sailing. Karen's missing. She fell over-board.'

Dad gave a funny, snorty little laugh. 'What's that, sweet-heart? Has Karen run off with a stripper?'

I repeated my news. Formentera. The yacht. Missing, possibly drowned.

Dad wasn't laughing any more.

And that's when my funeral fantasy didn't seem quite so

enticing any more either. I didn't think about the outfit I would wear, I thought about a body washed up on the shore. Bloated. Nibbled by fishes. I remembered the one line of Shakespeare I ever learned – Ariel's song from *The Tempest*. I committed it to memory for the sake of my GCSE English. 'Full fathom five thy father lies, Of his bones are coral made . . .'

Because I think I had my first inkling then, from my father's voice as he tried his best to make practical arrangements – 'Which airlines fly to Ibiza, Lindsey? Where do the BA flights leave from?' – that if Karen's body did wash up on shore with pearls for eyes, she wouldn't be the only one who suffered a sea change.

20

Nobody slept that night.

Dad arrived on the first flight the following morning. I took a taxi to the airport and met him there. I was relieved to have some time alone with him – Gemma had insisted on taking the *Afsaneh* out to look for Karen again – though it was hardly quality time. I could see Dad's agitation in the set of his shoulders the second he walked into the arrivals lounge. As we took another taxi to the police station, he made me go over and over what had happened on the boat.

'I lost my footing. She reached out to grab me, over-balanced and toppled.'

'So she was trying to stop you going in?'

'Absolutely. She was trying to save me.'

That was my story and I was sticking to it. It was the story I had honed during my sleepless night. I had been drunk. I had spilled some beer and slipped on my own wet patch. I was about to go into the drink and she was trying to save me when she lost her own balance and toppled herself. It made her sound like a heroine. More importantly, it made me sound innocent.

'Oh, Karen! Why does she always think about other people before herself?' Dad cried. I was slightly taken aback at the tone of his voice as he said it. He sounded annoyed as much as anything, as he might justifiably have been had I told him that

Karen went overboard trying to save a pet poodle rather than his daughter. 'Why did she do it?'

'Er, because otherwise I would have drowned instead,' I reminded him.

'Lindsey,' snapped Dad. 'Please do not use the word "drowned".'

But that was the truth, wasn't it? Fifteen hours after Karen fell off the boat with no life-jacket, could she honestly still be swimming around in circles, waiting for a passing whale?

At the police station, the mood was sombre. There was little of the frantic activity of the previous night, though the police chief confirmed that a couple of boats had gone out to continue the search as soon as it got light that morning. A few British ex-pats had offered their services too. In fact, the *Afsaneh* had gone out again that morning.

There was certainly no lack of goodwill. The minister for the largest English-speaking church on the island came to the station and told Dad that he would ask his congregation to pray for Karen's safe return. But I knew that even a betting man like Damien wouldn't have placed good money on the odds of this particular tale ending happily. The photographs of Karen that Dad had brought with him and which the police chief was photocopying to circulate among his staff, would more than likely be used to identify a corpse.

At midday, the skipper of one of the coastguard boats returned. He was bringing his boat in to await the distress call from the next unlucky overboard. I saw the chief nodding sadly. The official search for Karen was over.

'Rest assured we have not abandoned the search,' said the police chief to my father. But we knew that the Ibizan coastguards' efforts would now be scaled down to merely keeping an eye out for a bloated floater that needed to be caught before it washed up at the foot of someone's beach towel and spoiled their two weeks in the sun.

'What are we supposed to do now?' my father asked.

'Go back to your hotel. We will call you if anything happens. We can call you in England too if you want to go back there.'

'How on earth can I even leave this station without knowing what has happened to my fiancée?' Dad exclaimed.

'This is not a very relaxing place to wait,' the police chief tried.

'Do you think I'm going to be able to relax anywhere until I get some proper news about her?' Dad snapped.

I put my hand on Dad's arm in an attempt to calm him down. He was understandably distraught but I wasn't sure whether grief would be a big enough excuse to keep him out of jail if he decked the police chief in his agony.

I led him back into the waiting room while the girl on the desk called for a car.

'We'll be all right, Dad,' I told him over and over. 'We'll get over this together.'

Dad sobbed into his shirt. 'I can't believe it. I can't believe it. How could this have happened? If I could just hear her voice one more time. I would give anything to have her back with me. If I could only hear her voice.'

'Alex.'

Hang on. That *was* her voice!

I thought I was hearing things. I shook my head to dislodge any water I might still have in my ears.

'Lindsey.'

The same voice.

I definitely wasn't hearing things.

I looked up and there she was. Karen stood at the doorway

of the waiting room. Quite dry. Wrapped in a blanket. And very much alive.

'Oh, my God!' Dad jumped up and raced across the room to touch her, to prove that his eyes weren't playing tricks. He wrapped his arms around her tightly and kissed her face like a Labrador greeting a long-absent mistress. Karen stood strangely stiff in his embrace.

'Thank goodness. Thank goodness,' said Dad. 'What happened?'

'Gemma and her crew rescued me this morning. I'd been clinging on to a rock in the middle of the ocean all night. Good job they came when they did. I was just about ready to give up.'

Gemma appeared behind her now. Along with Damien. He had his arm wrapped protectively around Gemma's shoulder. A very rare picture of half-sibling solidarity.

'Gemma is a hero,' said Karen.

Gemma gave a humble little smile. 'What's the point of having a yacht if you can't use it to rescue your friends?'

'How did you fall off the boat in the first place?' Dad wanted to know. 'Why on earth weren't you wearing a life-jacket?'

Karen just shrugged in reply, but she looked straight at me over my father's shoulder. I thought I saw her eyes narrow just a little. International body language for, 'I'm going to get you, bitch,' I was sure.

'Thank goodness you're safe,' I said weakly.

'Yes. Thank goodness,' she agreed. 'We live to fight another day.'

'I'll need to make an interview of your side of the story,' the police chief told her. 'Just a formality,' he added.

'Of course,' said Karen.

'We'll come with you,' I suggested quickly. 'Just in case you can't remember everything.'

But the police chief barred my entry into his office.
'Madam will need to make her interview alone.'

There followed the longest half-hour in my entire life. My
glamorous grieving fantasies were swiftly replaced with something altogether less romantic. Every time a door opened on
to the bare-walled room where my father and I waited for
Karen to finish her interview, I was convinced that they were
coming for me with handcuffs. My father had Gemma tell
him the story of the rescue several times but I could only
concentrate on what was being said *outside* my earshot.

What was Karen saying in that interview room? That I
pushed her off the boat, of course. I knew it. She knew it. Over
and over again, the image of Karen's face as she fell from the
deck appeared in my mind's eye; her horror not at the thought
that she was about to hit the inky-black water but at the fact
that I had shoved her. I had actually pushed her into the water
and watched as she floated out to sea and to what, for any
woman who wasn't a super-fit champion swimmer, should
have been certain death. Did she know how long I had
watched her drifting before I even raised the alarm?

When I stopped thinking about the look in Karen's eyes as
she realized the extent of my betrayal, I started thinking about
prison. Would I go to prison here in Ibiza or would they allow
me to fly back and serve my sentence in England? I imagined
long lonely years in a Spanish jail, struggling to communicate
with a vocabulary that stopped short at ordering a beer. And if
I were to end up in a Spanish jail, none of my friends would be
able to visit me. Or my family. Though I was increasingly
uncertain whether Dad would even bother to visit me anyway
once he found out what I had done.

Was Karma finally catching up?

But no one came to arrest me. And after that hellish

half-hour, the police chief and Karen actually emerged smiling from his office. The police chief smiled at everybody. Even me.

'Well, I think that's the case completely closed,' he said. 'Simply an unfortunate accident.'

'Very unfortunate,' Karen agreed,

'Thank you, Miss Gemma, for all your efforts to save your friend. And you,' he wagged a finger at me, 'you just remember to check that you don't stand so near the edge next time. You English girls always drink so much. You need to take more care of yourself,' he added. I nodded double-quick.

'It's been a pleasure to meet you, Ms Spencer.' The police chief actually kissed Karen's hand as he bid her farewell. 'Whatever the circumstances. I hope your night at sea hasn't put you off visiting our beautiful island again.'

'Of course not,' she smiled gracefully. 'Though right now all I want to do is go home and get some sleep.'

'Your wish is my command,' said my father, leaping to his feet. 'I'll call the airline right away.'

There were only two spaces on the British Airways flight back to Gatwick that afternoon. I didn't much want to hang around in Ibiza myself but Karen told me that there was absolutely no need for me to cut short my holiday on her behalf. In fact, I should stay in Ibiza as long as I liked.

That should have been the clue. The wedding was just four weeks away and yet she merely shrugged her shoulders when I suggested that I should come home in time to make it to my bridesmaid's dress fitting that weekend.

'Really, don't worry about it,' she said. 'There's no need to hurry back at all.'

Dad and Karen were on their way home less than two hours after Karen finished her interview at the police station.

Gemma went into Ibiza Town for a while. I sat alone on the sun-deck of the *Afsaneh* and didn't know what to do with myself. I think I might have uttered a little grateful prayer that Karen hadn't drowned after all. I think I probably promised that in the future I would be the best stepdaughter anyone ever had. I had to accept it now, didn't I? And make the most of it. Karen was marrying my dad. Not even the great sea god Poseidon had dared intervene.

21

Eventually Gemma returned. Despite the fact that Karen was fine after all and everything was OK again, Gemma still looked drawn.

'Thank God she made it,' I said. 'I thought for a moment we were going to have to cancel the wedding.'

Gemma just looked at me.

'It was incredible,' I chattered on. 'One minute Dad and I were practically planning her funeral. The next she walks in through the door. Like a ghost. I almost died of shock.'

'She almost died by drowning,' Gemma pointed out.

'Hardly.' I forced a laugh. 'She told me she was only in the water for twenty minutes before she found that rock.'

'And what if she hadn't?'

'That would have been a shame,' I admitted.

'You pushed her, didn't you?' said Gemma then.

I was shocked by her directness.

'I didn't push anyone. She lost her balance.'

'You pushed her, Lindsey. I know you did.' Gemma's voice began to rise like a TV cop's realizing she's in the presence of a mild-mannered serial killer. 'You pushed your future stepmother off a moving yacht and into the middle of the sea.'

'You're being ridiculous. She slipped. She told you what happened herself.'

'Yes, but I've been talking to Damien about it. And he

agrees with me. Karen probably doesn't remember much about the whole thing because she's still in shock but there is no way she would have gone over that rail on her own. It was much too high. It's specifically designed to stop people from falling over when drunk. She had to have had some momentum behind her. Some *assistance*, as it were.' Gemma raised her eyebrows meaningfully.

'Well, I didn't give her any. I didn't push her, Gem.'

'The evidence suggests otherwise.'

'What evidence?'

'Damien said . . .'

'You're believing your stupid half-brother over me?'

'Karen might have died.'

'She's a stronger swimmer than she thinks she is.'

'You didn't know that. You meant for her to drown.'

'Gemma, don't be stupid. I didn't push her.'

'I'm not stupid. Just look at all the evidence! When you turned up on the island with Karen in tow, muttering darkly about how you would never wear your bridesmaid's dress, I thought you were kidding. But it all makes sense now. You were serious about getting rid of her. And when she wouldn't conveniently get off with Damien in front of your camera, you decided to turn to desperate measures. Your dad doesn't have bad taste in girlfriends at all. He just has a psychopath for a daughter.'

'You're the one who's gone psycho, Gemma. Accusing me of attempted murder. No one will believe a word you say.'

'Don't worry,' she sneered. 'I'm not going to tell anyone what you did. I don't want you to have to go to prison. But I don't particularly want to be your friend any more either.'

'Gemma. Don't say that.'

'You've never been much of a friend to me. You're so full of hatred and bitterness. I've spent almost fifteen years allowing you to influence me, Lindsey. At first I thought you were protecting me against all the snotty cows who picked on me at school, but now I see that what you've actually done is try to turn me into one of them. When I think what we did to Melinda Haverstock and Poupeh Gharani! I'm not naturally a bitch at heart. It's you who made me that way.'

It was a bit of an overreach, I thought – there had been times when Gemma's heart pumped pure acid round her veins – but it clearly wasn't the time to do anything but grovel.

'I'm sorry you feel like that,' I told her, remembering one of my favourite lines from family therapy with Trish. 'But I'm not going to be like that any more. I've seen how self-destructive my behaviour has been in the past. I'm not going to bitch about anybody ever again. I've decided to make an effort to be a nicer person from now on. I've seen how much Dad loves Karen and I'm going to try to love her too. I'm going to be a fabulous stepdaughter and one day all this will seem very funny.'

'No. No, it won't. I don't think attempted murder ever becomes something you can laugh about.'

I shook my head.

'If she had died, I would have had to live with that burden for the rest of my life. That someone died falling off my boat. Always wondering whether I might have saved her. And you would have let me.'

'I'm sorry. I'm sorry.' It was all I could say.

Gemma just rolled her eyes.

'I think you'd better go back to London tomorrow morning,' she said. 'I'll call a taxi to drive you to the airport.'

'Gemma, I don't want to go until we're friends. You've got to forgive me. You must understand that I only wanted to get rid of her because I love my dad. Because I love my mum.'

'And that's the way you show your love? You really think

your mum would want you to kill another woman to prove how much you care? Lindsey,' she said, 'you are fucked in the head.' She tapped her own forehead. 'You always have been. Your mother has been gone since 1981. Princess Diana has divorced and died since then. Concorde has stopped flying. The USSR has fallen apart. A quarter of a century has passed and your mother is never coming back. Never, never, never. You've got to give it up!'

She stalked into the bedroom and slammed the door behind her. In so much as the fabulously well-engineered doors on a Sunseeker are slammable.

But to my surprise, Gemma really wasn't kidding about not wanting to be my friend any more. Not a single further word passed between us that day, and the following morning I left for the airport before she'd even got out of bed. I left a note on the galley table, telling her once again that I was sorry we had fallen out (I drew the line at writing 'for pushing Karen off the boat' in case it wound up as evidence in my court case) and begging her to call me as soon as she could.

As the taxi pulled away from the harbour, I looked up at Gemma's bedroom port-holes until I couldn't see them any more. I was convinced that when she heard the crunch of the taxi's tyres on gravel, she would at least pop her head out and wave me off. I longed for just the slightest gesture that we might be reconciled. She was my soul sister after all. She had never managed to stay mad at me for so long before. But that morning Gemma was staying mad and she didn't wave goodbye.

I was so upset I didn't even bother to look round the airport duty-free shop before I boarded the plane. For the entire flight home, I couldn't even concentrate on the copy of *Heat* magazine I had failed to read on the way out to Ibiza. I felt so guilty and ashamed.

Plus, I was desperately trying to figure out how I could get into Karen's stupid fake Fendi handbag and retrieve that not-so-little packet of cocaine before she found it . . .

22

When the taxi pulled up outside the house where I had lived for the past twelve years, the first thing I noticed was that the curtains were drawn. I felt a shiver pass through me, remembering my grandmother who told me that curtains drawn during the day meant someone was dead. These days, it just meant that everyone was out or watching daytime TV and trying to keep the sun from reflecting off the telly. Dad didn't generally watch daytime television. And yet the door wasn't double-locked and when I opened it the burglar alarm didn't start beeping. There had to be someone in the house.

'Hello?' I called. 'Dad? Karen? It's Lindsey. I'm *ho-ome.*'

No one replied. Ordinarily, if Karen were in, she would have called back to me with her big friendly voice. And ordinarily, my heart would have sunk at the sound of it. But that day, I wanted to hear that we were friends again with her brightest, most annoying 'Hiya, babes!'

'Hel-lo-ooo?'

Nothing. Not even an echo greeted me that day. I walked around the ground floor of the house feeling increasingly creeped out, turning on lights as I went. Maybe Gran's drawn-curtain interpretation was right. It certainly felt as though someone had died while I'd been away.

'Dad?'

No answer.

Perhaps they had gone out and forgotten to put on the burglar alarm.

As I passed Dad and Karen's bedroom, I nudged the door just a little. But the bedroom was empty too. I dropped my case in my own room and continued my search.

Eventually I found Dad right at the top of the house in his attic study. He was sitting at his desk. A picture of him and Karen taken on the weekend they got engaged in Barcelona was propped up in front of him. He didn't hear me walk in behind him.

He was too busy crying.

'Dad?' I said quietly before I touched him on the shoulder. I didn't want to make him jump.

He turned around to face me, eyes glittering with tears. I couldn't help but gasp at the sight of him. He looked so young. So hopeless. It was a face I hadn't seen him wear for a very long time.

'Dad, what's wrong?'

He just gave a big snorting sob.

'Has something happened? Are you OK? Is Karen OK?'

Had she died from the late-onset complications of swallowing too much sea water? Was that possible?

'Are you OK? Say something, Dad, you're worrying me.'

'Karen has left me,' he managed to choke out at last.

It took a second before I realized what he had said.

'*She's* left *you*?'

'She says she's never coming back.'

'What? But why?'

My heart started edging its way up my windpipe as I waited

for him to say, 'Because you tried to kill her.' But he didn't say that. Instead, between loud, wet, teary snorts, Dad poured out the following explanation.

'She said she's been thinking about it for a long time. About whether or not we're really compatible. She said that she wasn't sure how we'd work in the long term. She said it's clear we're so different that it would be bound to get hard. She said she decided she had to end it while she was hanging on to that rock in the ocean.'

'Oh no.'

I covered my mouth with my hands. To be absolutely honest with you, I was a little bit scared I might laugh.

'I tried to tell her that she's all I ever wanted, but she told me that ultimately she thinks I'll get bored. She doesn't share any of my interests, is what she said. And one day I'll want to talk opera or politics and I'll realize I made a mistake.'

'She really said that?'

I couldn't believe it.

'I told her she was wrong but she just wouldn't listen to me. She said that she knows there's someone out there who is better suited to me than she is. Someone like Gemma's mother, for example. Can you believe she said that?' Dad laughed, but in a mirthless way. 'She's obviously never met Gemma's mum.'

'Tanya is very beautiful,' I threw in. Dad ignored me.

'Lindsey, I don't know what to do with myself. Karen's moved back in with her mother and refuses to take my calls. It happened as soon as we got back here. We had an argument on the drive from the airport. When we got here she wouldn't even have a cup of tea and talk about it properly. She just walked upstairs, packed a case and went to her mother's house. She came back while I was at work to pick up the rest of her stuff. I drove round to Marilyn's to see her last night but Marilyn said she would call the police if I came round again. Karen's Uncle Tony backed her up. Though he said he wouldn't call the cops but would break my legs himself. She's cut me out of her life. It's as though I never existed. It's as though I dreamt the last two years. Falling in love. Getting engaged. Planning the wedding. All that happiness. All that love we had. Gone in a minute.'

'And that's really all she said? That she thinks your different interests will eventually break you up?'

You're sure she said nothing about me at all, was what I wanted to ask. Nothing about the hideous argument we had before I pushed her off a yacht into the Mediterranean? Because she'd pretty much paraphrased the case I had presented to her just before doing it.

'That can't be her real reason for calling the wedding off,' I muttered.

'You're right,' said Dad. 'She's definitely lying to me. There must be someone else. What did she say while you were in Ibiza with her? Was she getting mysterious phone calls? Any text messages? Did she go off on her own? Did you have any clue at all that this would happen?'

'No,' I said. 'There definitely isn't someone else. She's not that kind of woman.' I knew that for a fact but decided against telling Dad about the evidence I'd accrued right then.

'Then why is she doing this?' Dad brought his fists down on the desk. 'Why? Why? Why? Why? Why?' He thumped the desk so hard I snatched his laptop out of the way before he broke it. But then he fell forward over his arms again and his shoulders heaved up and down as he cried more tears on to that photograph I hated so much.

'It'll be OK,' I said, placing my hand gently between his

shoulder blades. 'You've always got me, Dad. I'm not going anywhere. It's just you and me again. Against the world.'

I hardly dared believe it. When Dad had recovered himself a little. I suggested for form's sake that he try to call Karen one more time. He did and, once again, he got the nasty side of Marilyn. She shouted so much she gave herself another coughing fit. Karen didn't want to speak to Dad ever again, Marilyn yelled, so loud that I had to pull my ear away from the second phone in my bedroom I was using to listen in. The wedding was absolutely off. But there was still no mention of me as the cause.

Further conversation with Dad only confirmed that Karen hadn't cited me in her reasons for leaving. In fact she had told him that up until the boating 'accident', the trip to Ibiza had been a fantastic success. I was a wonderful girl. Fantastic company. Together with Gemma, I had done my very best to make the hen weekend special, she said. My father should be very, very proud of me. She even went so far as to say she would miss me.

'Did she really say that?' I asked.

'She did,' Dad nodded. And he clearly believed her.

The spectre of that attempted murder charge drifted a little further away.

Of course, it was hard to see Dad unhappy, but when I went to bed that night, I allowed myself a little moment of quiet contentment. What a turnaround! On that flight back from Ibiza, I had been utterly resigned to the fact that the wedding was going ahead. The last thing I had expected was for Karen to be the one who decided to call it off. Now I could dare to dream that eventually Dad would be back to normal and

Karen would still be gone. Which was what I had wanted all along.

Sometimes, it seemed, the most difficult wishes do come true.

23

A couple of days later, I moved some of my things into the spare bedroom that had been Karen's dressing room, assuring Dad that if she came back, I would move my stuff straight out again but that in the meantime, it was best for his mental health that we removed as many reminders of her from the house as we could.

I wasted no time in getting rid of the big 'canvas-style' photograph of Karen and Dad on their engagement weekend that hung above the fireplace in the dining room. After that, I whizzed around the rest of house with a bin bag, spring-cleaning every touch of my former nemesis's style into oblivion. Out went the 'comedy' fridge magnets, the dusty silk flowers on the landing, the pot-pourri on top of the cistern in the guest bathroom. Dad had asked me to keep everything I moved in the corner of the garage pending Karen's return, but most of it was so tatty I felt absolutely no guilt as I threw it straight into the wheelie-bin.

My tactics seemed to work. After that first day when I found him sitting at his desk, I didn't catch Dad crying again. Which isn't to say that he wasn't doing it, of course, just that he was managing to restrict his misery to the hours of darkness. And a week later, my heart gave a little skip of joy when I heard him mutter those immortal words, 'Plenty more fish in the sea' while talking on the phone to one of his old advertising buddies. The sound of Dad's familiar laugh when his friend made a joke in reply was the best thing I'd heard in years.

Everything was going to be all right.

After two weeks, during which I pretty much devoted myself to looking after Dad, I decided that it was time to try to bring some semblance of normality to the other important relationship in my life.

Gemma and I had been friends for such a long time and I missed her. Even when we were both jet-setting, we tried to speak every day, or at least instant-message if we were both at our computers. I had tried catching her that way for quite a few days but every time I logged on, it seemed she was just logging off. The period between my logging on and her logging off was so brief, I decided that she probably hadn't even seen that I had pinged her.

Eventually, I knew I was going to have to reach out the hard way. By telephone. Not even by text but by actually calling.

I dialled her number and was very relieved when she picked up at once. I had feared she would let me go through to her answerphone.

'Who is it?'

'It's me,' I said. 'Lindsey.'

'Oh. I didn't recognize your number.'

'Have you erased me from your mobile?' I asked incredulously. Erasing all numbers was the punishment I only meted out to ex-boyfriends. It was the ultimate snub.

'I guess I must have,' she said breezily.

'Well, it doesn't matter,' I choked. 'Look, I was wondering whether you wanted to do something this weekend? You're coming back, aren't you? Perhaps we could get lunch somewhere and do a bit of shopping.'

'I'm spending the weekend with Damien and some of his friends.'

'Your half-brother Damien, who you hate?'

'Used to hate. I've started to see him in an altogether better light since he saved Karen's life after you pushed her into the Mediterranean.'

'Gemma, you know I didn't mean to.'

'Ah-ha.' She seized upon my sentence. 'At least you're now accepting that you were involved in the "accident"!'

I could almost hear the inverted commas.

'No, I'm not!'

'Whatever. Is there anything else you need to say to me?'

'If you're busy all weekend, perhaps we could meet up again next week?'

'Lindsey,' said Gemma, 'I wasn't joking when I said that I don't want to be your friend any more. My therapist is quite insistent that I cut out all the negative influences in my life in order to move forward optimistically and you have definitely been one of my negative influences. Look, I hope that things turn out all right for you. I really do. I don't hate you for what you've done. I just feel sorry for you. And a little bit sad that I can't help you find peace with yourself. But I can't. You've got to admit you've got a problem to solve it. Goodbye.'

She hung up before I could protest.

I slammed my phone down helplessly.

Who needed Gemma anyway? Why would anyone need so unforgiving a friend? I'd been completely contrite about what happened on the boat in Ibiza. I'd apologized to everyone involved. Well, everyone except Karen. If Gemma couldn't find it in herself to offer me the olive branch then she was the bitch.

In the meantime, I had other friends. I flicked through the

numbers in my phone's memory for the girls I would usually hang out with if Gemma wasn't around. There weren't many of them. Gemma and I were almost always together.

But there was Katie Randolph. Katie had been in our class all through school and occasionally we'd let her hang out with us. Mostly because she was the daughter of Gemma's father's business partner and he had threatened to cut Gemma's allowance if she didn't make an effort to include Katie in our weekend and holiday plans . . .

Katie Randolph was a bit of a drag. She wouldn't smoke. She couldn't drink more than half a pint of lager without being sick or worrying that we would be stopped by the police and thrown into jail for under-age drinking. And despite having a top music producer for a dad and an ex-model / actress / whatever for a mother, which in turn gave her access to any number of extremely expensive stylists, she still didn't know how to dress. She was a real life *Ab Fab* Saffy – getting even geekier when she went to university to study Ancient History and Norse.

But a night out with Katie Randolph was better than no night out at all. I dialled her number. And couldn't quite believe how long it took her to pick up. What else did she have to do?

'Oh, Lindsey,' she said. 'I haven't heard from you in *ages*.' She put extra-heavy emphasis on that last word. 'Not since you didn't reply to the wedding invitation I sent you earlier this year.'

'You're getting married?' I spluttered.

'I *am* married. Since May the fifteenth. You were invited to the wedding.'

'The invitation never got to me,' I lied.

In reality, I remembered now that I had thrown over Katie Randolph's wedding invitation in favour of a weekend house-party with some much cooler people and simply hadn't got round to letting her know that I wouldn't be there.

'Congratulations,' I said feebly.

'His name is George,' she said. 'Since I don't imagine you can remember.'

'Of course I can remember.'

Gemma and I had always laughed at Katie's succession of red-faced and thoroughly hearty boyfriends with their tendency to wear jumpers knitted by their mothers. Hadn't all of them been called George?

'He's the chap with the ginger hair, yes? Nice guy.'

'He's blond.'

'So, I don't suppose you're up for a girls' night out?' I said.

'Not really. Not now I'm married.'

I waited for her to say that she would make an exception for me. She didn't. Instead she said, 'Gemma told me what happened in Ibiza.'

'Oh.'

'Lindsey, I've got the number of a very good chap if you feel like you might want to get some proper help. A professional. I met him while I was doing my training for the Samaritans. Have you got a pen?'

I dutifully pretended to write down a number.

'Call me again when you've had time to think about your life.'

'Thank you,' I said. 'Goodbye.'

I flicked the Vs at the receiver as I flung it back down on the cradle. Patronizing cow. Professional help? She was the one who needed professional help. She was probably still wearing Ugg boots.

I punched through a few more numbers but had to discount them since they were close friends of Katie's, probably had bothered to reply to her wedding invite and had discussed my need for professional help at some post-wedding gathering where everyone cooed over the photos.

And then I was at Z.

What about Poupeh?

Poupeh had actually called me a few days earlier. She'd tracked Dad down at his office and asked him for my number, which he gave, unaware of how I really felt about this 'dear old friend from school'. Not recognizing her number, I'd let her go straight through to my voicemail (not that I would have answered had I known it was Poupeh on the line). I hadn't called her back. I hadn't even properly looked at Poupeh's card since she pressed it into my hand outside Zara. It hadn't moved from the bottom of my bag. But now I dug it out and actually got round to reading what it said.

'Poupeh Gharani, Managing Director, PGI.'

PGI? What did that stand for? Poupeh Gharani Industries?

What did she do for a living? Perhaps she was a club promoter with a handful of VIP tickets for something amazing that night! In which case, I should definitely call her. Gemma would be sick as a dog to find out that Poupeh Gharani was no longer a geek but had a hip promotions business with direct access to Robbie Williams and she was my new best friend . . . Then again, Poupeh probably wasn't a club promoter.

Fact was, Poupeh would never be cool. I couldn't call her. I wasn't that lonely. Things would never get quite that bad.

24

After a month, during which I had nothing better to do than cook fabulous meals and generally make his life comfortable, I felt that Dad was finally beginning to accept that Karen really was gone for good. He had stopped calling her every day and given up sitting in his car outside the gym where she worked in the hope that she might come outside and talk to him at the end of her shift. And I had stopped hiding behind walls every time I heard a police siren in the distance (in case they were on their way to arrest me for the Ibiza incident at last). My guilt at almost having killed Karen had been totally replaced by relief that I hadn't and a sense of sheer joy that the woman I hadn't wanted for a stepmother had, in the end, taken herself out of the running. It was time for Dad and me to resume life as normal. The way it had been before he even knew Karen existed.

That week was the week of the wedding that never was. Worrying that Dad might have a relapse into self-pity in the run-up to the Big Day that didn't happen, I knew that it was important to give him plenty to occupy his thoughts. With that in mind, I decided to arrange a dinner party for a few of his friends. And a couple of choice single women . . .

That's right. I needed to find some single girls to put before my father. In my experience – and I had had enough nasty break-ups to test this theory pretty well – the best way to take your mind off someone who has rejected you is to flirt with someone else. In fact, it's the only way. Forget about meditation. Sleep with somebody new.

I called Dad's assistant, Clare, and asked her to make sure that he didn't work late the following Thursday. Then I set about trying to find a couple of suitable gals.

Where do you go to find single women these days? The answer was right at my fingertips of course. Not in my mobile phone address book – I'd already trawled that – but on the Internet. I set aside a day and started googling for dating sites.

It was pretty depressing to start with. Not knowing much about the business of cybersex, I went straight to a couple of big international sites that were as intimate as a supermarket and presented members about as enticing as own-brand baked beans. Since I knew that ultimately I could be shopping for a stepmother, this was a very serious business indeed. There was no way I could even consider someone who called herself 'Sexy Sadie' or 'Fluffybunny69'.

Eventually, I happened upon a site with a little more promise, a little more exclusivity – Bluesmatch.com. It was a site dedicated to people who had studied at Oxford or Cambridge. Perfect. Every woman on the site would at least be guaranteed to meet the strict academic requirements of the post of potential stepmother to me.

I fabricated my own education history to get on board, using the name and college address of Lukas Van De Posten, the total bum from an extremely good family who had sold me the cocaine I slipped into Karen's bag on the way to Ibiza. My ruse worked. Soon I was in the site and browsing for Ms Right. There were no pictures, unfortunately, but since I had already decided that there were more important qualities than the perfect turned-up nose, I persisted. I sent emails to four of the women I found, asking pertinent questions about marital history and career status and explaining that I was in fact looking for a date for my father. Two of the girls wrote back.

Jane and Louisa sounded like the perfect candidates. They were both in their late thirties (far closer to Dad's age than Karen. Much more appropriate). Neither had ever been married. Neither had kids and, at their age, no real potential for kids to come, which suited me just fine. Both owned their own homes. Jane had a First Class degree in history from Caius College, Cambridge. Louisa had a 2:1 in English from Corpus Christi, Oxford.

I called them both up and once I was pleasantly reassured that neither had a hideous regional accent I extended the invitation to dinner. Both accepted.

So I found myself cooking for six that Thursday night. Dad, me, the two potential dates, and Dad's best friends, Henry and Lydia.

I began my quest to create the perfect dinner party the second Dad left for work that Thursday morning. I had the food delivered by Ocado. Everything organic. I bought simply hundreds of candles at Habitat, having decided not to use any electric light at all to give Jane and Louisa a bit of help on smoothing out those wrinkles, should they need it. As any Hollywood actress will tell you, good lighting is by far the most important part of any woman's anti-aging regime.

The menu I chose for the evening had a slightly Moroccan theme – a lamb stew with couscous – and I dressed the table accordingly, with a bright pink tablecloth. Pink would have an added brightening effect on the ladies' complexions, I hoped.

Dad's secretary, Clare, duly sent him home from the office at six o'clock. I had already laid out his outfit for the evening on his bed. Now that he had lost a few pounds (I had no idea that the Dumping Diet worked for men too), he fitted into my favourite Dolce and Gabbana suit again. It was a pre-Karen purchase. She didn't like him in it – thought it made him look too skinny – but I considered it the best outfit he had. Together with a deep blue shirt, the effect was very Italian. He looked, I thought, absolutely fabulous. Jane and Louisa would fall in love on the spot.

But despite my efforts, Dad didn't seem terribly sparkly when he first got home from work that night. So, when he came downstairs in the clothes I had so carefully chosen, I handed him a martini mixed exactly as he liked it. A double. He seemed to loosen up a little after that.

'What is tonight in aid of again?' he asked.

'Just a little summer supper,' I said. 'To welcome Henry and Lydia back to London.'

Dad looked at the floor. I wondered if he was remembering the reason why Henry and Lydia had originally booked their flight to be in London that particular day.

'And the other guests?' he continued.

'Oh, you don't know them yet. I just thought it would be nice to mix things up a bit. I know these two girls from an Internet chat-room on politics and thought it would be nice to meet them face to face.'

The chat-room was a neat cover story, I thought. Louisa had come up with it.

'OK.'

Dad helped me put the finishing touches to the canapés. I topped up his martini, and by the time the first of the girls arrived, he was almost on top form.

Dad made excellent chit-chat while we waited for the other guests to arrive. There wasn't any immediate spark between him and Louisa but I hoped that when she relaxed a little, some witty conversation on her part would help him to overlook her lazy eye. Personally, I never quite got the hang of where she was looking and ignored several questions she addressed to me and answered several more that weren't.

Unfortunately, Jane also fitted the 'very attractive' mould in exactly the way I had expected. That is to say, she wasn't. She had an unusually thick neck and clearly hadn't referred to Trinny and Susannah before she bought the jet bead choker that only served to highlight the knotted veins that ran alongside the considerable muscles in her throat. It came as no surprise to learn that she had practised martial arts for several years, starting with karate and moving on to Tae Kwon Do. But she was nice. She helped me rescue the lamb from the oven before it was entirely cremated. She didn't even need to use oven gloves.

By this time, Dad's friends Henry and Lydia had arrived and the kitchen was buzzing. It didn't seem to matter how beautifully I decorated the sitting room, when guests arrived at our house they would always head straight for the kitchen and plonk themselves down on the old pine chairs or perch on the rail of the Aga that Trisha had once used as a ballet barre. I didn't mind as long as Dad was having a good time. Everyone else was. Particularly Jane, who had a laugh that could drive holes in concrete. Why hadn't I noticed that during our phone conversation? I had a suspicion that Henry, Dad's best friend, was deliberately trying to set her off.

Eventually, I managed to corral everyone into the dining room. I had made a seating plan, putting the new girls on either side of Dad, but Jane and Louisa seemed to have sensed that my father was a lost cause before they even finished their aperitifs. When we moved into the dining room, they didn't fight to sit next to him, instead they chose to sit next to each other at the end of the table and embarked on what was to be a long and fruitful conversation about their various small businesses. They continued to shout across the table to each other even when I moved everyone around for the dessert course, in the desperate hope that, a bottle of red wine later, Dad might have changed his mind and started to fancy one or other of them.

By the end of the evening the girls had swapped cards and made plans to get together and discuss how Jane's small chain of gift shops might be able to help promote Louisa's hand-poured scented candles. As they left, sharing a taxi, they thanked me for giving them the chance to get to know each other and promised to hold a dinner party of their own that I should attend. I made all the right noises but knew I would never see either of them again.

By eleven o'clock, considerably earlier than I expected, only Henry and Lydia remained. They joined Dad and me in the kitchen and helped to load the dishwasher. The smile that Dad had managed to keep on his face all night was finally starting to slip. He didn't look like an Italian stallion any more. He looked tired. I had been thinking lately that he suddenly looked his age. After years of being the Peter Pan (or Cliff Richard, as Henry would say) among all his frankly middle-aged-looking friends, Dad didn't look so strikingly young and healthy any more. Just exhausted. Even depressed.

25

'How have you been?' Lydia asked Dad. This was the first time he had seen his friends since the split from Karen. After many years in London, these days Lydia and Henry spent most of their time at their second home in France. Henry had made a fortune in the City while everyone else was losing them during the nineties and retired when he hit forty-five. Of course, they had tickets to fly back to London that week because they were expecting to be coming back for the wedding.

'Are you doing OK?' Lydia persisted.

'I'm just fine,' said Dad. 'Lindsey's been looking after me.'

'As she always has done,' said Lydia with an indulgent smile in my direction. 'What a good girl she is.'

I accepted her compliment with a nod.

'Got a boyfriend yet, Lindsey?' Henry asked.

'No,' I said flatly.

End of that conversation.

'Alex,' Lydia continued, 'we just didn't know what to say when Lindsey called to tell us that Karen had gone. We were so shocked. You guys seemed so right for each other. And when Lindsey told us what she said about not fitting in, well, we just felt so guilty. We tried our best to make her welcome in our circle,' she insisted. 'We were really looking forward to being here for the wedding.'

'We never thought she was anything other than the perfect woman for you,' Henry agreed.

'We certainly never called her the bimbo.' Lydia looked genuinely horrified at the thought.

'I know,' said Dad. 'I know you didn't. I don't know where she got that idea from. I told her it really isn't your style.'

'And she won't let you see her at all?' Lydia asked.

'The last time I went round there, Marilyn sent the dog out after me.'

'That stupid poodle? Couldn't you just have drop-kicked it?' I asked.

'At least you won't have to have Marilyn as a mother-in-law,' Henry shuddered.

Dad almost managed a smile at that. He had once joked that Marilyn was Karen's only bad point.

'Is there anything we can do?' Lydia persisted. 'Perhaps I could call her. I could reassure her that we always liked her very much and miss her just as much as you do? I did think, prior to this "bimbo" business, that she and I had quite a good rapport.'

'You did,' said Dad. 'I know she liked you very much. But I don't think that's going to help now.'

'She doesn't know what she's missing,' Henry said brusquely. 'If she's too stupid to get over whatever it is she's imagining is wrong between the pair of you, then there are plenty of women out there who'd be only too happy to take her place.'

'Hear, hear,' I said. 'You won't be single for long, Dad.'

'I get the feeling that Alex doesn't even want to imagine anyone could take Karen's place right now,' said Lydia quietly.

'Not either of those two dogs at the table tonight,' Henry continued regardless. 'Conan the Barbarian and Main Beam and Dip.' He did an impression of Louisa's crossed eyes. 'Where on earth did they come from?'

'They're friends of Lindsey's,' said Dad.

'Were they lesbians?'

'Henry, what have I told you about thinking before you open your mouth?' Lydia asked him. 'You're talking about Lindsey's friends.'

'That's OK,' I said. 'I didn't really know them that well. We met in an Internet chat-room. On politics.'

'Thank God for that,' said Henry. 'Was starting to think you'd gone lezza on us too.'

Lydia sent a cork from one of the bottles we'd finished that night sailing across the kitchen towards her husband's head and managed to get him right between the eyes.

'I married her for her aim,' said Henry, rubbing at the sore spot.

'And I married him because . . . well, to be honest with you, I'm still wondering why I married him.' Lydia gave an exaggerated sigh, but it had always been clear to me that theirs was what a marriage should be like. They'd been married for nearly twenty years. A proper double act. A union of two equals. And it's what I wanted for my Dad. It's how I imagined he had been with my mother.

'Time to go,' Lydia announced when all the drying up had been done. 'We've got an early start tomorrow. My niece is getting married in France on Saturday afternoon. She planned it ever so quickly. A total surprise.'

'Don't mention the "m" word,' said Henry.

'It's OK,' said Dad. 'I'll survive.'

'I'm sure Karen will come to her senses,' said Lydia, but I could tell from the way her brows were knitted together that she wasn't at all sure she was right. She kissed Dad tenderly on both cheeks and he helped her into her coat.

I saw them to the door. As we stood on the doorstep, Lydia

took my face between her hands. She and Henry had known me since the day I was born. And even though I was a good two inches taller than her these days, she squeezed my cheeks as though I was still a little girl. I didn't mind. I had always liked my 'Auntie Lydia'. If there had been a mother figure in my life since the dreadful day Mum left us, it was Lydia. She had taken me to buy my first bra. It was the one thing I had refused to let Dad do for me.

'You're a great daughter, looking after your dad so well. But you mustn't let what's going on with him and Karen stop you from getting out there and enjoying your own life, Linz. I know you've been spending an awful lot of time at home lately.'

'I'm happy looking after Dad.'

'Come on. I know you'd far rather be in Ibiza with Gemma.'

I blushed slightly at the mention of my ex-best friend's name.

'You know, whatever your father did to piss Karen off – and believe me, I'm sure that he's just as capable of saying the wrong thing as my Henry – I'm amazed that Karen hasn't been in touch with you. It's so unlike her. She cared so much about you.'

'She did?'

'Absolutely. Karen was always singing your praises. She was just as proud of you when you got your degree as your Dad was.'

'She was?'

'Oh yes. She planned a big surprise celebration dinner. Henry and I were invited. But I think you went to stay with some friends that night instead. You didn't pick up any of the calls she made to your mobile so you didn't know that we were all sitting there in the dark, waiting for you to come back so we could fire off the party poppers.'

'But she didn't ever mention it.'

'We all agreed not to. Karen didn't want you to feel bad that you hadn't come home when she made all that effort. You weren't to know. It's just a hazard of surprise celebrations. The guest of honour isn't always available.'

I remembered now that there had been a night the previous summer when Karen had called my mobile so many times I had switched it off, thinking after the third time she left a message that said, 'I'd love to see you as soon as you can get home tonight,' she wanted to ask some retarded question about the wedding plans. I figured she would have sounded a great deal more urgent and upset if anything had happened to Dad, and there was no other reason I would have wanted to talk to her.

'I can't believe she didn't tell me.'

I know that in the same circumstances I would have used the situation to score points for months.

'It's OK. We all enjoyed ourselves. None of the food went to waste with Henry around.'

Henry patted his stomach as he remembered. 'The cake was particularly good.'

'Goodnight, Lindsey,' said Lydia. 'Call us any time you like. Especially if Alex starts to drive you up the wall with his moping.'

'Kiss for your Uncle Henry?'

Henry rubbed his bristly beard against my cheek.

'Goodnight.'

26

I walked back into the kitchen. Dad had boiled the kettle and was pouring hot water over a couple of camomile tea-bags. I sat down at the table and gladly accepted my mug. I had forgotten how exhausting playing the hostess can be.

'You didn't have a very good time, did you, Dad?' I said.

'Poppet,' Dad replied, 'I had a lovely time. You cooked a wonderful meal. But I suppose, if I'm honest, I just didn't feel much like celebrating tonight.'

'That's OK,' I assured him.

'I suppose I should also tell you that I don't think I'm ready to be set up with another woman yet. And I suspect that is what tonight was all about.'

I tried to look innocent. 'Come on! Would I try to set my own father up with a date?'

'I believe you would,' Dad smiled. 'Where did you get those girls from again?'

'I met them in that Internet chat-room I told you about,' I lied. 'The one where we all discuss politics. I thought it would be nice to put some faces to the names. They're better by email,' I added.

'They were both very nice,' Dad said in an utterly uninterested way.

'You know, Dad,' I began then. 'I can see why you didn't fancy either of those girls tonight but I don't think you should be so quick to dismiss the possibility of starting to date again sometime soon. And the Internet actually isn't such a bad place to find someone these days.'

Dad snorted.

'No, Dad. Don't laugh. It's not just weirdos who go on dating sites any more. Everybody's doing it. And it's totally a guy's market. The girls tend to be much higher quality than the men. You'd have them falling at your feet.'

'Lindsey, I don't want to have anyone fall at my feet. It's not the right time.'

'I know you think you don't want to right *now*. But I think you've got to approach this area of your life like getting back behind the wheel of a car after you've had an accident. Or getting back on a horse after it's thrown you. Don't let yourself get the fear, Dad. The longer you stay out of the dating arena, the harder it will be to get back in.'

Dad shook his head but smiled as he did so, which I took as the cue I needed to carry on.

'Just try it. I'll show you how. Help you write your profile and choose a good photo. You don't even have to meet anyone face to face. Just a little bit of Internet flirting. Get you back into the swing. It will make you feel so much better.'

'I really can't imagine how it could.'

'There are millions of women on-line. There will be at least one you want to swap emails with. And it won't involve hours of trawling through hopeless profiles. There are specialist sites now so that you can make sure you're meeting women from the right background straight off the bat.'

'You mean there is a site for women who are specifically looking for a bad-tempered, washed-up copywriter who doesn't actually want to meet anyone?'

'I mean there are sites that you can't even get access to without the proper education and social credentials.'

'And what might they be?' Dad laughed. 'The proper credentials?'

'Having gone to the right schools. A degree-level education from a good university. Women who work in the law, in medicine, in the City. Serious jobs. That sort of thing.'

'I see.' Dad got up from the kitchen table to swill out his tea mug though I knew he was far from having finished drinking. He was trying to close the conversation, I knew. 'I appreciate what you're trying to do, Linz,' he said. 'But the last thing I want or need to do right now is get involved with someone new. Even someone with impeccable qualifications. Crikey. I definitely don't have those myself . . .' he mused.

'Dad, there could be someone perfect for you on-line right now. If you don't take action someone else might snap her up.'

'I still haven't entirely given up hope that Karen and I will be reconciled.'

'Well, I think you should!' I blurted out.

'What?'

'I think you should give up.'

Since that night when I found Dad crying in his office, we hadn't really had an explicit conversation about Karen at all. For the first few days, I would ask Dad every hour on the hour whether he had spoken to her and he would tell me 'No'. That was usually the end of the conversation. Thank goodness. I didn't want to have to sit there and commiserate and pretend I too was gutted that Karen was no longer with us. But the evening of the dinner party, the things he had said to Lydia and Henry, and this revelation that he hadn't given up hope, made it clear that I had been very, very wrong in my estimation of how far along Dad was in the grieving process.

It had been a month. A whole month. I would have lost

hope if someone still refused to return my calls after a *week*. Having any hope at all at the end of a month was just crazy. It was ridiculous and embarrassing to keep holding on in the face of such obvious disdain.

That night I decided, perhaps influenced by the five glasses of wine I had polished off over dinner, that what Dad needed was a dose of reality. He needed to know what he had really lost. A reminder of the real Karen, not the perfect, mythical Karen he had constructed in his mind, was the only thing that would give him some perspective. It was the only thing that would make him snap out of this ridiculous bout of self-pity.

'You really think I should give up on Karen?' he asked me, with a look of such pure pain I almost hesitated to tell him the truth right then. But I didn't.

'Yes, I do,' I said honestly. And the floodgates opened.

'I mean, look at what she's done to you, Dad. She jilted you a month before you were supposed to be married. She's been horrible to you ever since. She even won't talk to you. She had her mother set the dog on you.'

'I'm sure Karen doesn't know anything about the dog,' said Dad.

'I'm sure she does.'

'Marilyn thought she was doing her best for her daughter. I rather hope Karen and I will be able to laugh about it soon. And I know that you're just trying to defend me, sweetheart, but you really don't have to take my side so strongly that you don't remember how sweet Karen was to you.'

'Oh, come on,' I sighed. 'If she was anything towards me, she was patronizing.'

'Lindsey, don't take a stance that will be difficult to come back from when she does return.'

'But she won't come back! Don't you see? You've got to give it up, Dad. I hate to have to do the tough love thing on you but Karen clearly doesn't want you any more and you shouldn't want to see her either. You're hanging on to something that wasn't even right for you in the first place.'

'Lindsey, stop there . . .'

'No,' I continued. 'It's about time I was really honest with you.'

'Honest about what?'

'That as far as I'm concerned you had a lucky escape.'

Dad shook his head.

'You did,' I said. 'A jilting is far less difficult to go through than a divorce.'

Dad didn't look convinced.

'Really. You know what I'm saying is true. If Karen hadn't had the good sense to see how badly suited you were, you would have seen it yourself within months. And then what would you have done?'

'That moment would never have come,' said Dad. 'Karen and I were perfect for each other.'

'Like hell you were. Your relationship was like something out of *My Fair Lady*, which, as everybody knows, absolutely wouldn't have happened in real life. I'm not the only person who thought that you totally outclassed her. Lydia and Henry might say that they would never have called Karen a bimbo, but you can bet that most of your friends have been thinking it all along.'

Dad lifted his hand but the gesture was about as useful at stopping me as it would have been at stopping a juggernaut with no brakes on a 45-degree slope. I wasn't ready to stop. Not at all.

'Dad, she was beneath you,' I pushed on. 'If you had married her, you would have been marrying into a family of thugs. You would have been marrying into the kind of people who hang out with train robbers on the Costa del Sol. In fact, I'm pretty sure I've seen her mother and her Uncle Tony on *Crimewatch.*'

'Lindsey, please!'

'It's not even as though Karen is trying to better herself. She works in a bloody gym. She's never picked up a book. If she had a daughter she'd probably call her Chardonnay. Don't you remember the time she drank from the finger-bowl at that Thai restaurant? I was so embarrassed. And then there are the clothes she wears. She dresses like a footballer's wife. You should have seen her in Ibiza, Dad. She looked like a total slag. Skirts up here, tops down there.' I indicated thigh-high and deep cleavage. 'And the kind of shoes you only otherwise see on transvestites. You should have seen the dress she was going to wear to the wedding, Dad! Honestly, if she hadn't jilted you, you would have turned and run the minute you saw her at the altar anyway.

'I was always ashamed to be seen with her. You should have been ashamed of her too. Now you don't have to be embarrassed any more. She was a stupid, classless gold-digger. She made Christina Aguilera look like Gwyneth Paltrow. But she also had the sense to set you free. She's giving you the chance to get the love you truly deserve. And if she came to her senses while she was in the sea overnight, then I'm bloody glad I pushed her off the boat.'

I pushed her off the boat . . .

Oh, those six words which were to change my life. As I came to the end of my rant, my confession of my true feelings about Dad's ex-fiancée, I thought I finally knew what the Catholics were on about. I felt purged, cleansed, forgiven already. I was sure that having aired my thoughts I had offered Dad space for catharsis too. When he got over the shock he would see that for sure.

But the short silence I had expected soon became a long one. And eventually Dad got up from the table again and walked across the kitchen to the window. He stood there and looked out on to the dark street, still saying nothing.

'So you see,' I said, just to clarify matters, 'I know that what I did was childish and possibly cruel but I did it out of love for you.'

Still he said nothing.

'I just didn't want you to fall into the clutches of a gold-digger. I didn't want you to get hurt when you found out what she's really like.'

Dad didn't even turn to look at me.

'Dad?'

His gaze remained on the street outside. Only his shoulders rose slightly as he took a breath, with which to give me the light ticking-off I probably deserved, I assumed. Except that this was to be no light ticking-off.

'Dad?'

After a minute or so I realized that this was the longest period of time during an argument that Dad had ever remained speechless. Longer even than the day I was sent home from school for having cigarettes and a small bag of weed tucked inside my geography course-work folder (no one had been impressed by my argument that I was simply putting an extraordinary amount of effort into my project on the agricultural economies of south-east Asia).

This was far worse than that.

It was like the moment after you realize someone has taken the pin out of a grenade. Like the quiet but deadly click of a landmine beneath a soldier's boot.

'Get out.'

'What?'

'Get out,' he repeated quietly.

'Dad?' I said pleadingly. 'What do you mean?'

'What do you think I mean? I mean get out of my sight. Get out of my house!'

'You don't mean that. I was just saying what I—'

'Lindsey,' he interrupted me. 'I don't want to hear another word from you. Not one word. This morning I was merely concerned that you didn't seem to be putting a lot of effort into carving out a decent adult life of your own. Now it transpires that you have been putting a great deal of active effort into ruining mine.'

'But Dad . . .'

'Over the past twenty-four years you have cost me many sleepless nights and astronomical school fees, only to come back here after university and loll on the sofa as though you don't have an educated thought in your head. I was prepared to put up with that for a while. I know it isn't easy finding your way in the world. But now I find out that you have also cost me the woman I love.'

'But Dad, you don't really love her!'

'How dare you say that?'

'It's true!'

'Of course it bloody well isn't true. I love her more than you can possibly imagine. Clearly.'

'But how could you love a woman like that?'

'*Like that?* Have you got any idea what you sound like? I didn't raise you to be bitter and snobbish and judgmental, but that is exactly how you have turned out. What right did you have to decide that Karen wasn't good enough for me – was a gold-digger – when you yourself haven't done a day's work in your entire life?'

I decided it was the wrong moment to remind him about

the Saturday job at the local boutique that lasted approximately two weeks before I decided that getting up early on a weekend wasn't my style.

'What did I do wrong to raise such a nasty, flint-hearted girl?'

'I'm not flint-hearted, Dad. I told you. I did everything because I care about you!'

'If you cared about me, why didn't you approach me like an adult with your concerns so that I could have put you straight about my feelings for Karen before you almost killed her? To think that I thought you had changed! To think that I believed that by taking Karen away for her hen weekend you were finally thinking of someone else and showing some maturity! How could I not have guessed what you were planning to do when Karen called home to say that you had her on a boat?'

'I didn't intend for her to end up in the sea. It was a Sunseeker 105, Dad. It's not as though I took her out on a Hobie Cat.'

'You know full well that she's frightened of the water.'

'She didn't tell me.'

'She told you. You just didn't listen. Just like you didn't listen to me when I told you that I loved her. Because you didn't care, did you? It was all about your own agenda. I can't believe you took it upon yourself to decide what I want from my life. What on earth possessed you? Were you frightened about losing your inheritance?'

'Of course I wasn't!' I protested loudly. Before adding, 'My inheritance was always going to be protected by a pre-nup anyway, right?'

Dad shook his head.

'Right?' I wasn't sure whether he was telling me 'No, it wasn't protected' or just expressing sadness that I had asked.

'This is like something out of bloody Shakespeare,' he sighed.

He adopted a pretty Shakespearean posture then, clutching his head with both hands, scrunching up his hair and actually groaning.

I chewed my lip as I wondered what on earth to say next. Was there a magic phrase that would make everything better? I looked at the clock. It was almost midnight. If only I could make the hands whizz back by twenty minutes or so and shut my big fat mouth.

'Do you still want me to leave?' I squeaked eventually.

'Yes.'

It wasn't the answer I had hoped for.

'I think it would be a good idea. I need a bit of time on my own to think things through. It's not every day you find out you've raised a viper.'

'Dad!' I protested.

'I think you need a bit of time on your own to think things through as well.'

'But where should I go?'

'I don't know. You're nearly twenty-four years old. You work it out. Stay with one of your friends for a while. How about Gemma?'

Dad was one of the few people in London who didn't seem to know that Gemma and I were no longer on speaking terms.

'I don't think Gemma is in town right now,' I lied.

'Well, you've got a credit card. Book yourself into a hotel for a few days.'

'But I haven't got a job . . .'

Dad rolled his eyes. 'I'll take care of it, Lindsey. I just want to be on my own. And I want you to think about what you've done before you dare to talk to me again.'

'Do you want me to go right this minute?'

I pulled my cardigan tightly around me because suddenly I felt very cold and small. I hoped he'd notice.

'In the morning,' he conceded. 'I'd never send you any-where in the middle of the night. But get out of my sight now.'

I nodded and went straight to my room.

What else could I do? There was no point trying to argue any more. Dad wasn't going to calm down in the next ten minutes. But though I went to bed more than a little shaken by the strength of his reaction, I also went to bed confident that things would look a great deal better in the morning. Things always look better in the morning.

27

Things did not look better in the morning. Not at all.

By the time I woke up the next day, Dad had already left for the office. I suppose I should have made the effort to get up before nine and catch him at breakfast on that particular morning at least but I didn't. Organizing the ill-fated dinner party had left me completely wiped out and I didn't even hear him leave the house.

When I walked into the kitchen, my heart gave a little skip of relief when I found that Dad had left me a note on the table. But it dived straight back down into my boots again when I saw that the note was merely outlining the maximum amount per night Dad was prepared to pay for me to stay in a hotel until he felt he could speak to me again. I looked at the number he had scribbled on the Post-it and wondered if he had left off a nought. I mean, was it really possible to find a decent hotel room in Central London for less than *a hundred and fifty pounds* per night? He must have been joking. Yes, I decided. This was all a big joke. That pitiful figure on the Post-it was supposed to signal to me that Dad had thought better of kicking me out and was pulling my leg by suggesting that I try to survive on backpacker money in the second most expensive city in the world.

I called Dad's office to tell him that I was willing to accept his olive branch.

His assistant picked up.

'Hey, Clare. It's Lindsey.'

'Oh.' She didn't sound all that pleased to hear from me.

'Can I speak to my father?'

'Er . . . no.'

'No?'

Clare took a deep breath. 'He told me to tell you that the note he left tells you everything he wants to say to you for now. You can call if you have an emergency but otherwise you should do as he asked and wait for him to call you.'

'What?'

'I'm sorry, Lindsey. That's what he said. I'm sure he'll think better of it later today.'

'Are you in on the joke?' I asked.

'He didn't appear to be *joking*,' Clare said quietly. 'Look, I don't know what you guys have fallen out about but if I were you, I'd just lie low for a while. That's what I do when he's going off on one at me. It's a very difficult time for him right now. I mean, he was supposed to be getting married this week.'

'I do remember,' I said.

'That's probably why he's in such a foul mood.'

'Thanks, Clare. I appreciate your insight.'

Lying low didn't seem like an option to me. I decided to call Lydia, my fairy godmother, for a proper strategy discussion. She'd known Dad since they were teenagers. Lydia would know what to do. But because I had woken up so late, I had missed her too. She and Henry were already on a plane back to France. I left her a particularly pathetic-sounding message. And that was it. I had run out of people to call . . .

★   ★   ★

Lydia phoned back as soon as she and Henry landed in Lyons. I poured out the story. Well, most of it . . . I told her that Dad and I had argued because I told him what I really thought of Karen in quite unflattering terms. I didn't mention that I had also confessed to attempting to kill her.

'What do you think I should do?'

'Do as he asked?' suggested Lydia. Like Clare, she sounded oddly short with me. 'I think he probably does need a bit of time on his own, especially given the timing. Why don't you go and stay with Gemma for a while?'

'Gemma isn't talking to me!'

'Oh dear. But you two were always so close.'

'Not any more.'

'Well then, I guess you'll have to stay in a hotel. I would say you could move into our place, sweetheart, but Henry's insisting that we rent it out to some Russian family to pay for my credit card bills. You'll be fine in a hotel. Show your dad what a grown-up you can be. Chin up.'

Chin up? What kind of advice was that?

I sat down in front of *Trisha* and breakfasted on the remains of the food that hadn't been eaten at the dinner party the night before. But the warring families on the talk show didn't help me feel optimistic about my chances of reconciling with Dad and I soon lost my appetite.

'You got to give respect to get respect,' was about the only line that made any sense between the bleeped-out obscenities as fathers and daughters faced each other in a television studio. Maybe Lydia was right. Perhaps I did have to respect Dad's wishes for now. Perhaps that was the key.

But all the same I packed really slowly, lingering as I folded each item into my suitcase because the longer I took, the more time Dad would have to come home and tell me I was forgiven. By four o'clock, I had heard nothing. Five o'clock. Still nothing. Six o'clock. At half past six, I took a deep breath and walked out of the house to my little red Mini, feeling like the end of the world.

28

I was still feeling like the end of the world when I got to the beautifully appointed Charlotte Street Hotel and handed over my credit card for a small double room. No breakfast included.

The room was just a little over Dad's ridiculous budget. OK. It was a good two hundred pounds over budget. But I had considered the alternatives on the drive from Hampstead to Fitzrovia and decided that there were none. I wasn't about to risk catching body lice in some budget travellers' place, which was all I could have afforded on Dad's random figure. There were health *and* safety issues to consider. I would have been scared in a place I hadn't heard of. A hundred and fifty pounds per night? Dad clearly hadn't stayed in a London hotel for a while. He would understand why I had to ignore him. I could even pay back the difference if it was that big an issue. When I got back home, I would sell one of my handbags on E-bay or something.

Once in my room at the Charlotte Street, I booked an in-room massage. It was impossible to think clearly when my shoulders were up around my ears with stress. And then I ordered room service. I just didn't feel like eating anything except smoked salmon. And then I ordered a video on demand to take my mind off the worst of the previous night's row. And I did have a couple of drinks from the mini-bar to help me sleep.

All the time my mobile phone remained ominously silent.

★   ★   ★

The following morning – with still no word from Dad – I got up late and went for a walk. The Charlotte Street Hotel was very convenient for lots of good walks. Past lots of great shops. I decided to treat myself to a little something from Liberty. It was definitely a time for retail therapy. Then I jumped into a taxi and went for lunch at a new restaurant in Covent Garden that I had read about in *Vogue*. I kept to the set menu (forty pounds for three courses) but a half-bottle of Chablis seemed like a reasonable splurge under the circumstances.

After lunch I walked back to the hotel to save another cab fare. My route took me past the shoe shops. There are lots of good shoe shops in Covent Garden. I was enjoying my stroll so much that I bought two new pairs of trainers, thinking that rather than taking cabs or driving my Mini I could do this walking thing more often.

When I got back to the hotel late that afternoon, I felt altogether more cheerful. Dad still hadn't called, but I was optimistic that it wouldn't be long before he did. I tried on my new clothes, lit three Diptyque candles (I know they're thirty quid each but there really are no better scented candles out there), ordered more room service and treated myself to a half bottle of champagne. Vintage. I toasted myself. I could do independence very well. Perhaps this break from Dad was doing me good too.

The following day passed in a similar fashion, though I headed west to Selfridges for a change this time. They were having a sale. It would have been silly not to buy those lovely floppy Ghost trousers in all three of the colours that had been reduced. They're so useful for holidays.

I had lunch at a restaurant in store, then I treated myself to a pair of flip-flops from Jimmy Choo (when you find a pair of Jimmy Choo flip-flops in your size, price really is no object.

Do you know how quickly they walk out of the shops?). Then I headed back to the hotel. I booked another massage (carrying shopping bags really does for your shoulders). More room service. Another movie. Dad still hadn't called but I was feeling marvellous.

On the third morning, I decided I would make the most of my exile in Fitzrovia by getting in some culture at the British Museum. Fabulous Egyptian exhibits *and* a great gift shop. I was just walking out of the hotel when the receptionist called my name.

'Miss Parker?'

'Yes.'

'Can I bother you for just a moment?'

'Of course.' I walked across to the desk. 'Are you going to be able to sort out that room upgrade today?' I asked her. The room I had been in for the past couple of nights was nice enough but had a somewhat restricted view.

'Yes, we are,' the receptionist nodded. 'But I wonder if I might just ask you to close out your bill so far first. We have a policy here that we ask guests to settle their bills each time the total reaches fifteen hundred pounds. It's just a formality.'

'I understand.' I pulled my credit card out of my new Louis Vuitton wallet (Selfridges. Not in the sale) and handed it over. 'Here you go.'

'Thank you, Miss Parker,' said the receptionist. She swiped my platinum card with a smile and we waited for the machine to do its magic.

Her smile wavered. Just a little, but I definitely caught it.

'Is there a problem?' I asked.

'I shouldn't imagine so,' the receptionist assured me, turning that smile back on full blast again. 'It sometimes happens that there's a glitch in the computer system that means a perfectly good card is refused. Particularly if the transaction looks irregular. Would you mind waiting for a moment while I call your card issuer?'

I shrugged.

'It shouldn't take long.'

The receptionist called Delhi, or wherever it is that my credit card company has its call centre, and recited my card number down the phone. There was a pause while the digits were tapped in at the other end. I studied my nails while we waited and considered booking into Bliss for a manicure that afternoon.

'I see,' said the receptionist eventually. 'Thank you very much. Goodbye.'

'Is everything in order?' I asked.

'I'm afraid it isn't . . .' she said.

29

It couldn't be right. I had never been refused credit in my life. Dad had always made sure that my balance was paid off in full at the end of every month. I told the hotel receptionist as much.

'I'm sure you're telling the truth,' the receptionist said almost apologetically. 'But right now your card issuer says that you have reached your limit and we're unable to put the full amount of your bill so far through on this card.'

'What?' I spat in disbelief. 'You're kidding me. That card has a twenty-thousand-pound limit!'

'And you must have reached it.'

'That's impossible. Try this one.'

I handed over my American Express.

And was met with the same crazy result. My American Express was refused. I could have no more credit.

'That's ridiculous,' I said. 'I've got a ten thousand limit on that card too.'

My Egg card was similarly challenged. My Mastercard wilted before my eyes. My Harvey Nicks card was obviously useless outside Harvey Nicks. My cheque guarantee card was only good for five hundred. I had just three hundred pounds' cash in my bag.

'The bill is one thousand, six hundred and thirty-four pounds,' the receptionist reminded me.

'I know. But I don't usually carry that much on me!' I said, trying hard to keep the panic from my voice with sarcasm.

'There's a cash point near the tube station,' the receptionist suggested. 'Perhaps you could get some money out of your current account? If you leave your passport as security until you return, we'd be more than happy to accept the balance in cash.'

So that lunchtime, instead of heading to the British Museum for some culturally-related leisure and retail, I found myself totally clearing out both my current *and* my savings accounts to cover my Charlotte Street Hotel bill. There was only just enough money between the two accounts to settle it. I kept telling myself as I waited for the bank teller to allow a withdrawal of more than five hundred pounds in one day that there must be some mistake. Everything would be sorted out with a couple more phone calls. There was no way I could have run up forty thousand pounds' worth of credit card bills in the space of a month. Where had all the money gone?

I hadn't spent that much in Ibiza, had I? Of course not. We'd stayed for free on Gemma's boat and hadn't paid for a thing in Damien's club. I didn't think I'd been to the shops more than three times a week since getting home. Fair enough, I had bought an expensive leather jacket from Kenzo, and a handbag from Hogan that I probably could have managed without, and a couple of pairs of shoes from LK Bennett – OK, three pairs of shoes from LK Bennett – but I'd been pretty abstemious otherwise. For example, I'd budgeted on the things I needed for the dinner party by going to Habitat rather than the Conran Shop . . .

The sums just didn't add up. I could not have spent forty thousand pounds. Not even if I had been shopping in the company of Paris Hilton in my sleep. But whatever the truth of my disappearing cash was, right then I couldn't afford a single night more in my swanky hotel. Nor could I stand the embarrassment of trying to persuade them to give me time to get more credit. After I had settled my bill, I told the hotel receptionist that I would be checking out that day. There was no need for her to have me moved into the upgraded room after all.

'I've been called away suddenly on business,' I lied.

She nodded kindly.

'I've already spoken to all my credit card companies and asked them to look into what is clearly a terrible mistake,' I added.

Then I walked out with my head held as high as I could.

What had gone wrong? I settled myself in a corner of the nearest Starbucks with a double espresso and resolved to get to the bottom of my sudden financial embarrassment. Heads would roll. I'd demand apologies at the very highest level. I was an excellent customer. I called Visa and prepared to give the telephone operator there a large and ugly piece of my mind.

'My credit limit is twenty thousand pounds!' I shouted.

'Actually,' said the person at the other end. 'Your joint cardholder called us two days ago and requested that the limit on this particular card be reduced to just three thousand.'

'What?'

'He should have informed you.'

But he hadn't.

My joint cardholder was my father, of course. In fact, all my cards were registered in his name since no one would give me a card of my own while I didn't have a salary coming in. Each of the card issuers I called that day had the same tale to tell me. With just four phone calls over the space of one afternoon, my father had systematically reduced my credit limit from a total of forty thousand pounds to six.

'I can't believe he's allowed to do that!' I wailed.

'They are actually his credit cards,' the man at Egg reminded me. 'You're just a second signatory. He decides how much you get to spend.'

'How could he leave me with just six thousand pounds?'

'It must be hard,' said the man at Egg. Sarcastically.

'There are plenty of people who live on less than six thousand pounds a year,' Clare pointed out when I telephoned Dad at his office to rail at the injustice.

'But I can't. I'm up to my limit and I can't afford another night in my hotel. Does he want me to be on the street?' I cried. 'Put him on the phone at once.'

'He's in Amsterdam right now,' Clare told me. 'But when he checks in with me later this afternoon I'll tell him to call you right away.'

'What am I supposed to do until then?' I asked.

'I don't know.'

'You're not being very sympathetic, Clare.'

'Really? Maybe that's because I take home about fifteen thousand pounds a year after tax. I buy all my clothes at Top Shop and I share a flat in Balham with three guys who have never heard of a toilet brush. Please forgive me if my heart is beyond bleeding.'

'I'll have you sacked!' I shouted.

'I'd like to see you try it. Look, Lindsey.' Clare's voice softened just a little. 'I understand you're feeling a bit upset but it's really not the end of the world. Think of this as a challenge to your ingenuity. Why don't you start by taking back some of the things you've bought over the past few days? That would free up some credit.'

'You want me to take some things back to the shops?'

'Or start busking. Welcome to the real world,' said Clare.

I can't play any instruments so un-shopping was my only option right then. Though I begged *and* cried, none of the card issuers would increase my limit without Dad's say-so. I had to take *everything* back to the shops. Back went the three pairs of Ghost trousers. I can't tell you how that hurt. I mean, I'd saved almost two hundred pounds on their full price when I bought them and I knew for certain that I would have worn them until they fell apart! Back went the trainers in two colourways. That was a false economy, surely, since now I wouldn't be able to walk instead of driving or taking cabs. Still, I did it. I even gritted my teeth and went to return the three-hundred-pound flip-flops.

But the girl in the Jimmy Choo concession refused to take them.

'You've used them,' she said, looking at the soles and tossing the flip-flops back in the box as though they'd cost three pounds and not three hundred and fifteen.

'No, I haven't.'

'They're scuffed.'

'Hardly.'

'Look at this,' she said, waving the left flip-flop under my nose.

It was so unfair. I explained that I'd only worn them for three minutes, as I dashed across the road from the hotel to the newsagent's to buy a few magazines. I couldn't have taken more than twenty steps but apparently that was enough to void my right to change my mind.

'We get a lot of people trying to bring stuff back when they realize they've overspent,' the assistant said. 'You need to learn to stay within your budget.'

'I was well within my budget,' I protested. 'They just don't fit me properly.'

'Yeah, yeah. Haven't heard that one before.'

'You can't expect me to wear shoes that don't fit.'

'Feet grew overnight, did they? That's your lookout. These shoes were perfectly fit for sale. And you bought them. Excuse me . . .'

She pushed the shoe box back towards me and headed in the direction of another customer.

'You haven't finished with me yet!'

'I told you once, we're not taking them back.'

'That is ridiculous. You're being unfair. I'll never buy a pair of Jimmy Choos from this shop again!' I snarled.

'You probably won't ever be able to afford to,' said the sales assistant as I flounced towards the escalator. Her colleagues' nasty laughter followed me all the way to the ground floor. Even the customer she served right after me was laughing. Had they never needed a little help in their lives before? A little leeway in their consumer rights? How could people be so cruel?

Not being able to return the flip-flops and having already lit the Diptyque candles, I only managed to un-shop about five hundred pounds' worth of goods that afternoon. It would take at least three days for the money to be credited back to my account and even then it would cover less than two nights' worth of decent accommodation without touching the mini-bar.

'Please. Please, please extend my limit,' I begged Mr Visa one more time.

'Nope. Not without your father's permission.'

'He said it would be OK.'

'We need to talk to him in person.'

'I'll get him,' I said, covering the mouthpiece for a moment before I returned to the telephone with the deepest voice I could manage. 'Hello, this is Alex Parker.'

'Nice try, Miss Parker,' said Mr Visa.

I had to get hold of Dad. I understood *why* he had reduced my credit limits – he had set me a budget, after all – but I was certain that he would not have meant for me to experience so much upset and humiliation as a result. If he knew how bad things were he would be on the phone to Visa in a moment. I thought carefully and composed a desperate SMS rather than calling just in case he was in a meeting.

'Dad, I'm having an emergency,' I texted. 'Have run out of money. What should I do?'

I sat down on a bench in a garden square behind Selfridges and waited for Dad's reply. As I waited, I watched a woman dressed in a greasy duffel coat rifling through the bins and actually putting some of the things she found into her mouth! I winced. Fifteen minutes passed.

'Oh Lord,' I prayed, as the woman lit a cigarette butt to end her dustbin dinner. 'Just get Dad to raise my limit by five hundred pounds. Please, please, please don't let me end up like that.'

The woman in the duffel coat suddenly looked straight at me. I shrieked beneath her evil eye.

'Get a job,' Dad texted back.

Get a job????!!!!

I stared at that text message until the tears started to swim before my eyes. All I had left in the world was forty-seven pounds in my savings account, a nearly new Mini with half a tank of petrol and a pair of lightly worn Jimmy Choos. And my dad didn't care. He had abandoned me.

I was homeless. I was poor. And I was *fatherless*.

30

I picked up my car from the NCP car park – swiftly disposing of another thirty pounds in the process – and drove disconsolately around Earl's Court, trying to find a bed for the night. I slowed to a crawl as I passed the backpackers' hotels, trying to convince myself that I could do worse than spend a night there. Then I imagined the vast range of tropical ticks that might be living in those beds . . .

I couldn't do it. I was itching at the mere thought of it. Ticks, scabies, pubic hair in the plughole! There was no way I could sleep in a bed that might recently have been vacated by someone who had spent three months travelling around Europe with just two pairs of pants and a bottle of that dubious multi-purpose travel-wash that manages none of its stated purposes effectively.

I was crying so hard by this time, I couldn't actually see to drive properly. Horns blared as I swerved erratically from one side of the road to the other every time I wiped my eyes. Rather than continue to endanger my fellow road-users, I pulled up on a double red line outside a branch of Starbucks and went inside for a consolatory muffin, thinking dramatically that it might be the last meal I could afford. I added four sugars to my coffee for energy and slipped another six packets into my handbag. I might be grateful for them on the park bench that night, I sniffed.

I sat in the window of Starbucks for an hour. Eventually, I

managed to stop crying but was so dazed I didn't even notice the traffic warden slapping a ticket on the Mini's windscreen. Nor did I notice the towing van that turned up shortly afterwards and carted my beloved car off to the pound . . .

I couldn't afford to get my car back. I walked to the pound to save on taxi fares but the towing charge was two hundred pounds and I had nowhere near enough. The guy on the desk was as mean as the girl at Jimmy Choo when I told him my predicament.

'I'll write an IOU and come in again just as soon as my credit limit is restored,' I suggested.

'Get a bus,' he said.

'I'll write to Ken Livingstone about your rudeness!' I said.

'I'm sure he'll write back. He makes exceptions for every moron who parks on a double red line during the rush hour.'

He wouldn't even allow me to go into my car boot and get out a suitcase.

'Nobody is allowed in the yard without one of these,' he said, waving a slip of paper at me. 'And you don't get one of these unless you pay your fine.'

I kicked the desk in frustration, cursed the cashier and his mother and his mother's mother before her. Three burly guys immediately appeared to help defend their colleague, though in kicking the desk while wearing flip-flops, I had just hurt myself far more than I would ever be able to hurt him, snug behind his glass.

I limped away.

I had to call Dad again. I left a truly desperate message this time, not bothering to keep the wobble out of my voice. I told him that I would wait for his reply in Pâtisserie Valerie on Old Compton Street, just in case he wanted to send a car to pick me up. I couldn't go home and wait for him there, risking his wrath by heading back without an invitation, because my house keys were in a holdall in the back of the Mini.

'Dad, please call,' I said. 'I know I overspent your budget but I'm in serious doo-doo now. I've stupidly, completely, run out of cash and the car's just been towed, so I can't even sleep in that for the night.'

But he didn't call me back.

I sat upstairs at Pâtisserie Valerie making a millefeuille last until the place shut for the evening. Then I took myself to The Stockpot two streets down and made a three-course meal for five pounds last until the restaurant staff started to close up, but still my phone didn't ring. After that, I nursed an espresso in Bar Italia until they too started to stack chairs on tables to signify the end of the night. By this time I had less than twenty pounds to my name. Even the backpacker hostels I had turned my nose up at before were out of my price range now.

As I stepped out of Bar Italia and the staff locked the door shut behind me, Soho was quieter than I had ever seen it. It seemed that everyone who had a bed to go to had gone home to it. Everyone else was bedding down for the night in doorways and alleyways, swathed in filthy grey blankets and collapsed cardboard boxes. I had been regretting my choice of outfit (those stupid flip-flops) for quite some time already. I was freezing. Though it was July, I felt certain that if I lay down in one of those doorways I would go into a cold-induced coma and never wake up. Especially since there wasn't a spare cardboard box to be had. I looked longingly at a greasy sleeping bag in the doorway of All Bar One. A filthy head popped out of it.

'Fuck off,' the bag owner said.

His casual rudeness made my eyes begin to itch again.

I decided I had to keep moving to stay warm. I started to

trudge northwards, keeping my eyes firmly fixed ahead of me, careful not to attract any trouble. The streets I would happily walk down in the daytime looked altogether different in the dark. The tall London buildings seemed to be leaning in to cover me, like a vampire wrapping his cloak around a victim. I heard footsteps behind me but whirled round in terror to see nobody. Still, I quickened my pace. Soon I was walking past the Charlotte Street Hotel, its reception bathed in friendly light. I lingered like a Victorian urchin outside a cake shop as I remembered the big soft beds, the clean white sheets. Had I really been there just twenty-four hours ago?

Noticing me standing outside staring in, one of the hotel doormen started to walk towards me, to find out what it was I wanted. I scuttled away before he recognized me as the customer who had failed to tip him properly the previous night. I pushed on north to Regent's Park, imagining my grave there beneath a tree. I would lay down to sleep and be found white and frozen in the morning.

But then I had an idea.

31

Henry and Lydia lived just to the north of Regent's Park. They'd bought their enormous white stucco house as a wreck and lovingly restored it over fifteen years. Now the house, which had at one time been used as a squat by a communist collective, was worthy of any interiors magazine. It had a beautiful garden too.

The thing was, I knew the access code for their security gate – Lydia had told me when I had to let myself in to feed their cat while they went on holiday. Unfortunately the cat died before they got back. Lydia assured me that it was because the beloved mog was old and poorly and not because I had forgotten to feed it for three nights in a row.

Anyway, I might not be able to get into Henry and Lydia's house that night but I could definitely get into their garden *and* their shed. I quickened my pace. The pretty yet utterly impractical jewelling in those three-hundred-pound flip-flops was making mincemeat of my feet, but I didn't care. Henry and Lydia's shed awaited and I anticipated arriving there with almost as much enthusiasm as I had anticipated playing in it as a child.

Thankfully, the code was the same. 1987. It was a sentimental code – 1987 was the year that Henry and Lydia had married. I pushed the gate open as quietly as I could, not knowing whether the new Russian tenants were yet in residence. The gate gave an outraged little squeak. I froze, expecting immediate detection, but the house remained dark and silent. I slipped down the side alley into Henry and Lydia's beautiful garden, grateful they'd planted so many trees and deliriously thankful that they hadn't decided to get rid of the shed when they had the landscapers in.

It was still there. A very ordinary shed with a pointy roof made of corrugated plastic and a single dirty window. That shed had been the scene of many happy days for me. When I was a little girl, Henry and Lydia had kept their lawnmower under a tarpaulin so that I could have the empty shed for a Wendy House. I crept inside. The door didn't have a lock since Henry's view was that anyone desperate enough to steal fertilizer was welcome to it. Once inside, the moonlight on the wall illuminated the Laura Ashley wallpaper with which I had insisted they paper my new home. It was very expensive wallpaper, but I was a very sweet five-year-old, and Henry in particular could refuse me nothing.

There had been furniture too back then. A miniature table and chairs, painted white. A red gingham tablecloth. A pretend oven in which I baked mud pies. They were all gone. As were the old blankets with which I had made a pretend bed. The lawnmower was back in its rightful place . . .

But the shed still had an intact roof and a roof was all that I needed right then. Outside, I could hear the first rumblings of another summer storm. Seconds later, I heard the rain clattering hard on the corrugated plastic roof as though someone was shaking a big bag of frozen peas from the sky. Safe inside the shed, I pushed the creaking lawnmower to the far corner and found an old deckchair. I opened out the chair, shooed away the spiders that had taken up residence in its creases, and sat down. I folded one of Henry's old waxed jackets into a pillow and covered myself with a dust sheet.

And that was how I spent my first night in the real world.

32

Incredible as it sounds, I managed to have quite a comfortable night in that deckchair. In fact I slept quite deeply until nine o'clock when I awakened very abruptly indeed to the sound of someone rattling the latch.

'Come on, come on,' said a female voice. 'Bloody open up.'

It was a stiff latch, I knew that. But it wouldn't stay shut for ever. I sat bolt upright. What was I going to do? I looked about for a means of escape but there was none. There was just one door into the shed and one door out. Should I tell the person trying to get into the shed that I was Henry and Lydia's god-daughter, or should I just dash out as they came in and avoid any explanation?

I decided to take the latter course. I stood up and pushed the deckchair out of the way. I reached for the handle on the inside of the door and pulled just as the person on the other side put her shoulder into it. As a result, the intruder came tumbling in at some speed. I had planned to use the sudden disorientation this would cause to my advantage but I couldn't get past the body on the ground.

'My knees!' she cried. She'd landed badly.

'I'm sorry,' I said. 'I'm really sorry. Look, I haven't taken anything. I'm getting out of your way right now. Goodbye.'

'Not so fast, Lind-zay Parker!'

The prostrate body grabbed me by the ankle and used my legs to haul herself up to her feet.

'How do you know my name?'

She knew my name because she was Poupeh Gharani.

'What on earth are you doing in this shed?' she asked me.

'What on earth are *you* doing in this shed?' I countered.

'I am here on business,' said Poupeh.

'What possible business could you have in my godmother's garden?'

'I might ask the same question of you. Help me up.'

Poupeh dusted herself off and then pushed straight past me to look out through the dusty window.

'Damn. Duck!' she said suddenly.

I did.

'Why are we ducking?' I whispered as she kept me down on the floor.

'The lady who is renting the house has come back early.'

'You mean the lady renting the house doesn't know you're here either?'

'Absolutely not. Her husband has retained me to find out whether she's having an affair. Damn, I shouldn't have told you that . . .' Poupeh added. 'You didn't hear me say that, OK? You're sworn to secrecy.'

'OK,' I shrugged. 'But I still don't understand what you're doing in the shed.'

'I was looking for a good place to put one of these.' She reached into her shoulder bag and pulled out a teeny-tiny camera. 'I need to have a totally unobstructed view of the back door so I can keep tabs on who comes in and out when her husband isn't home.'

Poupeh straightened up just enough to get a peep out of the dust-covered window. 'She's on her way out again by the look of things. Must have forgotten something she needed. Yep,' said Poupeh, pressing an earpiece into her ear. 'That's the sound of the front door closing. She's gone. Thank goodness. We'd have been completely stuck if she decided to stay in for the day.' Poupeh stood up completely and dusted herself down again. Now I got a proper look at her. She was like a cabbage rose on legs in a pale pink kaftan layered over a matching tiered skirt. A toning scarf trailed behind her like a streamer from an errant toilet roll. Her outfit made me look down at my own clothes. My white Capri trousers weren't quite so bright any more.

'Well, Lind-zay Parker.' Poupeh extended her hand towards me to shake mine. 'We meet again. What a pleasant surprise.'

'It's certainly a surprise,' I agreed.

'Now you've probably guessed I'm a private detective, but your excuse for being in the shed is?'

I didn't want to tell her but it came out like a sneeze. I couldn't stop it.

'Poupeh,' I said. 'I'm homeless.'

'Oh, Lind-zay! This is terrible news.'

I was so hungry, I simply couldn't refuse Poupeh's offer of breakfast at a café in Primrose Hill while I told her the full story. I would have eaten dog food if she'd offered it. Funny what a night in the great outdoors does for your appetitite.

But first she made me rearrange everything in the shed exactly as I had found it the previous night.

'*Exactly* as you found it,' she told me. 'If the wife comes in here and sees that anything has been moved, she'll be more likely to look too closely and find my camera.'

'Is this really what you do for a living?' I asked as I hung Henry's coat back on its peg. 'Trap people who are being unfaithful?'

'It's just one of the things people ask me to do. But I do

surveillance for all sorts of reasons. I look out for fraud in the workplace. That takes up quite a bit of my time. Sometimes I trail children to find out whether they are skipping school. I keep an eye on students away from home for the first time to make sure they're not spending their allowance on drugs. I track down runaways. That's the most satisfying part of my job. Reuniting someone with his or her family.' She smiled. 'Come on, let's get out of here before she comes back. Just do exactly what I do and don't say anything until we get to the car.'

Poupeh sidled around the shed door and headed for the garden gate. She kept low to the ground at all times. Once we were on the other side of the gate, she stood up and strolled out on to the pavement quite casually.

'Look natural,' she hissed at me.

How natural could we possibly look? One girl dressed like a blancmange and another who'd slept rough in Capri pants and Jimmy Choos?

We reached Poupeh's car. It was a Smart Car. As she clambered into the driver's seat, I was reminded of the joke about the elephants in the Mini. We drove to a pâtisserie on Regent's Park Road. Poupeh chattered all the way as though we had stayed in touch since school and saw each other every day.

In the café, I let her buy me a croissant and a big cappuccino. Telling her my story seemed like a small price to pay in return.

Still she didn't seem overly distressed on my behalf when I told her that I had been kicked out of home after falling out with my father. But then Poupeh had hardly seen her parents since they shipped her off to boarding school aged twelve.

'But you can't live in a hotel,' she said.

'I know. I can't find anywhere around here for less than one hundred pounds a night and I have twenty pounds left to my name.'

'No, I mean I won't allow it.'

'What choice do I have?'

'Well, you must come and stay with me.'

'What?'

'I insist on it,' she said. 'My apartment is just around the corner from here. There is nothing in my spare room except my shoe racks. We will move the shoes out and you will move in.'

'That's very kind of you but . . .'

'This is no time for butting,' said Poupeh. 'You are coming to stay with me and that is that. I know that you would do the same for me under the circumstances.'

How wrong she was.

'Don't you dare say no to me, Lind-zay. It will give us time to get to know each other better.'

Getting to know Poupeh Gharani better was exactly the kind of prospect I would have thrown myself under a bus to avoid just a week or so earlier. But what else could I do but take her up on her offer? My night in the shed hadn't been so comfortable that I was particularly eager to repeat it. I still couldn't afford to get my car back from the pound so that I might at least have a change of clothes to slum in.

'Seriously, Lind-zay. I insist that you be my guest,' said Poupeh.

I nodded my thanks and started crying once more.

'I'm sorry,' I said.

'I know it's an emotional time,' Poupeh assured me. 'Leaving home. When I left home I cried for two weeks solid. It was very embarrassing. I mean, I was nearly thirteen years old, for goodness' sake. Some of the girls in my boarding house had been sent away at eight.'

That made me sob even harder – the thought of an eight-year-old girl leaving home.

My dad would never have sent me away to board. I was always a day girl at my Hampstead girls' school, even though it would have undoubtedly made Dad's life much easier not to have to rush home from the office every evening to make sure I wasn't smoking pot or sleeping with the gardener. I knew that some of his friends had suggested it might actually be good for me to go away to school but Dad had always insisted that home was the only place for me.

Oh, what had I done in return for his unwavering dedication to bringing me up all alone?

Since leaving Dad's house four days earlier, I had pretty much managed to avoid thinking over our last horrible conversation, but now that I couldn't distract myself by burning through his savings it all came rushing back.

Dad was right. He had made so many sacrifices for me and in return I had been a terrible daughter. I had lived a life of incredible privilege and managed to turn all my advantages to nothing. My expensive education amounted to a handful of certificates that I had never bothered to use in a job application. My bedroom was full of valuable trinkets I had begged for and discarded days later. I contributed nothing to the household except a couple of extra loads of washing a week. And I would have been happy to let Dad continue to pick up the tab for ever.

No wonder Clare had laughed at me when I called her and demanded that Dad increase my credit card limits at once. She had been earning her own living since she turned seventeen. The idea that her parents would continue to help her out financially was not only unrealistic, it was embarrassing to her.

How could I, who had never done a day's work in my life, have accused anyone else of taking advantage of Dad's kindness? I had become the type of woman I accused Karen of being. I had been spending my father's money far faster than she ever could. Forget about my outburst over Karen, now that I looked back, I could see that the really humiliating revelation was the discovery that my own father considered me to be a great big waste of space. A loafer. A sponge. A loser. No wonder he had finally lost patience with me.

I snorted into my cappuccino as I remembered Dad's harsh words and the 'Get a job' text. Noticing that the waterworks were about to start again, Poupeh moved my cup out of my reach.

'I think it's time we left,' she said, interrupting the beginning of my painful epiphany. 'Let's go back to my place and get you in the bath.'

33

I let Poupeh march me back to her Smart Car. Luckily it was only a short trip from the café in Primrose Hill to the big red apartment block that had been Poupeh's home since we left the Lady Margaret Heron School for Girls six years earlier.

'There was no way I could have gone back to living with my parents after school,' she said as we looked for a parking space within three miles of her apartment. 'I value my independence much too much.'

'Dad was always very good about giving me my own space,' I said sadly, remembering how I had insisted on having a lock put on my bedroom door just after meeting Karen because while Dad thought she was perfectly trustworthy, I told him that she still needed to prove herself to me. He'd been so embarrassed at having to explain my actions to her. I remembered her stoic smile as she assured me that I'd know I could trust her soon.

'Here we are.'

The doorman of Poupeh's building greeted her with a cheery 'Hello'. As did everyone we met as we navigated the lobby of Olympic House. It struck me that I didn't even know the names of the people who lived in the vast detached places to either side of my father's house though we had been living there for twelve years. I'd never considered it worth making the effort. They didn't interfere with me. I didn't interfere with them. Poupeh, by contrast, greeted everyone by name.

'I like to know my neighbours,' said Poupeh, when I commented that she seemed to know everybody. 'If you look out for other people, they'll look out for you.'

I know she didn't mean it that way, but Poupeh's comment seemed like a rebuke to me right then. You had to give attention and care to get it, was what she was saying. I had been learning that the hard way. I'd never previously imagined myself to be the kind of person who didn't have friends. There had always been someone to hang out with (Gemma), parties to go to (thrown by people Gemma knew) . . . I had felt as though I was never alone. Now I knew exactly how it felt.

What kind of a person was I that when it came to the crunch, when I found myself without a bed to sleep in for the night and Gemma wasn't speaking to me, there was nobody I could call? I'd had to spend the night in a *garden shed*.

Somehow I knew that Poupeh would never be short of a friend to put her up for the night. Her friendly neighbours would probably fight for the honour of having Poupeh to stay. Meanwhile, I would have been in the shed again if Poupeh hadn't played the good Samaritan. That's one of the ways it happens, I realized, how people end up sleeping rough. Caring for nobody and distrusting everybody is OK until you need someone to care for you. The loony woman in the duffel coat had probably been someone's beloved daughter too.

I didn't share my revelation with Poupeh.

Instead, I said, 'I think I would feel a bit claustrophobic, having everybody know me.'

Poupeh smiled. 'That's a shame.'

Her smile left me in no doubt that she thought I was talking rubbish.

Poupeh's apartment was on the top storey of the building, accessed via one of those old-fashioned lifts that get stuck between floors in horror movies. It was barely large enough for the two of us and Poupeh's shopping bags. The suffocating atmosphere was enhanced when Poupeh caught me trying to stifle another sniffle and pressed me against her chest for an impromptu hug.

'What was that for?'

'You needed it,' she said. 'I sense that you are a person who needs to be hugged quite often.'

'Not really,' I protested weakly, swiftly wiping away a tear.

Thank goodness the lift journey was a fast one, and thank goodness the size of the lift was not a harbinger of what was to come.

Poupeh's apartment was *huge*. Though there wasn't actually that much room to move about in it. This was a girl who could never have been accused of minimalism. The furniture, which reminded me of the decor on the *Afsaneh*, seemed to have been bought for a six-bedroom family home rather than a bachelorette pad. While Poupeh took my jacket and hung it on a hatstand that could have been more realistically described as a coat *hill*, I counted ten assorted dining chairs lined up along one wall, in addition to the four that flanked the marble-topped table.

Every available space was home to a knick-knack. Souvenirs from all over the world: flamenco dolls from Spain, dolls doing those twitchy hand-dances from Thailand, even miniature Eskimos, straw donkeys, clay houses, plastic castanets. You describe a piece of tourist tat, Poupeh had it. I felt my interior design cortex begin to throb.

'What do you think?' Poupeh asked.

Why do people always have to ask what you think when you least want to have to tell them? I searched for an adjective to describe the explosion of rubbish before me. 'It's very sumptuous,' I said. She seemed pleased with that.

'Thank you. I like things to be luxurious. Come on, let me show you where you'll be sleeping. I'm afraid it's the shoe room right now.'

The shoe room?

Unfortunately, Poupeh wasn't kidding. I think there may have been a bed in there somewhere, but it was obscured by those garment rails that you see backstage at catwalk shows and piles and piles of shoe-boxes. And loose shoes. Some in pairs. Some not.

'It's a little bit cluttered in here,' she said.

'No. Not at all,' I replied. Another social lie.

'Why don't you freshen up while I make that tea,' she said, handing me a fluffy gold towel. 'You can put this on until we fetch your car from the pound and get your own clothes back.' She tossed a bright green kaftan in my direction. I could have gone camping in it.

I didn't even make it to the bathroom. I was frozen to the spot in horror as I surveyed the mess around me.

'I'm going to go for a walk,' I told Poupeh then. 'I need to get some air.'

Well, wouldn't anybody need to get some air after discovering that they were going to be sharing a sleeping space with five hundred pairs of lightly worn size eights?

Outside the building I leaned against a wall and tried to take some deep, calming breaths. I managed deep but I definitely didn't manage calming.

I walked around the block. And then I walked around the

block again. I felt feeble. I was a far cry from the bolshie schoolgirl who didn't think anything of telling Poupeh Gharani that the clothes she wore on non-uniform day weren't fit for Oxfam. I cringed at the memory of my casual cruelty. Had she forgotten it? Perhaps this was her revenge, seeing me brought so low. Having to sleep in her shoe cupboard! If the fifteen-year-old Poupeh had known that one day, one of her worst tormentors would be homeless and have nowhere to stay but for her kindness . . .

No. I couldn't be that woman. I wouldn't. I was not going to throw myself on Poupeh Gharani's mercy. Accepting Poupeh's offer was a huge mistake made in a moment of weakness. I would have to go back in and tell her that I couldn't possibly impose on her. I wouldn't be able to sleep in that flat. I'd go back to the shed if I had to. It was horrible. If I could ever get over the idea that I was going to spend the night breathing used shoe fumes, then the glare of the gold flock wallpaper would keep me awake instead. Really, if they want to stop people falling asleep on motorways, they could do car interiors in yellow.

My mobile phone vibrated. I dived into my handbag to retrieve it, hoping, praying, that it would be a message from Dad telling me to come home at once, Karen was back in his arms and all was forgiven. I was ready to tell him that I would go out the following morning and get a job, any job, to prove to him that I was ready to be an adult at last. I'd clean toilets. Serve burgers. I'd pluck chickens if I had to. Just let me spend a night in my own bed again.

It wasn't Dad.

'Supper will be ready at seven,' said Poupeh's text message.

Well, I had to go back and at least have supper with her, didn't I? I decided in the lift to her apartment that I would tell her while we ate that Dad had asked me to go back home. Then I would head straight for Henry and Lydia's garden again.

But it wasn't to be. As soon as I walked back into Poupeh's flat, she laid in front of me a meal so fantastic that I knew I couldn't just stuff it down and go. With this wonderful dinner – a chicken roasted to perfection, roast potatoes that suggested she had grown up in an English country vicarage rather than Dubai – she served a fabulous bottle of wine, and with the fabulous wine, I served up my secrets.

34

There are some people who have a way about them that makes it impossible not to confide. Poupeh Gharani was one of those people. Looking back, I remembered now that she had been that way even at school. Almost every lunch-break, Gemma and I would slouch back into class to find Poupeh sitting at the back of the room with her arm slung comfortingly around the shoulder of a weeping nerd. She was always ready to dispense advice on boyfriends, acne and bad exam results to the pariahs of Lady Margaret Heron School's fifth form. Never in a million years did I suspect that one day I would be the nerd in need of comfort.

I always kept my own counsel. Or confided the less romantically lurid of my worries in Dad. Even Gemma didn't know the worst of my fears. But three glasses of wine and no Dad to confide in left me with a story that had to come out and no one but Poupeh to hear it.

'My father always seemed to pick the wrong girlfriends,' I began. 'Since the day I turned thirteen there was a constant stream of tarts and gold-diggers through my kitchen . . . I could tell Melanie was after his money from the moment she walked into the house. Dad was a partner in his company. She was a typist. But Melanie was clever. She told Dad she was attracted to the man underneath the success. Within six months she had persuaded him to marry her. Then I told

Dad I overheard a phone conversation in which she told one of her friends she didn't love him at all but was determined to get her hands on his cash.'

'The evil woman,' Poupeh exclaimed. 'I can't believe anyone would really say that.'

'That's because she didn't,' I admitted for the first time in my life. 'Poupeh, I made the whole conversation up. I wanted to get rid of Melanie and I took the easiest way. But I decided that for Dad to have believed me when it came to the crunch, he must have had an idea that what I claimed wasn't totally beyond the realms of possibility.'

'You're probably right,' said Poupeh. 'Sounds like you did him a favour.'

'I'm glad you think so. Because after her, there was Heather,' I continued. 'A model stroke actress who was perfecting the art of "resting".'

I made little quotation marks around most of the words in that sentence.

'Heather got to Dad by being a classic "Rules girl". Dad fell for it hook, line and ring. I couldn't believe it. She was mad as a mongoose. Couldn't get out of bed without reading the runes. She and Dad broke up because she started to hear voices.'

'Voices?' asked Poupeh.

'From the spirit world. Telling her to get out of the house. It all came to a head when she suggested that I should be exorcized.'

'That must have been terrifying,' said Poupeh sympathetically.

'Not really. You see, I bought a baby monitor and stuck one part of it to the underside of her bed. Those ghostly voices she heard were me, talking into the other part of the monitor in my room every time Dad wasn't at home.'

Poupeh's eyes opened wide with delight. 'Now that's what I call a creative solution,' she said.

I couldn't help indulging in a little smile. 'It was one of my prouder moments,' I said. 'Unlike what happened with Trisha . . .'

I dropped my voice for this one. Poupeh leaned closer.

'After Heather,' I explained, 'it was two years before Dad met anyone else he really liked. I was devastated when he brought Trisha home. The others were bad enough but at least they were too self-obsessed to interfere with what I got up to. Trisha, on the other hand, was always on my case. She was always bothering me about my schoolwork, my diet, my lack of exercise . . .'

'I wish someone had bothered about my diet and lack of exercise,' said Poupeh.

'Well, I know now that she was only doing her best for me,' I agreed. 'But the harder she tried to encourage me to do the right thing, the harder I fought against it. She refused to let me have coffee. I opened an account at Starbucks. She tried to stop me eating meat. I developed a passion for burgers. She told me not to smoke. I started smoking *drugs*. I never even touched a cigarette before Trisha came into my life.'

'What happened then?'

'We had a show-down. She caught me and Gemma with a joint. I was grounded for the entire summer hols.'

'I remember!' Poupeh exclaimed. 'You missed those great parties. And didn't your boyfriend go off with someone else because you were never allowed out?'

'That's right,' I said through gritted teeth. 'So you understand how I felt, don't you? I was sixteen years old. It should have been the best summer of my life and I spent it looking at ecclesiastical frescoes with my father and his girlfriend. I decided I needed to teach Trisha a lesson. She was about to go to Thailand on a yoga retreat . . .'

Poupeh nodded.

'So,' I said the rest quickly, 'I bought twenty grams of cocaine from the big brother of a girl at school and stitched them into the lining of Trish's duffel bag.'

Poupeh gasped.

'I thought she would be stopped at Heathrow,' I explained in mitigation. 'I had no idea she would get all the way out to Chiang Mai and be on her way back through Bangkok airport before she came across a sniffer dog. Really, what were the chances of that?'

'Did they throw her into prison?'

'They were going to throw away the key. Dad spent thousands of pounds getting her out of that place. Thousands and thousands of pounds. But he wouldn't marry her after that. Said he couldn't live with a hypocrite.'

'And you never confessed?'

'What do you think?' I slumped forward on to the table, with my head in my arms. 'So, you can see why I'm such a disappointment to my father,' I sniffed.

'But he doesn't know about all this,' reasoned Poupeh.

'No,' I admitted. 'He only knows for certain that I pushed Karen off the boat.'

Poupeh went 'Pfft'. 'Hen party high jinks.'

'I pushed her off a hundred-and-fifty-foot yacht travelling at fifty knots. And I didn't raise the alarm until I was pretty sure she would have drowned. I knew she couldn't swim very well. Poupeh, I wanted to *kill* her.'

I had achieved the impossible. Poupeh was struck dumb. She stayed silent for quite a while, though she did reach out and pat my shoulder a couple of times. I didn't raise my forehead

from the table. It was the first time I had ever told anybody the
real truth about all of Dad's exes. All of it. Not even Gemma
knew I had planted the coke in Trisha's bag.

Hearing the three stories out loud, capped by my murder
attempt on Karen, I was finally forced to admit that they
didn't sound much like the actions of a loving daughter bent
on protecting her dad from a bunch of women who didn't
deserve him. I sounded like a nut.

'I've lied, I've driven one woman mad, sent another to a
Thai jail and attempted to kill a fourth. You should probably
call the police right now,' I told Poupeh.

'I wouldn't do that,' said Poupeh. 'I won't repeat anything
you say to me within these four walls. Sometimes we do the
worst things with the best intentions. I still think you have a
good heart.'

'Poupeh, you think everybody has a good heart.' The way I
said it should have left her in no doubt that I considered such
generosity of spirit a fatal flaw.

'You must be very tired,' she said, ignoring my cynicism.
'Why don't you go to bed? Things will look better in the
morning.'

'People never look any better in the morning, so why
should my life?' I whined.

'It will,' Poupeh persisted. 'Get some sleep.' She started to
clear the plates away. 'Let me know if there's anything you
need. I've tidied up your bedroom.'

Oh no. I'd forgotten all about the shoe room.

But boy, had Poupeh tidied up while I took my long walk
around the block. The shoe room could now justifiably be
called a bedroom once more. You could actually see the
whole bed. There wasn't a single flip-flop in sight. Poupeh
had moved every last sandal and sneaker into her own bed-

room. She had wheeled the rickety garment rails, groaning under the weight of a thousand kaftans, out into the hall. She had cleared the folders from the bed and replaced the hideous gold counterpane that would have given Sleeping Beauty insomnia with soft white sheets. Frette, I noticed at once. The very best. Cotton soft as silk.

Poupeh had even turned the sheets back with the perfection of a hotel turn-down service. And there, on the pillow, was a single pink rosebud attached to a little card.

It was the size of a business card but it was pale pink and edged with gold. It was from one of those packets of cards you can buy at the counter in bookshops. *365 Fluffy Thoughts for the Year*, or something retarded like that. Gemma and I would occasionally flick through them and sneer. Had anyone told me that I would one day find one on my pillow, and that Poupeh Gharani would have put it there, I would have shuddered with disgust. But there it was.

I sat down on the fairytale-princess-thick mattress and picked the card up.

'Today is the first day of the rest of your life,' it said.

I started crying again.

35

All this blubbing came as quite a shock to me. You've probably guessed that I wasn't usually the kind of girl who cries. I mean, what's the point? Crying doesn't heal a grazed knee or ease the type of heartbreak that is really just embarrassment in disguise. But that night at Poupeh's, I cried twenty-three years' worth of tears for the first real pain I had felt in my life. I had disappointed my father. And the really stupid thing was, I had put such an enormous amount of effort and creativity into doing it.

I had never felt so lost as I did with my father refusing to speak to me. All day long I had expected Dad to think better of allowing me to find my way in the city without money, to call and demand that I come back home. But apart from Poupeh's text message, my mobile phone didn't ring again, no matter how many times I got it out of my bag and shook it to check that the battery hadn't gone flat.

With a heavy heart, I took off my clothes and put on the voluminous nightdress that Poupeh had left beneath my pillow. I cleaned my teeth with the new toothbrush she had placed by the basin in the guest bathroom. Seeing the cellophane-wrapped toiletries she had laid out for me made me feel even more like a refugee.

Thank goodness my most precious possession had been in my handbag and not in the boot of my car when it was towed.

Back in the bedroom, I took out the little framed photograph and put it on the bedside table.

'One careless lady owner?' the shop assistant had asked with a laugh when Karen said that she was going to be a second wife.

You want to know why it hurt so much? That careless lady owner was my mum. And the thing is, my mum wasn't careless with my dad. If she'd had her own way, I know she wouldn't have let him go at all. But Mum didn't have a say in whether or not she and Dad made it to their ruby anniversary. Or even their second.

Mum and Dad grew up in the same small West Country town. They lived within three streets of each other and attended sibling grammar schools. That's how they met. The girls in the fifth form at Mum's all-girls' school had a disco to celebrate the end of their O-levels to which the pupils from the boys' grammar were invited.

Dad has told me exactly what happened that night so many times I feel like I might have been there, sitting with the girls on Mum's side of the school gym, admiring the dress she bought from Chelsea Girl for the occasion. I've seen a photograph of her wearing it. It was a dark cherry red with a thin gold stripe. I'm sure it looked very fashionable in 1979.

Dad had seen Mum around before that night. He saw her waiting for the school bus in the mornings. In fact, he saw her almost every morning for five years without her ever seeming to notice him in return. But that night at the school disco Dad finally plucked up the courage to talk to her. Mum was momentarily separated from her cronies as she waited at the 'bar' for another can of Diet Coke.

'I've seen you at the bus stop,' was Dad's brilliant opening line.

'I know you have,' said my mother. 'We call you "he who stares".' And then she did an impression of Dad gawping at her, bugging out her eyes.

I suppose I should thank God that Dad didn't turn around and run for it then. I would have done. Instead, recovering somewhat magnificently, he said, 'Thanks. I was trying to work out whether your left eye was made of glass.'

Mum laughed. Dad had heard her laugh a hundred times before but this time it was just for him. He sensed he'd broken through and carried on. They swapped school-subject small talk. They were taking some of the same courses. Mum was a year behind Dad so he offered to lend her his first year A-level notes. They shared three more cans of Coke. They smooched to 'Chicago'. Mum wrote her phone number down on the back of the notebook Dad carried at all times (while he still thought he might be a novelist and hadn't even heard of advertising copywriters). He called her from a phone box in town that weekend. Her parents teased her about her first 'boyfriend'.

Mum's parents weren't quite so happy when those Saturday afternoons spent hanging out with a big gang of friends turned into something altogether more intimate. By the time Mum sat her mock A-level exams, she was almost three months pregnant.

Her parents tried to persuade her to have an abortion. As did her teachers. But Mum refused. She told them she could have a baby and still go to university. Other girls had done it. Mum's parents told her she wouldn't be able to do it without their help and they definitely didn't want to become de facto parents again at their time of life. They wouldn't have to, Mum assured them. Dad would support her. Rubbish. He'd be off like a shot as soon as he realized what an enormous responsibility a baby really was. Dad wasn't like that, Mum assured them. Of course he was like that. All young men were like that, was what everybody said.

But Dad really wasn't like that. Of course it wasn't exactly what he'd planned – eighteen years old, away from home for the first time, still getting used to doing his own laundry, and suddenly he found himself about to become a father. While his new friends spent every weekend getting drunk at the students' union, Dad caught a train back home to be with Mum.

She was studying for her A-levels from home. Her school had asked her to leave when the bump started to show, naming her a 'disruptive influence'. The teachers weren't the only adults to abandon her. By this time, she was actually living with my paternal grandparents. The situation at home had become too uncomfortable. Still, Mum wouldn't give up. I like to think of her around that time, setting her jaw, studying hard, determined to prove that she wasn't throwing her life away by giving me a chance.

When I was born, Dad's parents, Nana and Grand-pop, took over the middle of the night feed while Mum crammed for her exams. They loved her like a daughter and were delighted when Dad told them he wanted to make her their daughter-in-law as soon as he possible could.

Mum and Dad were married when I was six months old. It was a low-key affair. Her parents refused to come along, adamant that Mum was compounding her mistakes with a wedding. There were just five guests at the registry office: Dad's parents, Mum and Dad's best friends Henry and Lydia, who acted as witnesses, and me.

On the dressing table in my dad's room is a photograph taken as my parents emerged into the sunny street as man and wife. Dad is carrying me. Mum is reaching over to smooth down my flyaway hair. They are both smiling with the certainty of two people who know they have made all the right decisions.

'We were meant to be together,' Dad would tell me simply.

It was leukaemia that took her away from us. At first Mum put her tiredness down to her new life as a university student (she got A grades in all her exams and took up a place to study psychology) and the mother of a toddler. But tiredness couldn't explain the way her skin felt tender to touch or the fact that the slightest knock would leave a black bruise the size of a dinner plate. And then her hair started falling out in clumps each time she brushed it, leaving her looking almost as bald and ugly as I was at eighteen months old. It was my grandparents who marched her to the doctor. There were blood tests. The news was bad. The doctor couldn't promise her she would see me go to school. And she didn't. Less than two years after she and Dad married, Mum was dead.

So there you have it. I never really knew my mother. All I have is the stories Dad told me, and my photographs. When I try to think of Mum, I suppose the photographs are all I really see. I can't remember what her voice was like. But when I bring her to mind I do have a feeling of love that goes beyond anything anyone could describe to me. When I look at the photograph of us – me, Mum and Dad – outside the registry office, I can almost feel the warmth of her hand upon my head as she smoothes my hair and tries to make me look presentable for the cameras. When I look at the photograph of Mum on her own, the one that I packed in my handbag when I left home, I feel as though her eyes are seeking mine.

I've told that photograph so many secrets.

'Mum,' I told the picture then, 'I've made some terrible mistakes. I've been a useless and ungrateful daughter and I think I might have ruined Dad's life. Dad really loves Karen and Karen loves him back. Do you think they should be together?' I closed my eyes tightly for a moment or two, offering up a sort of prayer for guidance.

Nothing happened, of course. I don't know what I had been expecting. I'd managed to conjure some pretty convincing DIY spirits with a baby monitor, but right then I couldn't raise a thing. The window didn't bang open. The curtains didn't billow across the room as a spectral presence expressed her disapproval. The lights didn't flicker. Nothing.

My mother's face remained as still and serene as ever. Smiling her half-smile, refusing to show her teeth because she was still wearing a brace. Frozen and perfect. An eighteen-year-old schoolgirl. My mother as she was twenty-four years ago. She had been dead for longer than she had lived. And she had been younger yet far more mature when she died than I was that summer when I made such a fool of myself.

Nothing happened. Except inside me. As though I had suddenly worked out the secret of long division, everything became quite clear. I didn't need a message from another plane to tell me that of course Dad and Karen should be with each other. And as the one who had caused their break-up in the first place, I had to be the one to bring them back together. It was the only way to make amends.

I'd get started first thing in the morning.

36

So much for starting 'first thing'. I guess my night in the shed must have left me with some sleep-lag because I slept for ten hours straight and it was midday by the time I got up. Poupeh wasn't in the flat but she had left a note – and my car keys – next to the coffee machine in the kitchen. She had already been all the way across London to Fulham and retrieved my beloved Mini from the pound. Her note warned that if I didn't get a shift on and move it from its new parking place outside the apartment block before twelve, which was when the pay and display ticket expired, it would probably be back at the pound again.

I decided I had better forgo my kick-start coffee and headed out to find the car.

Thank goodness, I beat the traffic warden to it. If I'd left it just two minutes longer, he would have finished gleefully sticking a ticket to the window of a Bentley and started tapping one out for me. I leapt into the driver's seat and pulled out into the road. I decided there was no point trying to re-park. I should just get on with my mission. The sooner Karen and Dad were back together, the sooner I could go home.

I didn't know where Karen had been living since she moved out of Dad's house – I had never bothered to find out Marilyn's address – but I hoped that she wouldn't have changed her place of work as well. The other staff at the gym would be able to tell me how to get in contact with her. Perhaps she was even working that day. She often worked Saturdays, so with that in mind I headed straight for Hollywood Fitness.

I rehearsed my speech on the short drive across London. There was really nothing to do but grovel. 'Karen, I made a terrible mistake. Please come back to Dad and I promise never to interfere in your lives again,' seemed like a good start. I would even wear that bloody gold dress every day for the rest of my life if that was what it would take to convince her I was serious. I prayed that my apology would be enough and that she hadn't really believed her elegant little speech to Dad about the fatal differences between them.

I picked up a bunch of roses at a florist en route (always easier to have something in your hands when you've got to say something difficult). I even went so far as to buy a big, expensive bunch wrapped in three colours of tissue paper and tied with a raffia bow. It wiped out the last of my extremely meagre resources. I secretly hoped that once she had accepted my apology and the flowers, Karen would offer to buy me lunch. I drove the last few streets feeling extremely optimistic and wondering if I could persuade her to take me to Sardi's.

It turned out that Karen was working. She hadn't chosen to get out of town on the weekend of the wedding that never was. But neither was she wallowing in self-pity, red-eyed with tears and hollow-cheeked with misery at what might have been. Far from it.

Just as I pulled my car up opposite the gym, she pushed open the big glass doors and stepped out on to the pavement. She was bouncing like a girl in a shampoo ad. In fact, her hair was looking particularly good. While Dad had been looking more and more like the kind of chap you might avoid in the underpass at Waterloo station, Karen looked healthy and happy. Not heartbroken in the least.

I took a deep breath and prepared to get out of the car. I hoped this air of happy confidence didn't mean that Karen wouldn't be at all interested in my message of contrition and Dad's woe. She wasn't really happier *without* him, was she?

In the end, I didn't have a chance to find out. Even as I turned off my Mini's engine, a smart bright green car pulled up on the other side of the road, right alongside Karen. It was a Porsche 911. Brand-new. And Karen obviously knew the man who was driving it. As the car approached, her face was brightened even further by an enormous grin. The kind of grin that had split her face that lunchtime in Sardi's, the very first time I met her, when she looked across the room and saw my dad.

So I suppose I shouldn't have been surprised when the driver of the Porsche got out of the car and revealed himself to be a man of some considerable attractiveness. Tall and slim with thick brown hair. Nor should I have been surprised when Karen threw her arms about his neck and he picked her up off her feet and whirled her around like Dad used to spin me around when he had been away on business and I ran to meet him the second he put his key in the front door. Nor should I have been at all surprised when Karen's new friend reached back inside his car and brought out an enormous bouquet of roses – even bigger than the one I had bought – that she accepted with much excited squealing.

It could only mean one thing.

Karen was in love. And not with my father.

37

I had to abandon my plan. What possible point was there in telling Karen how much Dad missed her now, when she had so obviously moved on? And so quickly! I turned my car around and skidded away, gripping the steering wheel so hard in my annoyance that my knuckles soon started to go white.

I decided that as soon as I got to Poupeh's, I would pick up my stuff then head straight for Dad's. He would soon forgive me for having taken such a hard line on Karen when I revealed to him what a disloyal bitch his ex-fiancée really was. I had been right about her all along. Days after she was supposed to have married my father, she was whizzing about town with some Porsche-driving chancer. How could she have moved on from Dad to that wide boy with such obscene haste? What a fickle cow! Clearly anyone with cash would do for our Karen.

'I wanted to run across the road and pull her hair,' I told Poupeh. 'She broke my father's heart. And she's already shacked up with someone else. She obviously never cared about Dad at all.'

Poupeh had other ideas.

'Calm down,' she said to start with.

'How can I calm down?' I told her what I had seen. About Karen waiting outside the gym. The way she was all tarted up as though she was off on a date. The Porsche. The gorgeous-looking guy who was driving it. The flowers. The *enormous* bunch of flowers.

'They must be shagging.'

'Pffft,' said Poupeh, in that peculiar way she had.

'What do you mean, "Pfft?"' It all pointed to one thing as far as I was concerned.

'Nothing means one thing, Lind-zay.'

'That's the first mistake most civilians make,' Poupeh continued as she set about making another pot of what I had come to realize was her *trademark* tooth-rotting mint tea. 'Jumping to conclusions as you've done. But nothing means one thing. Every single scenario has more than one interpretation.'

'Well, sure, but . . . come on, Poupeh. The guy brought her flowers and she kissed him. How many explanations could there really be for what I saw this afternoon?'

'Dozens,' said Poupeh. 'For example,' she pulled me towards the window and pointed at a twenty-something couple on the street outside, 'take those two there. What's going on? What are they doing right now? Tell me everything that's happening.'

'Poupeh . . .' I began.

'Just humour me.'

As I watched, the girl wrapped her arms around the guy's neck and pressed herself against him.

'Well,' I said, 'obviously they're boyfriend and girlfriend. She's kissing him goodbye before she gets on the tube and goes off to work a late shift at a restaurant or something like that.'

'Maybe,' said Poupeh. 'Or maybe she's his drug dealer, passing a rock of crack to him using her mouth so as not to draw the attention of the police.'

'What?' I couldn't help pulling a face at the thought. 'Ugh.'

'Public displays of affection in particular are not always what they seem. Let me tell you. I once worked for a woman who thought her husband was having an affair because she saw him kissing a girl in the street outside his office. When I saw him kissing a guy in the street a few weeks later, I knew she had a very different problem on her hands.'

'He was sleeping with another woman *and* a man?'

'No. He was dealing in stolen jewellery. He was passing diamonds mouth to mouth.'

'So you're saying that the guy who picked Karen up from work is more likely to be a dodgy diamond dealer than her boyfriend?'

'He could be dealing anything. Drugs. Rare coins. Gemstones. Anything that fits in your mouth.'

'No,' I said. I didn't want to believe it. But it would certainly make me start looking at those embarrassing PDAs you see on every street corner differently.

'Well, it doesn't have to be a sign of crime,' Poupeh continued. 'Perhaps what you saw was one of Karen's clients taking her a bouquet of flowers to thank her for having transformed him from a couch potato into a love god. Perhaps she saved his marriage by getting him into such good shape that his wife decided not to have an affair with her tennis coach after all.'

'But they did a full body hug!'

'Pffft!!!!! You English people think that body contact can only mean one thing. Where I come from, men hold hands in the street quite openly without anyone assuming they're gay. Girlfriends kiss each other on the mouth.'

I stepped back subconsciously, hoping she wasn't about to try that with me.

'English mothers don't even kiss their own babies,' she concluded with a shake of her head.

'But isn't the simplest explanation usually the right one?' I persisted.

'Let me put it to you this way. If you had never seen a sheep before and the first sheep you saw was a black sheep, you might assume that all sheep were black. Right? But you would be wrong. Remember our science lessons. You can't draw conclusions from one single event. You've got to do a proper sample. You've seen Karen get into a stranger's car just once. That's no basis for assuming that she is head-over-heels in love with this Porsche driver and would no longer be interested in getting back together with your father.'

I nodded thoughtfully. It was a compelling argument. Perhaps Poupeh was right. Just because I had seen Karen embrace the guy with the Porsche as though he brought news of a multi-million lottery win *and* world peace, it didn't necessarily mean that they were headed up the aisle any time soon. Maybe they weren't romantically entangled at all.

'Lind-zay,' said Poupeh. 'I think I may be able to help you get your dad and Karen back together.'

'Just tell me how,' I begged her.

'You need to learn to think like a detective does. This could be your very first case.'

Poupeh would be my mentor.

'How can I think like a detective? How did *you* become a detective?' I asked Poupeh then.

Over another exotic tea-pot full of freshly crushed mint leaves, Poupeh finally revealed to me what she had been doing for a living since we both left Lady Margaret Heron School for Girls. While Gemma and I had spent a 'gap year' on the King's Road, Poupeh had travelled to New York. Once there, she got herself an extremely unusual internship. She spent twelve months working for a private eye.

'He took me on as a favour to my father,' Poupeh explained. 'Papa put a lot of business his way.'

I remembered now that Poupeh's father had been the subject of some speculation during our final year at school. I knew that he was embroiled in a big court case to do with his business. Now I learned that this private detective in New York had uncovered the evidence that sent Mr Gharani's dodgy adversaries to Sing Sing.

'And I had always wanted to be a detective after that terrible thing that happened to me,' she continued.

'What terrible thing?' I asked. I imagined there were many.

'Do you remember when I was accused of writing a love letter to Miss Hobson?'

'I don't remember that at all,' I said, and hoped that Poupeh's private detective training hadn't encompassed the secret body language of people in the process of telling a whopping great lie.

'Well, it was a terrible time for me. Someone forged my signature at the bottom of the most incredible piece of filth you can imagine. There were things in that letter that I didn't think were humanly possible. Still don't, in fact. I was almost expelled. Thank goodness, my previous good record eventually convinced the headmistress that I was absolutely innocent, but the real culprits were never found. I was so upset. I vowed that I would never be caught out like that again.'

'I can't say I blame you.'

'That summer I investigated many methods for tracking criminals down. I was frustrated at the time that the headmistress refused to fingerprint our entire year or allow me to do a proper desk-to-desk search. And so the crime went unpunished. But now I am grateful to the person who almost ruined my life because they unwittingly gave me my interest in detective methods at the same time.'

'Hmmm,' I nodded.

'So I spent a year in New York, trailing the best of the best. And then I came back here to set up PGI.'

I remembered the card she had given me that day outside Harrods. The curious initials.

'Poupeh Gharani *Investigations*,' she clarified.

'You're like Colombo,' I chipped in.

'I was thinking more along the lines of Cybill Shepherd in *Moonlighting*.'

'You could probably share clothes,' I said, without thinking. 'I mean, you have a similar elegant style.'

'Thank you. So that is how I came to know more about human behaviour than you could ever imagine.'

'And why you were hiding behind a newspaper outside Harrods.'

'Spot on. Surveillance.'

'So what are you proposing I do about Karen? Stalk her?'

'Not exactly. But you will have to do a little bit of surveillance work to find out what's really going on between her and that man. After that, we can look at your options again.'

'But what options do I have if they're together? It's game over then. Dad's lost her for ever and he'll never forgive me and let me go back home.'

'OK,' said Poupeh. 'So let's say they are together. Perhaps they're not right for each other. Karen is quite likely to be on the rebound. Perhaps they're just embarking on a relationship that will make them both desperately unhappy.'

She poured me another cup of tea, managed to get three sugars into it before I could stop her, then continued with her speech.

'You and I both know from experience that it's easy to be very enthusiastic about people when you first meet them. For all we know so far, Karen and the Porsche guy might have been on their very first date. Even as you drove home from your abortive mission, cursing Karen's fickleness, she might have been sitting in some restaurant, wondering how such a promising lunch date was turning out so badly. Perhaps receiving that enormous bouquet was the best bit and then Mr Porsche revealed himself to be a self-obsessed car nut who can only talk about his wheels and his seven-figure Christmas bonus, forcing Karen to reminisce sadly on your father's more wide-ranging interests and exceptional ability to small-talk. I've been out with plenty of good-looking City boys whose appeal was only as deep as the lacquer on their luxury sports cars,' Poupeh concluded with a wave of her hand.

'You have?'

I had assumed that Poupeh had never been on a date.

'Oh yes. Countless times. Karen's new toy-boy is almost certainly doomed. And you can help hurry his demise.'

'I don't want to have him killed!' I exclaimed.

Poupeh just laughed – long and wildly enough for me to start worrying – before she said, 'That wasn't *exactly* what I was thinking either . . .'

'Then what were you thinking?'

'Now, you have to understand that I don't have much experience of this. When it comes to relationship work, I just find out whether people are being unfaithful and leave it up to my client to decide what to do next . . . but there are agencies in Japan that offer something slightly different. They are "matchbreakers". People hire them to break up relationships. Perhaps your partner is seeing someone on the side and you want to end that affair without having to reveal that you know about it. Perhaps your best friend is seeing someone

unsuitable, you're scared for her but she's refusing to leave
the Bozo without a push. Perhaps you just know that the
object of your affections would be so much happier with you
rather than the girlfriend or boyfriend they have already.
Some people employ a matchbreaker to make someone
available. I think you would be quite good at that.'

'I don't think so.'

'But you've already done it. At least four times.'

Poupeh had a point. Since I turned thirteen, I had dedicated
an extraordinary amount of energy into breaking up Dad's
budding relationships. And I'd met with an extraordinary
amount of success. A matchbreaker was what I was. And a
good one. Poupeh suggested that all I had to do was channel
my efforts elsewhere. From defending my father from all-
comers to splitting up Karen and her new boyfriend, leaving
her single, a little bit sad and perfectly delighted to accept
Dad's attentions once again.

My optimism started to creep back. Yes. It would be easy.
There wasn't a relationship in the world that could remain
intact if I set my heart on dismembering it.

'Hooray for the matchbreaker!' said Poupeh.

38

But where would I begin? It had been easy to get access to
Dad's previous girlfriends, study their strengths and weak-
nesses and work out exactly how to scupper them. As soon as
any of those hapless girls moved into the Hampstead house,
they were unwittingly moving not closer to marrying Dad but
further into my realm of evil influence. Having moved out
again, Karen would be harder to get to.

'I don't know where to start,' I admitted.

'Your first step is to find out just who Karen's swanky new
boyfriend is.'

'How can I find out who he is? I can't just go to the gym and
ask her.'

'Use your imagination. Clues to a person's identity are all
about them,' Poupeh replied.

I stared at her blankly.

'Oh, for goodness' sake. Get back to the gym and stay there
until you get the registration number of his car.'

So the following day, that's what I did. I returned to Hollywood Fitness. But this time I was incognito. I left my distinctive Mini outside Poupeh's building and went to my
stake-out by tube and on foot. I wore a baseball cap and
sunglasses, though it wasn't sunny at all, it being the middle of
summer in London.

The previous night, Poupeh had really got me fired up

about this private detective thing. Who would have thought that she would turn out to have such an interesting job? She was a veritable encyclopaedia of surveillance techniques. To make sure that I wasn't going to be wasting my time that afternoon, on Poupeh's advice I had already ascertained that it wasn't Karen's day off by calling the gym earlier that morning under the pretence of wanting to set up some personal training sessions.

'My friend recommended Karen,' I lied.

'Oh yeah,' said the receptionist. 'Well, she's working until six tonight. Drop by any time before then and I'm sure she'll be delighted to discuss a training regime with you.'

Of course I had no intention whatsoever of dropping in to discuss a training regime but at six o'clock sharp, the end of Karen's shift, I was ensconced in the window of the café directly opposite the gym, newspaper shielding my face, just as Poupeh had demonstrated, watching the big glass doors of Hollywood Fitness for Karen's exit. Or, more importantly, for the arrival of the bright green Porsche I had seen her climb into the day before.

Six o'clock came and went. There was no sign of the car. But eventually Karen appeared, chatting on her mobile as she stepped out on to the street. She hesitated by the kerb, still talking on her phone. I wondered if she was calling Mr Porsche, telling him that she was ready to be picked up, but he didn't appear. Karen carried on chatting and then, suddenly, she seemed to look straight at me. I held the newspaper up higher. When I thought enough time had passed to be certain that she had looked away again, I lowered my paper shield. And saw that she was gone.

Damn. I slammed two pound coins on the table to pay for my coffee and dashed out into the street. I knew Porsches were fast but I didn't know they were so quiet. I scanned the traffic desperately. But the reason I hadn't heard the Porsche was because Karen hadn't been picked up after all. I finally caught sight of her still chatting away on her Nokia as she jumped aboard a bus heading for Earl's Court.

My stake-out had been a total waste of time.

'Patience, grasshopper,' said Poupeh when I got back to the flat in a vile mood.

I told her that if there was one thing guaranteed to make me lose my patience, it was being called 'grasshopper' by some-one who had been in the same class as me at school.

But at Poupeh's insistence, I did return to my post the following day. And the next day. And the next . . . I had to stake out the gym for a further three days before I saw the Porsche again. It appeared outside Hollywood Fitness at five to six, giving me plenty of time to jot down the registration number before Karen came out. It was drizzling. Karen's new boyfriend didn't get out of the car this time. He just popped the passenger door open for her. It was hard to see exactly what was going on inside the car's plush leather interior, but I was pretty sure it was the same guy in the driving seat. I was also pretty sure I saw her kiss him. And not in a friendly way, if you know what I mean.

I got drenched when I dashed out of the café to copy down the registration number but I didn't care. I was elated be-cause, as Poupeh had promised, once I had that number, I was away.

With the magical digits safely scribbled in my Smythson shopping notebook, I dashed straight back to Poupeh's flat. When I got there, I found her covered from head to toe in a black hijab.

'I didn't know you were a practising Muslim,' I said.

'I'm not. It's just that a hijab is the perfect disguise if you're stalking someone in Marks and Spencer Marble Arch,' she explained. That afternoon Poupeh had been in pursuit of a chap whose credit card bills had revealed several purchases of ladies' underwear that his wife definitely hadn't received.

'He bought two black camisoles in a size twenty-two just this afternoon,' Poupeh told me.

'He's not replacing his wife with a younger, slimmer model then.'

'No. I'm pretty sure he's buying them for himself.'

Poupeh was delighted with my efforts to track down Karen's new man. With the details in front of her, she put in a call to a 'friendly neighbourhood policeman' right away. There weren't many bright green Porsche Turbos about. And for the promise of fifty quid in used notes Poupeh's policeman friend was only too happy to fit a name to the registration number.

Less than two hours later I knew exactly whose car Karen was swanning about in. The Porsche was registered to one Barney Cavanagh, the policeman told Poupeh in a text. So that was the name of Karen's boyfriend. Unless her boyfriend had just borrowed his boss's car for the afternoon . . .

The name and an address came together. Barney Cavanagh, owner of a bright green Porsche with private plates, lived in a swanky ground-floor flat in Onslow Gardens, South Kensington. It was a pretty impressive address, Poupeh assured me. And he was definitely on the good side of the street.

Poupeh's pet copper also came up with the information that this Barney Cavanagh was in the fine art business. He traded under the name of 'Art East Limited' and had offices in London and Singapore. He must have been doing well. He bought his Porsche with cash.

With a name and an address in hand, more information poured out like coins from a slot machine hitting the jackpot as Poupeh tapped our target's details into financial services websites I had hoped that only bona fide financial service staff had access to. Not only did Cavanagh live in a swanky flat, he didn't have a mortgage. He'd paid that off two years before. His credit rating was impeccable. He paid all his utility bills on time. He had five credit cards and had never defaulted on a payment.

A quick visit to Google Images revealed that while it appeared he had never been married, he had once appeared in a society column in the *Straits Times*, Singapore's daily newspaper, pictured alongside a 'model friend'. The Internet was a valuable source of such colourful detail. Poupeh and I pored over the grainy picture on the newspaper's web page.

'Is this the man you saw get out of the car?' she asked.

'Definitely,' I was able to tell her.

In the photograph Cavanagh was smiling. There was something of a film-star twinkle about his eyes. Now that I'd had a chance to study his face properly, I had to admit that he was very good-looking. No wonder he was such a hit with the women. The 'model friend' snuggled into his side as though attached to him by several blood vessels and two major organs.

'Oh, and he clearly likes sushi,' Poupeh told me an hour or so later as she brought up on screen copies of Cavanagh's last three credit card statements, which documented no fewer than twelve visits to an extremely chi-chi Knightsbridge sushi restaurant called Kyoto.

'How on earth did you log into his credit card details?'

'We live in an information age.' Poupeh gave me her most 'enigmatic' smile.

'Terrifying,' I said.

But I was very interested in Cavanagh's eating habits. And surprised by the sushi revelation. Had Karen suddenly developed a liking for raw fish? While she lived with Dad, he often complained that she would never touch the stuff. Sushi was one of Dad's favourite things.

I felt a pang of jealousy on Dad's behalf when I noted that apart from sushi, Cavanagh had also been spending quite a lot of money with Interflora over the past months. The kind of sums that suggested more than the dozen red roses I had seen him press into Karen's arms outside the gym, to boot.

Anyway, by the time Poupeh had finished going through Cavanagh's files, I'm sure I knew a lot more about Karen's new boyfriend than she did. We even knew his shoe size.

'Thank you,' I said to Poupeh. Now the excitement of finding out all about Cavanagh was over, it struck me that I probably owed her a great deal of money for the search results.

'This information cost you quite a bit,' I said. 'I'm not sure when I'll be able to repay you. I'm absolutely skint. I need to get a job,' I added.

'I've been thinking about that,' said Poupeh.

'I don't think I'm qualified to do anything except serve Big Macs.'

'Or work for me,' Poupeh smiled. 'I've been thinking I should expand for some time. I'm starting to get more requests for my services than I can possibly deal with alone. And there are certain situations where a girl like me finds it quite hard to slip by unnoticed.'

'No,' I said, eyeing the emerald-green pajamas she had changed into now that she had discarded the hijab. 'You're really good at blending in.'

'I do my best. But there are definitely situations where I could use you. And when I do, I'll split the fee.'

I was delighted by the thought of my first pay cheque.

'I could get into this,' I said. 'Tracking people down and finding out whether they're having an affair is easy. It didn't take long to find out about Karen.'

'Oh no, grasshopper . . .'

I let her get away with it this time.

'You're still jumping the gun there,' said Poupeh. 'All we know is that Karen knows Cavanagh. We still don't know for certain they're together.'

A bit more surveillance was in order.

39

So I found myself waiting outside the gym once more at the end of Karen's shift. I had traded cars with Poupeh again, and with my baseball cap pulled down low over my eyes, I was pretty sure that I wouldn't be recognizable even if Karen, travelling in Cavanagh's passenger seat, glanced up at his rear-view mirror and started to wonder why there was always a Smart Car behind him.

I was in luck. Cavanagh was on pick-up duty that night. Once Karen was safely in the car, I pulled out into the traffic behind them. On a motorway, or even a dual carriageway, I would have had no chance of keeping up with the bright green Porsche in Poupeh's toy car, but in London traffic, keeping close behind them was easy. Even if I did have to jump one red light, sending some old biddy jumping back on to the pavement when she unwisely attempted to cross between hunter and the hunted.

I followed the Porsche as far as the big branch of Tesco on the Gloucester Road. Once there, Karen leapt out of the passenger seat and went in search of a trolley while Cavanagh looked for a space in the multi-storey car park attached. To my delight, I was able to park right behind him and followed him into the store. I picked up a basket to help me blend into the after-work grocery shopping crowd but I kept close behind Cavanagh while he browsed magazines in the news-agency section before calling Karen on his mobile to find out where she had got to.

It was surprisingly easy. Poupeh had told me not to worry too much about people noticing you're following them on foot. Most of us are too wrapped up in our own thoughts to take in the people around us properly. It's amazing how infrequently people look up. Or even behind themselves. We go through life like shire horses wearing blinkers. And that was the case with Cavanagh and Karen. Just as Cavanagh put down a car magazine, Karen rounded the corner with a trolley piled high with shopping. She almost knocked me over.

'Sorry,' she said. But she didn't even look at me. Her eyes were fixed firmly on her new boyfriend.

'You sod,' she said to Cavanagh. 'I knew you would lurk in the magazines until you could be sure I'd finished.'

She cuffed him playfully. Affectionately.

'You know you shop so much more quickly when I'm not in your way,' Cavanagh replied.

Aha. Clearly this supermarket shop was part of a regular routine.

'Besides, I'm paying.'

Karen was free-loading.

'Such a stickler for gender-defined roles,' Karen sighed.

I followed them to the till. Cavanagh took over the wheeling of the trolley. They were deep in banter. They weren't overly tactile with one another but it was pretty clear to me that they had the easy rapport that comes from knowing someone very well. Knowing and *loving* them. So much for Poupeh's reassurance that they probably didn't get on that well.

Once at the till, Karen sent Cavanagh off again in search of fresh rosemary, telling him she needed it for the chicken. He had to squeeze out of the aisle past me.

'Excuse me,' he said.

I looked down as I stepped out of the way, then resumed my place in the queue.

It was very strange to be standing so close to Karen. In fact, I don't think I had actually stood quite so close to her since the night I pushed her off the yacht. I was close enough to find out that she was wearing the perfume that I had hated so much when she lived in our house – continued to hate, in fact – and yet she still didn't look around. It just goes to show that people don't always have that 'sixth sense'.

As Karen loaded the contents of her trolley on to the conveyor belt, her face was expressionless. I suppose it's not that interesting a task, unloading a shopping trolley, but I might even go so far as to say she looked sad. What was she thinking about? She seemed to pause as she put a packet of chocolate biscuits on to the belt. They were the type of biscuits she had always bought for Dad, to be doled out one at a time to make sure he kept to the strict target weight she had for him. Was she sighing because she remembered that too? But when Cavanagh returned with the rosemary, she switched her smile back on.

'Was this all they had?' she asked as she looked at the little packet.

'You want me to change it?'

'No,' she said. 'I just want to get home.'

'Good call.'

Moments later, Cavanagh was signing the credit card receipt and they were off.

'Next,' said the cashier, looking at me.

I realized I had nothing in my basket.

But it was thanks to the fact that I had completely forgotten to do any shopping while pretending to be an authentic casual shopper that I was able to get to my car and be back behind the green Porsche before Cavanagh even got her out of the car park.

I needed to know where they were going next. Perhaps Cavanagh had offered to lend Karen his services for her weekly shop and they were going to drive back to her mother's house. It would be the ideal way to get her address. But they weren't going there. Instead, I followed the green Porsche closely through the streets of South Kensington. Eventually they pulled up outside the house in Onslow Gardens that I knew belonged to Cavanagh.

I parked a little further down the road and watched in my rear-view mirror as they unloaded the carrier bags and carried them up the steps to the big black-painted door with its shining brass knob. I worried a little that they might have noticed me park and not get out of my car. But I worried that if I got out then and tried to stroll off down the street looking casual, I would draw even more attention to myself. I stayed put, slinking as far down in my seat as I could without losing my view.

When Cavanagh and Karen had finished unpacking and disappeared into the house for the last time, I reversed up the street to a parking spot almost directly opposite. From there I had a much better lookout.

I got out the small pair of binoculars that I had borrowed from Poupeh and focused them on the window of the grand drawing room that was the only downstairs room visible from my side of the street. The curtains, thankfully, had been left wide open, allowing me a fantastic perspective with no obstructions. I took a close look at the artwork on the wall. I recognized a Sam Taylor Wood print of a vast, still lake. One of those gyroscopic Damien Hirst paintings hung above the fire-place. A curious pot that might have been made by that Turner prizewinner who likes to wear dresses graced the mantelpiece. I couldn't help but be impressed. Barney Cavanagh was clearly a man of some taste when it came to art.

While I was trying to get a better look at that strange pot, Karen suddenly walked into the room. She had taken off her leather jacket and was carrying a vase of tall white lilies that she arranged in the centre of the dining table. She looked very much at home as she plucked off a single dead leaf. Then she turned her head at the sound of someone's voice. Must have been Cavanagh's. She laughed at a joke. She always laughed so easily. It was one of the things about her that Dad had liked most. I always thought it was a sign of simple-mindedness. Anyway, she finished arranging the flowers and left the room once more.

There followed half an hour during which the scene in my binocular sights didn't change at all. The front room remained empty and still. There were no other lights on upstairs or downstairs. I wasn't sure how many floors of the building Cavanagh had. The street was equally quiet. I put Poupeh's binoculars on maximum power and tried to read the titles of the books on Cavanagh's bookshelves. One thing Poupeh hadn't mentioned was how tedious surveillance could be.

After that half-hour, I sank down in my seat at the sound of a pair of high heels clipping along the pavement behind me. Glancing in the rear-view mirror, I saw a tall blonde woman leaning on the arm of a man much older and shorter than she was. There were at least six inches and twice as many years between them. He must have been loaded. I thought they were going to walk right past my stake-out, but they crossed the road before they drew level with me and walked up the steps to Cavanagh's house.

The woman rang the door-bell and a second later Karen answered the door, air-kissing the blonde and stooping to hug her mini-mogul. Karen was every inch the gracious hostess, helping the blonde take her jacket off before the door closed behind them. Ten minutes later another couple arrived. This time, they were more evenly matched in height and age. Once again, it was Karen who greeted them at the door like the firm friends they obviously were.

His friends? Her friends? Their friends?

I kept watch as the party drifted through into the reception room. Karen handed out glasses. Cavanagh popped the cork on a bottle of champagne and filled Karen's flute first. Their guests raised a toast to them both. Cavanagh pulled Karen towards him and gave her a one-armed hug. She kissed him on the cheek.

What a happy, happy scene . . .

I threw Poupeh's binoculars on to the passenger seat and started the car.

I had felt something begin to form in my heart. It was just like an ice crystal. I was getting pretty used to being angry and upset on behalf of my father, but as I sat there in my car, watching Karen and her new man host a dinner party together, a new, equally uncomfortable feeling was spreading cold fingers throughout me. I realized that part of me was envious of Karen and her life as it was now. I wanted a man like Cavanagh to raise a toast to me.

40

At last Poupeh agreed with my conclusion that Karen and Cavanagh were 'together' in the biblical sense.

What to do next?

'Break them up,' said Poupeh simply. 'If you still want to.'

I did.

Unfortunately, the extensive notes Poupeh and her pet policeman had produced for me, while extremely informative on Cavanagh's shopping and eating habits, had not thrown up any other information that could obviously be used against him. No short spell in prison that he might have neglected to mention to his new girlfriend. There was probably no point putting in an anonymous call to the police suggesting that his 'import–export' practices might require a little scrutiny. Not so much as three points for speeding on his driving licence. How could you own a brand-new Porsche and not get a speeding fine, I marvelled.

As Poupeh and I sat down to discuss my options, I suggested that one way to get rid of Cavanagh would be to fabricate my sushi chef credentials, moonlight at Kyoto and present the crazy fish fan with the poisonous part of a puffer-fish. Painful (for him) but effective.

Poupeh responded with the simplest way, which would be to put a letter through Cavanagh's letter-box claiming I was a 'friend' who had seen Karen out and about with yet another man, kissing him in a nightclub. Cavanagh would be furious and dump her.

It was less dramatic or likely to land me in jail than my puffer-fish solution but it wasn't quite what I wanted either.

I had quickly realized that one of the most important things about this mission to get between Karen and Cavanagh was that Karen had to be the one who did the dumping. She had to think that Cavanagh was a dickhead so that Dad would appear wonderful in comparison. I didn't want to have to wait while Karen got over Cavanagh before she agreed to see Dad again. There was also the very slim danger that Dad might have a sudden attack of pride and not want Karen back if he thought she was only coming back to him because another man had thrown her over. It was crucial that whatever I had to do to break them up, I didn't besmirch Karen's good name.

'You've got to work on him,' Poupeh agreed. 'Karen must remain blameless.'

How easy would it be?

The picture in the paper suggested that Cavanagh was a big hit with the ladies. Perhaps it wouldn't be hard to put temptation in his way and take a couple of compromising pictures that could mysteriously appear in Karen's pigeonhole at the gym. But how could I guarantee I would catch him with another woman?

'Hire a professional,' said Poupeh.

Of course, Poupeh had the number of a honey-trapper. It was both depressing and enlightening to learn that the particular honey-trapping agency Poupeh occasionally used was responsible for somewhere in the region of three considerable divorce settlements a week, providing taped evidence or clear colour photographs of unequivocally unreasonable behaviour.

The following morning, Poupeh sent me to meet the boss.

The honey-trappers' office was pretty innocuous. I'm not sure what I had expected. A Soho address? Lots of velvet, perhaps? Instead, Poupeh sent me to Pimlico. A small brass sign in the street outside announced that the 'Victoria Sturgeon Agency' was on the third floor. I walked up the tidy stairs and was welcomed into a bright, magnolia-painted waiting room, complete with a neat yet slightly incongruous pile of *Good Housekeeping* to browse through while I waited for my appointment with Victoria Sturgeon herself. Assuming that was her real name.

On the walls were a series of framed headshots. I wondered whether these were the girls who were sent out to tempt the men of London. There were a couple of guys too. I couldn't imagine being tempted by either of them myself. They put me in mind of those photos you see in old-fashioned barber-shop windows. All Brylcreem and dodgy moustaches. The overall impression was of a provincial actors' agency rather than a place where so many marriages began to end.

I had time to read an entire article on how to make the perfect roast potato before Victoria was ready to see me. Clearly, her previous appointment had overrun for emotional reasons. An elegant middle-aged woman exited clutching a brown paper envelope and blowing her nose very loudly.

'At least you know he hasn't been unfaithful.' Victoria patted her sobbing client on the back in an attempt to comfort her.

'But he's been wearing my clothes to the supermarket!' the woman wailed. 'And to think I threatened to sue the dry cleaner for stretching my Missoni sweater-dress! If he's been wearing my Armani I will kill him.'

Victoria shrugged her shoulders sympathetically and deftly manoeuvred the woman into the corridor.

She paused for a moment before she turned around and walked back in. I imagined her taking a breath, shaking off the psychic weight of what had just transpired like an actress preparing to step on-stage.

'Lindsey?'

'That's me.'

'You look much younger than I expected,' Victoria said.

And she looked much more, well, ordinary than I'd expected. In her smart beige skirt and white blouse she was less like a femme fatale and more like Dad's rather mumsy housekeeper.

'How did you find us again? Ah yes, PGI. How is the lovely Poupch? Come on in.'

I followed her into her office, which was decorated with yet more headshots of the probably not rich and the definitely not famous. She directed me to the chair on the opposite side of her desk to the Dallas boardroom-style swivel monstrosity from which she conducted her business.

'Now, tell me what I can do for you.'

I told her the sorry tale. My 'client' was dating a man she suspected to be the unfaithful kind. She'd asked me to find out for sure.

The most important thing about Victoria's business, I learned then, was to set the right kind of trap. Different men go for different kinds of women. That much was obvious. You had to tailor your bait to the catch. What did I think this Cavanagh bloke was attracted to? Perhaps the easiest way to work that out was to describe the woman he was already with, Victoria suggested.

'Karen? Hmmm. Well, I suppose she's very attractive,' I began.

'All our field workers are very attractive,' Victoria informed me.

'Of course.'

'What's her style?'

How on earth could I describe it without sounding like a complete cow?

'Somewhere between Britney Spears and Christina Aguilera dressing to visit the mother-in-law?' I said frankly.

Victoria frowned and made a note.

'You'll have to be more specific.'

'She works in a gym, so her daywear is sort of sporty. She has a penchant for those velour tracksuits by Juicy. She wears lots of trousers with slogans on the bum. If she's going out in the evening, she might wear a skirt but always a short one.'

Victoria nodded.

'Hair?'

'Light brown. Long. Brutally straightened.'

'Build?'

'Athletic.'

'Of course, since she works in a gym. Class?'

'Lower middle?' I said.

'Not much then.' Victoria smiled meanly. 'Well, you've given me quite a picture,' she said. 'And I think we've got someone who can do the style you've described. Now all we need to do is fix a date to get out there and trap him. We need to know where the target's going to be and what he looks like.'

'This is the man.' I slid a printout from the Internet across the desk.

'Very good-looking,' Victoria said admiringly. 'They are usually the worst ones,' she added with a sudden snarl. 'They think they can get away with anything and fix everything with a smile. But don't you worry, Lindsey. If he isn't worth your client's love and devotion then we'll give you all the evidence you need to prove it to her. Got any idea when we might get started on this?'

'I know where he lives and where his office is.'

'Does he go to a bar near work?'

'I don't know.'

'You need to find a venue and get him to be there.' Victoria flicked through the pages of her big black diary. 'I have someone available on Wednesday night. If you can get him to a rendezvous and your cheque has cleared in time . . .' she added.

'No need to worry about that.' I pulled the brown envelope, fat with fifty-pound notes, out of my bag. Poupeh had warned me that small businesses like the Victoria Sturgeon Agency rarely accepted American Express and given me an advance on my wages.

'I'd like to be there too,' I said.

Victoria raised an eyebrow. 'If you want.'

'Poupeh thought it would be a good idea for me to see how your girls work.'

'Tell her she'd better not be thinking of moving into my field,' Victoria laughed. But there was a hint of steel beneath her statement.

'Of course,' I agreed. 'How did you get into this?' I couldn't resist asking.

'I set up the agency with my divorce settlement,' she smiled.

41

Now all I had to do was get Cavanagh in a position to be honey-trapped. I investigated the area around his office and found a place called Frogmortons. It was a chi-chi bar / gastro-pub and looked like the type of place a man like Cavanagh would go to.

With a location chosen, I got Poupeh to call Cavanagh's office and make an appointment for an evening when I knew Karen would be at work.

I had Poupeh claim to be interested in having Cavanagh's company source some exciting artwork for a new company headquarters in the city. So far, so authentic. But for some reason Poupeh, who claimed to be a mistress of mystery accents (she'd done an acting course – lots of PIs do, she told me), chose to arrange the rendezvous in the character of a Glaswegian called Doreen.

'Och, hello,' she began. 'Am I speaking to Mr Cavanagh, begorrah?'

She suggested an early Wednesday evening rendezvous at Frogmortons and described herself as five feet five, slim, with long red hair. 'Like Bree from *Desperate Housewives*,' she added.

'Do you think he'll be there?' I asked anxiously when Poupeh got off the phone. 'Do you think he thought you were genuine?'

'Why wouldn't he?' Poupeh asked.

'Because your accent wavered alarmingly between broad Glaswegian and Irish. You sounded like you didn't know where you were from.'

'My accent was fine.'

'Poupeh, how many Scots do you know who use the word "begorrah"?'

'He'll be there,' said Poupeh somewhat irritably. 'I was totally convincing.'

'I'm sorry. I didn't mean to suggest . . . It's just that you know how important this is to me . . .'

Poupeh was still bristling.

'What are you doing this afternoon?' I asked conversationally.

'A stake-out.'

'Who are you staking?'

'A dog-walking company. One of my clients thinks they're not giving her labra-doodle the fifteen laps of the park that she's paying for.'

'What do you think?'

'I don't know yet. I'm going to get out there with my lap-counter.'

'Good luck,' I said.

Poupeh was already putting on a Humphrey Bogart hat, pulling it low over her eyes and wrapping a scarf around the bottom half of her face though it really wasn't scarf weather. Sometimes, hanging out with Poupeh, I felt as though I was on the set of a 1940s spy movie. Sometimes it was more like being on the set of a *Carry On* film. She couldn't have looked more conspicuous if she'd tried.

I watched from the window as Poupeh got on to her bicycle and headed off shakily in the direction of Regent's Park.

★   ★   ★

That Wednesday night, I arranged to meet 'Wendy' from the honey-trapping agency in a pub just across the street from Frogmortons. I don't know quite who or what I had been expecting. I suppose I was probably thinking of someone more along the lines of the traditional femme fatale. All thick black eyeliner and pouting red lips, a low, husky voice and a cigarette constantly on the go. There were a couple of women who actually did look like that in the pub, but neither of them was the mid-range Mata Hari I had paid for.

My accomplice for the evening was the woman in the Burberry check mini-skirt and matching baseball cap.

'Wendy?' I asked, hoping I was wrong. I had already 'Wendy-ed' the two femmes fatales. The barman had started looking at me in a very strange way, as though he suspected me of waiting for a lesbian blind date and hoped if he kept the drinks coming fast and strong enough the mystery woman and I might invite him back to make the video.

'That's right,' said Burberry woman. 'Are you the girl-friend?' She lowered her voice. I sensed she was appraising me, making a note of the reasons why my man would want to stray. Considering what I was wearing that night, she could probably list at least ten.

'The girlfriend is my client. I'm a detective,' I said, slightly stretching the truth.

I couldn't help staring at Wendy's outfit in return. She looked as though she had escaped from the audience on *Top of the Pops*. But then, I suppose, I had described Karen as Britney meets Aguilera. Wendy probably dressed in a far classier fashion in her downtime, I thought generously. Maybe not.

'Where is the shit then?' Wendy asked.

'I'm sorry?'

"The shit. The man we're after. That's the code we honey-trappers at the VS Agency use.'

'Ah, right. Very, er . . . subtle. I'm hoping he's in that bar across the road.' I gestured towards Frogmortons. 'I had my colleague call and pretend to be interested in his business. They arranged a meeting for seven-thirty. He should be in there waiting for her to turn up.'

On the other side of the street, the doorman was just opening Frogmortons' door for a couple of archetypal Chelsea girls, all long legs encased in Seven Jeans and straight blonde hair down to their bottoms. In fact every woman who went to Frogmortons wore Seven Jeans and had straight blonde hair down to her bum. If Cavanagh was in there, I thought, there was absolutely no guarantee that Wendy would be allowed in to try to honey-trap him wearing that terrible Burberry plaid skirt and matching, er . . . poncho.

'Bit cold in here,' Wendy said, as she slipped the hideous poncho thing on over her head. 'And I'll need a drink before I get started,' she informed me. I realized quickly that I was supposed to buy it. I forked out for a vodka tonic for her and another glass of mineral water for me. I couldn't risk touching a drop. I was driving and needed to maintain the capability for a decent getaway speed if that evening's plan went wrong.

'How long have you been doing this job?' I asked politely as Wendy guzzled her drink and suggested that another double might make it even easier for her to pretend that she found Karen's boyfriend attractive.

'A couple of years.'

'And how did you get into it?'

'I used to be a lap-dancer.'

'What was that like?'

'Good money. But my knees started to go.'

'Oh.'

'The money dries up when you can't go upside down on the pole any more.'

'I can imagine.'

'So, Victoria was setting up her agency. And the first guy she was asked to stitch up just happened to be a guy who came into the lap-dance bar where I worked every Wednesday night and always asked for me. She approached me as I was leaving my shift one night. Showed me this guy's picture and asked whether I knew him. He'd spent three hundred pounds on me that very evening. She asked whether I'd like a bigger cut. So, the following Wednesday night, I slipped him a note and asked him to meet me in the alley when the club closed. He got a quick grope. Victoria got her pictures. And some poor woman got a divorce. It was easy money.'

I couldn't help shuddering at the matter-of-fact tone to Wendy's voice. 'But how do you make sure that you convince a man to cheat?' I asked. 'What if it turns out you're not his type? What if he isn't a cheat?'

'Honey, every man is a cheat if he's given the opportunity and thinks that he won't get caught. It's in their DNA. And as for whether or not I'm his type, darlin', I am like the Mounties. I always get my man.'

Fascinating though Wendy was, I was mightily relieved when it was time to deploy her on her mission. Before she went, she handed me the little listening and recording device that would pick up signals from the wire she wore under her tight jumper. The idea was that she would engage Cavanagh in conversation and we would get him telling her he didn't have a girlfriend on tape. If she managed to get further than that, I was armed with a digital camera to snap compromising pictures in the alley behind Frogmortons, which was where Wendy would drag Cavanagh if she could.

I inserted the earpiece as Wendy left the pub and heard her clearing her throat and hawking into the gutter as she crossed the road and wiggled straight into Frogmortons. Watching through the window, I noticed that while Wendy may not have been dressed like the club's usual clientele, the bouncer not only opened the door for her, he even gave her a little bow.

'Good evening, madam,' he said. 'That's a beautiful poncho.'

I couldn't believe it. I had always thought that men were almost as horrified of ponchos as they are of getting accidentally engaged! I was horrified and pleased. Perhaps Wendy wasn't exaggerating. If she could get a guy to compliment a poncho then perhaps she really did have something that no red-blooded man could resist. I felt much more confident that she would be able to frame Cavanagh now.

I left a few minutes before I followed her across the road. I almost got myself run over, distracted as I was by the live feed from Wendy's mike.

'Double vodka and tonic,' I heard her say. It was her third that evening and it would be going on my bill. I remembered too late that Poupeh had advised me to try to agree a bar-bill cap before the evening started.

'These girls aren't always entirely honest,' she said.

'Well, I suppose it's safe to say that honey-trapping attracts a different type of girl from teaching primary school,' I'd replied.

I reached Frogmortons. The doorman who had complimented Wendy barely nodded at me as I pushed open the door myself. But then, I was wearing my 'disguise'. My full-length Prada duffel coat made me look like a walking duvet. It was hardly suitable for the late summer evening but it covered me from nose to knees and that was what really mattered. Once inside, I kept it done up while I went to the bar and ordered another water, unzipping it only when I was safely installed in a very dark corner table and thought I might be about to faint with the heat.

Meanwhile, Wendy had positioned herself at a high table in the middle of the room. She had slipped off the poncho and hitched up her skirt so that it showed the very top of her stockings. All eyes were on her. The girls, disgusted. The guys, delighted.

'He isn't here yet, is he?' Wendy muttered into the microphone she had secreted in her crêpey cleavage.

I shook my head, hoping she and no one else caught the gesture. A man sitting diagonally across from me narrowed his eyes at me as though I had escaped from a secure ward. It was a pretty fair assumption. I was inappropriately dressed and talking to myself. I slid down into the squishy leather cushions, trying to make myself less conspicuous.

It was another ten minutes before Cavanagh walked in.

I sat up to get a better look.

Barney Cavanagh knew how to make an impressive entrance. As he strolled through the room, he nodded at a couple of the cookie-cutter blondes. They immediately sat to attention. He was wearing a blue shirt tucked into black jeans. His dark hair was smoothed back from his forehead. By the time he reached the bar, the cocktail waitress had already made his drink. A tall drink. A vodka and tonic, I wondered. Not a white wine spritzer, I hoped for Karen's sake. I've always thought that a very bad sign in a man.

'Thank you, Shelley,' said Cavanagh to the barmaid.

Wendy's mic picked up his voice! This was going to be good, I decided.

Cavanagh chose a seat at the bar and brought out a paperback novel. From time to time, he looked up and shared a smile with the girl who had served him. Wendy gave Cavanagh just a couple of minutes before she left her table in the centre of the room, pulled up a stool and sat back down again right beside him.

'What's a nice boy like you doing in a place like this?' was her opening gambit.

Zero points for originality.

'Having a nice evening?' she continued.

Cavanagh glanced up from his book for just a nano-second and gave Wendy a friendly nod.

'Great,' he said. 'Thanks.' Then he moved his glass a little further away from her, subconsciously, or perhaps not so subconsciously, marking the distinction between his space and hers. I knew these things from a book on body language Gemma and I had once read with the intention of becoming irresistible.

Undeterred, Wendy ordered a drink from the barmaid. Another vodka tonic. They poured doubles in this bar. I was surprised she could still see. Then she cracked a joke with the barmaid and looked to Cavanagh to see if she had got his attention too. She hadn't. Nor did she manage to get his attention when she crossed her legs and hitched her skirt up again. She took a thoughtful sip from her drink as she considered her next move, re-crossing her legs as she did so.

Wendy's next move was to reach into her handbag for a packet of fags. She slipped a cigarette between her lips and leaned across to Cavanagh.

'Have you got a light?' she hissed out of the corner of her mouth.

Cavanagh pressed his lips together and shook his head. 'No, I don't smoke. There are some matches on the bar over there.'

Wendy glanced in the direction of the jar full of match-books but didn't bother picking any up. She put the cigarette back in the packet instead.

'Never mind. Supposed to be giving up anyway. What are you reading?' she tried then.

Cavanagh didn't answer her. He didn't even seem to hear her the first time she asked, so she actually took the book out of his hands to look at the cover.

'*Confederacy of Dunces*? What's that about then?'

Even I could see Cavanagh's brow crinkle minutely in annoyance. He managed to keep smiling as Wendy read the blurb on the back of the book out loud. But by the time he eventually plucked the book back from her hands he still hadn't actually spoken a word.

This was going to be a tough one.

'Go on. Tell me what happens in your book,' said Wendy. You had to admire her dogged approach.

'It's too complicated to explain quickly,' said Cavanagh.

'Then explain it to me *slowly*,' Wendy slurred.

'Some other time perhaps,' he replied. 'Do you mind if I carry on reading? I'm getting to a good bit.'

'You're not being very social.'

'I didn't really come here to socialize.'

It wasn't going well. Ten minutes after her first attempt to catch his attention, Wendy was practically horizontal along the bar but Cavanagh still resisted all her attempts to start a conversation, replying monosyllabically when he couldn't get away with not answering at all.

By this time, even an anthropologist from outer space would have been able to tell by Cavanagh's body language that he simply wasn't interested. In fact, if anything, he seemed to be actively repulsed. Cavanagh's body was turned away from Wendy's. It wouldn't be long before he was actually showing her his back. Having given up on getting enough peace to carry on reading, his eyes were fixed on a point in the distance as Wendy tried every trick in her book to get him to listen to her.

'Come on,' she said finally. 'Give me your hand.'

She made a last-ditch attempt to engage him by actually offering to *read his palm*.

'I can tell that you're a red-hot lover,' she said.

'That's interesting,' he said, disinterestedly.

'Some people think that palm-reading is rubbish but I bet you're the one man who could make me believe it . . . What do you say? Shall we go outside and test the theory? Or have you got a girlfriend?'

I sat up straight and pushed the earpiece a little further into my ear so that I caught every word of his answer. I checked also that every word of that answer would be recorded. Wendy had asked the million-dollar question. I held my breath.

But then the most unexpected thing happened. Cavanagh made his excuses, got up from the bar and made a beeline straight for me.

42

What was he doing? I considered making a run for it but there simply wasn't time. Cavanagh was across the room and upon me before I could even push myself up out of the ridiculously squishy leather cushions that were sucking me down like quicksand.

Why on earth was he heading for me? He hadn't recognized me, had he? There was no reason why he should know who I was. Could Karen have shown him a photograph? No, Cavanagh didn't know me. I was sure of that. Perhaps he had mistaken me for someone else. I noticed when he was reading his book that he had held it quite closely, like someone whose sight wasn't exactly 20/20.

Yet as he approached, his smile only grew wider and more genuine, as if he not only thought we had met before but decided that we liked each other to boot.

What could I do? I chanced a smile back.

'Thank God you're here,' he said loudly. 'Have you been sitting there long? I haven't got my glasses on so I couldn't see you from across the room.'

Wendy gawped in confusion as Cavanagh sat down on the banquette beside me.

Her whispered 'What the fuck?' went straight into my ear, making me flinch.

'Look,' said Cavanagh then, lowering his voice and leaning in close to the ear that didn't have the earpiece in it. 'I know this is a bit odd – I'm a total stranger and you've got no reason to want to help me out at all – but do you think you could just pretend to know me for a little while? Just look like you're happy to see me, would you? I've come here tonight to meet a potential client but she seems to be running late and that bizarre woman at the bar just will not leave me alone.'

Oh-mi-god, I thought.

'OK,' I said in a voice a good octave higher than usual. On the pretence of pushing back my hair, I surreptitiously pulled the earpiece out before Cavanagh spotted it.

'I think she might be a professional,' he added confidentially.

'What do you mean?' I squeaked, fearing at once that Wendy's honey-trapping reputation had preceded her.

'A lady of the night . . . I'm sorry. That's an awful thing to say about a girl. She probably works in the City or PR like all the rest of the girls in here. It's just that she's being terribly persistent in trying to chat me up. And those clothes . . .'

He glanced sidelong in her direction and actually gave a small shudder.

'Where do they sell that kind of gear? Anyway,' he said, recovering from the horror, 'since I'm imposing myself on you, I suppose I should introduce myself. My name is Barney. Barney Cavanagh. And you are?'

Who was I? To him?

'Er, Jane,' I lied, giving Cavanagh my second name. I was way too discombobulated by the fact that he was suddenly sitting next to me to think of an alibi surname fast enough. Thankfully, he didn't seem to notice and didn't ask for one.

'Well, Not-At-All-Plain-Jane,' he smiled, 'thank you for agreeing to rescue me. I will be eternally grateful. I hope you'll let me buy you a drink in return?'

What should I say?

'I'll have a glass of sparkling water,' I said.

'Cheap date,' he laughed. 'One bottle of sparkling water coming up.' He waved in the direction of one of the club hostesses. She jumped to attention and was at Cavanagh's side with a smile within a nano-second. And I could absolutely see why she was smiling.

I had already discerned what gave Cavanagh appeal from a distance. There were plenty of women for whom the mere fact that he drove a brand-new Porsche would be quite enough. I knew he was good-looking. Tall, svelte, well dressed. And chivalrous too. I'd seen him leap out of the car to open the passenger door for Karen when it wasn't raining – but I hadn't really experienced the full force of the Cavanagh effect until that moment.

Now that he was just a metre away from me – maybe less – I could see that his skin was perfect, with the clarity that speaks of mineral water, organic food and long hours spent in the great outdoors. His hair was thick, dark and glossy: the kind of hair you see shining in the 'after' shots of an anti-dandruff commercial, while a super-model with long red nails runs her hands through it and sighs. His eyes really did have that film-star twinkle I'd noticed in the society column photograph. The twinkle was far more effective in the flesh.

'Are you waiting for someone?' Cavanagh asked me then. 'I don't want to interrupt anything. Or get you into trouble with your boyfriend. If this is at all awkward . . .'

It was. But not in any way he could possibly have imagined.

'No,' I said, still squeaking. 'I'm not waiting for anyone.'

'Oh. Good. So, what is a nice girl like you doing in a place like this? On her own? And drinking mineral water?'

'Soaking up the ambience?' I lied.

'Well, personally I think the ambience is much better

diluted with alcohol,' Cavanagh quipped. 'But it is nice and quiet on a week night, I suppose. I often come in here after work to wind down before I go home. Or to take a meeting. My office is just around the corner. Do you work near here?'

I shook my head.

'Shall I be cheesy and ask what you do?'

Oh dear. It probably wouldn't have been helpful to tell him that right then, I spent office hours working on breaking up his relationship so my father could have another shot at getting married to the love of his life (Mum not included). Instead, I racked my brains for a job I could lay claim to without risking Cavanagh having insider knowledge that would quickly winkle out my lie. Doctor was the first job that sprang to mind. It was always the first job that sprang to mind. Then nurse. But I had a superstitious fear of pretending to be a medical professional, in case someone in the bar choked on a peanut and I failed to administer the Heimlich manoeuvre properly. I could be sued.

I needed a job that I could bluff with some confidence. I really should have had one rehearsed. Poupeh had warned me as much in our latest 'Private Detective 101'. Fortunately, I was crunching an ice-cube, which gave me the perfect excuse not to speak right away and a few all-important extra moments. Eventually, ice-cube completely crunched, I plumped for the job that I would have most liked to have.

'I'm an interior designer,' I said.

'Oh. Nice,' said Cavanagh. 'Who do you work for?'

'Self-employed. My offices are in Brixton,' I continued. Highly unlikely that Cavanagh would ever risk taking his Porsche that far south of the river. 'But I heard this club was getting popular and wanted to find out why.'

I allowed myself a small moment of being pleased with my story. It had come out pretty naturally in the end.

'So, what do you think?' Cavanagh asked. 'What is its appeal?'

'Comfy seats,' I said weakly.

Cavanagh bounced up and down on the cushions as though he was checking my claim. 'They're not too bad. What a great job, Jane. Where did you train?'

'I did a degree at Exeter.'

That part, at least, was true – though my degree had been in psychology and not design.

'Lucky you. I was always interested in design but my teachers pushed me towards law. Dull, dull, dull. I've sort of come back to design now though.'

'You have?' I panicked.

'Yes. I have a business that imports fine art from the Far East. You know, maybe you should drop by my office one day. Might give you some inspiration.'

'Maybe, but the Eastern look is . . .'

'A bit passé?'

'No, I was just going to say it isn't really my style.'

'Then what is your style?'

'Um. Eclectic?' I tried.

'Hmmm.' Cavanagh nodded as though either of us really knew what I had meant. He glanced at his watch. 'Well, it's eight o'clock. Looks like I've been stood up. You can't see anyone in here who looks like a red-haired Glaswegian called Doreen, can you?'

'No.'

'I should have guessed. Someone's been winding me up. It's probably one of my mates. Happens all the time. This "Doreen" woman's accent was all over the place. One minute she was Scottish. The next she was Irish. To be honest, I'm not entirely convinced she was even female.'

I forced a titter.

'But you can't just come out and say you think someone's having a laugh just in case they are the real thing and you insult them out of putting some business your way. I got caught out really badly once. I got a phone-call from my credit card company. The guy on the phone had such a funny voice I burst out laughing and said, "That's the worst Indian accent I've ever heard, Richard." My friend Richard is big on stupid voices. But of course, this call really was coming from Delhi.'

'Embarrassing,' I said.

'Yes, I don't think that bank will be raising my credit limit any time soon. Ah well. Doreen from Glasgow may have stood me up but I don't feel as though it's been an entirely wasted evening.'

And then he smiled at me.

I was saved from having to think of any kind of response to that by the arrival of Cavanagh's friend. He was one of the guys I had seen through the window at the dinner party. The short bloke with the Amazonian girlfriend. She wasn't with him that night. He looked much taller without her.

'Richard!' Cavanagh jumped up. 'I knew it was you, you sod.'

'Knew what, you twat?'

Oh, the lovely way that English guys of a certain class greet each other.

'That set me up. I've been waiting here since half past seven for one "Doreen Stewart" from Glasgow. Or was it County Cork? Your comedy accents get worse all the time. Nice touch though, pretending to be a woman.'

'I don't know what you're bloody talking about.'

'Sure you don't. I'll be billing you for my wasted time. Richard, this is Jane.' Cavanagh patted his friend on the back and introduced us. 'Jane has been providing an invaluable service, keeping me safe from the ladies of the night.'

Richard shook my hand quite jovially but I thought he narrowed his eyes at me. As though he wondered where he had seen me before. Had he noticed me lurking in Poupeh's Smart Car outside Cavanagh's flat that night?

'Jane's an interior designer,' Cavanagh continued. 'Richard is having his house refurbished. Perhaps the pair of you should have a conversation. In fact, you definitely should. His sitting room already looks like something from an eighties Argos catalogue. You need to rescue him before he fits a cocktail bar in his bedroom.'

'I don't do houses,' I said hurriedly. 'Only commercial.'

'Oh.'

'And I've got an early meeting tomorrow. I'd better go.'

Richard was still looking at me quizzically. Perhaps it was just the way his eyes were set – a little close together. But perhaps he was going to rumble me. I decided I had better not push my luck by staying a moment longer. Besides which, Wendy was staring at me quite openly by now and making gestures I took to mean that she wanted to talk to me. Or shoot me. One or the other. Perhaps she was just drawing my attention to the fact that I was no longer wearing my earpiece. Whatever, it was only a matter of time before one of the men noticed Wendy's angry gesticulating and realized that she knew me.

I struggled back into my duvet coat.

'It's July out there!' Cavanagh joked.

'I've got bad circulation. Look, it's been really nice to meet you both. Bye.'

I managed just half a step before Cavanagh caught my arm.

'Wait! You can't just go like that. Can I have your phone number?' he asked me. 'I'd really like to see you again.'

'I don't give strange men my phone number.'

'And he certainly is strange,' said Richard.

'Then let this strange man give you his number,' Cavanagh insisted. He reached into his pocket and brought out a card. 'Call me. Really. I'd love to talk more about cushions.'

'Sure. Goodbye.' I nodded quickly and fled.

Outside, Wendy was leaning against a wall, smoking. She'd clearly found her own lighter, having had no luck at the bar. She didn't look too happy.

'What the hell was going on in there?' she asked.

'I was going to ask the same of you! What kind of rubbish were you saying to him? He came to talk to me to escape from you.'

'I'll still need my money.'

'But you didn't do your job,' I said angrily. 'You didn't seduce him. You scared him straight towards me! It was a total disaster. I had to make up an alibi. He ended up asking for my number for heaven's sake.'

'So?' said Wendy. 'He fancied the wrong girl. You still found out that he's prepared to be unfaithful, didn't you?'

'But I've got no evidence to present to my client, have I? No photographs of you and him together. No incriminating recording of him whispering sweet nothings in your ear.'

'Why don't you just tell her that he came on to you instead?'

'It isn't that simple.'

Wendy shrugged. 'You know, you looked pretty hot under the collar when he came and sat next to you,' she commented. 'That's always a sign.'

'Of what?'

'That you fancy someone.'

'That's ridiculous.'

'I'm just saying what I saw. Look, are you going to give me

that money or not? I've got another job booked in for ten o'clock.'

'But you didn't do what you were supposed to. I want a reduction.'

'Look,' said Wendy. 'I work for a honey-trapping agency, not Marks and bloody Spencers. We don't give no money-back guarantees. If the quarry doesn't act like he's supposed to, then that's the end of the story. Not my issue. You've still got to pay for my time and expertise.'

Expertise? Wendy's seduction technique was as sophisti-cated as trying to catch fish with dynamite. I fought the urge to snort and kept my hands firmly in my pockets.

'Don't make me enforce our payment policy,' Wendy sighed.

She wasn't much bigger than me but her change of tone right then left me under no illusion that she was much, much harder. Reluctantly, I got my wallet out and handed over the last instalment of the payment I had promised.

'Thanks for nothing,' I said.

'Ta.' She rolled the crisp new notes into a tube and tucked them into her bra. I guess that old lap-dancing habits die hard. Then Wendy and her poncho tottered off in the direction of tube station. An angel of destruction in a Burberry mini-skirt, ready to catch out the next skank with her classy looks and repartee. I hoped that evening's next client got better results for her money than I had.

43

What a disaster. Five hundred pounds down and no evidence of Cavanagh's tendency to cheat whatsoever.

I considered my next move on the drive back to Poupeh's flat. Should I hire a different honey-trapper? One with a bit more class? Was there such a thing, I wondered, thinking about Wendy and the other women pictured on the walls of the Victoria Sturgeon Agency's office.

Poupeh was eager to hear how my mission had proceeded. She agreed that Wendy hadn't fulfilled her brief.

'But at least you got to know your quarry better,' she said. 'And information is power. What was he like?'

'He was all right,' I said, surprising myself. 'Really normal. I don't know what I was expecting. Someone smoother, I think.'

'Of course, the very smooth ones know how to come across as not being smooth at all,' Poupeh reminded me. 'Anything else?'

'He drinks vodka. He's got some cheesy mates who like to make prank phone calls. He thought your Doreen was one of them. And that's about it.'

'Well, I think the most important piece of information we've gathered so far is that Barney Cavanagh likes you.'

I felt a peculiar flutter. 'He was just trying to escape from Wendy.'

'Pfft,' said Poupeh. 'He could have left the bar altogether. Why shouldn't he like you?'

I caught a glimpse of myself in the mirror above Poupeh's fireplace. Was I blushing?

I suppose it was possible that he did fancy me, wasn't it? There were any number of single women in that bar he could have chosen to rescue him from Wendy. It would have made much more sense for him to go up to those girls he had nodded at as he walked into the bar if all he wanted was a cover. He'd obviously met them before. Why didn't he ask them for help? Unless he specifically wanted a reason to engage *me* in conversation . . .

I felt a peculiar thrill go through me at the thought that a man with as much taste as Cavanagh had found me attractive. But I shook it off at once. Cavanagh was a jerk who was prepared to cheat on his girlfriend and there is no point being flattered by the attentions of an arse-hole.

Poupeh interrupted my reverie.

'So, you have to become our honey-trap . . .'

'No,' I said firmly.

'You've got his number. He asked for a date. So go on that date and we'll wire you up.'

'What possible good could it do? If I try to persuade Karen to get back together with Dad by presenting her with tape and photos of *me* seducing her boyfriend, I really don't think it's going to help her decide that I'm the kind of balanced and not-at-all conniving woman she wants for a stepdaughter.'

'She doesn't have to know it's you. We can distort your voice on tape. If I get any photos, I'll make sure that your face isn't showing in any of the shots. Change your hairstyle a bit. The lighting will be dim. Trust me, if people aren't looking for something they often don't notice that it's sitting right under their nose. Why would she expect to see her boyfriend with her ex-fiancé's daughter? Set up a date and we could have the photographs in Karen's hands by the end of the week.'

'Do you really think it's a good idea?'

'Right now it's my only idea,' said Poupeh.

I didn't have anything better to add.

All this required me to meet Cavanagh again and for that I needed to call him. How long should I wait? Ordinarily, The Rules stated that I should have waited at least three days, giving him plenty of time to think about me and wonder whether he had impressed me at all. But I didn't have the luxury of time. As soon as Poupeh had convinced me that this plan to use me as the honey-trap might work, I pulled his card out of my wallet and dialled his number right away, using one of the five mobile phones Poupeh kept for her various investigative persona.

'This will be "Jane's" phone,' she said, handing over a Nokia with a pink clip-on cover.

Cavanagh answered at once.

'Oh, hi, Barney. It's Linz,' I stuttered. 'I mean, it's Jane.'

'Lynne?'

'Jane. Sorry, bad line. We met earlier tonight at Frogmortons?'

'Oh, Jane!' His voice was suddenly flooded with what sounded like enthusiasm. 'I'm still there! Sitting in the nice warm seat you left behind. The mysterious Doreen didn't ever turn up but Richard won't let me leave. I'm so glad you called! I've been thinking about you.'

'You have?' I squeaked. 'I mean, you have?' I said in a slightly less excited tone.

'Yes. I've been thinking I should have insisted that you joined Richard and me for dinner. I let you get away much too easily. I was convinced I had made such a bad impression by accusing that poor woman at the bar of being a prostitute that I'd never hear from you again. I'm glad I was wrong.'

I hadn't expected him to be quite so pleased to hear from me.

'You know, she left the bar seconds after you did. Richard said she must be going outside to pick a fight with you for hitting on her man. I was all for running to your defence.'

I laughed. Nervously.

'So?' said Cavanagh.

'So?'

'So, does this mean you are going to let me take you out and buy you a proper drink this time? Or dinner?'

'Yes. I suppose it does.'

'Fantastic. When are you free? I can do just about any night this week. My diary is sadly very empty.'

Because Karen is working late all week, I thought.

'How about tomorrow?'

I mouthed 'Tomorrow' at Poupeh, who had been sitting opposite me all the time I was talking. She flicked through her desk diary and nodded.

'Very short notice, I know,' said Cavanagh. 'I'll understand if you can't. I imagine you've got something in your diary already.'

'A cancellation,' I lied.

'Fantastic,' said Cavanagh. 'I mean, fantastic for me. You weren't terribly disappointed, I hope.'

'It'll be rescheduled. Where are we going?' I asked.

'How about Kyoto?' he said.

★   ★   ★

'Excellent,' said Poupeh, when I put down the phone. 'I will be there tomorrow night with my camera.'

'You know what,' I told her. 'I'm sort of excited . . . About taking another step closer to getting Dad and Karen back together,' I clarified.

44

Getting ready for my first 'date' with Barney Cavanagh was less like preparing for a romantic assignation than preparing for war. First, I had to choose my outfit. But the ordinary rules for date-dressing did not apply that afternoon. Poupeh stood beside me as I went through my clothes, giving her expert opinion on each item as I picked it up.

I held out my favourite dress. A black jersey wrap by Diane von Furstenberg. Simple, classic, dangerously sexy low neckline. It was a sure-fire winner. Cavanagh would not be able to resist.

'No,' said Poupeh. 'Far too big a risk.'

It wasn't my honour she was worried about but where I would hide my microphone. Not only did the wrap dress have too low a neckline for Poupeh to be able to conceal the mic to her satisfaction, it fitted too closely all over, she explained. The wires trailing from the mic to the transmitter pack would show clearly through the slinky material.

Poupeh rejected most of my wardrobe for the same reasons. I started to wonder whether I was going to have to borrow one of her voluminous kaftans. I could have hidden a whole extra spy inside one of those. But eventually we compromised on another dress – a green jersey number that had a proper collar, inside which Poupeh pinned a microphone just a little bigger than a matchstick. After that we had a practice run to make sure that the mic was properly transmitting to Poupeh's digital recorder.

I walked to the other end of the flat and sat at the kitchen table, talking to myself for a while.

'You've got to stop swishing your hair,' Poupeh told me when the test was over. 'All I could hear every other minute was "swoosh, swoosh". We'll pin it up.'

'I don't flick my hair all the time,' I protested.

'You do,' Poupeh assured me. 'It's one of your most irritating habits.'

I bit my tongue. I would have liked to point out some of Poupeh's own irritating habits – pfft – but since I didn't want to go back to Henry and Lydia's shed, I just assured her that I would sort my hair out. I reminded myself that she was being very kind to me. I didn't know how long I was going to need to prevail upon her kindness. Dad still hadn't called. I had no idea how long it would be before I persuaded Karen to give him another chance and was thus able to return to Hampstead in triumph.

As promised, Poupeh had even given me something of a job. She wasn't sure that I was ready to be let loose on a real case just yet, but that morning I had made a start on the termite hill of receipts that was Poupeh's filing system. In return I got my bed, board and credit towards the money I owed her for liberating my car from the pound, paying the honey-trapper and bribing a policeman on my behalf.

'OK. So you know how to turn it on?' said Poupeh.

I dutifully flicked the mic switch to 'on' and we both got a shot of hideous feedback.

'Great,' said Poupeh, turning the volume down.

I was wired for sound.

After that we had to practise my new persona. Poupeh had been impressed that I had managed to think of an alibi at all when Cavanagh descended on me at Frogmortons, but she wanted the character of 'Jane' to be far better thought out before I headed for Kyoto. We sat down at the kitchen table and I answered all the questions I might reasonably expect to be asked on a date.

'Where were you born?' Poupeh began.

She advised me that when creating an alter ego, it was a good idea to stick relatively close to the truth to avoid having to talk about subjects you weren't really familiar with.

'If you tell him you were born and raised in Liverpool, you run the risk of Cavanagh having a dear aunt he visits in Liverpool every other weekend and it's going to sound strange when you can't tell him which suburb in particular you grew up in.'

And so we decided that, like me, Jane would have been born in a small West Country town but spent most of her life in London, having moved to the capital aged four. She would have attended the state girls' school near the private school that Poupeh and I had attended. That way, I knew I would get the uniform colour right at least. Jane studied interior design in Exeter. She had lived on the street where I lodged as a student. Now she lived in Brixton with a girl she had met there who would, should I need to answer questions on her, be based on Poupeh.

'Good,' said Poupeh. 'Almost believable. What's her sur-name?'

'Smith,' I smiled. 'What do I do now?'

'Just do what you always do when you're going on a hot date,' Poupeh told me then.

It had been quite a while since I'd really got ready for a hot date but I thought I could remember.

I lounged in a bath full of Poupeh's Jo Malone oil, reading first-date tips from *How to Make Anyone Fall in Love with*

You. Unfortunately, it was a bit too late to make a blinding first impression – why, oh why did Cavanagh have to notice me for the first time when I was wearing a *duffel coat* for goodness' sake? – but I was determined that my second impression would be flawless. After making sure that I was up to speed with the body language guaranteed to drive any man into a frenzy of desire, I flicked through copies of *The Times* and the *Guardian* to bone up on the day's big news stories so that I wouldn't be stuck for small talk either. I narrowed my topics down to the war on terrorism, a Tory Party scandal and some new research on the sex habits of the bonobo chimpanzee that I would trot out if either of the previous conversation pieces looked set to start a row.

I emerged from the bath an hour later as wrinkled as an eighty-one-year-old. I slapped on a generous helping of Poupeh's body lotion, then I strapped myself into my most flattering underwear and pulled the green dress on over my head. Dress on, I presented myself to Poupeh, who attached the mic and the transmitter unit once more.

'Give me a twirl,' she said, to make sure that my surveillance equipment was invisible from all angles.

'Perfect. Can't see a thing. Do you want me to do your make-up now?'

Not really, I didn't. It was one thing letting Poupeh choose what I was going to wear, but letting her do my make-up too? It didn't seem like a good idea. In addition to dressing in the kind of colours that would make a parrot look drab, Poupeh's make-up skills were on a par with those girls who work the cosmetics counters at Heathrow duty-free. That is to say, she looked as though she had never been allowed to use foundation and mascara before that morning and she was damn well going to make up for lost time now. I sometimes wondered if she took her face off in one piece every night, like a mask. I felt sure that if I allowed Poupeh to do my make-up, I would only have to undo it all again before I left for my date so that I didn't get mistaken for a transvestite.

'If I do your hair and make-up, it will help ensure you don't look quite like yourself just in case I catch too much of your face in the pictures,' Poupeh reasoned.

She obviously wasn't going to let me get away with it.

I settled down on the pink satin-covered stool in front of Poupeh's dressing table and submitted myself to her hands. She had me turn to face her so that I couldn't see what she was doing to me until the final 'reveal'.

'I can't stand it when someone makes comments on a work in progress,' she explained.

My shoulders tensed as Poupeh picked up a purple eye pencil.

'Purple? That is not one of my colours! Don't make me look like a clown,' I pleaded.

'Are you saying that I would do that to you? I don't look like a clown, do I?'

'Well, no. But you know,' I added carefully, 'even when we were at school, Gemma and I used to look at you and wonder why you wore so much foundation when you had such flawless skin.'

'Did you really think that?' Poupeh stopped blending something unnaturally orange on to my cheeks and rocked back on her heels.

'Yes,' I said. 'And you've got really beautiful eyes. A little less mascara might actually help us to see them better.'

Poupeh grinned. 'That's a very lovely thing to hear.'

She looked happy and I found that I was glad to have made her feel that way. Even if my comments didn't seem to have had any bearing on the amount of slap she was administering to my face. I winced as she brought out that green make-up that is supposed to tone down redness but just makes people look, well, green.

'Your make-up is finished,' she announced after a final puff of powder. 'Are you ready? Ta da!' Poupeh spun me round to face the mirror. 'And I think that wearing a little more mascara is what makes your beautiful eyes stand out!'

I was wearing so much mascara that I wasn't sure I would be able to open my eyes again if I blinked before the stuff had dried, but the effect was wonderful. That purple pencil had been surprisingly effective. Poupeh had blended a butterfly wing of colour on to each of my eyelids, my cheeks were sculpted and my lips looked as though I had already spent half a day kissing. I had never worn so much make-up in my life. But it looked amazing. Poupeh was right.

'Thank you,' I said. And I meant it.

'Irresistible,' she pronounced. 'You are officially a femme fatale.'

Femme fatale. That sounded good. I felt extremely sexy in a Bond girl sort of way with my hidden mic and my perfectly applied lipstick. I gave myself a little pout in the mirror.

'Now I had better get to work on myself so that I blend into the crowd,' said Poupeh. 'What do you think I should wear?'

'Something black?' I suggested. Kyoto attracted a pretty hip crowd.

'I don't have a single black outfit in my wardrobe.'

'Of course you don't.'

'Except that hijab . . .'

'Don't wear that,' I pleaded.

Poupeh went for something pink. Surprise, surprise. She put the recording device for my mic in a matching handbag. She had a huge array of handbags that had been specially customized for her work. She showed me how this particular innocuous pink suede number had a special hole through which poked the lens of a little digital camera.

As Poupeh applied her own make-up, the curious evening started to take on a party feel. I had poured us both a glass of wine to help us settle into our roles but it felt as though we were two friends getting ready for a girls' night out. Two real friends.

I realized I was starting to like Poupeh Gharani.

45

Poupeh and I travelled towards Kyoto in the same cab, but we had the driver stop just a little way down Knightsbridge so that Poupeh could jump out and have a quick coffee in Starbucks before she completed her journey to the restaurant. That way, there was no danger of us bumping into Cavanagh on the way in and having him rumble that we were together. It was especially important since Poupeh planned to sit very close in order to get her snaps.

As it was, I was pretty sure that he would already be safely inside the restaurant when I got there. I had timed my arrival so that I was exactly ten minutes late. There's nothing worse than being first to the rendezvous if you're the girl. I hate sitting there all dressed up, knowing that everyone is looking at you and wondering whether your beau will show. Gemma used to tell me that I was being silly, that no one was interested in whether or not I was going to be stood up. I guess I was still slightly traumatized by the time my date really didn't turn up.

Of course it was Valentine's Night. I was seventeen years old. It was the first time I had been invited to dinner in a proper restaurant – Café Rouge off High Street Kensington. I spent three months' allowance on a dress from Armani. And Matthew Charlton stood me up. He spent the evening laughing about it with his friends – and his girlfriend – at Po Na Na.

I had no idea at the time that his girlfriend was Melinda Haverstock, who had suffered so much at my hands during the previous six years.

Anyway, there's another good reason to turn up slightly later than your date. The walk across the floor is an all-important part of the seduction process. There's no point wearing a fabulous dress if the man you're hoping to impress isn't going to get the full benefit of your sashay through the restaurant because you're already sitting down.

I stopped by the hostess podium just inside Kyoto's big wooden door.

'I'm here to meet Barney Cavanagh,' I told the girl.

'Oh, Barney!' she smiled broadly. Of course she knew him. He practically paid her wages single-handed. 'He's here already. Waiting for you at the bar.'

She jerked her head in his direction while she relieved me of my jacket. I spotted him at once.

Cavanagh was sitting on a high stool at the bar, seemingly mesmerized by the flames that leaped from the exotic display behind glass shelves full of spirits. He hadn't noticed me yet, giving me a good chance to take a look at him.

He was wearing a soft blue shirt tucked into a pair of dark black jeans again. Very slightly different from the ones he had been wearing the night at Frogmortons but similar enough to suggest a man who found it difficult to put an outfit together. I don't know why I found that endearing. It reminded me of Dad, I suppose. His entire wardrobe is black, white and blue. As a child, I used to check that he wasn't wearing anything that clashed before he left the house.

I let my eyes travel over the reflection of Cavanagh's face in the mirror. I liked the way his hair curled over the back of his collar too. I wanted to touch it.

Stop it. I pulled myself up short. This was not a proper date. It was a mission.

Time to get to work. I checked that the transmitting device I had tucked into my bra was still in place and turned on, then I set off on the walk across the room. But so much for my idea that I would sashay like a supermodel. The restaurant was full of real supermodels (or post-op sex-change recipients – some of them were suspiciously tall for girls) who impeded my progress by moving more closely together like a magic forest as I tried to get to Cavanagh. By the time I reached him, I was considerably less cool than I had felt as I stood at the door, both literally and psychologically. My carefully pinned-up hair was starting to fall down. Still, this crowd was a good thing, I told myself. All the better to camouflage Poupeh when she arrived to take those all-important pictures.

'I was beginning to think you'd stood me up!' Cavanagh jumped off his stool when he saw me.

'I'm only ten minutes late.'

'Ten minutes is a very long time when you've been looking forward to seeing someone all day.'

Cavanagh knew all the best lines.

'You have?'

'I have. Here, I took the liberty of ordering this for you.'

He handed me a tall glass of champagne. Good stuff. I could tell from the tiny bubbles.

'You look fabulous. Green really is your colour.'

'And blue is yours,' I commented.

Cavanagh blushed. 'I should warn you that just about my entire wardrobe is blue and black. I find it hard to know what suits me. Here. Sit down.'

He motioned me to the stool he had vacated.

'It's such a zoo in here,' he sighed. 'Perhaps we should go

someone quieter so we can get to know each other properly
without having to repeat ourselves all the time?' He got out his
mobile phone. 'I'll ring my second favourite restaurant and
see if they've got a table, if you want.'

'No,' I insisted. 'It's nice here.'

'Well, if you're sure. I suppose it gives me an excuse to lean
in close to you. Only so you can hear what I'm saying, of
course.'

He did lean in close. I felt the tickly fingers of delight at the
bottom of my spine as his breath tickled my hair.

'Oh, my hair's falling down,' I said, leaning away from him
and fiddling with my pins to get some space.

'Leave it down,' said Cavanagh. 'You've got beautiful hair.'

'Have I?'

'When someone pays you a truthful compliment you
should just say thank you.'

I blushed. But fortunately, I was distracted by the sudden
appearance of Poupeh, red-faced herself with having fought her
way through the crowds that had given me such trouble. Her
presence gave me a shot of confidence and another reminder of
why I was there. Poupeh positioned herself a few barstools
down. I gave her a surreptitious nod while Cavanagh was
turning towards the barman to tell him that we were about to
go to our table. Poupeh gave me a big wink in reply.

'More champagne. A toast to your hair!' Cavanagh said
when he turned back towards me.

Poupeh's eyes widened approvingly and I knew she was
getting a good feed from the mic pinned to my dress.

After a second glass of champagne, I felt surprisingly relaxed.
At Frogmortons Cavanagh had taken me by surprise, but that
evening at Kyoto was the culmination of a whole day of
preparation. My new dress was giving me confidence, and

glancing at my reflection in a mirror just behind Cavanagh, I was reassured that, with Poupeh's make-up, I was looking my very best.

I answered all his questions about 'Jane' with the non-chalance of a well-briefed executive at an interview for a job she already knew was hers. In fact, at one point, Cavanagh laughed that our conversation was more like the grilling he gave prospective employees. There was just one sticky moment when Cavanagh asked which school I had attended and responded when I told him that he once had an employee who had been there. Thankfully, she was ten years older than me and so I could justifiably excuse not recognizing her name.

'Brothers and sisters?' he asked.

'None,' I said. 'Only child.'

'Me too. Until I got a stepsister.'

I automatically pulled a sympathetic face.

'No. She's all right,' said Cavanagh. 'We get on really well. Didn't you ever want to have brothers and sisters? Are your parents still together?'

'I'm not answering that,' I said. All this chat was very well but none of it was incriminating. The time had come to ask some questions of my own.

'Do you have a girlfriend?'

I came straight out with it.

Cavanagh looked slightly taken aback but he answered.

'No,' he said. 'Of course I don't.' I could imagine Poupeh smiling when she heard that. 'I've been single for a while.'

'An eligible guy like you?'

'I'm picky.'

He looked me straight in the eye and I found myself blushing at the implied compliment.

'So, when did you last go out with someone?'

'What is this? Your revenge for my being so nosy? Twenty questions?'

'I'll stop at ten.'

'Thank God,' he laughed. 'OK. Let me see. My last relationship ended a year ago. When I was still out in Singapore.'

'Who was she?'

'Her name was Michelle. She was a model.'

Ah. She must have been the Siamese Twin from the *Straits Times*.

'What happened?' I asked.

'I knew that I was going to be coming back to the UK and I'm afraid that instantly brought the relationship under the microscope.'

'What does that mean?'

'Well, she said that she couldn't give up her career in Singapore and move to England with me unless I could promise her a ring. And I couldn't promise her a ring because I couldn't promise her a future.'

'I see.'

'She was a wonderful girl. I didn't want it to end. At least not then. But because I knew it would end eventually, I couldn't waste any more of her time.'

'That's very thoughtful,' I said. As it was. Either that or the well-polished spiel of a serial philanderer. 'And since her there's really been no one?'

'No one at all.'

'When you say "No one at all", do you mean absolutely no one or just that there's been no one special?'

Here was his cue to tell me that Karen meant nothing.

'I haven't even been on a date,' he persisted. 'I've been really busy since I got back from the Far East. Moving my business over here has been a lot of work.'

He clearly wasn't going to crack. I just had to hope that a straightforward denial that he was seeing anyone would be enough to convince Karen that he didn't care.

'What about you?' he asked.

I smiled into my glass with the intention of looking mysterious.

46

Had we been on a real date, I could genuinely have said there wasn't much going on with my love life. Hadn't been for quite some time. In fact, the last time I had properly kissed a guy was at the end-of-year ball for my final year at university. No one had drifted across my path that I even remotely fancied since then. Sometimes I wondered why not. Was I perhaps just not noticing them, as Karen had once suggested?

Any man who was interested in me had a lot to live up to. They say that all girls subconsciously look for someone with all their fathers' best qualities. Well, there was no subconscious about it for me and there weren't many twenty-something guys around that I thought were a patch on my Dad. Whenever I met a new guy, I tried to imagine how he would cope if he found himself widowed and alone with a baby at the tender age of twenty-one. Would he be able to juggle raising a daughter and having a brilliant career? Once I'd applied that test, the field dwindled even more dramatically.

Right then, just out of interest, I looked at Cavanagh and tried to imagine him changing a nappy. Wearing his Armani shirt. Nope. Couldn't quite see it.

'Come on, Jane. Tell me about the broken hearts you've left in your wake.'

Our food arrived, saving me from having to answer his variation on my own question. At the same time, the waitress brought a bottle of sake. Cavanagh had insisted that we drink it cold, which is, apparently, the only way to drink the good stuff. 'If a restaurant only offers warm sake,' he explained. 'It's usually because it's of a lower quality.'

'I didn't know that.'

I also didn't know that I would be expected to drink the sake from a little wooden box. When the waitress poured the ice-cold rice wine into two little crates, I had to wait for Cavanagh to take the first sip. I didn't have a clue whether to drink from one of the sides or a corner. Dad and I had always been to sushi restaurants where the sake came in little pottery cups.

'Here's to you.' He toasted me with the strange square. 'But don't think you've got away without telling me your secrets . . .'

'Here's to secrets,' I toasted. Just at that moment, a flash went off somewhere. I hoped that it was Poupeh.

'This stuff is glorious,' said Cavanagh. 'So refreshing. Deceptively so, in fact. I can't tell you the number of times I have found myself in trouble drinking sake.'

I took a sip of my sake and winced.

'Don't you like it?' Cavanagh asked.

'It's not that,' I said. 'I think I've got a splinter.'

I put the sake box down and peered at my hand. I did indeed have a splinter, right there in the softest part of my middle finger. The light in the restaurant was dim. I couldn't see how far in the splinter had managed to work itself.

'Let me have a look.'

Cavanagh took my hand and held it near to a candle, peering closely to assess the damage.

'Does it hurt?'

'Just a little.'

Then he reached into his jacket pocket and pulled out a miniature Swiss army knife.

'We'll have to amputate,' he joked, when he saw my eyes widen in horror. 'Don't worry, I'm not going to use a blade.' Instead, he pulled out the tiny pair of tweezers that fitted into the case. 'Hold still,' he whispered.

I held still and held my breath as he delicately took hold of one end of the pale blond splinter and pulled it out. I felt that little sharp sting as the wood tugged on my skin on exit. Like an insect biting. And then the splinter was gone, leaving behind just the tiniest speck of blood.

But Cavanagh still held my hand.

'How's that?'

'Thank you,' I said. 'Good job you had that penknife.'

'I subscribe to the Boy Scout motto,' he said, closing the knife with his free hand and slipping it back into his pocket.

Then he dipped his head towards my finger and kissed the tender spot better.

Flash! Flash! Poupeh was all over the gesture like a professional paparazzo. Cavanagh looked up in the direction of the light. I turned to see where his eyes were focused but Poupeh was already gone.

She had caught the moment and it was over. Cavanagh let go of my hand. Now he was suddenly businesslike again, using his chopsticks to place morsels of fish on my plate.

'We should eat this before it goes cold,' he joked as he passed me a slice of sashimi that had been presented on a bed of crushed ice.

Looking over his shoulder, I saw Poupeh slip out through the big wooden door and on to the street. She must have been confident that she had everything we needed to stitch Cavanagh up like a kipper. As they say.

*   *   *

I don't know where the time went after that but pretty soon the crowds had thinned down and the staff started hovering to make it clear that they would like to be going home too. We took the hint. Cavanagh offered me his arm as we walked towards Knightsbridge and waited for a cab.

'I had a really nice time tonight,' he said when we were outside.

'Me too.' I looked at my shoes.

'Can we do this again sometime?'

I wasn't sure what I should answer.

'Perhaps you're free on Thursday to join me to see this play I have tickets for at the Wyndham Theatre.'

'Perhaps. I ought to ring you,' I said.

He looked disappointed, but quickly plastered on that smile again.

'OK. But I'm not going to let you go until you promise me you will call. Promise on your mother's life.'

'I don't like to do that,' I said,

'I'm sorry. But, you know, Jane, I am determined to see you again. I don't think I have ever felt such an instant connection with anyone,' he told me. 'I really like you.'

'I like you too,' I said, surprisingly truthfully.

Cavanagh's smile suddenly looked much more self-assured again.

'Then why don't we just arrange to meet on Thursday night, in the lobby of the theatre at about seven-thirty? You have my number. If by the time Thursday rolls around, you've been over everything we talked about tonight and come to the conclusion that I'm just a pretentious old arse and you've no interest in seeing me ever again, I'd appreciate it if you'd give me a call before you stand me up.'

'I will,' I said. I didn't promise.

A taxi with its yellow sign aglow was heading towards us.

Cavanagh practically threw himself in front of the cab to make it stop. He opened the door for me and I climbed inside.

'Make sure this wonderful woman gets home safely,' he told the cab driver. 'I've got nothing to live for but seeing her again on Thursday night. Farewell, sweet princess!'

What a line!

47

Poupeh was waiting for me when I got home. She immediately abandoned her report on the dishonest dog-walker for a debrief on my mission.

'It went perfectly from what I heard,' she said. 'What a swine, pretending that he hasn't even been on a date since he got back from Singapore! It's always the good-looking ones. What an arrogant sod!'

'I know,' I said. 'I couldn't believe he was such a brazen liar. Did you get it all on tape?'

'Better than tape,' said Poupeh. 'We got it on digital.'

She waved the little recording device at me. 'Want to listen to this now and decide which section you want to put on a CD to send to Karen?'

'No time like the present.' I nodded eagerly and joined Poupeh at her computer. She plugged the device into a USB port with the intention of listening to my conversation through her PC speakers.

'Here goes,' she said.

Here goes nothing.

'Have you got the volume turned up?' I asked after a minute of ominous silence.

Poupeh confirmed that she had.

'Then why can't we hear anything?'

Poupeh looked from her computer screen to the device and back again. 'Oh dear,' she said eventually.

'Oh dear what?'

'I think I may have wiped it.'

I stared at her in disbelief.

'Oh, Lind-zay, I'm sorry. I'm afraid I've done this before. That's the problem with computers. It's all very quick and convenient except sometimes it's too quick and before you know it you've accidentally erased the evidence when you thought you were transferring it to the hard drive. I must remember not to do that. Why am I such a Luddite?'

I tried not to be too annoyed.

'At least we have the pictures.'

'Ah. Yes,' said Poupeh.

'I noticed the flash go off when he was kissing my finger,' I said. 'Did you get that?'

'I'm not sure.'

Poupeh plugged her digital camera into her PC and we waited while the pictures were downloaded.

'I took hundreds,' she said.

There were three.

'The battery in my camera ran out.'

I stared at the screen.

'And the flash didn't go off.'

I had soon realized that the camera flashes I had seen in the restaurant couldn't have been Poupeh's. The photographs she was showing me could have been photographs of a bat in the night sky. I could see nothing.

'There's bound to be one we could use.'

Poupeh began to play with the photo settings. But it was no use. The two figures could have been anybody. Male or female. Black or white. I could have been having dinner with Lenny Henry or Liberace for all you could tell from this photograph. No amount of digital tweaking gave us a useful image.

'Karen might recognize the shape of Cavanagh's head,' Poupeh suggested.

'These are useless,' I sighed.

Poupeh had to agree.

'The entire evening was a total waste of time.'

'At least you got to eat sushi!' said Poupeh. 'I was starving.'

'But we're no closer to having anything that will split Cavanagh and Karen up as a result. We can't send her any of these shots. We've got no recording of him telling me he's not seeing anyone.'

'All is not lost,' said Poupeh.

'You always say that,' I complained. 'Your optimism really is the most irritating thing about you.'

Poupeh looked slightly crestfallen.

'I'm sorry,' I said. 'I don't think I meant to say that. But what are we really going to do next?'

'Try to get the photos and a recording somewhere else. Did he suggest another date?'

'The theatre. Thursday night.'

'See, I knew all is not lost. You're going to the theatre. And I will make sure I get more batteries for my camera.'

So I agreed that I would go out with Cavanagh again. Purely for the sake of the mission, as I told Poupeh.

But as I lay in bed that night, I couldn't help replaying some of that evening's conversation in a not altogether disinterested way.

If I hadn't known better, I would have said that Cavanagh was very interested in me and not just because he had yet to see me with my clothes off. He gave the impression of being the very best kind of date. He had listened intently to everything I said. He had asked interested questions. He had been chivalrous to a fault, opening doors, pulling out my chair, even standing up when I left the table to go to the ladies' room. If I were an alien anthropologist regarding our interactions from outer space, I would have been convinced that we were headed for a long and happy romance. He was the perfect gentleman.

Except that he was someone else's perfect gentleman.

With that in mind, I dug out Karen's work timetable. I had called her gym that week using several different accents in an attempt to find out when she would be there. I saw to my surprise that she wasn't working late that Thursday night. How brazen Cavanagh was! Would he get ready for our date in front of her? Would he ask her to help him choose a tie? How would he explain his arrangements for that night? Would he tell her that he was entertaining 'a client'?

Totally unbidden, the memory of Cavanagh kissing my finger after he removed the splinter popped into my head. He knew all the moves.

Only because he was a cad!

Ah well. Good job. I was going to save Karen from any heartache he might be storing up for her.

Soon it was Thursday. Once again, Poupeh helped me choose my outfit for the date. I managed to convince her that my cream linen trousers and a matching off-the-shoulder top would work.

Poupeh approved. Sort of.

'It is very classy. But men prefer pink,' she assured me. 'Shall I do your make-up?'

Once again she transformed me into 'not at all plain Jane'. And then I let her persuade me to wrap a pink scarf around my neck. I could always take it off when she wasn't looking and claim it had made me itchy if she asked.

'Now, you know where we're going to be this evening?' I asked her.

Poupeh recited the name and address of the theatre. We had decided that she would be there for the end of the performance, at which time I would endeavour to emerge with my arm linked through Cavanagh's and Poupeh would snap us while I planted a kiss of thanks on his cheek.

'On his mouth,' said Poupeh.

'OK,' I said with a pained expression on my face. 'On his mouth.'

To make sure that Poupeh got the perfect angle, she and I had actually done a walk-through the day before. Poupeh was going to position herself in the doorway of the Chinese restaurant on the opposite side of the road. I had to make sure that Cavanagh and I emerged from the most westerly doorway and that I was standing on his left as we did so. That way, Poupeh would get the back of my head and his face, as we needed.

Meanwhile, I was also going to be wired again. Though obviously that wouldn't be terribly useful until the interval.

I got a taxi to the theatre. On the way there I ran through the routine and wondered whether it would seem natural for me to wind my arm through Cavanagh's at the end of the play. Of course it would. He had offered me his arm on the way out of Kyoto. I couldn't help smiling at the memory.

Was I was looking forward to that evening? I told myself that if anything I was looking forward to the chance to see a fading Hollywood actor taking to the London stage. Nothing to do with the company. Nothing at all.

48

Cavanagh was already at the theatre when I arrived. He was leaning against a wall in the lobby with what was clearly *studied* nonchalance. I knew he was only pretending to read his programme because in the few seconds it took for me to reach him, I noticed him scan the crowd for me several times. When he saw me, he broke into a smile.

'I was beginning to think you wouldn't come,' he said.

'I'm only two minutes late,' I protested.

'Five,' he said, showing me his watch. 'You're clearly perpetually tardy. But you're here now.'

He went to kiss me, aiming straight for my mouth. I instinctively offered him my cheek. We clashed noses.

'Sorry,' we chimed as one.

'Jinx,' said Cavanagh.

It seemed a geeky thing for such a smooth guy to say.

'We should go on in.'

The bell that heralded the start of the performance was already ringing. Cavanagh took me by the elbow and guided me towards our seats. They were, of course, the best in the house, close enough to the stage so that we would be able to see the actors sweat, but not so close that we might get wet if someone sweaty made a grand hair-tossing gesture. Cavanagh helped me slip my jacket off and insisted we swap places when a very tall chap with an unusually big head sat down in the previously empty seat in front of me.

The theatre was absolutely packed. I had guessed that it would be. The star of the show had been the love interest in a long-running American soap and as such was a guaranteed crowd-puller. A quick glance around the crowd told me that there were several people there who would have turned up to see him recite from a shopping list.

The house lights dipped and the chattering crowd quietened like starlings at nightfall.

'You can hold my hand if you get scared.' Cavanagh's whisper was the last thing I heard before the music began.

I didn't think I was likely to be scared but the play did start on a somewhat dramatic note. It was set in a mental hospital and the opening scene took place in the middle of a storm. A crack of stage thunder made me jump but I kept my hands firmly in my lap and didn't even look at Cavanagh, though from the corner of my eye, I could tell that he was looking at me to see how I was reacting.

When the star lumbered on-stage, the audience erupted in spontaneous applause. Cavanagh clapped too. And when he'd finished clapping, he put his hand back down on the arm-rest that I had assumed belonged to my seat.

For the rest of the first half of the play, I kept my hands in my lap and my eyes half on the stage and half on Cavanagh's encroaching fingers. Cavanagh's hand didn't move. I wondered if he was aware that he was in my space. It was incredibly distracting.

At the interval, we went to the bar and Cavanagh retrieved the two glasses of champagne that he had already ordered.

'Champagne again. How very celebratory!' I commented.

'You turned up. That's something to celebrate.'

We talked politely about the week that had passed. And about the play. Which was terrible.

'Not that great,' said Cavanagh. 'Perhaps we should bail out now.'

'No,' I insisted. 'We should watch to the end.'

Of course I was thinking of Poupeh.

'You're right,' Cavanagh conceded. 'It might get better.'

I'm not sure if the play did get better after that. I have to admit that my mind wasn't really on the action that was taking place on stage.

When we got back into the auditorium, I decided that I would stake my claim to the arm-rest first. I let my hand rest there, all casually. Cavanagh's hand was on his own arm-rest and it stayed there for at least half an hour as though my surreptitious glances were pinning it there. Then, on stage, an actor cracked a joke that had the whole theatre in uproar. Cavanagh slapped his arm-rest in glee, and brought his hand down to rest on top of mine.

I looked at him from the corner of my eye. He was still looking straight ahead at the stage. But slowly his fingers moved so that they wrapped around my own. Entwined with them in fact. I felt my heart beat just a little faster.

It wasn't long before the curtains came down for the final time. The house lights came up. I pulled my hand away in order to clap. And to wipe my forehead.

'What did you think?'

I wouldn't be able to answer detailed questions on the second half, so I just told him, 'I'm glad we stayed.' Then I rubbed my nose and caught the scent of his aftershave on my hand and after that I was so discombobulated that I didn't notice we were headed for the wrong exit until we were outside the back of the theatre.

*   *   *

'Where are we?' I must have seemed a little distressed as I registered that Cavanagh had led me from the theatre by a fire exit and we were standing on a completely different street from the one where Poupeh and her heretofore not-terribly-trusty camera would be waiting for us to emerge.

'Always best to leave by the back door,' said Cavanagh. 'The West End is a zoo at this time of night. I hate getting stuck in that crush by the front entrance.'

'But . . .' I began.

'What's the matter?'

I could hardly tell him, could I? 'Nothing,' I replied.

'I thought we might get a bite to eat now. Is that OK with you? You haven't got to be anywhere else?'

I did have somewhere to be. I imagined Poupeh waiting outside the front of the theatre. I couldn't leave her there.

'I've got to go,' I said. 'I've got an early meeting with a client in the morning.'

'You're kidding,' said Cavanagh.

'I wish I was.'

'It's not even ten o'clock.'

'I need a lot of sleep.'

'Well, OK. At least let me drive you home. My car is parked over . . .'

'It's all right,' I interrupted. 'There's a taxi.'

'But my car is just over there.'

'No,' I said. 'Brixton is totally out of your way.'

'I think you're worth going out of my way for.'

'I'll get a cab,' I told him. 'It will take you hours to get all the way down to South London and back. I'd feel too guilty. Look, there's another cab.' I flagged an empty one down. The cabbie mounted the pavement just in front of us.

'Jane,' Cavanagh pleaded. 'I hate seeing you drive off in a taxi. Let me take you home.'

'Next time,' I promised, jumping into the cab so quickly that he didn't have time to kiss me goodbye.

'Does that mean I can see you again?' Cavanagh yelled after us.

I sort of nodded as I waved.

'Drive as though you're heading towards Brixton,' I told the driver. 'Then, when he's out of sight, turn around and head for the front of the theatre.'

Poupeh was still standing in the doorway of the Chinese restaurant, camera still poised as the crowd exiting the theatre dwindled to nothing. We picked her up and headed back to mission control for more mint tea and a debrief.

'At least I got a photo of Joanna Lumley,' said Poupeh. 'Did you know she was at the theatre tonight?'

49

I wasn't in the mood to be impressed by Poupeh's paparazzi shots of Joanna Lumley. I was furious with Cavanagh for having distracted me from my plan and even more furious with myself when I realized that I had forgotten to turn my wire on during the interval when Cavanagh said a couple of things that might have been incriminating.

How hard could it possibly be to get something on tape or a couple of decent photos of Cavanagh out on the town with a woman who most definitely wasn't his girlfriend? That night at the theatre it was almost as though he had some sixth sense about what was going on as he steered me towards the back door.

I was starting to get impatient.

'Sometimes these things take longer than you would expect,' said Poupeh. 'I think you should see him again. We may be just one more date away from a breakthrough. Do you think you could handle that?'

I had to admit that my assignment wasn't as arduous as most of Poupeh's jobs seemed to be. Having given the dog-owner enough evidence to confront the short-changing dog-walker, Poupeh had just taken on an assignment that would require her to spend a week working undercover in a kebab restaurant to find out who was fiddling the takings. So far, my mission had required me to go to the theatre and one of the best sushi restaurants in town with a very interesting companion.

Just one more date.

I had nothing better to do.

When I called Cavanagh this time he tried a new tactic.

'This time I'm coming to you,' he said. 'I can't have you coming north of the river to see me all the time. Where's your house? I'll pick you up in my car.'

'I'd rather meet you somewhere,' I said quickly. 'My house is a mess.'

'There's no need to tidy up on my behalf.'

'I know. It's just that I share with another girl and she's so nosy. I don't want to put you through having to meet her yet.'

'Are you sure that it's not that you think she wouldn't like me? That I'd embarrass you?' Cavanagh teased.

'No. I'm sure she would like you.'

'So, where shall I meet you? Are there any restaurants you like to go to down there where taxis never venture?'

Oh, bugger. As far as I could remember, I had never eaten at a restaurant south of the river in my life. Then, thank goodness, I remembered the name of a place I had been to for an old schoolfriend's eighteenth birthday party. I hoped it still existed.

'Buchans?' I suggested.

'I know it,' said Cavanagh. 'I was there just a couple of weeks ago.'

'You were?'

'Absolutely. It's by Battersea Bridge, isn't it?'

'That's the one,' I said. 'Battersea Bridge . . .'

'Road,' Cavanagh finished the sentence for me. 'Eight o'clock.'

'Sounds ideal.'

If I could find the bloody place.

*   *   *

I called ahead and asked for detailed cab instructions from Hampstead to the godforsaken south. You might have thought I was planning a trip down the Amazon. Poupeh and I left her flat with forty-five minutes to spare for the twenty-minute journey. She dropped me off on the wrong side of Battersea Bridge before she went in search of a parking spot.

It was a good job I hadn't let her drop me off right in front of the restaurant. The waiter led me to a seat at the window and from there I saw the distinctive green flash as Cavanagh whizzed by in search of a parking place, almost fifteen minutes before we were actually due to meet. Poupeh passed by the window a few seconds later. Her Smart Car was easy to find a place for. She entered the restaurant and took a seat at a table behind me long before Cavanagh turned up.

Seeing Cavanagh's Porsche pass by, I felt a smile settle on my mouth at the knowledge that he hadn't stood me up. There was no doubt about it. I was actually looking forward to seeing him.

It took him a full twenty minutes to find somewhere to leave his car. When he walked into the restaurant he looked slightly panicked. That expression was quickly replaced by a beam when he saw me.

'I can't believe I'm so late. I thought you might have given up on me.'

This time we managed to coordinate our kiss so that no one risked a broken nose.

'I'd forgotten how nice this place is. Do you come here often?' he asked.

'Oh yes,' I lied. 'All the time.'

While Cavanagh perused the menu I excused myself to the ladies' room. Poupeh followed at a discreet distance.

*   *   *

'How's the angle from where you're sitting?' I asked.

'Perfect,' she told me. 'Let's hope this works.'

That night, Poupeh was going to be using a hidden camera whose lens poked out through one of her button-holes. The restaurant was too small for her to risk using her ordinary digital SLR.

'Isn't the lens a bit obstructed by your cleavage?' I suggested.

Poupeh demonstrated how she would lean back in her chair so that her boobs didn't get in the way.

'All we need now is for you to get lovey-dovey,' she said. 'What are the chances?'

Poupeh needn't have worried about my ability to entice Cavanagh from across the table. Before long, Cavanagh was encroaching on my personal space again.

It was the stuff of all those articles on body language that Gemma and I had devoured when we were still at school and trying to work out how on earth you tell if somebody likes you. While we waited for the food to arrive, I picked up the matchbox from the ashtray and turned it over a couple of times. I put it down. Cavanagh picked the matchbox up straightaway and started to play with it himself. I leaned my head on one hand. Cavanagh followed suit. He was echoing me. A sure sign. Or was I in fact echoing him?

When our food came, Cavanagh offered me a bite of his main course, insisting on feeding me himself rather than letting me take his fork. Then, when the plates had been taken away, he asked for a closer look at the ring I was wearing on the little finger of my right hand. He held my hand gently in both of his while he peered at it.

All the time, Poupeh was stretching back in her chair,

looking a little bit demented but hopefully getting everything on camera while I got all our conversation on my wire.

'Pudding?' Cavanagh suggested.

He ordered one bowl of ice cream and two spoons. I thought I heard Poupeh's boob-camera click as Cavanagh spooned the first bite into my mouth.

When the meal was over. Cavanagh paid the bill again. Insisted on it.

'Trust me,' he said. 'When you get that contract to refit the Metropolitan Hotel, the drinks will be on you.'

And then we were outside the restaurant.

But it was still only half past nine.

'Well, thank you for a lovely evening,' I said.

'You're not going alrcady. Isn't thcre somc fabulous secret cocktail bar around here that you can take me to?'

'It's not that kind of area,' I said. Really, I had no idea whether it was that kind of area or not. For all I knew, the best cocktail bar in the whole of London town might have been within two minutes' walking distance.

'Pity. It's such a beautiful night. Perhaps we should go for a walk.'

'Around here? Where?'

'Er,' Cavanagh nodded his head behind him. 'By the river? To Battersea Park?'

Forget cocktail bars, we were within two minutes' walking distance of one of the most beautiful parks in London.

'We can walk along the river from here. I can show you the building where I thought about buying an apartment when I first got back to London.'

From where we were standing, he pointed out the back of an enormous building that looked like a giant steel-clad bubble. I started to tell him that the place where he had chosen to live was altogether more elegant but remembered just in time that I wasn't supposed to know he lived in Onslow Gardens and had works by some of the major contemporary British artists on his walls.

'Shall we go?'

He offered me his arm.

'Hold on a sec,' I said. 'I think I might have left something in the restaurant.'

I dashed back inside. Poupeh was just paying her bill. I gestured that she should follow me to the toilets just in case Cavanagh glanced in through the big plate-glass windows at the front of the restaurant and caught us talking.

'He's asked me to go for a walk with him,' I told her.

'I heard. You should go.'

'Should I?'

'Yes. I'll follow you for a while. Take a few more snaps. Though try not to walk too quickly, will you? I'm feeling rather stuffed. Good food here.'

So Cavanagh and I set off on our walk along the riverside path. It was busy with people enjoying the long summer evening. On the balconies of the enormous new apartment blocks that had sprung up along the river over the past few years, residents enjoyed the little bit of outside space and the views that they had paid so much for. Roller-bladers weaved in and out of the promenading pedestrians. London felt almost continental.

'Reminds me of Paris,' said Cavanagh. 'Have you been to Paris?'

'Not lately,' I said. 'At least, not as a grown-up.'

My last visit to Paris had been on a school trip while Dad was still engaged to Trisha. Dad had planned to take advantage of my being away to take Trisha to a hotel in the

Cotswolds, but I had to come home early – suspected appendicitis again – and they didn't get away.

'I'll take you to Paris,' said Cavanagh.

'That sounds good,' I said.

It was a nice fantasy.

Cavanagh offered me his arm again and I linked mine through it. As we walked, I wondered for how long Poupeh was intending to trail us with her camera. It was already starting to get dark and as far as I knew, her boob-cam didn't have a flash. I glanced behind whenever I could but didn't see her. She was very good at this trailing thing. Either that or she had gone back to the flat already.

Cavanagh and I reached the park and descended into the shade of the trees. We kept to the river side and soon reached the Buddhist temple – the beautiful white and gold monstrosity that has broken up what was once the longest undeveloped stretch of riverside in London.

'I don't know if I like it,' I admitted. 'It looks sort of out of place here.'

'I love it,' said Cavanagh. 'And I love that it is so unexpected. Just like you.'

'What does that mean?' I asked him.

'Well, I never expected to meet someone so enchanting in a dive like Frogmortons.'

'That place is full of gorgeous women.'

'And they all look exactly the same. You seemed very exotic compared to all the Brompton Blondes.'

'I'm a natural blonde,' I reminded him.

'Exactly,' he laughed. 'I like that. You know, Jane, you're so mysterious.'

'Hardly.'

'No, you are. All this insistence on not meeting at your place and not letting me take you home. I'm beginning to think you don't live with another girl at all. You've got a husband. Or a boyfriend at the very least.'

I couldn't help laughing at that.

'So?' he said.

'What?'

'Are you secretly married?'

'Of course I'm not.'

'Do you have a boyfriend?'

'No.'

'Do you want to have one?' he smiled.

'I don't know. Anyway,' I said, 'you're not the only one being mysterious about his home life. I don't know where you live. How do I know you haven't got a wife? Or a girlfriend?'

'I told you I don't. I wouldn't be here if I did.'

He looked me straight in the eye as he said that. A very honest gesture if I hadn't known otherwise. Poupeh had given me enough coaching for me to know that the very best liars make sure they are practised at body language. Cavanagh doubtless knew that direct eye contact is usually taken to mean that someone has nothing to hide. It isn't that easy to fake. Hell, I'd done it enough times myself.

'So why don't you invite me back to your place right now?' he asked.

'On our third date? What kind of a girl do you think I am?'

'A fabulous one?' he tried.

We continued to walk along the Embankment. The evening was so still and balmy, we could actually hear when Big Ben started to strike eleven.

Eleven? 'I've got to go,' I said. I had promised Poupeh that I would check in with her at half past ten.

'Who are you? Cinderella? It's only eleven o'clock.'

'I've just got to go,' I insisted.

We had walked right through the park and reached the road by Chelsea Bridge. I quickly climbed the steps. Cavanagh was close behind me.

'Come on, Jane. What's with all this dramatic rushing off? I'm starting to think you don't really like me.'

I started to trot across Chelsea Bridge. It's the next bridge east from Albert Bridge, which is the one where all London romances begin in the movies – the pretty one. Chelsea Bridge isn't nearly so delicate. It's rusty red to Albert Bridge's pink and white and there's always way too much traffic on Chelsea Bridge for a romantic comedy moment. My explanation that I had to get up for work early in the morning was drowned out by three 137 buses passing in convoy, as buses do.

'But you're going in the wrong direction.' Cavanagh was confused. 'You live south of the river.'

'Easier to catch a taxi from the other side,' I said quickly as I realized my mistake.

'Wait,' he said. He grabbed my hand. 'You don't need a cab. Jane, this is ridiculous. I'm not letting another evening end with you jumping into the taxi like you're afraid you're going to turn into a pumpkin if you stay a second longer. Or if I kiss you.'

If he kissed me? I thought that's what he said. A Triumph Daytona was passing at exactly the wrong time. I stopped looking for a cab for a moment. I'm not sure why.

'What did you just say?' I had to ask.

He didn't repeat himself. He just did it. Cavanagh didn't have to pull hard to bring me towards him. I was like a yo-yo rewinding into his hand. And then he wrapped his arms right around me so that I was pressed against his chest and my face had nowhere to be but directly in front of his. Nose to nose.

Oh, God.

I closed my eyes.
And it happened.

Cavanagh's kiss totally took me by surprise. It wasn't exactly the fact that he had kissed me – the whole idea, after all had been to make him fall for me and commit an indiscretion that Poupeh could commit to film – but that in the few seconds between the moment I realized what he was intending to do and the moment his lips first brushed against mine, I had reacted in such a dizzy manner.

I had intended all along to retain the sangfroid of a professional honey-trapper, to remain as cold and detached as Wendy had been. Instead, when he took my hand, I found my heart speeding up to the point where I could hear my pulse inside my head and thought I might faint if he didn't do the deed before the pressure blew the top of my head off. The world around us seemed to blur and recede until there was nothing left but us, me and Cavanagh, in a pool of light that we ourselves were generating.

Even the traffic disappeared. Although I have no doubt that the constant stream of four-by-fours and double-deckers continued, I couldn't hear anything but the rush of my blood and the sound of our breathing, and dirty old Chelsea Bridge suddenly didn't seem the poor cousin to Albert Bridge's wedding-cake beauty after all.

Cavanagh had tasted minty. He must have slipped himself a Smint or something on the walk from the restaurant. I don't know why I found that touching. I suppose it suggested a slight insecurity that I really didn't expect from the kind of guy who was photographed squiring models to exclusive cocktail parties.

And it was such a gentlemanly kiss. He didn't force his tongue into my mouth and yet there was still enough passion behind it to disturb the flock of butterflies that hadn't moved from the bottom of my stomach for a very long time. It was soft and tender and yet so full of intent. If a picture is worth a thousand words, then I had just discovered that a kiss could say even more. I don't think I had ever been kissed so well.

When we finally pulled apart, Cavanagh was gazing at me with a look I would have captioned 'love' had I seen it photographed in a magazine. I gazed back.

'I really do have to go!'

A squeal of brakes on the other side of the road woke me up and the second Cavanagh loosened his grasp on my waist I ran away again.

'Jane!' he shouted after me.

I was already hailing a cab.

'Jane, you are a nutter!' said Cavanagh.

'Where to, love?' the taxi driver asked.

'Hampstead,' I told him. Completely forgetting that I was supposed to be living on the other side of the river.

'Jane, you better call me!'

As the cab pulled away, I glanced back to see Cavanagh still standing on the spot where he had kissed me. He gave a Gallic shrug and shook his head, then started to walk back west.

In the taxi on the way back to Poupeh's house, I found myself listening closely to the lyrics of a Celine Dion song.

It had been a very serious kiss indeed.

50

'I got some fantastic pictures,' said Poupeh as soon as I walked into the flat.

There had been no comedy cock-ups this time. Poupeh's camera had worked perfectly. She had already printed the pictures and laid them out on the dining table for my perusal. 'This one is particularly good.' She pointed out a shot she had taken in the restaurant with her boob-cam. 'You can see his face really well but you're pretty much unrecognizable in the shadows.'

'Great,' I said faintly as I turned from the table and hung up my jacket on the coat hill.

'But I think this is the one you should send.'

Poupeh pushed a different photograph towards me. I picked it up. Cavanagh's face was perfectly illuminated in the street light. Poupeh hadn't gone straight home from the restaurant after all, because this was a photograph of me and Cavanagh on the bridge.

'Pretty good work, eh?'

She had captured the split second before we kissed. Cavanagh's hands were spread on my back. My face was tilted upwards towards his but mostly obscured. However, I didn't have to be able to see my expression to know what it had been. Seeing that second captured in a photograph, a feeling of melting warmth spread through me as it had done in the very moment.

'I didn't know you were still following us,' I said.

'Good job I did, eh? I was hiding in the bushes by the entrance to the park. I had my SLR with the telephoto lens in my handbag. I got three clear shots before I was disturbed by somebody's Labrador.'

'You're bloody good at stalking,' I commented.

'Thank you. I don't think Karen can argue with the evidence here,' Poupeh continued. 'Everything else could be interpreted as Cavanagh being flirtatious with a potential client. The hand-holding. The feeding you from his plate. But this . . . Look at where his hands are positioned. Look at the expression in his eyes.'

I looked. He looked entranced. I could hardly believe he had really been directing that gaze at me.

'This time we've got him bang to rights,' said Poupeh with a faint note of triumph in her voice. 'Much more effective than a CD of your conversation, I think. You could post these pictures tomorrow morning and Karen could be on a date with your Dad by Monday night.'

I nodded.

'And you could be back home on Tuesday. Not that I'm keen to get rid of you or anything,' she added quickly. 'I do like having someone around the flat. Anyway, that's my part of the mission accomplished. The rest I'll leave to you.'

Poupeh gathered up the rest of the photos, plucked the one I had been holding out of my hand and put all of them back into a big brown envelope. Then she handed the brown envelope to me.

'Have to say, you guys looked pretty passionate out there. Talk about dedication to your mission.'

'Well,' I admitted. 'It was nice to be kissed.'

'Was he good?'

'He was excellent.'

'He's well practised.'

'I haven't been kissed like that in a long time,' I sighed.

Poupeh must have noticed my slightly wistful gaze.

'You know,' she said. 'I find it incredible that you don't have a boyfriend. You're beautiful, you're funny, you were very popular at school.'

'Only because people were afraid not to be my friend,' I said.

'Not just because of that,' said Poupeh. 'You played some great practical jokes.'

I cringed inwardly at the thought of some of the practical jokes I had played on her. Not just the love letter to Miss Hobson. A particularly memorable one was filling her trainers with quick-setting jelly.

'Anyway, I'm surprised you haven't been snapped up.'

'I'm surprised too,' I said flatly.

'I think it's because you're afraid of being alone,' Poupeh announced.

'That doesn't make any sense!' I snorted. 'If I was afraid of being alone, I'd never be out of a relationship. I can manage perfectly well without anyone.'

'Sure. Most people can. Manage, that is. It's the ultimate low-risk strategy.'

'What do you mean by that?'

'Falling in love with someone gives them the power to hurt you. When I say that you're afraid of being alone, I suppose that more specifically, I think you're afraid of being left alone. You haven't opened your heart up to anyone because you're frightened of the hole they would leave if they went away again. I can sort of understand it. Because of what happened with your mother, you know only too well that love isn't enough to keep people with us for ever.'

'What happened with Mum was different. The reason why

I haven't shacked up with anyone is because I haven't met anyone who lives up to my standards.'

'I don't think you'd recognize someone who did,' said Poupeh.

'Poupeh,' I said. 'You really do talk some crap.'

But Poupeh was right about one thing that night. At last we had everything we needed to blow Karen and Cavanagh apart. So why wasn't I feeling happier?

In the silence of the spare room, I got the photos out again. I looked at them in chronological order and found myself reliving the events of the evening as I flipped through the blurry boob-cam shots and the clearer ones Poupeh had taken with her SLR.

Poupeh had taken plenty of pictures that evening. Everything had been captured for posterity. As I saw a photo of Barney walking into Buchans, looking so out of breath and flustered, I remembered the kiss on the cheek he had given me when he arrived at the restaurant. A picture of us poring over our menus reminded me of the lame joke he had made as we waited for our food to arrive.

'Two goldfish in a tank,' he began. 'One of them says to the other one, "How do you drive this thing?"'

I remembered the way he had given me a piece of his fish to taste, insisting that he fed me though I protested that I didn't trust him enough to be sure he wouldn't get hollandaise all over my nose.

And there we were eating icecream. I looked as though I was laughing. What had he been saying to me then? Ah yes, he was telling me about the hideous fate of his first pet hamster, whirled to oblivion from a makeshift 'Wheel of Death' fashioned from an upturned open umbrella.

There we were in the park. I was tucking my hair behind

my ear. Probably blushing. Barney must have just paid me a compliment.

And there we were on the bridge again.

I remembered every moment captured in those frames . . .

Without telling Poupeh anything about it, I made arrangements to meet Barney just one more time.

51

I don't know what I was thinking. I had entered into my bizarre acquaintanceship with Barney with the sole purpose of breaking up his relationship with Karen. Now I had the means to complete my mission but I still felt compelled to see him just one more time. To see him, and, if I'm honest, to kiss him.

I told myself that seeing Barney again was just like having one last bite of chocolate ice cream before you give it up for Lent. There was no harm to it if I intended to be good for ever after . . . But that kiss. Something had changed in me when Barney kissed me. A part of myself that I hadn't taken any notice of for years – not since my last proto-relationship was felled by Karen in that mini-dress distracting my date from my far less considerable charms – was suddenly awake again and stretching its limbs. My body was telling me to go for it, get as much as I could, because it might be a long, long time before I met anyone else I felt like kissing again.

So the following Friday night at seven o'clock, I was waiting for Barney and his Porsche outside South Kensington tube station exactly as promised.

'Jump in,' he said. 'We've got a bit of a drive ahead.'

I knew that he had been planning a surprise, but when he said a 'bit of a drive', I thought perhaps we were going at most as far as Putney. I didn't expect that we would soon be out of

London and racing along the A40 in the direction of Oxford.
Racing was the word. On the motorway, Barney really let the
Porsche do its worst. We stayed in the fast lane all the way.
But I didn't feel unsafe with him behind the wheel.

'Where are we going?' I asked.

I suspected that we might be heading for Le Manoir Aux
Quat' Saisons. It was the only restaurant of any reputation I
knew outside the M25. 'Le Manoir?' I guessed.

'No. Somewhere much better than that.'

'Is there such a place?'

An hour later, we passed signs for Woodstock. I knew there
were some good gastro-pubs there, but that wasn't our
destination either. We shot through village after village,
passing plenty of places where we might at least have got a
cheese sandwich and a pint. I was starting to get hungry and
the sky was already beginning to turn pink when Barney
finally pulled the car to a halt by the side of a country road.

We had stopped right in the middle of nowhere. I could see
no Michelin-starred establishment on the horizon. Not even
one of those kebab vans that catered for the truckers. Perhaps
we had just stopped so that Barney could check the map.

No. He got out of the car and came around to let me out
too.

'We're here,' he said.

'Where's here?'

'Seconds away from the most perfect view in the world.'

Now he waved his arm in the direction of the fields to either
side of us.

'Come on.'

'In these shoes?'

I was wearing kitten heels.

'I don't think so. How about in these?'

He propped open the trunk of the car to reveal a picnic

basket and two sets of wellington boots. One huge green pair, for him. One brightly coloured and girl-sized – Karen-sized? – that were presumably for me.

'Put these on,' he instructed.

I took the wellies from him and surreptitiously turned them over so I could get a look at the soles. These boots had never seen the outside of a shoe shop. So they were new. But that didn't mean to say they hadn't been bought for someone else.

'Are they the right size?' he asked. 'I had to try and guess what size feet you have by asking my, er, sister. She's about the same height as you.'

His sister?

'I didn't know you had a sister.'

'You know. My stepsister. I just don't like to call her that. Come on,' he changed the subject, 'you sit on the bonnet of the car and I'll help get these boots on.' He sat me on the bonnet of his Porsche and slipped my kitten heels off with incredible reverence. I was reminded of holidays with Dad and the way he would sit me on the boot of the car while he washed sand off my feet. 'Do they fit?' Barney asked when I jumped down to get my feet properly inside the wellies.

'They'll do,' I said. 'We haven't got to go far, have we?'

'Just over this gate.'

He threw the basket over and clambered up himself. He held out his hand to me.

I was a little bit worried by the gate. It wasn't just my shoes that were impractical. I had teamed the kitten heels with a knee-length skirt that really didn't have much kick in it. I just couldn't see how I was going to be able to get my leg over that bar.

'Hitch your skirt up, silly,' Barney said to me then. His eyes twinkled as he added, 'Show me some of those fabulous thighs.'

After that, it was a wonder I didn't fall face first into the mud on the other side.

'OK. You just look at the view for a moment while I get this set up.'

Barney opened the picnic basket and pulled out a blanket that he flourished like a matador before allowing it to settle on the only perfectly flat piece of ground in the field. He motioned for me to sit down while he set about getting out the picnic. Three Tupperware boxes of diminishing size contained the most delicately cut sandwiches I had ever seen and four small but perfectly formed scones already dripping with jam and cream.

'Where did you buy this lot from?' I asked. 'I want the name of your deli.'

'The "deli" is Sainsburys. I will have you know that I made these sandwiches myself. I even sliced the bread.'

After the sandwiches, he brought out a bottle of sparkling water. Some elderflower cordial. And, of course, the requisite bottle of champagne.

'Still cold,' he said, holding its bottom. 'Here.'

He handed me two perfect crystal flutes.

'You love your bubbly,' I said.

'Always something to celebrate with you.'

We were just in time to catch the best of the sunset. In the darkening sky, starlings wheeled in groups so large and dense they looked like swarms of bees.

'Horrible birds,' said Barney. 'But they always put on quite a spectacle at sunset. This is a great place to see them.'

'You've been here before.'

'When I was a kid,' he said. 'And as a teenager, drinking cider with my friends.'

'But you're telling me you've never been here with one girl and two glasses of champagne.'

'That's exactly what I'm telling you,' he smiled. 'Here's to you. The first girl I've kissed in this field.'

He clinked his glass against mine and simultaneously planted a kiss on my lips. It was the first time we had kissed properly since the Bridge. When I got into the car, we'd done a rather awkward 'mwah mwah' over the gear-stick. My imagination, remembering that kiss on Chelsea Bridge, hadn't run as wild as I suspected. He was good. Even with just half a glass of champagne inside me as opposed to the half bottle of wine I drank at Buchans that night, I could tell that much.

'I have been waiting all day for that,' he said.

'So have I,' I told him. I couldn't help myself.

'Now let's watch the sun go down.'

It happened surprisingly quickly. The starlings stopped their dizzy swirling about the sky and seemed to pour, like rice grains from a bowl, into the reed beds where they would spend the night. Almost simultaneously, the sun slipped behind the trees on the far side of the valley. For a short while, the sky continued to glow as though lit by a fallen flare. But then the darkness started to creep in behind us and the stars began to appear, one by one, as though an unseen hand was turning them on individually.

I hadn't spent an evening watching the sun go down for a long time. There aren't many places in London where you can see a decent sunset. On Ibiza, I had been too consumed with my own misery really to notice the way that even the worst day can end as beautifully as a Turner painting. I was filled with a feeling of such calm, such gratitude for that moment. For being in a field, for watching the sun go down with a glass of champagne in my hand, for being with Barney . . .

He squeezed my hand. I had to say something stupid.

★   ★   ★

'So I suppose this is the point in the evening where we lie on our backs and you start to tell me about the constellations,' I said to break the silence.

'Nope,' said Barney. 'I know nothing about the stars.'

'Does anybody? I thought you guys just had a book of star facts to reel out to impress chicks and get them into vulnerable positions?'

'How can someone so pretty be so cynical? I thought I might sing to you instead.'

'That other well-known boy trick.'

'Well, it usually works,' he admitted. With that, he lay back on the blanket and pulled me backwards so that I lay beside him. He wove his fingers between mine and began.

I couldn't believe it when he started to sing one of my favourite songs, 'What Are You Doing for the Rest of Your Life?' An old Sinatra tune that Dad often played when I was a girl. Barney's voice stayed perfectly true to the lilting melody. Even though he was lying on his back, and thus not in a particularly good singing position, his voice came out clear and strong.

'That's a lovely song,' I said when he finished.

'I'll sing it again. If you'll dance.'

'I'll dance,' I said.

He got to his feet and pulled me up after him. I was a little giddy from the champagne and he had to hold me tight against him to stop me from stumbling. But even when I had found my balance, he didn't loosen his hold on me at all. He started to sing again and we swayed between the cowpats, as graceful as it is possible to be in a pair of too-big wellington boots.

'You dance beautifully,' he told me.

'You lead so well,' I replied.

We danced our way through another round of '*What are*

you doing . . .' After that, he sang 'Moon River' and 'The Way You Look Tonight'. My own personal favourite. It never fails to make me cry. And it didn't fail that time.

'Are you all right?' he stopped singing to ask. 'Are you crying?'

'Just shivering,' I murmured into his shoulder so that I wouldn't have to look at him. 'It's getting cold.'

He took off his jacket and draped it around my shoulders.

'Now you'll be cold too,' I complained.

'I'm tough,' he said.

'But it's freezing.'

'Are you trying to tell me you'd like to get back in the car?'

I didn't want to, but I said, 'I suppose you should take me back to London soon.'

'I suppose I should.'

I was surprisingly disappointed when Barney didn't protest, but instead began to pack away the picnic and fold up the rug. Soon he was helping me back over the fence. I wanted just one last dance. I'd wanted him to kiss me one more time, out there in that field. This would never happen again.

Before we got into the car, Barney obliged me with the softest, warmest kiss I have ever known. It warmed me far more effectively than his jacket.

52

I could still feel the heat from that kiss as I settled into the passenger seat of the Porsche again and Barney turned his key in the ignition. And the car refused to start.

'What the—?'

The throaty roar that ordinarily heralded the Porsche springing into life and going from 0 to 60 in 2.4 seconds had been replaced by a petrol-powered smoker's cough that made Karen's mother Marilyn sound quite healthy.

'Shit,' said Barney. Then, 'Sorry. Shouldn't swear in front of a lady.'

'It's absolutely a swearing matter,' I told him as the car continued to splutter. 'What do you think is wrong?'

'Much as it pains me to admit it,' he said, 'I have absolutely no idea. I think I'm missing the motoring gene that would compel another man to get out and look under the bonnet at this sort of time.'

He turned the key again. The Porsche groaned some more.

'I don't think that's going to work,' I said. The noise was making me feel queasy. 'Did you leave the lights on?' I suggested knowledgeably. 'Perhaps the battery has just run down?'

He looked at me. I remembered that men don't like it when girls know more about cars than they do. But Barney wasn't looking at me with any kind of disdain, more embarrassment on his own behalf. 'You know what, you're probably right,' he said. 'I must have left the CD player on or something. I was just so keen to get you in that field. Now we'll get to spend the whole night there.' He smiled cheekily.

'Call the AA,' I said. 'It's cold out here.'

I could see the pleasure on the AA guy's face when he finally pulled up alongside us forty-five minutes later. This was something to tell the lads about. A brand-new 911 going nowhere, much less at 100 mph. So much for German engineering, eh? It probably made his day to see us sitting there in the lay-by unable to get the damn thing started.

'This the car?' he asked.

'No,' said Barney. 'We just got in this one to keep warm.'

The AA guy ignored Barney's sarcasm and climbed into the driver's seat. Despite having heard Barney's description of the problem in so far as we could describe it, Mr AA turned the key just as Barney had done. The Porsche coughed.

'Sounds like the battery's flat,' he said. 'Did you leave the lights on?'

'Probably,' said Barney.

The AA guy's night was getting better and better. Even the faux pas he made in opening the front of the car to get to the engine couldn't suppress his delight at getting his hands on a Porsche 911. A new one. Barney could only watch helplessly as the guy got his jump-leads out and prepared to perform an auto-resuscitation.

Standing on the side of the road, still wearing Barney's jacket around my shoulders, I instinctively wove my arm through his and around his waist. He was chewing his lip. Such a dejected expression. I knew how Dad felt about his cars. You could take anything from his house and he wouldn't bat an eyelid. Even burn the house down if you felt like it. But scratch his car and Dad would go to war. For poor old

Barney, watching Mr AA trail a pair of filthy jump-leads across the Porsche's exquisite paint job was probably the equivalent of seeing your favourite dog undergo surgery.

I waited for him to bark out, 'Be careful.' But he didn't. He just bit his lip and watched.

It didn't work.

A check of all the 'obvious' things that might be wrong (obvious to whom, I wondered) yielded no results either.

'This is beyond me now,' the AA chap admitted. 'Don't want to mess with a machine like this too much. We're going to have to take her into a garage.'

Funny how cars are always female, I thought.

'You've got the Home Start option, right?'

'Yes.'

'So where is home?'

'London,' Barney sighed.

'Hop in the truck,' said the AA driver. 'I'll drive you back.'

'You're proposing to tow a Porsche 911 all the way back to London?' said Barney. He couldn't hide his distress now.

'I can take it somewhere nearer.'

'But then I'll have to come back and get the car tomorrow.'

'It's up to you.'

'Unless . . .'

Barney turned towards me.

'We could stay in a hotel out here?'

The AA man smirked.

'A hotel?' I coughed. 'You and me?'

'You're right. I shouldn't even have suggested that. Sorry. Of course you're not going to say yes.'

'Oh, go on,' said the AA man to me. 'After all the effort he's gone to. Driving you all the way out here. Making a picnic. Buying champagne. Seeing his poor little car bite the dust.'

Barney cringed. 'Don't let that make you change your mind,' he told me.

I rolled my eyes in sympathy and turned further towards him so that the AA guy had a view of my back.

'Give the man a break,' he persisted.

But I couldn't spend the night with Barney. Could I?

I shouldn't have even seen him again after the kiss on Chelsea Bridge. I shouldn't have been seeing him in the first place! I could and should have disappeared from his life the moment Poupeh got the shots we needed. But I had agreed to this outing. And now we were standing by his disabled car in the middle of the countryside in the middle of the night.

Insisting on driving back now would be like shutting the stable door long after the horse had bolted and been made into glue . . .

'OK,' I said. 'I suppose it makes more sense.'

If I didn't think about it too much, it did.

'Where do you suggest?' I asked the AA guy.

'I know a place in Woodstock that's supposed to be nice,' he said.

'That'll do me. All right for you, Barney?'

Barney's face betrayed that he really couldn't believe I had agreed.

'I'll drive you over there now,' said the AA man.

We were lucky. Ordinarily, the little hotel in Woodstock would have been packed out with American tourists en route to the Cotswolds at this stage of the summer, but that day they had just one cancellation.

'We'd have to share the room,' said Barney.

I made a show of agreeing grudgingly – though in reality it

hadn't crossed my mind that we would get *two* rooms – and we followed the hotel manager upstairs.

It was a lovely suite. One of the best in the hotel, we were assured, though we would be getting it for a good rate since the manager had expected that it would stay empty that night. The small doorway, that Barney and I both had to stoop to get through, led into a room with a beamed ceiling. In the centre was a big bed covered in floral linen and piled high with chi-chi cushions embroidered with legends such as 'Home sweet home'. It was very different from the minimal chic of the hotels I typically stayed in on my shopping jaunts around the world. This was much more old-fashioned. Romantic.

'Will this do?' the manager asked.

'It's great,' I assured him.

'No luggage?' he asked again.

'We didn't expect to be spending the night,' Barney clarified.

I certainly hadn't expected it. Though I wasn't sure I would have know what to pack if I had. This would be the first time I had actually spent the night with a man in three years.

By the time we got to Woodstock it was pretty late. The effect of the champagne had long since worn off and the hotel bar downstairs was closed so we couldn't get a top-up. There was nowhere else in the town that could oblige us. Woodstock was far from being a city that never sleeps. It was more of a village that rarely woke up. There was nothing to do but get into bed with a couple of hot drinks and watch television.

With the hotel manager gone, Barney and I continued to stand exactly where he'd left us in the middle of the room like two characters in a play waiting for someone to give us our lines.

'I'll go into the bathroom while you get into bed,' said

Barney eventually. 'And we'll put all those silly cushions down the middle so that you're not tempted to molest me.'

'Good idea,' I said.

'Shall I make you some Horlicks while you're getting ready?' he asked, shaking out a sachet from the collection by the 'tea-making facilities'.

'Yes,' I said. 'That will help me drop off more quickly.'

I don't think I have ever drunk Horlicks in my life.

'How do you actually make Horlicks?' Barney asked, betraying that he probably wasn't a big fan either.

'I'll have some decaff coffee if they've got that,' I said.

So I went into the bathroom. It was just as romantic as the bedroom. A claw-footed bath hulked beneath a dormer window. A pile of pink towels was topped off with a face-cloth that had been folded into a fan. I felt a little bit guilty for disturbing it.

I may not have been prepared for a whole night away, but at least I always carried make-up remover wipes in my handbag. After all, a girl never knows when she's going to get grit in her eye and ruin her mascara in the process of getting it out.

As I smoothed away the mascara that had begun to settle in the creases beneath my eyes, giving me the look of someone who hadn't slept in too long, I could hear Barney moving about the bedroom. I heard the click as he turned on the little plastic kettle on the tea-making tray. I heard the clink of cups and saucers. I heard the whoosh of the water in the kettle as it began to boil. Then I heard the sound of a zip . . .

I stopped in the middle of cleaning up my right eye. Was Barney taking off his trousers?

Up until that moment, I hadn't really considered what we were going to wear to bed. What would be appropriate? Would I look like a weirdo if I got beneath the covers with

all my clothes still on? How about if I just wore my underwear? What if I came out of the bathroom dressed in nothing
but a robe to find that Barney intended to sleep in everything
but his boots? I pulled out the old key in the bathroom lock
and tried to look through into the bedroom. I thought I caught
a glimpse of naked leg. I jumped back. He didn't have his
trousers on.

I decided that I would at least take off my highly crease-
prone skirt. I slipped it off slowly, moving my zip as silently as
possible as though if he couldn't hear me undressing, then I
wasn't. Then I took off my bra, unclipping it and pulling it out
through the arm-hole of my T-shirt rather than taking that off
too, even though I was behind a locked door. Skirt removed
and squarely folded, with my bra tucked demurely inside it, I
slipped into the enormous dressing gown that hung behind
the bathroom door. I knocked from the inside of the bathroom
before I stepped out.

'Are you decent?' I called.

'As I'll ever be,' said Barney.

I pushed the door open slowly to give him time to be sure.

He was sitting on the edge of the bed. Also in one of those
enormous fluffy dressing gowns.

'I made your coffee.'

'Thanks. There's only one toothbrush in the emergency
kit,' I said, handing it over.

'I don't mind sharing if you don't.'

As we passed in the bathroom doorway, he brushed his lips
against my hair. I felt my legs melt.

I lay in bed, waiting for him to come out of the bathroom, in a
state of high anxiety. I had taken the dressing gown off to slip
between the sheets but now I wondered whether I should take
my T-shirt off as well. Barney was bare-chested beneath his

gown, I assumed. I leaned over to look at his not so neatly folded pile of clothes. I made an inventory of the garments he had taken off. I couldn't see his underpants!

I heard him spit toothpaste into the basin. I heard him rinse and flush the toilet. I pulled my T-shirt half off, then put it on again.

Barney had gone quiet.

Then I heard it. The unmistakable 'beep, beep, beep' that told me he was sending a text.

What was he telling her?

'Car broke down. On my own in a Travel Inn, thinking of you'?

What had I been thinking? I'd been acting as though Karen didn't exist.

I tucked my T-shirt into my knickers for extra protection, turned to face the wall and pretended to be asleep.

53

A few minutes later, Barney exited the bathroom and, I assume from what I could hear, let his gown drop to the floor as he stood by the bed. I felt the bed dip as he climbed in on the other side of the pillow barricade that he had indeed built down the length of the mattress as promised.

I kept my eyes tightly shut.

'Are you asleep?' he whispered.

I didn't respond.

I heard him roll over.

'Not quite,' I said.

Barney immediately turned back to face me and strained over the pillow barrier to kiss me on the nose.

'I'm sorry that the evening has ended like this,' he told me. 'I promise I didn't plan it. German engineering, eh?'

'It's OK,' I said.

'I'll get you back to London first thing in the morning. I'm sure you've got lots to hurry back for.'

'Yes,' I lied. 'How about you?'

'I just texted my doubles partner to tell him he'll have to find someone else to play with.'

I wanted so much to believe him.

'Did you?' I couldn't help asking for him to say it again. 'I didn't know you played tennis.'

'I don't. At least, not well. I probably should have called him, shouldn't I? It's a bit off to let someone down by text.'

He was so convincing. Perhaps he was telling the truth.

'Are you disappointed that I didn't take you to Le Manoir?' Barney asked me in a whisper.

'No,' I said. 'Our private picnic was much more romantic.' I meant it.

'Am I allowed to put one arm over the barrier?'

'Just one arm.'

He stroked his hand down my arm.

'How about a foot?' he asked.

'Just one foot.'

I felt his foot touch mine.

'Your feet are freezing,' he said. 'Would you like me to warm them up?'

'Maybe.'

I reached between us and started to pull the wall of pillows apart.

'I need an extra one under my head,' I lied as I removed the first one.

'Me too,' said Barney, removing a second. 'In fact, I like to sleep on three.'

Soon there were no pillows at all between us. Without saying anything, we moved across the bed until the backs of my legs were resting against his hairy thighs and my bottom nestled in his lap. He wrapped an arm around my waist and planted a kiss at the nape of my neck. I rolled over so that we were face to face.

'I'm glad the car broke down,' he said.

'So am I.'

He pushed my hair back from my face and started to kiss me on the lips. I responded instantly and pressed my body more closely against his. I soon felt his hands moving up my back beneath my T-shirt. I shifted so that he could pull it off over my head and we found ourselves skin to skin.

In that moment, I forgot all about the reasons why I shouldn't be there. I forgot about the text message and who might have been the recipient. I forgot all the reasons why I shouldn't even *like* a boy like Barney Cavanagh. Instead I let him tuck his fingers inside my black cotton bikinis and wiggle them down my hips. I helped him out of his own white and blue striped boxer shorts. I wrapped my legs around his and sighed with happiness when he moved so that his weight was right on top of me.

The sound of his breathing drowned out the sound of my conscience. I wanted him so much that the thought of just one night with him finally tipped the scales against the disappointment that would certainly follow.

I let him make love to me.

Later, as we lay in the dark, our bodies moulded into each other like spoons nestling in a kitchen drawer, Barney kissed the back of my neck again with a tenderness that made me believe that it hadn't simply been sex for him either.

And then he whispered, 'I think I am falling in love with you.'

I didn't respond. I thought it was best to pretend that I hadn't heard. But as Barney's breath deepened and I knew he had fallen asleep, I found a little voice in my head was whispering, 'If only this were real. If only this were real.'

54

The following morning was one of the most beautiful we had seen that summer. Barney was still asleep when I opened my eyes. I watched him for a moment. His dark hair was plastered to his forehead. His mouth had settled into a smile that I wanted to kiss. Instead, I slipped out of bed as slowly and quietly as I could and went to the bedroom window. Pulling the curtains aside, I saw that even at eight o'clock it was warm enough for dog-walkers to be out in T-shirts. On the opposite side of the street, a cat bathed in a puddle of sunlight, too lazy even to twitch as a Labrador was dragged past on its lead.

The village was picture-postcard pretty. I opened the window so that I could smell the summer too.

The gentle breeze whispered across Barney's bare shoulder and stirred him awake.

'Hey,' he murmured.

'I've been watching you sleep,' I said.

'Ordinarily,' he told me, as he sat up and rubbed at his eyes, 'that would give me the creeps.'

'But not this morning?'

'No.'

I sat back down on the bed beside him. He kissed me in reply.

'Sleep well?' he asked.

'I don't think I've ever slept better,' I said.

'You snored,' said Barney.

'No I didn't!' I belted him with a cushion. He snatched it from my hands, then wrestled me down on to the mattress. Pinning me with the weight of his body, he kissed me with intent. I kissed him back.

There was a knock at the door.

Such bad timing.

'Oh, bum. I took the liberty of filling out the breakfast-in-bed card while you were in the bathroom last night,' Barney explained. He sprang off me and ran across the room to retrieve a dressing gown before answering the door. The sight of his bare, perfect bottom made me bite my lip and remember having dug my fingers into it the night before. I blushed at the thought.

We didn't eat much. I got a mouthful of orange juice before Barney started kissing me again and tasting him seemed so much more compelling than tucking into the fast-cooling toast.

We stayed in bed until eleven. Check-out time.

That's when I started to feel sad again. As I watched Barney pull on his jeans, I was only too aware that I wasn't going to be seeing him without them again. When he kissed my breast-bone while I still had my T-shirt only half on, I tugged it off again and pressed him to me as though I was trying to make an indent of myself on his skin.

'We'll have to come back here,' he said.

I agreed.

Then all too quickly we were in a taxi on our way to the garage where the Porsche had spent the night. I sat on a bench outside, taking a last few breaths of country air while Barney and the garage mechanic discussed the Porsche's problems.

'Permanent damage?' I asked, when Barney pulled the car into the forecourt.

'Just expensive. I'm too happy to care,' he said, kissing the inside of my wrist.

The car didn't seem to be having too much trouble as we headed back into London, not exactly taking it slowly as the mechanic had advised. Yet I wanted to take it slowly. In fact, I wanted the damn thing to break down again.

On the motorway, when he wasn't changing gear, Barney reached across the gear-stick and held my hand. I squeezed hard in response and looked out of my window to hide the fact that I thought I might be about to cry.

'You're very quiet this afternoon,' he noticed.

'Thinking about work,' I said. It was almost true.

He wanted to drive me home but I insisted that he drop me off at the tube station where he had picked me up the previous evening. I claimed that I needed to head into town to buy a birthday present for a friend before making for home. He didn't argue with that. But he did say, 'I want to see you as soon as I can.'

'I'll call you later,' I lied.

'Brilliant.'

'Thank you for a lovely evening,' I told him.

'It turned out to be far lovelier than I planned.'

'Much lovelier.'

I gave him one last kiss.

A kiss goodbye.

55

'Where were you?' asked Poupeh the moment I walked through the door. 'I was so worried about you when you didn't come home and didn't reply to any of my messages.'

'I'm sorry,' I said. 'I know I should have called.'

'What were you doing?'

'I went to see an old friend in Oxford, that's all. I didn't think I had to tell you everything,' I snapped.

'I don't care who you see,' said Poupeh. 'But why do you look so sad?'

'Time of the month,' I lied.

'Anyway, your father has called here. He wanted to speak to you.'

I noticed then that Dad had called my mobile several times too. I'd had it switched to 'vibrate' the whole time I'd been with Barney and hadn't bothered to check to see if anyone had called. No one usually did. And I had given up on Dad in particular. Now I felt strangely flat when I saw his name in the call history.

'Are you going to call him?' asked Poupeh.

I said I would later. There was something I had to do first. Something I knew I had to do before I chickened out.

I had to send Karen those pictures.

Barney had told me that he loved me and I had wanted to tell him that I thought I loved him too. But the fact was he knew next to nothing about me and I knew way too much about him. I had been stupid. I had allowed myself to indulge in a very dangerous fantasy. The biggest and most important fact was that Barney was Karen's boyfriend.

I just had to forget about that night in Woodstock. I had to forget about the way he held my face in his hands and kissed me so tenderly that I thought I might cry. It was all an illusion. He could turn that kind of tenderness on with any woman. He was going out with Karen. She had a key to his flat! She co-hosted his dinner parties. Even as he had kissed me for the first time to the sound of Big Ben striking eleven, she was probably sitting on the sofa in that flat waiting for him to come home. No doubt he kissed her just as tenderly when he walked into the house.

My mission had been to break Karen and Barney up. And I still had to complete that mission. There was no point wondering what might have been between Barney and me. He was a cheater. I knew that much for sure. What would I want with a man like that? Karen needed to know the truth too and the sooner the better. Eventually she would be grateful. When she was married to my dad.

There was no way on earth that Barney and I could ever be together.

I sat down at the desk in my bedroom and began to write the anonymous letter I had been planning for weeks.

'Dear Karen,' the letter began.

'You don't know me, but I know your boyfriend Barney Cavanagh. In fact, I know him very well. We have been going out together whenever you are working the evening shift since he picked me up in Frogmortons about a month ago. Last night, we spent the whole night

*together for the first time. You probably don't believe me
and I'm sure if you ask him about it, he will deny all
knowledge of my existence. But I can prove to you that
he has been unfaithful . . .'*

I hesitated then. Would the photos be enough? The one
photograph I could risk including – that shot from Chelsea
Bridge – didn't prove that much to someone who hadn't been
there, despite what Poupeh said. He might have been looking
for grit in my eye. So, to make sure that Karen couldn't ignore
the evidence, I wrote, cringing as I tapped the words into the
keyboard: *'He has a birthmark in the shape of Africa on his left
inner thigh.'*

That was definitely the kind of knowledge that only came
through intimacy.

*'I know that this news will probably come as a terrible shock to
you,'* I continued. *'Maybe Barney hasn't been unfaithful before
and you might feel as though you can forgive him. You've no
reason to trust me, but I would definitely advise you not to let this
incident slide. In my experience, leopards never change their spots.
If you let him get away with it once, he'll definitely try it again. To
continue to see Barney is to store up so much future unhappiness.
So my advice to you is to call your relationship off and look for
someone who really values you.'*

I didn't add 'someone like my dad'.

*'Rest assured that I have no ulterior motive for telling you that you
should dump Barney as soon as you can. I certainly am not waiting
for him to be mine and mine alone. Why would I want such a loser?'*

I finished my letter, *'With best wishes from a friend.'*

Then I took one last look at the photograph of our first kiss.
A bubble of sadness started to rise up in my throat. As I sealed
the envelope, I could feel tears pricking at the back of my eyes.
But I couldn't stop now.

'This feeling won't last long,' I told myself. I had known Barney properly for less than a fortnight. That was nothing. Of course I wouldn't be sad for long. When I broke up with my college boyfriend after four months together I had grieved for him for approximately two days. On that scale, I would have forgotten all about Barney by bedtime.

I thought about posting the letter but decided that a hand delivery was best. The postal service couldn't be relied upon and if I posted the letter straight through Barney's door, he might open it before he passed it on. If I delivered the letter to the gym, I could be sure that Karen had received it. I knew from my chart of her hours that Karen wasn't going to be working that day, so I could safely drop the letter off without risking bumping into her and she would get it first thing the following morning.

Aware that every moment I hesitated would make my mission harder, I got into my Mini and drove straight to Hollywood Fitness. The gym was closed for the night. I poked the letter into the letter-box but didn't quite let it go. For a couple of breaths, I stood there, still holding on to the very edge of the letter. Finally I released it. And with it, I released all hope I had of my own happy ever after.

56

The following morning, I woke with a heavy heart. How different from the way I had felt waking up in the Woodstock Hotel with Barney beside me!

It was eight in the morning. If my chart was right, Karen would be arriving at the gym by now. I imagined her walking into her office and finding the brown envelope on her desk. I imagined her turning it over, wondering about the handwriting before she opened it (I had gone to great lengths to disguise my scrawl). How would her face look when she saw what I had sent her? Would she believe it right away? Would she bother to read the whole letter? Would she try to continue her day at the gym as though nothing had happened? Or would she plead a personal emergency and go straight home to confront him?

And what would happen then? Would Barney be able to talk her round? Would he want to? Would he deny that we had ever met?

Now I realized that I wanted him to tell her that yes, not only had he had an affair, he had fallen in love with me while he was at it. He wanted to be with me and not her!

'Have you called your dad?' asked Poupeh when I shuffled into the kitchen after another hour lying in bed and gazing at the ceiling as though the answer might materialize upon it.

'Not yet,' I had to admit.

I didn't want to call Dad while I was feeling so low. I had breakfast and took a bath. I told myself that I would call him when I got out. But I sat in the bath until the water was cold and metallic with burst bubbles and still didn't feel any better for it.

'I bet there are fireworks going on at Karen's house today!' said Poupeh when I joined her in the kitchen. She knew that I had finally posted the photograph.

'I bet there are.'

'Soon we will be celebrating your first mission accomplished! I hope you will still think about working for me when you move back to your father's house. You are clearly the femme fatale I need. I'll even make you a partner.'

'Thanks,' I said. Though the last thing I felt like doing then was trying to entice someone else away from his commitments, church-blessed or otherwise.

'Phone your father,' Poupeh reminded me as she headed off for another surveillance shift at the kebab shop.

'I will.'

But I didn't have time to call Dad. I was just about to dial him when my mobile rang. A shiver ran through me as I looked at the screen and saw Karen's number there.

I didn't pick up, of course. I let her go through to voicemail. But within seconds Karen's number appeared on the screen again. And she just kept on calling. Again and again and again, hanging up and redialling each time she got voicemail. She was determined not to leave a message but to talk to me herself. Eventually, I had to give in.

'Lindsey.'

Her familiar voice sounded *pitying*.

'Oh, hello, Karen,' I said. 'I didn't expect to hear from you.'

'No,' she said flatly. 'I don't suppose you did.'

'How are things?' I burbled. 'Keeping yourself busy? Still working at the gym?'

'Well, you should know the answer to that one,' she said.

'I'm sorry?'

'Lindsey,' said Karen. 'I think you and I need to have a *talk*.'

'About anything in particular?' I asked.

'I got your letter.'

'What letter?'

'The letter you left at the gym.'

'I don't know what you're talking about.'

'Lindsey, you were captured on CCTV.'

All that subterfuge and I had been caught out in such an elementary way. Poupeh would be furious.

'We get a nice full-face shot of everyone who goes any-where near the door of the gym,' Karen told me.

Of course. Why on earth hadn't I thought of that?

'I couldn't believe it when I saw you,' she said.

There was no point denying it now. I decided instead to brazen it out. The outcome could still be the same.

'So are you going to tell me what's been going on?' Karen persisted.

'I've told you all you need to know in the letter,' I said.

'Aren't you going to give me a chance to respond? I'd like to see you face to face.'

'Why? So you can rip mine off? It takes two to tango.' I scraped up every gram of defiance left in my body. 'Barney's the one you should be angry with.'

'Lindsey, just stop acting like a child for one tiny moment,' Karen interrupted. 'If you could be grown-up enough to face facts rather than creating some fantasy world, you might be a whole lot happier.'

Fantasy world? My heart sank. Had Barney denied all knowledge of me? But then I remembered that he could justifiably deny all knowledge of Lindsey. After all, he still knew me as Jane.

'He thinks I'm called Jane,' I said. 'If he's been telling you that he doesn't know who I am, it's because I didn't tell him my real name.'

'We worked that much out.'

We?

'Lindsey, I am going to be at Sardi's in thirty minutes. I want you to be there and we'll get to the bottom of this mess together.'

Then she hung up.

I sat on my bed for the next twenty-five minutes, paralysed with despair. Karen had used the word 'we'. She and Barney must still be on speaking terms. Was there really any point in my going to Sardi's now?

After the full half-hour had passed, my mobile rang again. It was Karen.

'Don't make me come round to Poupeh's and get you,' she said.

I was in so much turmoil that it didn't even occur to me to wonder how she knew where I was. Instead I promised Karen that I was putting on my coat even as we spoke.

When I eventually arrived at the restaurant, forty-five minutes later than Karen had asked, I was on the verge of crying. Karen was sitting at our table. The table Dad liked best. We had last been there together on the day I offered to arrange her hen night. She'd been so happy then. Karen just looked irritated now. She was playing with a matchbox, turning it over and over between her fingers. Her mouth was drawn in a

thin, hard line. When she saw me, she just shook her head and
tutted in a way that reminded me of my school headmistress
hearing that Gemma and I had been caught smoking. Again.

'Sit down,' she instructed.

I did as I was told. The headmistress impression was that
good.

'What do you want? Caffè latte or something stronger?'

'Caffè latte,' I said quietly. 'Decaff. Semi-skimmed.'

'I know how you like it,' said Karen.

I nodded meekly. 'Thank you.'

A waiter placed the coffee in front of me and retreated
quickly to a safe distance as though he had been warned of the
fireworks likely to ensue.

'We haven't been out together since Ibiza,' Karen ob-
served, all faux brightness. 'Since the day of that fabulous
trip to Formentera on Gemma's yacht.'

I instantly pushed my coffee away in case she had slipped
me some arsenic.

'Now,' she said. 'I want you to tell me once again what you
wrote in the letter that you left for me at the gym. Start at the
very beginning,' she added. 'And don't miss anything out.'

'From the beginning?'

She meant to torture me.

'Yes. Because I'm sure it will make for a good hour or so's
entertainment, hearing how you've been sleeping with my
boyfriend.'

'I didn't mean for it to go so far!' I blurted. 'I didn't want to
like him. I didn't expect to. I just thought we would go on a
couple of dates and I would persuade him to dump you and
then you would be single and consider getting back with Dad
again.'

Karen's mouth twitched at the corners.

'How did you find out about Barney?' she asked me.

'I came to apologize to you at the gym and saw him meet you in his Porsche. I gave Poupeh his number-plate details and she had a policeman she knows look him up.'

'So you deliberately tracked him down?'

I nodded. 'Doesn't sound good, I know.'

'Not really. And where did you meet him?'

I told her how Poupeh and I had set up the meeting at Frogmortons and about the honey-trapper who had unwittingly pushed him in my direction like a beater rushing a pheasant to a shoot.

'I couldn't believe that he would fancy me. The honey-trapper was a lot more like you.'

This time Karen smiled into her coffee. 'I'm not even going to ask you how,' she said. 'Carry on.'

'Do you really want me to?'

'I want you to tell me everything.'

So I told her about the night at Kyoto, the evening at the theatre, the kiss on the bridge. I told her how I found myself wanting to see him again, stealing one last night in his company before I blew everything apart.

'I don't know why I did it. I suppose I thought it wouldn't matter. The last thing I expected to find was that I'd fallen in love . . .'

Karen snorted.

'You're telling me you actually "fell in love" with Barney?'

'Yes,' I had to admit.

'Well, I wouldn't have believed you had it in you.'

That seemed unnecessarily nasty, I thought.

'Little Lindsey fell in love.'

'I'm not ashamed of having feelings! Even though I knew he was a lying, cheating swine. Oh, Karen, you are better off without him. Really, you are. We're both better off.'

I felt the tears that had been pricking at my eyes all day get that little bit closer to spilling over.

'He's not worth wasting a moment's more thought on. You'll soon forget all about him.'

Karen couldn't stop herself from laughing at that.

'Lindsey,' she said. 'You are a total idiot.'

'I've saved you from a broken heart.'

'You've saved me from diddly squat . . .'

57

'Barney isn't my boyfriend,' said Karen. 'He's my step-brother. He's been living out of the country for a while but when he came back and moved into his new flat, he asked me to move in and keep him company. I was only too grateful to move out of Mum's. And because Barney doesn't have many friends in London after spending so much time abroad, I've also been trying to help him broaden his social circle. I'm his stepsister and his lodger. That is all.'

'How come you never spoke about him to me?' I protested.

'I seem to remember that you weren't terribly interested in anything I had to say,' said Karen flatly. 'But I'm pretty sure I did mention him. I was excited that he was going to fly back from Singapore for the wedding.'

When she said the word 'wedding', her eyes grew slightly damp. And then I remembered the conversation in Ibiza, when she'd told Gemma that her stepbrother was a catch.

'It didn't occur to me that your stepbrother would be someone like Barney,' I said.

'Well, when he said he'd been seeing a fantastic, kind and generous-hearted woman, you're not exactly the first person who sprang to my mind either,' Karen spat back.

'He's really your stepbrother?'

Karen just sighed.

'Oh, Karen, I've been so evil to you.'

She cocked her head to suggest she agreed.

'That stuff that I said on the boat before I . . . well, it was horrible! But I didn't know what I was talking about. When Dad told me that you said it was because you were from different backgrounds that you had to leave him, I hoped you were just using it as an excuse. Because you didn't want to say that you were leaving because I tried to drown you.'

'Did you try to drown me?'

'Not consciously.'

'That's what I thought. So what was the point flinging accusations of attempted murder around?'

'To get your own back on me for being such a cow?'

'Well, I have to admit that I did want to throttle you when I found the cocaine in my handbag. But what would that have achieved?'

I'd been so busy on my mission to split Karen and Barney, I'd almost forgotten about the drugs.

'I quickly guessed what really happened to poor old Trisha . . .'

'What did you do with the coke?' I asked.

'Had one fantastic night.'

My eyes widened.

'I flushed it down the toilet, you idiot. Honestly, Lindsey, you could have landed us both in some serious trouble. Thank God I left my bag in the taxi.'

'I'm sorry. Thanks for not telling anyone about it. You haven't told anybody about it, have you?'

'I haven't.' She shook her head.

The glimpse into Karen's decency that I got when I heard that she had planned that secret party for me but never told me when I didn't turn up, was supported by how she had behaved since. Then it dawned on me why she had been so forebearing. I realized she felt sorry for me.

'You didn't try to mess up my relationship with Dad because you knew that it was all I had, didn't you?'

Karen nodded.

'Loving me didn't make your father love you any less, Lindsey.'

'I know that now.'

'And I think you also now know that it's possible for you to meet someone and fall in love and perhaps have a family of your own and then you won't have time for your dad any more.'

'I'll always have time for Dad.'

'I know you will on one level. But maybe you've had too much time for him. I think that's a big part of why you're so unhappy. You've closed your eyes to the opportunities for love in your own life because you don't want him to think you're deserting him. But believe me, your father is perfectly capable of finding ways to fill his time when you're not around.'

'You haven't been seeing anyone since you and Dad split up, have you?' I asked then.

'No, I haven't.'

'Then will you call him now?'

A smile spread across Karen's face.

'Lindsey, I've already moved back in.'

Half an hour later, while Karen and I were finishing our coffee and chatting amiably about everyday subjects like her job at the gym, the door to Sardi's swung open and Dad walked in. He had a melon-slice smile on his face. He made a beeline for us and hugged me close to him.

'You loony,' he said to me. Affectionately.

When he finished hugging me, he turned to Karen. I wiped at a tear as they embraced each other. But it wasn't a tear of anger or jealousy this time. It was just the kind of tear you shed when you see people who make each other so happy doing exactly that.

It turned out that Dad and Karen had been reunited for a couple of weeks. While I had been busy playing the temptress, they had been slowly piecing their relationship back together, discussing the reasons for their split and what they could do about it. More specifically, what they could do about me.

Karen had been reluctant at first to enter back into a relationship with Dad. She had admitted to him that I had been making her unhappy for quite some time before the Ibiza incident. All those months she had plastered on a happy face and pretended not to hear me when I sniped at just about everything about her were starting to take their toll long before she took her dip in the Mediterranean.

She took a lot of persuading. But eventually she agreed to give it another go. The idea that I seemed to be carving out a life of my own, living with an old schoolfriend and, as the rumour went, actually doing a *job*, reassured her that perhaps I wasn't irredeemably idle and wicked.

'How did you know that I was working?' I asked Dad. 'As far as you knew, I was living on the street.'

'Lindsey, I knew you were never in any danger,' said Dad. 'I had you followed from day one.'

'You had *me* followed?'

'Absolutely. I wanted you to learn a few lessons about standing on your own two feet but I needed to be sure that you wouldn't come to any harm in the process. I hired a private detective to trail you around and be ready to step in if things started to get hairy.'

'Well, that was a total waste of money,' I said. 'I'd have

known if someone was trailing me, Dad. But I didn't see anyone at all. I don't think your private dick actually did the surveillance you asked for. I mean, I walked all the way across Regent's Park in the middle of the night on my own! It doesn't get much hairier than that. Surely that would have been the moment for your detective to step in? Or how about when I spent the night in Henry and Lydia's shed? Did he assure you that I was tucked up in bed in some hotel?'

Karen smirked. Dad shook his head.

'Darling, I knew exactly where you were. *She* watched you all night and came to your rescue first thing in the morning.'

Slowly it dawned on me.

'Poupeh? You hired Poupeh to keep an eye on me, didn't you?'

Dad nodded.

'She's pretty good, eh?'

'But she said she was doing surveillance on the woman who was renting the house.'

'Decent of Henry and Lydia's lodgers to play along. Poupeh persuaded them. They had actually already called the police when they saw you staggering down the garden path. You've Poupeh to thank that you got to spend the night in the shed and not in a cell.'

'How did you find her?'

'Poupeh found *me*. She called my office again the day you left home, trying to find out how to get hold of you since you hadn't returned her call. She wanted to invite you to a party. I remembered her from your school open days. We got talking. She told me what she'd been doing since she left school and when I admitted to her that I didn't know where you were as of that morning, she promised to track you down. Of course, you made it easier by not leaving the house until six o'clock that afternoon.'

'I thought Poupeh was my friend.'

'She is. She's one of the best friends you've got. Especially when you consider what you did to her at school.'

'She knows about the letter . . .'

'As I told you, Poupeh is a first-rate private detective.'

'But if Poupeh told you that I was working for her, why didn't she tell you how hard I was trying to get you and Karen back together?'

'She did.'

'And you didn't tell her to stop me?'

'I thought it might be fun to see how far you were prepared to go.'

'And Barney?'

Karen and Dad shared a smile.

Barney had been in on it too.

58

The blood rushed to my face. It was Valentine's Day all over again. Waiting for Matt Charlton to never turn up. Everybody laughing. Everybody in on the joke except me. I got up and rushed from the restaurant, convinced I could still hear Dad and Karen laughing as I stormed down the street. And Barney. What a kidder. What an actor.

When Karen first told me that Barney was her stepbrother, I had experienced such a jolt of happiness. If he wasn't her boyfriend then he was free to be mine. But now that I knew he had been her stooge, everything was different again. All those wonderful things he had said to me. Karen and my father had handed him a script.

My tears were in full flow as I got into my Mini and turned the ignition key. I didn't bother with 'mirror, signal, manoeuvre'. I just put pedal to metal, wrenched the gear stick into reverse and, rather than beginning an elegant exit from my parking space, I began an accident.

I slammed straight backwards into the front of Barney's Porsche as he pulled into the parking space behind me.

'Don't expect me to be sorry!' I shouted at him over his crumpled bumper. 'You lied to me.'

'If I did then you got it on tape! You tried to set me up!'

'I had a good reason. I thought you were going out with Karen.'

'Why on earth did you think that?'

'You bought her flowers.'

'She had helped unpack all the boxes I had sent from Singapore to my flat!'

'You looked so cosy when you were going around the supermarket.'

'You followed us round a *supermarket*? Lindsey, you are nuts.'

'You should have told me she was your stepsister.'

'You shouldn't have had me stalked. Have you any idea how it feels to find out that someone has spied on you? Let me tell you, it doesn't feel good.'

'It's not as though you didn't know what was going on. Every time we met you reported back to Poupeh and my Dad.'

'Not every time,' said Barney. 'Not the last time.'

'You mean in Woodstock, when you told me that . . .'

'We both strayed away from the script there. I knew you weren't wearing a wire that night.'

I leaned against my car.

'I almost wish you had been,' he continued. 'I'd love to play it back.'

'Stop teasing me,' I said.

'I'm not teasing.'

Cavanagh reached for my hand and lifted it to his lips. He kissed the finger from which he'd pulled the splinter all those weeks ago.

'Shall we start again?' he said. 'I'm going to need your phone number for insurance purposes. That's your real number, Lindsey Parker . . .'

59

Later that night, I found myself back in Hampstead, having supper at the kitchen table I had missed so badly. The day couldn't have turned out more differently than I had expected when I woke that morning at Poupeh's flat. I was back at home with my dad.

Even Gemma was back in my life. Karen had prodded me to reach out to Gemma one more time. I'd called her and been surprised to find that she burst into totally over-emotional tears of happiness when I suggested that we should be friends again.

'I've missed you so much,' she said. 'You've got no idea how dull my life is without your sarcasm and cynicism.'

'Then you won't be pleased to hear that I'm giving both those things up . . .'

After supper, Karen left Dad and me alone. I decided it was time to ask Dad to tell me why he loved Karen so much and this time I was prepared to hear the good stuff.

'I fell in love with Karen because she reminded me of your mother.'

It wasn't what I had expected to hear. But as Dad elaborated, it began to make sense.

'Your mother wasn't exactly the woman you always thought she was, sweetheart. I don't know why I let you build up the fantasy picture you did. Sure, she was beautiful.

She was bright. She was funny. She was smart. But she was also rather ordinary. Just like me.'

'You're not ordinary, Dad,' I protested.

'Yes I am, love. This is the only life you've known. The "right house". The "right school", the "right university", the "right clothes", the "right friends". When I met your mother, I had never eaten sushi. I didn't know my Armani from my arse. We were children. When we met each other, we had no criteria for falling in love other than that we made each other simply joyful. She didn't fall in love with me because she saw that one day I would be a partner in an advertising firm and we'd live in a great big house. She wouldn't have been bothered about whether or not I could get reservations in the best restaurants, or tickets to opening nights at Covent Garden. She loved me just for me.

'Lindsey, I meet so many people who judge everyone on what they have rather than what they are. Your mother wasn't like that. Karen isn't like that either. And she allows me to be the person I really am. I don't have to pretend I like opera for a start.'

'Don't you like opera?' I was surprised,

'I like some of it. The bits that get used in car adverts.'

'But you bought a season ticket.'

'To entertain pretentious clients . . . The funny thing is, I never feel so energized as when I'm *not* being the advertising go-getter. When I'm just being Alex, eating chips and listening to Led Zeppelin, that's when I'm at my happiest. I can be like that around Karen and I love her because there are no layers of society bullshit to wade through to find her heart. She is exactly who she says she is. And she loves you.'

I knew that now.

'Your mum would have liked her, you know.'

EPILOGUE

I think I grew up that summer. My stupid, impulsive action on the *Afsaneh* almost robbed me and my father of everything important in our lives. Instead, as the summer drew to a close, I had more in my life than ever before.

Though Dad had forgiven me for being such an idiot, I decided it probably wasn't a good idea to move back home properly. Dad and Karen definitely needed some time alone together, but, more than that, I found that I didn't want to live at home any more. I was twenty-four years old, for heaven's sake. It was about time I had my own space. I *wanted* my own space. Or at least, for as long as she could bear to sleep in the same room as her shoes, a shared space with Poupeh.

I had a job too, as partner in PGI. Poupeh had been serious about wanting me on board. I mostly took care of the paperwork but gradually she let me do fieldwork as well. Of course, I am much more careful when investigating other people's situations than I was when I investigated Barney.

I still had Barney. Thank goodness. Despite my having caved in the front of his car, Barney really was willing to take our relationship from fantasy to reality. And the reality was even better than the fantasy.

Last but not least, I had a wedding to go to.

So, for the final time, I found myself back in the bridal department of Selfridges. The original gold dress would, thank goodness, go unworn – it wouldn't look right at the newly rescheduled winter wedding – but I knew as Karen and I walked arm in arm into the store that I would be happy to wear whatever she wanted me to as she walked down the aisle with my dad. Gold, peach, lilac, whatever . . . (though preferably, I prayed, not lilac).

Eventually, Karen and I settled on a beautiful silver-blue dress that would make me look like an ice princess.

'And you must be the bride's little sister, right?' asked the bridal assistant as she pinned the dress tightly around me.

'Actually,' I said. 'Karen is going to be my mum.'